PERFECT ORDER

by

Kate Coscarelli

AN ONYX BOOK

NEW AMERICAN LIBRARY

PUBLISHED BY
THE NEW AMERICAN LIBRARY
OF CANADA LIMITED

PUBLISHER'S NOTE

This novel is a work of fiction. Names, characters, places, and incidents
either are the product of the author's imagination or are used fictitiously,
and any resemblance to actual persons, living or dead, events, or locales
is entirely coincidental.

PULLING OUT ALL THE STOPS

CAKE, the ordinary L.A. housewife, who decides
to pack up her dull life and move to Manhattan
in search of Red O'Shea, the only man she has ever
really loved . . .

VANESSA, the renegade heiress with a deadly
secret, who has the power to save Red's presidential
campaign—or destroy it . . .

MILLIE, the beautiful, fabulously rich "hippie,"
who comes down from her elegant penthouse to
become the dynamic force of the campaign . . .

*Together they move into high gear and discover
how it really is in the most super-rich, super-
sexy, super-powerful, exciting city in the world. . . .*

PERFECT ORDER

*This book is dedicated with love
to my husband, Don,
whose confidence is my strength.*

BOUQUETS TO

my agent, Joan Stewart,
and my editor, Maureen Baron

1

Almost Too Perfect

With a quick, expert twist, Cake Halliday pulled the last pink napkin into the shape of a calla lily, thrust it into the large crystal goblet, and stepped back to admire her creation. The tables looked beautiful with their gray linen cloths, pink-rimmed china, and centerpieces of fresh tiger lilies set amid chunks of volcanic rock. An inspired combination of textures, she thought, and congratulated herself on her handiwork.

The sound of the grandfather clock striking six caused a look of panic to brush across her face. "Good grief. . . it can't be that late!" she exclaimed to the air, and wondered where the caterer was. Mary wasn't usually late. Dan would be home in an hour, and she wanted everything to be in perfect order when he arrived.

She should get ready now, but if she got into the shower, she wouldn't hear the doorbell to let Mary in. Damn! She had to move quickly. She hurried into the kitchen and scribbled a note that read, "Mary, come in. The door is unlocked. I'm in the shower." Then she taped the note to the front door and dashed up the stairs.

An hour later Dan Halliday arrived home to find two middle-aged women in black uniforms with frilly white aprons bustling about in the kitchen.

"Mary . . . Greta . . . hmm . . . something smells good."

"Good evening, Mr. Halliday. Your wife is upstairs dressing."

"Good, I better get myself ready too. Our guests will be arriving about seven-thirty. Is the bartender here yet?"

"Yes, he is, Mr. Halliday. The bar is all set up. He went out to his car for a quick cigarette."

Dan left the kitchen, stopped briefly to sort through the mail on the hall credenza, and then walked up the stairs. A tall man with the lean and muscular body of an athlete, Dan Halliday had brown hair lightly frosted with silver, a square jaw, and large dark eyes that seemed to judge all they surveyed.

When he entered the bedroom, he saw that his wife's blue dress, the one he had chosen for her at Giorgio's as a birthday gift last year, was draped across the bed. He was annoyed. Good God, wasn't she dressed yet? Did she always have to be late?

"Cake," he called, "I'm home." There was no answer. The shower wasn't running, either. He strode into the large, luxurious bathroom that they had added to the house two years before, but his wife wasn't there. Perplexed, he searched all the bedrooms, but she was nowhere to be found. He hurried down to the kitchen.

"Mary, Cake isn't upstairs. Do you have any idea where she might be?"

Mary looked surprised. "No sir, I haven't seen her. She left this note on the front door for us, and we came right in."

As Dan read the note, a small cold worm of fear inched its way into his soul. "God, what a stupid thing for her to do. Anybody could have walked in that door!" He turned and rushed through the house toward the yard.

"Maybe she ran to the store to pick up something . . ." Mary suggested to his retreating back, but he answered, "I don't think so—her car is in the garage. She's probably at the Conways'." He switched on the patio lights in the backyard and strode toward the garage. Damn her, she better not be out there messing with one of those infernal paintings of hers. There were no lights on, but just to be sure, he opened the door and threw a switch in the small room where he had banished her after the smell of turpentine in the house had finally gotten to him. A quick glance told him she wasn't there. As he headed back to the house, he suddenly became aware of what he'd seen. Cake had finally cleaned up her studio. It was about time.

At his wife's desk in the study, he picked up her telephone book and dialed her best friend, Joyce, but there was no answer. With growing alarm he tried the numbers of other people in the neighborhood whom she saw frequently. Although none of them were particular friends of his, he knew that she talked with them often.

No one had seen Cake that day or had any idea where she might be. He checked the time. It was now close to seven-thirty. If she wasn't there by the time the guests arrived, he would call the police. Cake would never walk out and desert her home, never, especially with company coming. She loved to entertain. But what if someone *had* walked through that unlocked front door and . . . But no, he could not accept that. He hurried up the stairs to their bedroom and looked at it once more. Everything was in perfect order . . . almost too perfect. He opened the closet that held his wife's clothes, and everything seemed to be there, arranged neatly, shoes lined up in even rows on the floor. It looked strange to him. Cake wasn't ordinarily that tidy. He moved to her chest of drawers.

One by one he opened the drawers, and there, too, everything was organized perfectly. What had happened to the usual jumble of bras and panties that she was always rummaging through? A compulsively organized person himself, he had forever despaired of her lack of organization and often had complained about it. God knows she'd tried, but neatness had always been just beyond her reach.

Dan sat down on the bed and put his head in his hands. Was it possible his wife had left him? Could the ordered drawers and closets be her way of telling him something? No, it didn't make sense. She had always been happy in their marriage . . . happier than he was, actually. She had no reason to go . . . and certainly not like this. Someone must have forced her out of the house. She would never have gone of her own free will. . . .

2

Please Don't Interfere

The mausoleum was cold. Vanessa checked her watch. It was almost five o'clock and they would be closing soon, but she wasn't worried. She had spent hours walking the marble corridors since her father had been sealed into one of the tombs at Morningside the week before, and the place had become familiar and comfortable to her. In fact, she felt almost as secure here as she had ever felt in that huge mausoleum of a house where she had lived all of her life. Now, tonight, she planned to remain here, if she could manage to stay out of the caretaker's sight. It wouldn't be too difficult, she reasoned. The place was huge, and no one was worried about people getting locked in by mistake. Most people were scared silly of being surrounded by the dead, but Vanessa knew that the living were far more dangerous.

All the lights were suddenly turned off, and as soon as she was sure that she was alone, she walked very softly toward the ladies' room on the first floor. There the carpeting was thick and quiet, and since there were no windows, she could turn on a light and save the batteries of the tiny flashlights she carried. The sounds of the last of the staff leaving and locking the doors behind them echoed through the huge building. She hoped that the man who had been following her for the last few days would think he had lost

13

her in the crowd of mourners that had left the chapel several hours earlier. If he bothered to check with her chauffeur, he would learn that she had told him not to return for her, since she would be picked up by a friend. She was certain it would never occur to him that she would stay in the mausoleum alone all night. He was probably already looking elsewhere. But it didn't matter. In the morning she would be someone else.

There was no time to waste. Leaving her handbag and coat on a chair in the lounge, by flashlight she made her way back to the chapel. Every day in the last week she had come here, ostensibly to visit her father's tomb, but in reality to smuggle in the things she would need and to hide them one by one in nooks and crannies among the private burial chambers. Now she went about gathering up the small packages without any trouble. She had worried that the cleaning personnel might find some of them, but apparently they were no more thorough than staff cleaners anywhere.

Back in the rest room, she laid out the contents of the packages on a small couch and checked to be sure everything was there.

She had a sweater, skirt, shoes, a new pouchy handbag, and the reversible coat she had worn that day. Good. She would walk out in clothes entirely different from those she'd worn only hours before. Now she had to do something with her hair.

Not bothering to remove the dress she had on, she set to work cutting her long dark hair, which she had worn pulled back with a barrette for most of her adult life. Her hair was rich and thick and curly, and without a pang of remorse she cut it to shoulder length, leaving just enough so that it could be properly styled when she got to New York. She had never fussed much with her hair, because it had always seemed to look good no matter what she did to it. And besides, Mike had always liked it to look natural.

When she finished, she unfolded a large trash bag and

carefully swept the bits of hair into it. Then, reading the directions carefully, she mixed a bowl of bleach and combed it through her hair. Would she have more fun as a blond? She was certain she couldn't have less.

While she waited for the bleach to work, she opened the lunch she had packed that morning and stashed in her purse before the servants were awake. Two cartons of pineapple juice, a ham sandwich, and an apple. She ate slowly. It would be a long time before she had access to any more food. She regretted her decision not to bring at least a small bottle of wine.

She had also brought the latest *Time* magazine and a paperback copy of a recent best-seller about women taking control of their lives. Maybe she could learn something from it.

She tried to concentrate on the magazine, but her mind would not focus. As she flipped through the pages, her eye fastened on a picture of Senator Red O'Shea. Interesting and ironic, she mused, but not surprising. He was a magnet for journalists because he had real star quality. Well, she had to admit he was attractive. A lot like Kennedy. He was even Irish. She wondered if he had as strong a libidinous drive as Kennedy supposedly had. It would certainly be interesting to meet him and find out. She wished she had paid closer attention when they talked about him. She wished she had paid a lot closer attention to everything. It was important that she try to remember as many details as possible.

Half an hour later, she dampened a paper towel and wiped the bleach from a tiny strand of her hair to check the color. Good heavens, it had turned bright orange. Well, she'd just have to wait and hope that it would turn lighter. How stupid women were to put themselves through this miserable kind of routine just to look better . . . or think they did.

Feeling a little claustrophobic in the small room, she decided to take a walk through the mausoleum and stretch her legs. It was dark, but she knew her way around the huge place well enough. She turned on the flashlight and made her way back to her father's tomb.

Running her fingers over the bronze plate on which his name was engraved, she spoke in a whisper.

"This will probably be my last visit, Mike. I know you wouldn't understand what I'm going to do . . . and if you were still alive, I'd never have the courage, that's for sure. I stayed with you till the end, in spite of everything you'd done to me, but you're gone, and I can't wait any longer. If there's a hell, you're in it, and I have no intention of joining you there. I'm going to make one last stab at saving my immortal soul. Did you hear that, Mike? I know you wanted to possess my soul and my spirit too. My whole life wasn't enough, was it? Nothing was ever enough for you. You know, I tried so hard to please you, but I never quite succeeded. Funny, even when I rebelled, I tried to hurt myself, and not you."

She paused and pressed her hands against her eyes for a moment before continuing. "Why did I love you? I guess it was because you were all I ever had . . . and I had to love somebody, didn't I? A person can't go through life loving nobody. If you can hear me, Mike, do one thing for me. Please don't interfere. Let me get one thing right."

Vanessa slowly made her way through the dark echoing halls, back into the light of the rest room. Half an hour later, she checked the color of her hair again and saw that it was still not light enough. Oh well, there wasn't any hurry. She had all night.

3

Without Coercion

The doorbell rang, and Dan hurried down the steps to answer it, hoping it would be his wife returned from some foolish, thoughtless errand. But it was not. The first two couples of the twenty guests invited stood at the door. Dan could not bring himself to tell them the truth. Perhaps Cake would reappear any moment, and then he would look ridiculous.

"Sally . . . George, good to see you. Come in. Hello, Brett . . . Nadine, you look lovely." He shook hands with the men and kissed the women. Then, taking the women's wraps, he directed everyone to the living room.

"Please go on into the den. There's a bartender there to take care of you. I'll be back in a few minutes. Make yourselves at home. The others will be arriving shortly, and we're running a little late."

"Go right ahead, Dan. We can take care of ourselves. Say, I'm really looking forward to meeting your wife," Brett remarked graciously, making Dan feel even more awkward and discomfited. Brett was the president of a dynamic new group of real-estate men who were developing a racetrack in Riverside County. He had just awarded the engineering contract to Dan's firm, and Dan was not anxious for him to find out about Cake's disappearance.

The contracts were not yet signed. Smiling, Dan backed out of the room with a promise to return immediately.

"Mary, some of our guests are here. Will you take care of them for me and see that they have everything they need? And please let the others in when they arrive. I'm going up to the bedroom to call the police."

"The police?" Mary asked in alarm.

"I'm afraid not to. I haven't been able to locate anyone who's seen Cake. Don't mention any of this to the guests, okay?"

Dan ran up the stairs to look once more—somewhere in the back of his mind hoping to find Cake in their bedroom, the way one finally sees a lost key or a letter on the very desk that has previously been thoroughly searched. No luck. No Cake.

He picked up the telephone, dialed the police, and asked them to send someone to the house.

"For what reason?" the voice asked.

"My wife is missing."

"How long's she been gone?"

"I'm not sure . . . an hour, more or less." God, how dumb he sounded.

"An hour? I'm sorry, sir, but we don't list adults as missing until forty-eight hours have passed. Unless, of course, you have reason to suspect foul play."

Dan looked around at the unusually perfect order the room was in and replied, "Yes, something is very wrong here. Please send someone right away." He gave his name and address, then hung up the telephone and collapsed into a chair and buried his face in his hands.

Looking up, he stared at his now haggard face in the mirror. As he peered into the reflection of his own eyes, Dan wondered at the macabre nature of his feelings. Why was it less frightening to believe she had been forcibly abducted by a murderer or a rapist than to believe she had walked out of her own free will?

Dan stayed in his room and listened to the guests arriving. He did not emerge until he heard the police ask for him. As the two young policemen in uniform stepped inside, George, who was the comptroller of Dan's firm, appeared from the living room, startled to see policemen in the house. "Dan, is something wrong?" he asked.

"Really, it's nothing serious. I'm sure it will all be cleared up soon. Please don't say anything to anyone. I'll join you all and explain in a little while. Right now I have to talk privately with these officers." He called to the caterer, "Mary, if dinner's ready, go ahead and serve. I'll be in my study."

Dan signaled the officers to follow him, and once in the study, he closed the doors so they could talk privately. Quickly he explained the situation and showed them the note Cake had left on the unlocked front door. The policemen listened and made notes, and when Dan was finished, one of them asked, "Have you and your wife been having any marital difficulties lately?"

Dan was indignant. "Of course not! Do you think I would have called you if that had been the case?" he snapped.

"Sorry, but we had to ask. Do you have any children in the house?"

"We have two children, but our son is at the University of Oregon and our daughter is studying art at the Sorbonne in France."

"Have they lived away from home long?"

"Rob is in his first year of college, and Trina left for France just three months ago."

"Have you talked to either one of them?"

"No, I wouldn't want to worry them."

"May we have a look around, Mr. Halliday?"

"Certainly," Dan replied, hoping they were beginning to take him seriously.

Dan took them on a tour of the house, and then outside to check the grounds. Finally, one of them said, "Mr. Halliday, I think we should talk to your neighbors, ask them if they saw anyone around the house or if they saw her leave.''

"I've already done that," Dan responded irritably.

"I know it's hard to face, sir, but it looks to me as if she left without coercion. If I were you, I'd talk to everyone close to her. You might find out more than we could.''

"Thanks, for nothing," Dan replied testily.

"Sorry we couldn't be of more help. Keep in touch with us. We'll put this on file for now.''

Dan slammed the door on their retreating figures. Now he had to go into the dining room and face his guests. What the shit was he going to tell them!

4

Is It Really You?

Trish Delaney awakened at ten in the morning and for a moment was disoriented by the strangeness of her surroundings. God, what was she doing in New York in this tiny hotel room? It hadn't looked so bad when she checked in late the night before, but the sunlight streaming through the thin curtains brought all its ratty little details into sharp focus. "Small, but cozy and homey," the brochure had said. It was certainly right about small.

Stretching, she contemplated the day before her, then looked at the telephone. It was time to make that call. Should she do it now, this very minute . . . get it over with . . . find out, for better or worse? Or should she postpone it one more day, give herself a chance to relax? No. She had to do it now. It wouldn't be any easier tomorrow.

She got out of bed, took a small piece of paper out of her purse, and dialed the number written on it. After one ring, a voice answered, "Senator O'Shea's office, may I help you?"

Trish answered nervously, "Yes, this is Trish Delaney, an old friend of the senator's. Is he in?"

"No, I'm sorry, he's not, but if you'll leave your telephone number, I'll see that his personal secretary gets your message."

"I'd like to speak to her myself, please."

A few moments later, a deep masculine voice came on the line. Trish's heart skipped. Had she gotten Red himself by mistake? "Red?" she gasped.

"No, this is his secretary. Is there something I can do for you?"

"Oh . . . of course. I'm an old friend of the senator's. Is he in town now, or is he still in Washington?"

"I believe he's here in New York, but I'm not sure. I haven't heard from him yet today. Would you like to leave your name and number?"

Trish gave the man her name and the hotel number and then got back into bed to wait for Red's return call. Surely he would call her, wouldn't he? He couldn't have forgotten her when she remembered him so well . . . and often . . . and vividly.

Trish curled herself up into a tight ball of nerves as she thought back to the years when she and Red had been the most popular couple at Farragut High School in Dayton, Ohio. She was the head cheerleader, and Red O'Shea the football star. What glorious days those had been. Too bad she'd been such a tight-assed little virgin, or they might have been even better. Someone once said that you only regret the things you don't do. That's for sure, she muttered bitterly into the pillow.

Her thoughts roamed back in time, and she had just begun to doze again when the telephone jangled her to alertness. She picked up the receiver and was thrilled to hear a voice that was still familiar—partly through the magic of television—despite the years. "Delaney, for God's sake, is it really you?"

"Red, it's so good to hear you say my name. Nobody has called me Delaney since I last saw you." Her heart was racing with excitement.

"You sound wonderful. What've you been doing for the past twenty years?"

"Oh, you know, the usual. Nothing as exciting as you, I'm afraid."

"Are you still married?"

"Not really," she answered a beat too quickly. "I was hoping we could get together for a drink or something. I thought it might be fun to talk over the old days."

"I'd love to see you, Delaney. How long will you be in town?" Did she imagine it, or had his voice suddenly taken on a tone of reticence?

"I'm not quite sure. It depends on several things. A few days, maybe."

"Look, I'm tied up tonight, but what would you say if we had lunch tomorrow?"

"That would be wonderful. Where?"

"Four Seasons . . . at one, okay?"

"I'll be there. Do you think you'll remember me without my pom-poms?"

"Delaney, I could never forget you . . . or your damn pom-poms."

Trish put down the telephone, and her hands were shaking with excitement and joy. He had remembered her! He wanted to see her again. Not for dinner, of course—he was too smart to commit himself to an evening with someone who might very well have grown old and fat. Trish leapt out of bed and crossed the room to look at herself in the mirror. Lord, would she seem old to him? After all, he was remembering a nubile seventeen-year-old.

She picked up the telephone book—there wasn't a moment to be wasted—and found the number of Mr. Kenneth's salon. But though she pleaded and cajoled, she could not get an appointment for two weeks. Damn, why hadn't she thought of that?

Telephoning Elizabeth Arden's, she affected the slightest trace of a Texas accent and said, "Hello, this is Mrs. Delaney's secretary. We've just arrived from Dallas, and she needs an appointment this afternoon for a styling and coloring. I'm sure she'll want a pedicure and a manicure too, and if you can work it in, a facial. What time should she be there?''

There was a slight pause before the reply. "Tell Mrs. Delaney that we'll work her in at one. May I have a telephone number where she can be reached?''

Trish gave her the number and hoped the girl wouldn't check and find out she was staying in a fleabag. Now, she'd better get going. She needed food and a visit to Saks or Bergdorf's.

The morning was bright and clear. Feeling the need to stretch her legs, Trish walked from her hotel on the West Side, near Carnegie Hall, over to the Brasserie on the East Side. She ordered a light breakfast of juice and a poached egg, but when she caught sight of the fluffy, high kugelhopf, coffee cake filled with raisins, she blew calorie caution to the winds and asked for a slice. When she finished eating, Trish walked back to Fifth Avenue to browse at Saks. She didn't want to spend too much on her outfit for tomorrow because she might get a second chance for a dinner date, and for that she'd have to shoot the moon.

She walked through the store hoping for inspiration, but keeping track of the time. Suddenly she saw what she wanted. She knew whatever the cost, that was what Red O'Shea would first see her in. It was a muted gray-green suit of sheer wool by Anne Klein with a calf-length pleated skirt, a marvelous jacket with one huge lapel, and a matching silk blouse, high-necked with tucks and ruffles. She tried on the outfit, and it did just what she wanted it to do for her. It brought out the green in her large almond-shaped eyes and made her look tall and slim. The clerks exclaimed that she looked terrific in it, and she agreed.

Trying not to think of the price, Trish paid for the suit, then hurried up to the shoe department. There was nothing right for the outfit, and she was almost out of time. Well, either later that afternoon or tomorrow morning, she would surely find something.

Struggling with her packages, she walked the few blocks

up Fifth Avenue to the salon. She felt exhilarated and stimulated to be a part of the hurrying crowd, although she walked slowly to enjoy the experience and also to inspect the vast array of goods in the elegant shop windows. It was such an exciting day, she reflected with satisfaction. She felt like an adventuress.

At Elizabeth Arden's, she changed into a smock and was ushered into a small private room where an attractive young woman greeted her.

"Mrs. Delaney? I'm Noreen, your stylist. Please sit here in the chair, and we'll have a look. Did you have any particular hairstyle in mind?"

"Not really. I'd just like to look younger . . . by about twenty years if you could manage it," Trish replied with a laugh.

Noreen smiled. "Well, first of all, I think we should lighten the color. Not all over, of course, but just put in a few highlights to blend in with the strands of gray and your natural dark blond. All right?"

"Whatever you say."

As the young woman continued to talk, she ran her fingers through Trish's hair, lifting and separating the strands. "Then I think we'll shorten it on the sides and top so that we can lift it up and away from the face, although I'd like to leave enough length in the back to give it a nice full appearance."

"Do whatever you think is best," Trish murmured. "Just so you make me look beautiful."

5

The Jazzy Blond

Vanessa had slept on the small couch in the ladies' room of Morningside Mausoleum, but not very well. The room was miserably cold, the couch was not long enough for her, and the rollers in her hair dug into her scalp, already tender from the bleach.

She looked at her watch. It was almost six. She had better get moving. Quickly she took the rollers out of her hair and brushed through the curls. Actually the hair looked a lot better than she had expected it to. The color was a little brassy, but then, that was really the look she was aiming for, because it was so different from her normal elegant but subdued appearance. Hesitantly she then began to apply the makeup that would change her face as much as possible. She had practiced it in the privacy of her home, so she knew how different she could look.

First, a base with a lot of pink in it to give herself a glow, and then, painstakingly, she covered her eyelids with a bright teal shadow. At first it looked a little bizarre to her, but after she finished outlining her eyes with dark brown pencil and applying mascara to her lashes, the startling effect of the blue was diminished. She powdered her heavy dark eyebrows to soften them and wished she'd used a little bleach, but it was too late for that now. When she was finished, she had to admit that her efforts were successful. No one would ever mistake the jazzy blond looking out from the mirror for the forty-year-old rich lady who had slipped into this room yesterday.

Her next change was the color of her eyes. Removing the contact lenses she was wearing, she substituted a pair that were tinted green, and her dark brown eyes suddenly looked hazel. Not a total change, but enough, she hoped.

Quickly she slipped out of her clothes. Taking off her bra, she put on one that was heavily padded, pulled a thick angora sweater over it, and stepped into a heavy wool pleated skirt. She looked a good ten pounds heavier and a lot more robust. Her mid-heel Ferragamo pumps were replaced by a pair of pumps with stiletto heels from Charles Jourdan. She had practiced walking in them around the house, so they were not uncomfortable, and they certainly made walking with a hippy sway a lot easier.

Time was moving too fast. Swiftly she transferred everything from her old handbag into the new one. Then she gathered up everything else, including her old clothes, the bleach, the curlers, the shoes, and stuffed them into the garbage bag. When she was sure that the room showed no traces of her visit, she turned her coat inside out so the beige fabric was on the outside instead of the dark brown, and slipped it on. A bright teal-and-orange scarf at her neck completed the outfit. Picking up the trash bag and her purse, she headed for the crematorium.

She had to walk on her toes. The click-click of the high heels echoed too much, and although it was still early, she was afraid someone might have arrived at work ahead of schedule. As she walked through the chapel, she could see the sky lightening with the dawn. She moved faster. At the front of the chapel she used her flashlight to find the button that moved the sliding door, and pressed it. The carved oaken panel slid silently open, and she hurried into the crematorium behind. Striding to the oven, she grasped the handle and turned it to open the heavy metal door. Quickly she put the trash bag inside, placing it near the front corner where it could not be seen. She closed the door, locked it, and retraced her steps, carefully wiping her feet so that the fine ash that covered everything in the crematorium would not be carried onto the carpeting and leave telltale footprints.

So far, so good. Now all she had to do was wait until the doors were opened by the staff. The next service was scheduled for ten-thirty, and she planned to be among the mourners.

6

Her New Self

As Trish walked up Fifth Avenue she tried to catch glimpses of herself in the glass store windows. She looked great, if she did say so herself. That Noreen was a terrific hairdresser. The lightened hair had done a lot for her, too. She looked and felt younger, especially with the beautiful eye makeup. She hoped she could remember how to do it herself.

Suddenly she caught sight of a pair of supple gray calf boots in Gucci's window. They would look perfect with her new outfit, she decided, and pushed open the door of the shop.

Half an hour later, carrying her new suit, the boots, and a matching handbag, she struggled to find a cab. It was rush hour and hopeless. Her hotel wasn't too far away, but she was tired and loaded down, in no mood to walk. The Plaza was so close. Why not? She'd stop in at the Palm Court and treat herself to a little snack and a glass of wine. Then she could have the doorman get a taxi for her.

As she walked into the charming art-deco tearoom in the lobby of the historic old hotel, she was dismayed to find that half of New York had the same idea.

She simply didn't feel like standing in line holding all of her purchases just to have a drink. Perhaps she should pop into the Oak Bar. She remembered it as being dark and comfortable, and hoped it wouldn't be quite so crowded. She walked through the lobby into the shadowy wood-paneled room, which was filled with smoke and dark three-piece suits. She pushed her way to a small table and dropped into a chair. God, it felt good to put everything down and relax.

She gave the waiter her order and minutes later was served a glass of white wine. Sipping it slowly, she looked about, observing the people around her. There weren't too many women in the room and those present were involved in animated conversations. In fact, she was the only person in the room drinking alone. She began to feel awkward and ill-at-ease. Good grief, what was she doing spending her money sitting in a bar drinking alone? Then her other self, her new self, took over. And why the devil shouldn't she be there if that's where she wanted to be? After all, she was a free person, wasn't she? She didn't have to answer to anyone, thank you, she reassured herself.

As Trish sat ruminating, a man who was with a group at a nearby table got up and walked toward her. He was tall and thin, his bearing erect and graceful. Both his hair and his neatly trimmed mustache were pure white and contrasted handsomely with his complexion, which was remarkably tan for a New Yorker. And he was extremely attractive for a man she guessed to be about sixty.

"How do you do?" the man said courteously. "Would you mind if I sat down here with you? Everyone at that table is smoking, and my eyes are beginning to water."

Trish sympathized. There was no such thing as rights for nonsmokers in bars. "Of course," she replied. "The air in here is really a bit thick."

The man sat down, and she noticed that he was dressed in a perfectly tailored and expensive suit—Saville Row no doubt—and on his hand he wore a magnificent heavy gold ring.

"My name is Richard Terhune, and I'd be very pleased if you would let me buy you a drink."

"Thank you, but no. I just got this one, and I'm afraid one glass is about my limit."

"Smart girl. Waiter, please bring me another Chivas and water . . . no ice."

"No ice?" Trish asked curiously.

"Yes, just a little habit I picked up when I lived in London. Now, tell me your name, or do you intend to make me guess?"

Trish was intrigued. He was charming and she didn't feel at all threatened by him. "If you were to guess, what do you think I'd be called?" she replied in a tone that sounded more coy than she had intended.

He smiled, enjoying the little game. "Hmm, let's see. It would have to be a name that has dignity. . . . You're very dignified, you know."

Trish was surprised. No one had ever said she was dignified before. "What a strange thing to say. This new haircut must have really changed me."

"I meant it in the best possible way. You strike me as being. . . well, ladylike really. I'd guess you to be kind and gentle, and generally very comfortable with people."

Trish smiled. "You're being evasive, in a nice way, but you still haven't made a guess about my name."

"It's Jessica . . . right?"

"Jessica? What a lovely guess, but no, it's Trish . . . Trish Delaney."

"And where are you from Trish Trish Delaney?" His eyes were twinkling with amusement.

"Just one Trish. . . and I'm from. . . nowhere."

"Hmmm, I know the place well. Been there many times myself."

"Are you a New Yorker?" she asked.

"Good God, no. I'm from Los Angeles."

Trish was dismayed. How strange that she would meet someone in New York from her own city. Oh well, Los Angeles was a big place.

"What brings you here?" she asked.

He smiled ruefully. "Business. Messy business."

"I see." Trish decided she didn't want to hear any more. She sipped her wine and thought about getting up and leaving. She hadn't had anything to eat since breakfast, and the wine was making her a little queasy. She reached for her purse to get the money to pay the check, but Terhune touched her arm lightly. "No, please . . . permit me. It has been my pleasure to be able to talk with such a lovely lady for a few minutes. Are you a guest here at the hotel?"

Trish shook her head. "No, I'm not, and I would really prefer to pay for my own drink. I enjoyed talking to you, too."

"I don't suppose you'd consider having dinner with a lonely old man, would you? There's a dining room right here at the hotel. The food's pretty good, and there's a nice view of Fifth Avenue and the horse-drawn cabs."

Trish hesitated. Although she was tempted, the idea of being picked up in a bar seemed a little adventurous for her first night in the big city.

"Look, Trish. It's just for dinner, I promise you. I haven't propositioned a lovely lady I've just met in a bar for a long, long time. When dinner is over, I'll see that you're put into a cab and sent safely back to . . . nowhere. Cross my heart."

Trish relented. Why not? What trouble could she get into? And what was she worried about anyway? "All right, but could we start soon? I'm starved, and I have to get to bed early tonight. I have an important appointment tomorrow."

They had a quiet and delightful evening together in the Edwardian Room. Richard was full of stories about famous people he knew, and Trish was fascinated by him. He was witty and worldly and intelligent, his demeanor gentle and courtly. She was seated by the windows on Fifth Avenue, and during the infrequent lulls in the conversation she watched the people hurrying by in the cold night air with the lights of the city casting a glow of excitement over everything. A small group of musicians played music that was romantic and danceable, the kind her son described as elevator music, but she loved it. God, how she loved New York.

"Now, I suspect that you don't want to tell me about yourself, so how about telling me about your dreams. Don't tell me that you don't have any. We all have them," Richard said gently. There was a slight twinkle in his eye, and he seemed to be enjoying himself a great deal.

"My dreams. . . goodness, yes, I have lots of dreams. My parents thought I was impractical because I was such a daydreamer. My dad always said if I didn't get my act together the world would pass me by."

"What kind of dreams?"

Trish smiled at him impishly. She was feeling relaxed and a trifle reckless. "You tell me your dreams, and I'll tell you mine."

Richard laughed out loud. "Good God, you're too young to remember that old song."

"What do you want out of life?"

He shrugged his shoulders. "I don't know. I've already had success and fame. I've won cases that everyone said were unwinnable. I suppose I just want to keep on doing what I do because I do it well. I don't really want life ever to get too easy or too simple. I'm comfortable living on the edge."

As he spoke, Trish suddenly made the connection, and she was embarrassed that she'd been so obtuse. "Good heavens, you're Richard Terhune, the attorney who won that big suit against, uh . . ." She faltered, trying to remember the details.

"Against the whole world," he interjected.

"And you defend criminals too, don't you?"

"I prefer to think of them as the 'unjustly accused.' Now it's your turn."

Trish tried to digest the fact that she was dining with a

celebrity without acting unduly impressed. "Well, Richard, if you promise not to think me silly, my dream has always been to paint. I wanted to go to art school, but my parents thought that secretarial school was more practical. All these years, I've dabbled at it without a smidgen of encouragement from anyone. The only people who were ever impressed with my talent were my children when they were very little. As they got older and wiser, they too began to see my efforts as puny and uninspired. Luckily, my daughter was blessed with the talent I wanted and didn't have, so I suppose I shouldn't be greedy."

"Don't ever give up on a dream, Trish, and never, ever march to the beat of someone else's drums. What do you think of the work you turn out?"

Trish cupped her hand around the wineglass and smiled sheepishly. "I always thought it was rather good."

He touched her hand lightly and reassuringly. "You're the only critic that counts, my dear. Great artists work only to please themselves. Remember that. It's never too late."

Trish tried not to eat too much, but the food was delicious, and the bottle of Château Pétrus that he ordered was too special to resist.

After the espresso, Trish decided it was time for her to leave. "Richard, this has been a perfectly marvelous evening. I can't thank you enough, but I must go now."

"Of course you must. And please don't thank me. It was wonderful of you to accept my invitation. You made me forget for a while what a shabby place the world is."

They both stood up, and he walked her to the coach entrance of the hotel. As they stepped through the revolving door, a uniformed driver approached them. Terhune nodded to him, and the driver turned and sprinted to the other side of the circle and got into a long black limousine, which he quickly maneuvered directly in front of them.

Trish was dismayed. "Oh no, Richard, I can't afford one of these. I just need a cab," she protested.

He laughed. "Don't worry. This car is one of the perks of my job here, and I certainly don't need it tonight. I'm going right up to my room to go to sleep. The driver will take you wherever you want to go. Your packages are already inside. And don't pay him a thing, you understand?"

As he spoke, Richard took her arm and gently pressed her into the luxurious car. Without another word, he closed the door, saluted her, and turned to go back inside. She told the chauffeur the name of her hotel and settled back to inspect her surroundings. Good grief, the interior of the limousine was almost as big as her hotel room, and certainly a lot nicer. She wished she could go to sleep right there.

As the big car moved through the light traffic of the evening, taking her the few blocks to her hotel, she wondered why Richard Terhune had singled her out . . . and if she would ever see him again.

7

Macabre Overtones

Dan awakened the next morning to the still and lifeless house, and he felt eerily alone. All his married life he had complained about the tumult of the children, their friends, and the dog. Now they were all gone. Old Baldpate and his incessant bark had been stilled forever through the mercy of a vet just a month before Rob and Trina had left for school. And now Cake was gone. And he felt abandoned.

As he shaved and showered, he tried not to think of the dreadful evening before with its macabre overtones, nor to dwell too much on Selena's obvious delight in his solitude. Why had he felt so trapped when he talked to her on the telephone just before he had gone to bed? The nerve of her to actually suggest that she come over to spend the night with him. He hoped he had conveyed strongly enough to her the message that Cake's disappearance was temporary. At least he hoped it was temporary.

When he was dressed, he walked out of the house and across the street to see if Joyce, Cake's closest friend, knew anything. She looked surprised to see him.

"Dan! I was expecting Cake." She looked genuinely concerned. "Is she all right?"

"You tell *me*, Joyce. She was gone when I got home last night. Have you any idea where she could be?"

"No! Come in . . . come in."

Dan went into the house and sat down in the living room to give her the few details he knew.

Joyce listened intently, and when he finished, she let out a low exclamatory, "Jesus!"

"What do you think, Joyce? You're her closest friend. Can you explain it to me?"

"I'd like to think she's finally gotten smart and left you, but that would be out of character. That dumb wife of yours thinks you shit pearls."

"You do have a way with words, Joyce."

"Sorry. I didn't intend to put you down in your misery, Dan, but I don't really think I can help you. I didn't see Cake at all yesterday. She told me several days ago that she couldn't play tennis or go shopping this week because she had to get the house in shape for the party last night. The last time I saw her was at the hospital on Friday. It was a hellish day there because a lot of the regular staff was out with the flu, and they really leaned on the volunteers. Cake was on the pediatric ward feeding babies, and I was pushing wheelchairs. We had a quick cup of coffee together, and she seemed perfectly fine. I can't even remember what we talked about. Nothing much.

"Well, she certainly did work hard. The house is clean and in absolutely perfect order—including her closets and dresser drawers."

"Are you kidding me?" Joyce asked.

"No. It's certainly not normal, is it?"

"That's for sure. She always said, 'Show me a house with orderly closets, and I'll show you a wife with a disordered mind.' It sounds like she's telling you something." Suddenly Joyce grinned. "Hot damn! I bet she's left you. Whatta you know."

"Thanks a lot for your words of comfort," he replied testily.

"Sorry, that wasn't very nice, was it? But isn't it better to think that she walked out of her own free will than to think she was abducted?'' Joyce sensed his ambivalence and reacted. "You're a jerk, you know that? Your wife is one of the nicest, kindest, most unselfish people I've ever met. If she's finally gotten the smarts and left you, fine, but she's so damn naive and trusting that I'm worried about her being out there alone in a world filled with savages and creeps.''

"For your information, I'm worried about her too!" Dan got to his feet. There was no point in staying there to be insulted when Joyce could not give him any information. "Well, let me know if you think of anything.''

After Dan left Joyce's house, he drove to the convalescent hospital to see his mother. Cake rarely let more than two days pass without visiting her, so perhaps his mother could tell him something. On the way, he began to think about the awful prospect of telling Rob and Trina. Would they blame him as Joyce had?

Thoughts of Cake filled his mind. He tried to remember when they had last made love, but he couldn't remember exactly when. Funny. Had their sex become as commonplace as the morning coffee? Was it possible that she had ceased to find sexual satisfaction with him as he had with her? The possibility made him very uncomfortable, and he thrust it away.

Dan arrived at the hospital where his mother had lived since her stroke. Cake had tried to bring her home to live with them, but his mother would have none of it. A fiercely independent woman, she'd declared that she had no intention of living in a house with two noisy teenagers, but everyone knew that was only her excuse to keep from being a burden to a family she loved dearly.

Dan walked quickly through the hospital corridor, trying to avoid looking directly at the patients, those poor remnants of human beings who had outlived their minds and their bodies. Modern medicine had not really prolonged life—it had just managed to lengthen the process of dying.

It was depressing. He hated to come there. It was too great a reminder of his own mortality.

Elizabeth Halliday was propped up in bed with a dinner tray in front of her. She had barely touched the food, and her lack of appetite was evident in the frailness of her body.

Dan stood in the doorway and studied the woman who had borne and raised him, her only child. Her head was resting on the pillow, and her eyes were closed. He approached her silently and looked down at her delicate body, her transparent skin, wrinkled like crumpled tissue paper, that barely concealed her fragile bone structure. He could almost see the skeleton that was now so close to the surface. Good God, how much longer could she live like this?

Gently he leaned down and touched his lips to her forehead. He could smell the urine and feces that were now her constant companions. She had been such a lovely, meticulously groomed woman. She did not deserve to be robbed of her dignity this way.

Slowly she opened her eyes and looked up at the son she loved so much. It took a few moments for the words to form on her lips. "Dan . . is that you?"

"Yes, Mother. How are you feeling?"

A brief smile flickered across her face. "Oh, as well as can be expected. Where's Cake?"

Dan hesitated. Cake was important to Elizabeth, perhaps even more important than he was, since he had been too busy to devote much time to his mother. "I don't know, Mother. Do you?"

Elizabeth's eyes opened wide, and she suddenly seemed more her alert self. "What are you saying, son? Has Cake left you?"

Dan shook his head. "I really don't know. She wasn't home when I got there last night."

"Tell me about it," she whispered, and her eyes were bright and interested.

Briefly Dan gave her the details of his homecoming, the

police, the tidy closets, and his complete bafflement. His mother listened attentively, nodding her head with each revelation. When he was finished, she said, "You're right, Dan. She's left you, but perhaps not for good."

"How do you know that?"

"Because she didn't leave a note . . . or tell you it was all over. She went out, but she left the door unlocked so that she could come back."

"Why would she do that?"

"She probably still loves you, although I'm not sure why."

Dan was stung by his mother's words. Was her mind going as well as her body? "Why would you say something like that?"

The old woman closed her eyes for a moment, as if gathering courage to speak a painful truth. "My darling son . . . because of the way you treat her—the way you treat everyone who loves you. God help me, but I've often wondered if I was the cause . . . maybe I loved you too much when you were a child. Perhaps I exaggerated your place in the scheme of things. I just don't know." Her voice trailed off, and she turned her head away from him to gaze out the window.

"Mother, did Cake ever say anything to you about . . . the way I treated her?"

Slowly she shook her head, so slightly that the movement was almost imperceptible. "No, Dan, but there is something you should know . . ." She paused, again closing her eyes momentarily before continuing. "Several months ago, I asked Cake to take some money that I'd kept in my savings account and put it into an account in her name. I wanted to give it to her before I died. It was an account I'd had for many years. Your father never knew about it. It was my own little secret, but it gave me a . . . a sense of freedom, knowing that I had that little nest egg. Well, I wanted Cake to have one too . . . some money that was all hers. I told her to use it any way she wanted.''

"And she accepted it?" he asked, unable to control the tremor in his voice at the thought that Cake could just walk out on him like that.

"Not readily. She kept refusing, but I finally managed to convince her that it was of no use to me and that it would make me happy if she would take it. The account was much bigger than I expected it to be. I hadn't touched it in years, you know. It came to more than twelve thousand dollars. I was surprised and pleased that I had that much to give her. She's been so kind to me. She was the daughter I always wanted, and I love her as much as if she were really my own child.''

"How long ago did this happen?"

"I'm not sure. One day just melts into the next, and I lose track of time nowadays. It could have been a month ago . . . perhaps three . . . I'm just not sure."

"Do you know what bank she put it in?"

"I have no idea. It's her money now."

"Well, that certainly solves the problem of where she got the money to leave, doesn't it?" His voice betrayed bitterness that his own mother had somehow been an accomplice.

"Son, Cake must have been awfully unhappy with you to use money that I gave her to leave you. I'm sorry she's gone. For my sake as well as yours. But I will never regret giving it to her, and there is nothing that she could do that would destroy my faith in her.''

"I have to go now, Mother. I have a lot to do."

"Will you come back to see me, son? You're not angry with me?" Her voice had lost its resolute tone, and against her will had become a trifle pleading.

"Of course I will," he responded, suddenly touched by her frailty, and as his lips brushed her forehead, he felt a pang of longing for the vibrant woman his mother had once been. At the door he smiled reassuringly. "Don't worry, Mother . . . I promise to be here at least as often as Cake was.'' And as he left the room, he vowed that he would keep his promise.

Climbing into his car, he decided not to go to the office. A hopeful little voice inside him told him to go home instead. Cake would probably be back by now. He felt it in his bones.

8

Atonement and Revenge

Vanessa managed to stay out of sight until the first of the mourners entered the chapel for the funeral services. Then she emerged and took a seat in the middle of a pew not too far from the rear. The coffin was rolled in from the slumber room of the mortuary located at the far side of the cemetery. From the many flowers, Vanessa was sure there would be a sizable crowd in attendance. The man who had died was going to be cremated, so there would be no graveside service. She had ordered a cab to pick her up and take her to the airport. She hoped it would arrive on time because she couldn't afford to linger here after the others had gone. Surely someone was already looking for her by now, but he wouldn't expect to find her in a cemetery . . . not quite yet, anyway.

The organist played softly on the giant organ, and the pews began to fill up. Vanessa soon found herself hemmed in on both sides, and she tried to stifle her uneasiness. She was uncomfortable when people got too close, for she hated to be touched, especially by strangers. She had learned very early in her life that touching could be very unpleasant and threatening, and she always recoiled from casual human contact.

She tried to turn her mind back to the happy time, when her daughter was born and the world was full of hope, but the grim years kept intruding. If she managed to stay alive until she finished what she had set out to do, would she ever be happy again? Not likely. She had lost too much: her innocence . . . her dreams . . . love. There were also too many secrets, too many dark pages in her life, and the course she had laid out was too full of chances for disaster. Nor did she have much hope for success in this desperate, last-ditch adventure.

But, "One does what has to be done," her father had said. How insulted Mike would be if he heard her use his own words as a reason to betray him. What a devil he had been. Did that make her a devil worshiper? He was all she'd ever had. Her mother had died when she was just a little girl and her father had refused to talk about his wife ever, even when Vanessa begged him. As a child, she had learned the folly of crossing him in matters that he considered important. She had done it once, and she would suffer all her life for it. But now he was dead, her child was lost to her, and she had nothing to live for except atonement and revenge. Could she manage both in one daring mission? It was almost like cheating, putting her life on the line for something that was so important, when in reality her life had no meaning at all—neither for herself nor for anybody else.

The funeral service was brief and cursory. Although the deceased had once been a man of wealth and influence, he had outlived most of his contemporaries, and those that came to pay their respects did so with no sense of loss.

When the service was over and everyone began moving toward the chapel doors, Vanessa tried to stay in the middle of the crowd. As she emerged from the building and walked toward the street, she saw a cab parked in front of the long line of limousines. She resisted the urge to run toward it. A distinguished older man was walking beside her. He seemed to be alone. She decided to chance talking with him briefly so that she would not look so solitary, just in case someone was watching.

"That was a nice service, wasn't it?" she murmured to the man beside her.

He looked at her in surprise and curiosity. "What, what did you say?" he asked.

She repeated the words a little louder, afraid that she might draw too much attention to herself. Obviously, from the elevated tone of his voice, he was slightly hard of hearing.

His reply, too, was loud enough to make her a little uncomfortable. "Yes, it was. Did you know George?"

She smiled and shook her head. She had already prepared an answer, just in case anyone asked. "No, but my family did. Have a nice day," she replied, hurrying away from him and into the cab.

As soon as she settled into the back seat, she looked out the windows to see if there was anyone around who looked even slightly familiar. But she saw no one, and as the cab carried her away, she began to feel that perhaps she had made it.

She had the cabdriver drop her at the Pan Am terminal, and just to be sure, she walked inside and stayed at the newsstand until the cab picked up another fare and left. Then she hurried out to the TWA building and went upstairs to the gift shop, where she purchased a small carry-on bag, a newspaper, and a few magazines. Carrying her purchases into the ladies' room, she entered a toilet stall and stuffed the reading matter into the hand luggage, adding her small cosmetic bag as well. She had already printed the name "Mrs. John Fitzgerald" on a luggage tag and she affixed it to the carry-on.

So far, so good, she thought as she checked her watch. Damn, she was still wearing her telltale diamond-encrusted Cartier watch. She had planned to dispose of it along with everything else, but she'd forgotten. Quickly she stripped the watch off her wrist, threw it into the toilet, and flushed it away without a touch of regret.

At the TWA counter she purchased a round-trip coach

ticket to New York City. Would anyone who was on a fatal mission buy a round-trip ticket? Not likely.

She had never in her life flown any way except first class or by private jet, and she dreaded the thought of being hemmed in by strange human flesh for five and a half hours. Although she wanted to sit on the aisle, she felt that she would be less visible near the window, but there were no window seats left in the nonsmoking section. She chose to sit with the smokers and hoped she'd be able to breathe. How amusing. Here she was risking her life on an extremely risky cause, and she was worrying about cigarette smoke. Now, there was a thought. Why shouldn't she smoke?

While she was waiting for the flight to be called, she returned to the gift shop and bought herself an inexpensive Timex wristwatch. It was certainly more suitable for the life she would be living than the expensive one she'd just thrown away. As she buckled the watch on her wrist, she suddenly realized that for the first time she could remember, she felt free. Was it because she was out of her father's house . . . or that she was finally, once and for all, defying him?

She didn't know the answer to that, but one thing she knew for certain: she might not have much time left to live, but by God, she was going to live it for the first time as a free person. No one—no one at all—would ever again tell her what to do.

9

Politics

Trish had trouble falling asleep. The mattress sagged, and she felt alone and threatened in the dingy hotel room. Though she had put a chair under the doorknob and made sure the window was locked tight, she still did not feel secure. Damn! Her eyes would probably have bags big enough to carry groceries in. The harder she tried to relax, the more tense she became, until finally she gave up altogether and turned on the television set. She watched a rerun of the old Marlon Brando version of *Mutiny on the Bounty* until her eyes began to close. At four in the morning she finally dozed off into a dream-filled sleep which lasted until nine, when the hotel maid's knock awakened her.

By then it was too late to go out for breakfast and a walk, so she called room service and ordered toast and coffee, which did not arrive until almost ten. The coffee was cold and bitter, and the toast was made of pale and soggy white sandwich bread. There was one consolation: the thought that lunch would be better.

She also ordered a bucket of ice. Recalling Faye Dunaway's first scene in *Mommie Dearest*, Trish decided to test for herself the restorative powers of ice. She scooped up a handful of cubes and held them to her face. Within seconds, the pain became unbearable, and she dropped them into the sink. God, she wasn't cut out to be glamorous. She tried once more, but she could manage to keep the ice on her face for only a few moments. What a miserable way to start the day. She dried her face and scrutinized herself in the mirror. She couldn't tell much difference except that her face was red.

Taking a shower was nothing less than an ordeal, with alternating surges of scalding and icy water every time someone in the hotel flushed a toilet or turned on a faucet. Afterward, wrapped in a towel, she carried her makeup to the window and applied it by the gray light of day filtering through the filthy window that looked out on a dank and dismal air shaft.

She worked patiently, carefully patting the foundation under her eyes to cover the circles, shading the shadow on her eyelids, and separating each lash with the mascara brush. When she was finished, she brushed her hair out just as Noreen had instructed her, and it fell into place perfectly. So far, so good. Then she put on her beautiful new clothes and handsome new boots, switched her stuff from the old handbag to the new, and she was ready. Look out, Senator, here I come, the new woman looking out at her from the dresser mirror seemed to be saying.

Trish arrived at the Four Seasons early and took her time devouring every detail of the magnificent marble-and-art-filled aerie as she ascended the grand staircase to the dining rooms. The maître d' was busy seating other guests, so she studied the high ceilings and the profusion of greenery. No cozy and intimate place this, she reflected. Elegant, but not really designed for the encounter she had in mind. When she learned that Red had not yet arrived, she declined to be seated since she thought it would be better strategically for him to sit down first. She would go to the ladies' room to check herself over as well as to make one last pit stop. Why did her bladder have such a small capacity when she was nervous?

In the lounge, she lingered for a full ten minutes, luxuriating in the long mirrors that gave her the opportunity to admire her new, very fashionable appearance. When the attendant began to look at her quizzically, Trish diverted her by asking, "Do you think the hem is even on this skirt?" Immediately the woman became involved in checking it out, and they struck up a friendly conversation. Finally Trish decided it was time to leave. She pressed two dollars into the grateful woman's hand and swept back up the stairs.

Her timing was perfect. As the pink-jacketed attendant led her across the marble-and-glass walkway beneath an imposing Picasso tapestry, past hundreds of bottles of wine shielded by glass, and into the large room with a raised pool of water at its center, her host was just being seated. She felt a tiny quiver of anticipation at the sight of his tall, lean frame and that shock of red hair, not so bright as it had once been, but still brilliant enough to make him easy to spot in a crowd. She waited until he got settled onto the leather banquette and then walked toward him, silently willing him to look up so that he would see her in all her fashionable glory. When she was within five feet of the table, he did, and the smile on his face was all she had hoped it would be.

"Delaney, my God, you look magnificent—you've made time stand still." Standing, he greeted her with a light kiss and a quick hug, and then they both quickly sat down as they realized that all eyes had turned toward them.

"You look just wonderful, Red, you haven't changed at all," she remarked.

"Oh, yes, I have. It's just that you've been watching me grow old gradually through the magic of the media. So tell me—what's going on in your life?"

"Nothing as exciting as yours, I'm afraid. I've been reading in the newspapers that your marriage is headed for the rocks too. Is it true?" Good grief! Now, why did she bring up that subject so soon?

"Let's have a drink. What would you like?"

"A Bloody Mary, please."

He ordered their drinks, and then he leaned his folded arms on the table and looked closely into Trish's eyes as he spoke. "You know all those dirty lies that have been printed about Gloria and me?"

Trish nodded. She had read everything she could get her hands on about him since he had become a celebrity.

He smiled sardonically. "Well, don't ever tell anyone I said this, but they're all true."

Trish was shocked. "All of them?"

"Well, maybe not all, but they're right about my distant relationship with my wife. Gloria and I have what you might call a polite marriage. We treat each other with kindness and civility, and I can't remember having a conversation of any depth with her in over a year. And we certainly never fight. That would be much too personal." His tone was light and amused, but Trish sensed some bitterness.

"Why are you still together?"

"Politics, Delaney, politics. I'm looking for the nomination for president. If I get it, she's agreed to hang in there and play goody-two-shoes until after the election. She promises nothing beyond that, although it's my gut feeling that she won't be able to resist playing the role of first lady. Power corrupts, you know."

"You don't sound as if you care very much for her."

The senator sighed and took a deep swallow of the Scotch and soda that had been placed in front of him. "She never was the big love of my life, but I liked her and respected her a lot when we got married."

Trish wanted to ask him who was the big love of his life, but she had better sense. He might tell her, and she wouldn't like the answer. "That doesn't sound very romantic," she commented.

"Well, all marriages can't be made in heaven. It's just too bad that so many are made in hell."

There was an awkward lull, and Trish decided that the conversation had taken off too far in the wrong direction.

"Red, do you remember our last date? The night before you left for West Point?"

He looked at her thoughtfully for a moment before answering, "Yes. Do you?"

Trish felt herself begin to blush. "What do you suppose would have happened if . . . we'd done things differently that night?"

Red smiled and took her hand, examining her fingers as he spoke. "Well, I don't know, but I might have told the Army to go to hell and stayed in Ohio. You might have gotten pregnant, and I would have had to get a job pumping gas to support you and the kid. We'd probably be living in a tract house, and I'd be playing poker on Friday nights with the guys and drinking beer and watching football on TV. But you know what?"

"What?"

"I still wish you'd said yes."

Trish looked up at him, and she felt the tears begin to fill her eyes. "Red, you always did say just the right thing. No wonder everybody votes for you."

"Well, not quite everybody. Let's order lunch. How long are you going to be in New York?"

"I don't know. I'm thinking about staying for a while. I really have no place special to go, but I need to look for a job."

"Really? Why don't you come to work for me?"

"Doing what?"

"Working on my campaign. You know, I've been pretty well-funded since that last poll showed me leading everybody in the party. The boys in the back room are calling me the next JFK. The job wouldn't pay much, but it's exciting working on a presidential campaign . . . and it would give us a perfectly valid reason to be seen together in public. What do you think?"

"I . . . I'd love it, if you think I could really be of any help to you." Her heart skipped at the revelation that he wanted to be with her.

"It's settled. Now, if you want to taste something really different, try the apple vichyssoise, and the lobster soufflé is excellent."

They ordered, and the food was delicious, made even more delightful by the hilarity and sentimentality of their reminiscences. Finally coffee was served, and Red looked at his watch. "I've got to go. Though I wish we could stay here all day. Now, here's a card with the address of my headquarters. Talk only to Joe Franklin. He'll make all the arrangements. Okay?"

"Fine, and thank you for a terrific lunch. I had a wonderful time."

"So did I. I have to go to Washington this evening, but with a little luck, I'll be back here by Saturday. Let's have dinner together. Where can I reach you?"

Trish reached into her purse and took out a matchbook from her hotel and handed it to him. "Here's where I'm staying . . . temporarily, I hope."

"Great. I've got to dash, I'm afraid. Take your time with your coffee . . . or order anything else you might want. They'll put it on my tab. You know, Delaney, you're even more beautiful than I remembered."

As she watched him leave, Trish was assailed by conflicting emotions. She was elated that he had remembered and regretted as much as she had, but she was depressed that she would have to wait three days alone in this overpowering and forbidding city where she was a stranger. She drank her coffee slowly and allowed her cup to be filled again. Now, what would she do? She couldn't go to his campaign headquarters until tomorrow. Maybe she should hit the shopping trail again and pick out something for Saturday night. It was now more important than ever to be beautiful. But there was plenty of time for that. First she would head over to the newly remodeled Museum of Modern Art. She needed to replenish her soul with Monet's water lilies.

10

Alone at Last

The flight took off on schedule, and Vanessa was uncomfortable from the start as she struggled to find enough room in her narrow seat so that she could avoid touching the elbow of the huge, burly man seated next to her. She purchased a set of earphones and clamped them on, hoping to lose herself in the music. No luck. Just as she thought she had accommodated herself to the small space allotted her, the man in front of her reclined his seat as far as it would go, and she found herself with the back of the seat practically in her lap. She was in bloody steerage, and she was outraged. Why in the world would the public accept such conditions? It was criminal, she fumed.

The air around her became blue with smoke, and her eyes began to sting. It was all so dreadful. She was tempted to ask for a change of seat, but the plane looked nearly full, and she didn't want to draw attention to herself. She ordered two gin and tonics. Maybe that would help. She tried to read, but she couldn't concentrate. She was not accustomed to having people so close to her, and being hedged in by the bodies of complete strangers distracted and annoyed her.

Quickly she consumed both drinks, then ordered some wine with her dinner. But when the food came, the sight of the unattractive meal piled on the tiny plate made her nauseous. She ate the cold roll with butter, drank the wine, and began to feel light-headed. She suddenly realized that she'd better stop drinking. The combination of altitude and alcohol could be devastating, and she needed to keep her wits about her. She still had a long way to go.

She wanted to get up and walk around, to escape to the toilet, but there were two people between her and the aisle, and she couldn't bring herself to make a scene by asking them to stand up with trays in hand to let her out. Closing her eyes, she rested her head against the seat. How stupid of her to have had those drinks. After what seemed an eternity, the stewardess brought coffee, and Vanessa gratefully sipped the hot liquid. It was the first thing that tasted good to her.

When the trays were finally picked up, Vanessa managed to squeeze past the passengers and walk back to the lavatories. There was a long line of passengers—which was fine with her. She was glad for the excuse not to return to her seat, and she wondered if it would look strange if she walked around for the rest of the flight.

When she finally got her turn, she entered the tiny stall and shut the door with relief. She had no intention of rushing back out, in spite of the fact that the rest rooms for the smoking section were in the tail of the plane and subject to a lot of motion. Having a little privacy at last more than compensated.

Even under the heavy makeup, her skin had taken on a ghastly gray color, and her hands were shaking. She leaned over the toilet, hoping that she could vomit and get rid of the liquor, but nothing happened. Wetting a paper towel with cold water, she applied it to her forehead and then her neck.

After a while she began to feel a little better, and she washed her hands and ran a brush through her hair. Although she didn't much feel like it, she repaired her makeup and opened the door. The cabin had been darkened, and the movie had begun. Thank heaven for Hollywood.

When the flight landed, thirty minutes late because of traffic at Kennedy, Vanessa pushed to be one of the first off the plane. As she walked through the passageway enjoying the rush of the cold New York night air that seeped in, she felt both relieved and elevated.

Since she had no luggage to wait for, she hurried to the cab stand. A man asked if she was going to Manhattan and would be interested in sharing, but she told him she was on her way somewhere else. There was no way she would endure being closeted in a cab with another stranger tonight. When the man in charge of dispatching the cabs asked her destination, she just said, "Manhattan," because she was feeling a little paranoid, and there was no sense in telling anybody anything that wasn't absolutely necessary. She later directed the driver to take her to the Pierre, and when she arrived there, she went into the lobby for only a brief moment. As soon as the cab was gone, she walked out into the night.

She was tired, but the freedom and the cold fresh air were a tonic to her. Walking had always been her favorite exercise, and the distance to the hotel she had chosen was not that great.

She walked slowly but purposefully, enjoying the hubbub of the city and the traffic, but most of all the anonymity. New York was the best place for someone to disappear.

It didn't take her long to get to the Maybelle Hotel. It was an old, unfashionable place, now catering primarily to salesmen on limited charge accounts. Even in its day, it had been a commercial hotel, but it was slightly seedy now and no longer attracted conventions. It was certainly not the kind of hotel where any of her friends would stay. That's why it was perfect. She went to the desk and asked for her reservation in the name of Fitzgerald.

"Yes, ma'am, we have it here. A small suite, right?" the desk clerk asked.

"I hope it's ready, I'm very tired."

"You've had a long flight from . . . Seattle, correct?"

Vanessa nodded and said no more. There was a secret to lying, her father had told her, and that was to say as little as possible.

"Luggage . . . is your luggage outside?" the clerk asked.

"No," Vanessa replied wearily, "it's been lost. Please, if the airline delivers it during the night, just hold it for me. I don't want to be awakened."

"How long will you be with us, Miss Fitzgerald?"

"At least two weeks. May I have my key now?"

The desk clerk handed her key to the waiting bellman, who picked up her hand luggage. Vanessa was glad that she'd had the foresight to write her new name on the tag. They entered the elevator and stopped at the eleventh floor. Her room was not far down the hall, and when they arrived, she quickly tipped the bellman and dismissed him. As she shut and bolted the door, she sighed. Alone at last—thank God.

11

A Virgin

As she stood in line at the museum waiting to buy a ticket, Trish looked up at the threatening skies and wished she'd gone back to the hotel and changed out of her new clothes. She couldn't work up any real concern, however, because she was still so elated by her first encounter with Red. Everything had worked out just as she had dreamed it would, since he was quite obviously interested in resuming their relationship. She would have a job that would help pay some of her expenses, too. And she would be in New York, where she could wallow in its museums and galleries, where art was treated as an adventure, a stretching into the unknown and untried to find new and different perspectives on life. Glancing up at the new tower that had been built on top of the museum, she wished momentarily that she could afford to buy one of the condominiums up there. Daydreaming again.

She walked into the cool, austere lobby of the museum and stepped onto the escalator. As she ascended to the next level, she stared out the tall glass windows at the gray apartment buildings looking down on the sculpture garden. How funny all those air conditioners looked hanging outside the windows. Some of them seemed to be secured very poorly, and she wondered if anyone had ever been killed by one falling. Death from the sky, she mused. How mundane.

Standing before Monet's *Water Lilies*, her eyes melting into the limpid flowers, she thought about the artist and his inspiration and courage in splashing those large areas of color over so massive a canvas. How free and daring and confident he was, how sure of his own artistry and genius.

Inspecting the canvas from both near and far, she walked back and forth for a long time. As she studied it, she thought back to her own life and her own desires. She had never been one to paint with a small brush either. She loved to work in brilliant colors with bold strokes, but whenever she set out to paint something, it always turned out to be different from what she had planned it to be. Something inside her would never let her paint things as she saw them with her eyes; instead she painted with her emotions. Perhaps that was why she could never bring herself to show anyone what she was doing. Those closest to her didn't understand what she had done, because her work was not representational. And she didn't have enough confidence to show anyone with expertise, for fear of being told she was wasting her time.

When she left the museum an hour later, she was in the mood to do some serious shopping. It still hadn't started to rain, so she walked up Fifth Avenue.

At Bergdorf's she found a spectacular slinky black Mary McFadden silk cocktail dress and a silk-and-lace teddy to wear underneath it. Since she had not brought any of her jewelry, she also splurged on a pair of large chunky faux diamond earrings set in black enamel. At I. Miller's she found a pair of high-heeled black satin pumps that were fairly comfortable, considering that the heels were skyscraper height. She considered buying a black French angora cardigan by Gloria Sachs to throw around her shoulders, but five hundred dollars was more than she felt she could spend on something not absolutely essential. She'd go without a wrap. After all, the dress had long sleeves, and she would be going by car from the hotel to the restaurant. If it rained, she'd wear the light raincoat she'd brought with her.

Feeling better but considerably poorer, she returned to her hotel room around six-thirty. As she dropped her boxes onto the bed, she noticed a piece of paper that had been slipped under the door. The note said that Richard Terhune had called and left his number for her to call him back. Though she had enjoyed her evening with the lawyer, she had almost forgotten him in the excitement of having seen Red again.

Curious, Trish dialed the number, which turned out to be that of a law office. The switchboard operator put her call through directly to Richard.

"Trish, I'm so glad you returned my call. How has your visit to the big city been so far?"

"Just wonderful. It's so exciting being in New York."

"Good, I'm glad to hear someone's having fun here. I called to see if perhaps you might consider having dinner with me this evening. I'll take you to a very special place. The food will be wonderful, I promise you . . . and we won't stay out too late, since I have to be in court early in the morning with some pretrial motions. How about it?"

Trish's spirits lifted appreciably. "I'd love it, Richard. I have no plans at all for tonight, and I enjoyed last evening so much."

"Good. I'll have the car pick you up at seven, if that will be all right, and then you can come by for me. I have a meeting that will last until then."

"Should I wear a cocktail dress . . . or would a suit do?"

"A cocktail dress, by all means. See you then, my dear."

Trish put down the telephone and looked at the booty on the bed. "Well, fellas, it looks as if you're going to have a trial run."

Promptly at seven the desk called to tell her the car was waiting. Trish took one more look in the mirror at the new woman who was wearing a costly black designer gown and shoes and blithely hummed "If They Could See Me Now." Then she hurried down to the lobby and out to the limousine. Settling herself into the upholstery, she suddenly regretted not buying the sweater. Not only was it beginning to get awfully cold, but she was afraid she looked a little foolish without a wrap. After all, she wasn't used to New York weather, and she certainly didn't want to catch a cold.

The car picked Richard up in front of a building on Park Avenue, and he greeted her with great warmth and affection. "Trish, you are a vision for these jaded eyes. I can't tell you how much I was looking forward to another evening with you."

She laughed. "Just wait till you see me standing up. I spent the afternoon shopping for this outfit."

"Gilding the lily, my dear. I'm certain you would look absolutely dazzling in an old robe and slippers," he remarked as he lifted her hand and kissed it lightly.

For the second time in the same day, two dynamic and attractive men had paid her extravagant compliments, and suddenly she was ready to believe them. Amazing how one could become what another sees. It had to be the clothes. All her life she had been thrifty and prudent about clothes and could never understand women who squandered their time and money covering their bodies, but maybe they knew something she hadn't known—until now.

"I'm glad you called, Richard. I've had a perfectly wonderful day, and it's so nice to finish it off as well as it began."

"Good. I was thinking about calling you to see how you were doing, when I was offered the chance to dine at a very special restaurant. I'm so happy you were able to join me."

"Where are we going?"

"Some place I'm sure you've never heard of. It's so exclusive, you see, that it even has an unlisted telephone number."

"Are you serious?"

"Absolutely. It's called Ventidue. Do you know what that means?"

"No, but it sounds Italian."

"It is. It means twenty-two in Italian. It's a little joke, you see. The man who started the place got angry at the treatment he received at Twenty-One one evening, and he decided to open his own restaurant and go it one better."

"That's pretty funny. He must be very rich."

"True. He's a powerful and very private man, and one of my clients. I serve as sort of an adviser to make sure that he doesn't get into trouble with the law, ever. Well, anyway, he persuaded several of his friends to join him in this venture. They decided to create an intimate and extraordinary place to dine and to entertain friends and business associates. They enticed one of Italy's greatest chefs to come to New York and organize the place and run it, for which he is paid quite handsomely. The owners were not looking for profits, you understand, but for pleasure and convenience."

"Sounds like an expensive undertaking, but why did they bring a chef from Italy and not France?" she asked.

Richard smiled. "Tsk, tsk, my dear, the cuisine of Italy is the mother of the cuisine of France. And besides, the owners are Italian, as are many of their friends."

"They're not Mafia, are they?" she asked curiously.

"Shame on you, Trish. No, they certainly aren't. Not all wealthy Italians are gangsters, you know. As a matter of fact, my mother was Italian, as is our popular governor."

"Sorry. Dumb question." Trish really did feel gauche.

"Yes, but you're forgiven. Now, here we are."

The limousine pulled up in front of a new glass-and-steel skyscraper, and a doorman in gold-trimmed livery emerged from under the canopy on which only the address was written. Though they were in the upper Eighties on Lexington, the place seemed to be an office building. They walked through the brightly lighted marble lobby, past a pair of guards seated behind a desk banked with television monitors, and entered an elevator.

As they ascended to the penthouse, Richard continued to

explain. "My client got the idea for the restaurant while he was in Japan. There the finest places are very small, very private, and one's privilege of being a guest is handed down from father to son. In Japan, of course, they do not generally entertain women."

"I'm glad it's not that way here," Trish commented as the elevator doors slid open to reveal a dimly lit room surrounded by tall windows revealing the sparkling panorama of city lights far below. The darkened ceiling was studded with tiny lights that looked very much like the stars in the night sky and added to the feeling that the room was floating in space. As they emerged from the elevator, a small man in a dinner jacket greeted them.

"Good evening, Mr. Terhune. Your table is ready. Miss Delaney, welcome to Ventidue. I hope you enjoy your first evening with us."

The maître d' escorted them to a banquette of dark blue leather. Looking out into the vastness of the city, Trish remarked softly, "Do they know the names of everyone before they arrive?"

Richard nodded and replied, "You tell them when you make the reservation, and you're expected to call if there's any change."

Trish focused her attention on the loveliness of the surroundings. The table was covered with a cloth of pale blue damask, the wine and the water goblets were heavy cut crystal, and the silverware was massive and obviously solid sterling. A sleek oval silver bowl filled with fresh blue irises and a lighted candle sat on the table, as well as tiny white place cards with their names on them.

Trish had to rise slightly from her seat to see the table next to them because the restaurant had been designed so that no table had a direct view of another, thus assuring privacy in the midst of a feeling of spaciousness. She was impressed with the ingenuity of the design.

"The rich do know how to live, don't they?" Richard observed.

"They certainly do. How many tables are there?"

"Not as many as you might think. It's those huge areas of glass that make it look spacious. Actually, I don't think they can accommodate more than twenty tables."

"Are there enough customers to keep the place busy?"

He laughed. "God, yes. Not only is this the best place in town, it's also reasonable for the quality of the meal. If you're given the opportunity to dine here, you don't pass it up. And they are not as generous with invitations as they once were."

The captain came to the table and greeted them by name. "Good evening, Miss Delaney, Mr. Terhune. I am Carlo. Would you care for a cocktail, or shall I send the sommelier to help you choose some wine?"

"I'd like wine," Trish responded, and Richard nodded. "Good. So would I."

Within moments an elderly man with a dark complexion and shiny black hair approached them. He wore a dinner jacket, and hanging around his neck were two silver chains. At the end of one chain hung a silver *taste-vin*, the small shallow cup for sampling wine, and the other held an impressive ring of keys.

Richard ordered a bottle of Taittinger Rose champagne, and the sommelier served it with a murmur of admiration for his excellent choice. As they sipped the wine, Trish and Richard talked as if they were old friends. Richard told her that the case he was working on would take more time than he had anticipated and would necessitate his staying in New York longer than he'd intended to, and Trish told him that she had just found a job and would also be a resident of the big city for a while.

The dinner was as wonderful as he had promised, and as Trish tasted the feathery *gnocchi verdi*, she contemplated the sudden wonderful change of course her life had taken.

Everything went smoothly until she asked, "Richard, can you tell me about the case that's keeping you in New York?"

"It's nothing I'd want to discuss during a lovely dinner like this, and believe me, Trish, it's nothing you would want to hear." There was only a short awkward pause before he continued, but his face had clouded with annoyance. "A lawyer often finds himself associating with people for whom the law has no meaning. It can be very disillusioning, but under our system, every man has a right to be defended . . . ." His voice trailed off, and he seemed lost in thought.

Trish was apologetic. "I'm sorry—just tell me when I'm prying. I won't be offended, honestly. There are certain things in my life that I can't tell anyone either. I not only won't talk about them, I won't even allow myself to think about them. You know, it's funny, but I used to be such a worrier. When something went wrong, I would stew and fret over it until it became much larger than it should have been. Then something happened that was so much worse than anything I'd ever experienced before that I couldn't deal with it at all. I had to get rid of it . . . to put it away from me, or God knows what I would have done. Something awful, I'm sure."

The expression on her face was so troubled that Richard covered her hand with his. She seemed suddenly vulnerable, and he wanted to comfort and protect her. "Trish, my dear, you're right not to think about it. We can't afford to let the miseries of life dominate us, can we?" He smiled reassuringly and looked pleased when she responded, "Of course we can't. And I've taken a vow not to let it happen. Life is meant to be enjoyed, not just endured."

"Now, who was the wonderful philosopher who said that?"

Trish burst out laughing. "Me."

He looked at her in surprise and delight. "Really? Well, where was it written that wise philosophers had to be old and dead anyway?" The spirit of the evening was revived.

Trish was back at her hotel room before eleven-thirty after having promised her host that she would have dinner with him again on the first evening they were both free. She showered before she got into bed, but she wasn't at all sleepy, so she decided to read for a while.

The next thing she knew, the telephone was ringing and the operator was announcing her seven-o'clock wake-up call. As she put the phone down, she reflected that she was finally beginning to feel at home in the cramped room and on the wretched mattress. She had fallen asleep with her glasses and the light on. A body gets accustomed to almost anything, she observed.

Dressed in a suit, she headed for Red's campaign office. It was a chilly gray morning, and the wind penetrated her lightweight jacket. If she was going to stay in New York, she decided she had better invest in a heavy coat.

Stopping in a coffee shop for a Danish and hot coffee to accompany her perusal of the *Times*, she was surprised to see Red's face smiling at her from the front page of the newspaper. Eagerly she read the copy: "Senator Jonathan (Red) O'Shea leaves the Senate's chambers in triumph after leading a floor fight that successfully defeated the Whitcomb-Sandhill bill. Senator O'Shea remarked that the defeat was a victory for the workingman over the special-interests lobby, although it is not likely to endear him to the conservative elements in his party."

Trish felt a tingle of excitement. If only she had someone she could share it with. A sense of loneliness enveloped her—she missed her friends—but she shook it off. She would make new friends. She would not let herself sink into a miasma of self-pity and nostalgia. She would be strong.

The campaign office was bustling with people telephoning, typing, and talking. A young woman greeted Trish. "Hello, can I help you?"

"I'm looking for Joe Franklin," Trish responded.

"He's in the back office. Just go on in. He's not on the phone right now."

Trish walked through the office to a small cubicle cordoned off from the rest of the desks by a glass partition. A man in his late thirties, with dark hair carefully blow-dried and combed to cover the scalp peeking through, looked up as she approached. "Hi, can I help you?" he asked.

"Are you Joe Franklin?" she asked. He nodded, and she continued, "I'm Trish Delaney, and Red told me—" She did not finish, however, for as soon as she said her name, he jumped to his feet and offered his hand.

"Well, of course. Hi, come in and sit down. Red told me you'd be here today. I understand you're going to work for us."

Trish was relieved that Red had cleared the way for her until Franklin asked, "What kind of experience do you have? Can you type?"

Trish didn't quite know how to answer. "Is typing absolutely necessary for this job?"

"Well, to tell you the truth, I really don't know what your job will be. The senator just told me to find a spot for you on the staff, and that's what I'm trying to do." His voice had an unmistakable edge of disdain.

Suddenly Trish found herself annoyed, and she snapped, "Well, if I had been a man, would you have asked me that question first?"

Joe was irritated that he had been suddenly put on the defensive, but he was also relieved that she was not some bimbo who would take up space and money without pulling any weight. She obviously had a brain—and a mouth. "Okay, I apologize. The last thing I want to do is get Red in trouble with the women in the country. I'll try to be more sensitive about those things."

"Maybe what Senator O'Shea needs on his staff is someone who is alert to women's issues," Trish suggested, and was pleased with herself for not only thinking about it but also having the nerve to suggest it.

Joe Franklin had gotten where he was by being flexible and able to roll with the punches. This lady might very well be the senator's latest bed partner, but he had an idea that she could also be useful to him. He decided it would be wise to be friends with her, at least for the time being.

"Would you be interested in working on that aspect of the campaign? I take it you're concerned about women's issues?"

"Yes, I suppose I am, but I've got to confess that I've never done anything about it. I guess it's just been a feeling inside of me that I've never really expressed." She tried to speak forthrightly and honestly, in keeping with her new image of herself. When she came to New York, she had decided she would never be a doormat again.

"Good, then that's it. Maybe the fact that you're a virgin in the women's movement will work to our advantage. You won't be carrying over any hostile baggage from other encounters. Did the senator mention anything about salary?" he asked.

"Only that it probably wouldn't be very big. I'll need enough to pay my expenses. I don't have unlimited funds."

"Well, let me talk it over with him, okay? I'll do my best. Nobody gets rich in this business—at least not until after the election." His short bitter laugh came out more like a snort. "By the way, Mrs. Delaney . . . it is Mrs., isn't it? Have you known the senator very long?"

"If Red's campaign is going to be sensitive to women, then I think we should have a policy of using the title Ms., unless otherwise requested, don't you? And, yes, I've known the senator for a very long time." She was pleased with herself for evading the subject of her being married. She also sensed that she'd better not tell Franklin anything that wasn't absolutely necessary. She detected in him a desire for control, and instinctively didn't trust him.

"Well, when do I start?" she asked.

He smiled with half of his mouth. "Do you want to start today? Or would you rather wait until I find out how much we can pay you?"

"I've already promised Red that I'd work on his campaign. He'll be a terrific president, and I'd like to have a part in helping him get to the White House. I'm new at this, so I'd better get started right away. Have you got a desk for me?'' Trish got to her feet. She wanted to end the conversation before he could ask her any questions about her relationship with Red that would be awkward to answer. It was obvious that he already knew that it was important to his boss to have her around.

Joe introduced her to several people in the office, and she was assigned to a small desk covered with stacks of bumper stickers that proclaimed ''All the Way with Red O'Shea.'' They were obviously planning to exploit the connection with the JFK image.

While she was clearing the desk and stowing the campaign literature on nearby shelves, a tall thin woman dressed in faded denim skirt and blouse and boots came over and perched on the desk corner. She had long stringy hair parted in the middle, and she looked very much like a refugee from the early seventies. ''Hi, I'm Millie Burton. Will you answer a question for me?''

Trish looked up at the woman and laughed. ''Hi, I'm Trish Delaney, and I'll try, but I don't know very much.''

''If you had to choose between Mary Worth and Joanie Caucus, who would it be?''

Trish grinned. ''It depends.''

''On what?'' Millie asked, and her eyes narrowed in amusement behind her rimless heavily tinted eyeglasses.

''On whether I was looking for a little guilt or an interesting conversation.''

''C'mon, you're waffling, as they like to say in these parts,'' Millie insisted.

''Okay, okay. There's really no contest. I much prefer Joanie.'' Trish laughed and wondered what Millie was trying to prove.

''Good. You passed the test. Now we can be friends. I refuse to have anything to do with anyone who doesn't read *Doonesbury*.''

''Wasn't it awful when Trudeau took that hiatus to write

a play or something? The comic pages just weren't the same without him, although I must confess that *Peanuts* is still my favorite."

"Well, nobody's perfect, and I'm sort of a Snoopy fan myself. Charlie Brown, however, is very hard for me to laugh at. Sometimes I think Schulz was eavesdropping on my childhood. Anyway, you're a godsend. This place is just full of overblown assholes who think they're on some divine mission. They look down their noses on anybody who reads the funnies, for God's sake. Somewhere along the line they've lost sight of the fact that they're working for a redheaded Irish human being. I signed on because he has a great sense of humor . . . and God knows we need somebody who doesn't take himself too seriously, or for sure we'll all go up in a mushroom cloud of smoke one of these days." She had lowered her voice and leaned closer to Trish as she talked.

Trish smiled at her and realized she had just made a friend, and she was delighted. "Millie, I'm so glad you're here. What made you decide to work for the senator?"

"I'm thirty-five, and I long for the good old days at Berkeley. I thought maybe I could bring 'em back if we could revive Camelot, you know."

"Are you from California?"

"Not anymore. I was born and raised in North Carolina. I attended undergraduate school at Berkeley, and my whole life changed there. I tried going back to teach, but it's not the same place it was."

"What did you teach?"

"History. I wanted my students to know how important it was to understand history so that they *wouldn't* be 'doomed to repeat it.' But they really didn't give a shit. They were worried about grades and jobs. Very legitimate concerns that I couldn't quarrel with, but I just wasn't comfortable with them. I suddenly found myself on the wrong side of the generation gap. Say, let's go have lunch. I'm starved, and there's a great little coffee shop two blocks from here, but you have to get there before twelve or forget it."

"Good idea. Let's go."

As they headed for the door, Joe came out of his office, and Millie informed him that they were taking an early lunch and would be back in less than an hour.

As they walked down the crowded street, they chatted about the fun of living in New York. Trish found Millie to be a charming and intelligent woman, and when they were finally settled in one of the worn red leather booths with mugs of hot coffee in front of them, she decided to find out what the situation was in the campaign office.

"Millie, what do you think of Joe Franklin?"

"Not much. He's a chauvinistic bastard, but that's not why I don't trust him. I've been in that place for three months, and although I can't give you any specific reasons for feeling that way, his ambition seems a little too intense. He sees himself running the White House for Red. I think he would do anything, absolutely anything to get the senator elected. So just stay out of his way as much as possible. Have you met Senator O'Shea yet?"

Trish stared down into the steam rising from her cup. What would this nice, direct woman think of her if she knew what her real motives were? "Yes, I have, as a matter of fact. I knew Red in high school. When I got here, I called him and asked him if he could help me find a job. He offered me a spot in his campaign. Naturally, I was very pleased. I've followed his career over the years, and I think he would be a wonderful president." Her cheeks were hot with embarrassment and deception. She hoped Millie wouldn't notice.

"Yeah, I know what you mean. I'm worried about the world. During the sixties, I was sure we had all the answers. We, the youth of the nation, would band together in love and harmony. We'd put an end to war. It didn't work out the way we planned. But . . . anyway, I like Red O'Shea. He's a decent man, and he's very bright. We're not always on the same side of every issue, but he's never taken a stand that I think is immoral. I must admit, however, that sometimes I look in the mirror and say, 'Millie Burton, what the hell are you doing working to elect a Republican who spent over ten years of his life as a goddamn officer in the Army?' But then, I believe in his platform now, so why should I hold it against him for doing what he thought was right? Enough—tell me about yourself.''

Trish had hoped to keep Millie talking and avoid having to equivocate, but the question was too direct. "Oh, there's not all that much to tell. I just wanted to spend some time in New York. And one day I realized I wasn't getting any younger. If I didn't do it soon, I'd never do it. So here I am.''

"Found a place to live?" Millie asked.

"For the time being, I'm at a cheap hotel. It's small, and not too nice, but it'll do until I see how things work out. If I like it here and decide to stay, then I'll have to do something about finding an apartment."

"Well, if you'd be interested in sharing, I have a decent little place on the Upper East Side. I'd love to have somebody to share the rent."

"That's awfully nice of you to offer, but it's just too soon for me to make that kind of commitment. I'm not saying no, you understand. I just need some time."

They ate a light lunch, drank a lot of coffee, and walked back to the office. As they talked, Trish wondered what Millie would think if she knew that her ambitions for Red O'Shea were not to get him into the White House but to get him into bed.

12

Make-believe

For the first time in weeks, Vanessa slept long and soundly, in spite of the lumpiness of the mattress. When she awakened, she felt refreshed and rested. It was invigorating to have embarked on an adventure that carried so much risk with it. At nine o'clock she got out of bed and stepped into the shower. The underwear and pantyhose she had washed out the night before were still slightly damp so she laid them out on a towel on the radiator.

The sight of her blond image in the mirror startled her. Well, it was obvious that she had to get her hair shaped and toned down and buy herself some new clothes. She gazed out the window down on the busy thoroughfare that was Sixth Avenue and wondered where she should go to shop to avoid meeting anyone who might recognize her. Macy's would be a safe bet. She'd never shopped there, but it was a big store, and it would probably have a beauty shop. Most of the women she knew rarely ventured south of Fiftieth Street in New York unless they were heading for a quaint little restaurant. She dressed quickly and strode through the lobby out to the taxi stand. She would have liked to walk to clear her head, but it was too far.

At Macy's she went into the beauty salon and made an appointment for half an hour later, and then walked through the store until she found a lunch counter. The bowl of yogurt with granola and fruit tasted remarkably good, although she was somewhat distracted by a little elderly woman who sat on the stool next to her and read the *Times* aloud in a singsong whisper.

In the beauty salon, she had her hair lightened further so that it would have a more sophisticated ash tint, and she allowed the hairdresser to style it into a soft, curly halo that made her look younger. While she was there, she had a manicure. When she got the bill, she was startled at the low price. It wasn't Rodeo Drive, but she was not at all unhappy with the way she looked. She tipped the hairdresser extravagantly and then cursed herself. Dammit, she had to be more discreet. A middle-class housewife would not give a beauty operator a twenty-dollar bill.

Later she bought herself a new wardrobe, wistfully passing up the pricier designer clothes in favor of the less expensive Liz Claibornes and Evan Picones. She found several outfits that looked extremely good on her despite their inexpensive labels. She was surprised to realize that now that her hair was blond, she could wear drabber colors, the browns and greens, that she usually avoided in favor of brighter reds and purples and blues. A comfortable pair of shoes and a pair of boots for rainy and cold weather were added to her purchases, and finally a suitcase to put everything in. When no one would agree to deliver the heavy suitcase to the hotel that afternoon, she realized there were some drawbacks to shopping in an ordinary department store.

Taking a cab back to the hotel, she tipped the doorman to have the luggage put in her room and set off walking, to find a place to eat. She settled on a small buffet restaurant, decorated in natural woods and hanging plants, where she passed up the rich and fattening trays of pastries in favor of a large raw-vegetable salad. When she finished and was out on the street again, she passed an inviting bar, but she managed to quell the urge to stop in for one quick drink to bolster her courage. From long experience she knew that if she had one drink, she wouldn't stop, and that would be the end of her glorious quest. She stepped to the curb and lifted her arm in the typical salute of the New Yorker in search of a cab. She was lucky, and within ten minutes she was at Red O'Shea's campaign office.

She was met by Millie Burton, who greeted her in a friendly manner. "Hi, can I help you?"

"I'm not sure. I was . . . wondering . . . if maybe you needed volunteers . . ."

"That's the magic word, ma'am. We always need volunteers. Do you live here in Manhattan?"

"Well, temporarily. You see, my husband was transferred here from Seattle. I stayed home and sold the house and packed, but I no sooner got here than they sent him to Saudi Arabia for two months. They wouldn't let me go with him." Vanessa was enjoying the story. She had always loved make-believe, and in fact had become particularly adept at it.

"Gee, that's tough," Millie sympathized. "Where are you staying?"

"Oh, I have a very nice suite at the Maybelle Hotel. The company is paying for it. There's no point in looking for something permanent, because my husband thinks we'll be going to Alaska when he returns."

"Alaska? What in God's name does your husband do?" Millie asked in surprise.

"He's a geologist. Petroleum." Vanessa smiled proudly. A good wife always spoke with pride about her husband's work. Vanessa was impressed with her own glibness.

"So you want something to fill the time until he gets back. . . . Are you sure this is what you want to do? The hospitals are crying for volunteers all the time."

"Oh, no. I hate hospitals. They depress me terribly. Besides, I love politics. I work on the polls during elections whenever I can, and I just think Senator O'Shea will make a wonderful president. He's so handsome."

Millie's expression changed only slightly at the re-vealtion that this nice but naive lady wanted to help elect a man because he would look good in the White House. "Yeah, well, he's smart too. What would you like to do?"

"Well, I'm not much good at secretarial work. My typing is terrible, but I could stuff envelopes or something. I'm not fussy."

Millie laughed. "Well, that's a unique approach. Most of the people who come off the street want to start out writing speeches. How are you at begging?"

"Begging?"

"Yeah, telephone soliciting. We're mounting a grass-roots campaign, you see. Trying to get a lot of little people to donate. You know, if you can get the citizens to put their money on the candidate, they're more likely to get out on election day, even if it's raining, and vote for him."

"What a clever idea." Vanessa looked terribly impressed.

"Yeah, well, it's pretty basic," Millie replied, and tried not to sound condescending.

"Do you have any material I could read to sort of bone up, you know, in case anybody asks where he stands on issues?"

"Come on over and sit down. By the way, what's your name?"

"Mrs. John Fitzgerald, but please call me Ann."

"Nice to meet you, Ann. I'm Millie Burton. The cof-feepot is in that little room over there. Help yourself, but if you drink the last cup, you have to put another pot on. The rest rooms are back there. Quitting time is five, but since you're a volunteer, you can make your own hours."

"What time do you start in the morning?"

"Someone's usually here at eight . . . eight-fifteen."

"Good, then I'll be here too. I intend to work the same hours as everybody else."

"Yeah? Well, that's terrific. Then I'll assign you a desk that will be just yours, okay?"

"Oh, how nice. My own desk."

"You're sure easy to please. How about this one over by the window? Joe likes to put the pretty women up front where they can be seen."

"Who's Joe?"

"Joe Franklin, the senator's right-hand man. He'll probably be back in the morning. He's in Washington with the senator today, but he's in charge of things here." Millie paused and then impulsively asked, "What do you think of Joanie Caucus?"

For the first time, Vanessa looked nonplussed. "What?" she asked.

Millie smiled. "Nothing. It's just a joke."

"I see. Well, I suppose I should get started."

Vanessa sat down at the desk, and Millie gave her a number of papers to read, mostly copies of speeches that Red had made. She also gave her press clippings and editorials. Vanessa was delighted. She was looking for information about the presidential candidate, and here it was being thrust upon her.

By the time she had finished reading all the material, it was close to five o'clock. She said good night to Millie and promised to return first thing in the morning.

Since it was rush hour and almost impossible to find a cab, she walked slowly back toward the hotel. She passed the Russian Tea Room and longingly wished she could go in for some vodka and coulibiac, but she didn't dare. Someone she knew might be dining there. She would have to find an inexpensive little place that the people she knew wouldn't be caught dead in.

She passed several places that were possible, but could not force herself to go into them. They were crowded and not very inviting. As she got nearer to the hotel, she had an idea. Stopping at a liquor store, she bought herself an expensive bottle of Puligny Montrachet and carried it back to her hotel. Then she called room service and had dinner sent up.

Her father had always told her that a good bottle of wine would make a lackluster meal special. And God knows the hotel food needed something just to make it edible.

13

Charade

The next two days passed quickly for Trish. Millie had been great about helping her to familiarize herself with the routine in the campaign office, and Joe Franklin had not been around much to watch her with his speculating stare.

Most of the staff had been hired by Joe, and they were all loyal to him. Millie indicated that it would probably not be a good idea for Trish to say anything to them she wouldn't want Joe to know. A serious and hardworking group of people, they kept the telephones busy as they attempted to solicit donations and schedule events. Trish was especially interested in the campaign literature. There was something about it that bothered her, and she asked Millie who had written it.

"They've got some professional media consultants who work on image and stuff. We don't have anything to do with it. Why?"

Trish shrugged. "I don't know. I just think the campaign logo could be better. Red's got so many good things going for him, but this stuff looks dry and uninteresting."

"Boring, you mean."

"That's the word."

"Got any ideas? I'm sure they'd be happy to have them."

Trish shook her head. "What would I know? After all, these are experts."

"Want to hear Millie's Law? There are no experts . . . period. On anything."

Trish laughed at Millie's plain and wise view of the world and felt very lucky to have met her.

Early on Saturday morning Red telephoned to tell Trish he was back in town and was looking forward to seeing her that night. In spite of the gloomy weather forecast for an early snowfall, Trish's spirits were high.

She spent most of the day in her hotel room, and its limitations were beginning to annoy her. It was a pain to have to call room service for everything, and it was expensive too. How she longed for a refrigerator where she could have ice or a soda, or a stove so that she could have a cup of tea when she wanted it. She had begun to think seriously of accepting Millie's invitation to share her apartment, but she wanted to see just how things worked out with Red before she made any permanent arrangements. It was entirely possible that this would be only a one-night stand. After all, Red had been around a lot, and he obviously had many women. What did she have to offer that was special enough for him to want to get deeply involved? True, she represented a memory of his youth, but would the glow of that memory be extinguished by the reality of her older self?

Pushing aside the ghosts of self-doubt, she concentrated on preparing herself for the big event. She shampooed, manicured, pedicured, shaved, powdered, and painted, and was studying the results critically when the call from the desk came.

"Ms. Delaney, there's a car here to pick you up," the clerk announced in a respectful tone of voice.

Trish took one more look in the mirror, picked up her expensive new sweater, and strode toward an event that had been played a thousand times in her imagination over the past twenty years. Could the reality possibly live up to her expectations?

The first sign that all was not what she had hoped for

was that the driver waiting to deliver her to her assignation was not a faceless uniformed type like the one Richard had sent for her. Instead, she was greeted by Joe Franklin, whose sardonic expression of amusement at her surprise immediately irritated her.

"Joe! What are you doing here? Where's Red's driver?"

Taking her elbow, he steered her to the doors. "We'll talk about it in the car," he replied softly.

Joe's small, uninviting Toyota sedan waited at the entrance for them. Looking at the car, Trish knew what Cinderella must have felt when her carriage suddenly changed back into a pumpkin. Good grief, she'd spent a fortune on her dress and wrap for this!

"Where are we going?" she asked as she carefully folded her expensively clad body into the untidy sedan filled with campaign literature.

Joe did not answer any of her questions until he was behind the wheel, pulling away from the curb.

"You're going to meet the senator at Lutèce for dinner, Trish, but I'll be with you. For the benefit of the public and the press, you're my date tonight, not Red's. You didn't actually think you could go out alone in public with him, did you?"

Trish was mortified, and for the first time she felt the soil of a clandestine relationship. Where was the thrill?

"Don't tell me that Red's bringing his wife along too?" she asked bitterly.

Joe snorted. "Huh, you don't have to worry about that. Gloria only makes scheduled appearances, and only at very special functions. She and Red never have dinner alone together. I wish to hell they would. It's not easy trying to protect his image as a devoted husband, I can tell you that."

"I have a funny suspicion that you plan to spend the whole evening with us. Am I right?"

"Well, not really *all* evening . . . just while you're out in public. When you're in . . . private, I'll leave you alone."

His sarcastic tone angered her. He made her feel like some kind of a cheap prostitute, and she could not resist lashing back at him.

"Tell me, Joe, how long have you been pimping for the senator?"

The anger in his voice told her that the remark had stung. "Look, Miss Delaney, this wasn't my idea, you know. I'm just doing the best I can with the job I have to do. I can't help it if the people want to believe that politicians only sleep with their wives. What Red does is his own business, and I don't think he should be penalized for having married the wrong woman. It's just too bad that he didn't realize it and get rid of her years ago, but he can't do it now. As far as I'm concerned, he's the best man for the job . . . there's nobody else who even comes close . . . and if I have to do a few things I don't want to do, I can handle it. I just hope you can too. I don't know where he found you, but you better be aware that there's nothing permanent in sight, understand?"

"I don't feel that I have to discuss my relationship with Red with you or anybody else, but for your information, Joe, we've been friends for over twenty years. We grew up together. We went to the same high school, and our parents were friends."

There was a tense silence between them as Joe maneuvered the car through the dense traffic. When they reached the restaurant, the doorman opened the door and helped Trish out.

As Joe took her arm and guided her inside, he had the last word: "Just remember, he's not the same man you knew twenty years ago. He's going to be the leader of the free world."

While they waited to be shown to their table, Trish tried to calm her temper by looking around the famous restaurant, drinking in the details. There was a tiny room in the front with a small bar and wicker chairs where a group was having cocktails and chatting amiably with the bartender.

An elegant woman dressed in a chic black dress approached them and smiled. "Ah, good evening, Mr. Franklin. The senator's table is ready. Please follow me."

They walked through a narrow corridor and then through the antegarden, a cozy little room with green-fern-print wallpaper and glass paneling that looked onto the garden proper. Stepping out into a veritable fantasy of white latticework and whitewashed brick among pink stucco walls, they walked across flagstones under a vaulted glass skylight. They were seated in deep wicker chairs at a table set with white linen and gleaming crystal and silver. It was a serene and beautiful place, and Trish wished that Joe would just evaporate into thin air and leave her alone to enjoy it.

The table was set for three, but Red had not yet arrived. Once they were seated, the captain approached and handed Joe a note. He read it quickly and then handed it to Trish. "Here, read this so you'll know what's going on."

She was confused. It was a list of names with times and numbers after them. Some of the names, like Mary Tyler Moore and author Fred Mustard Stewart, were familiar, but most were not. "What does this mean?"

"That's the list of reservations and the table numbers where they'll be sitting. Red needs to know who is around him all the time. Donors and supporters hate not to be recognized by a politician they've shelled out big bucks to."

"Is there anybody here tonight that falls in that category?"

"Not as far as I can tell, but you never know. They could be here as somebody's guests. Don't worry, I have a great memory for faces and names. Besides, that's all I really have to do tonight, except enjoy the food and wine. I'm extremely good at making myself invisible. I've had a lot of practice with my randy boss." He looked at her through narrowed eyes with a simpering smirk on his face, and she hated him. Obviously he wanted to humiliate her by letting her know she was just one of a crowd.

"Tell me, Joe. Do you hang around hoping to get his leftovers?" she asked, bringing their conversation to an end.

The sommelier was just opening the wine when Red came through the door and walked toward them, nodding and smiling at the other diners. He generated a special spark of electricity that brought the room to attention, and everyone paused to look at him as he passed.

Joe rose to greet him. They shook hands, and before he sat down, Red leaned over and gave Trish a small social kiss on the cheek. She felt herself warmed by his presence, and the cold nagging doubts evaporated. She was glad she was here.

"Trish, you look beautiful. Do you mind if Joe and I talk business first?"

Without waiting for her response, he directed his next words to his campaign-office manager. "Joe, we've got to schedule a meeting tomorrow morning. Something's come up about that Stellano deal."

Joe looked surprised and concerned. "I knew that thing would come back to haunt us. We should never have taken the money."

"It's a damn good thing we gave it back as fast as we did," Red replied.

"Sam Fulton got you into that. His support is more of a liability than an asset."

"Don't I know? His good-ol'-boy image doesn't really fit in with mine either."

"Yeah, but let's face it, it's the good ol' boys who come up with the dough. Maybe I'd better get on the telephone right now and set things up before anybody starts talking to the press." Joe rose to his feet, and a slight smirk crossed his face as he said to Trish, "I hope you'll excuse me for a while. I'll use the telephone in the office." Taking a small notepad and pen out of his breast pocket, he laid it on the table beside Trish and left.

"What's this for? Am I supposed to take notes?" Trish asked Red.

"That's just a prop. If anyone from the press wanders in, it will look like a business meeting. After all, you are on my campaign staff now."

"Red, do you know how depressing this charade is?"

He moved his hand under the table to touch her knee lightly, and said, "Don't let it be a charade, Trish. All this subterfuge is not my idea, but I understand the reason for it. Besides, it helps to keep what's between us private and personal, and that's not a bad thing to have when everything else in your life is in the public domain."

She smiled at him tenderly, and the warmth of his fingers through the silk of her dress awakened her hunger for him.

"It's funny, but when you're near me, it's just like it was when we were young. We're the same people we were then, but when we're apart, we're not the same at all. You're the hope of the Western world, and I'm . . . nobody."

"Pick up that pen and write this down. I want you to commit it to memory," he demanded sternly.

She hesitated, and then, seeing that he was quite serious, she complied.

"Everybody is somebody. Write that down and remember it always. That's the key to my success in politics . . . and in life. I believe that everybody is important. We have no throwaway people in this country. Now, let's go ahead and order. I don't want to spend my whole evening sitting here in this restaurant not being able to touch you."

Trish was flattered and thrilled. So totally swept away by his attention was she that she felt that she had been transported to a place where only the two of them existed. Then Joe returned to the table, and the political talk resumed. The conversation swirled around her, but all she could think of was that tonight she would live her fantasy. Would it be as wonderful as she had imagined?

14

A Woman with Means

Dan sat at the desk in his office for almost four hours. He took numerous telephone calls and initialed several sets of blueprints, but he couldn't remember a single thing that he had done because his mind was so full of Cake. Funny, he couldn't ever recall a time that she had dominated his thoughts as she did now.

If someone had told him a week ago that he would be devastated by her absence, he would have laughed. For the past few years, ever since his engineering firm was awarded its first really big contract for a Navy hospital, Cake had been little more than a fixture in his life. She took care of his home, his clothes, his children. She prepared meals, entertained, and occasionally provided sex for him. If he thought about her at all, it was usually with annoyance. No matter how hard she tried, she never was able to achieve the sleek, well-groomed look of a woman with means. Selena, his secretary, had a fraction of the money to spend that Cake had, and yet she always looked wonderfully turned out.

Looking up, Dan saw Selena standing inside the door watching him. "Well, think of the devil," he remarked a little too softly for her to hear. He motioned to her to come in and close the door. As she walked across the room toward his desk, he followed the slow and sinuous movements of her body. She was not tall, but her legs were long, and she moved with the grace of a dancer. No, not exactly a dancer, he thought. She moved with a more natural ease, like an animal moves when stalking its prey.

Her dark hair was pulled sleekly back into a tight bun at the nape of her neck, and the severity of her hairstyle served to focus attention on her large dark eyes, which were enhanced by a dusky ring of kohl and heavily mascaraed lashes. The only jewelry she wore was the diamond studs in her ears that Dan had given her for her birthday and the gold Cartier tank watch that he had bought the day after they had made love for the first time.

"Sit down, over here," he commanded with a nod. Selena glided across the thick maroon rug and settled herself in the leather chair opposite his desk. She was one of those rare women who could sit quietly and wait for one to finish thinking important thoughts. She was totally composed. Silence did not upset her.

Finally Dan looked at his watch. "Good God, it's past six. Why didn't you tell me it was so late?"

"I've looked in on you several times, but you were so absorbed in your thoughts, I didn't want to disturb you. Cake's leaving has really upset you, hasn't it?"

He didn't reply but got up from his chair and walked to the window to look out over the city. His office was at the top of the tallest building in Century City, and the view was breathtaking, especially on a clear night. When he had moved into the spacious and expensive offices, he felt that he had finally arrived at the pinnacle, and whenever he was worried or depressed, the view helped to remind him of how far he had come. Up here in his office, he felt that he could touch the stars.

Selena watched Dan closely. Had she made a miscalculation? Had she grown too impatient? She must be very careful at this point. Somehow she had to find a way to convince him that he was better off with his wife out of the way. His pride was hurting, and she needed to provide a little diversion.

"Why don't you go on over to the apartment, Selena. I'll join you in a little while."

She hesitated. If she left without him, he might change his mind and not join her. He certainly didn't look much in the mood for sex, but she'd fix that.

"Why don't I make us a drink here . . . maybe it will help you unwind a bit."

Without waiting for him to answer, she went to the cabinet that held a fully stocked bar, glasses, and an ice machine. Quickly, before he could say no, she had put ice cubes into two of the heavy crystal tumblers, splashed a good portion of Chivas Regal into them, and offered one to him.

He took the glass from her hand, and she caught his eyes as he lifted hers for a toast. "To us," she said huskily, clinked her glass against his, and drank deeply. He followed her lead.

She put her arm in his to move him away from the window. "Come on, let's sit over on the couch and relax together for a little while. Everyone's gone, I've locked the doors to the corridor, and nothing is pressuring us to hurry. We can just sit here quietly and talk for a while."

Realizing that he was being manipulated, but seeing no reason to resist, Dan complied. As they settled down on the soft leather couch, Selena pressed her body close to his.

"Cake's got to be crazy, Dan. No woman in her right mind would walk out on a man who's been as good a husband as you've been. She never really appreciated you the way she should. You've been a wonderful husband to her."

He took a long swallow of the liquor, and it warmed him. He suddenly became aware of Selena's musky, sensual perfume. How different it was from Cake's clean, natural scent. Cake disdained perfume of all kinds, even to the point of buying unscented cosmetics. He inhaled deeply and closed his eyes. Funny, he liked the way both of them smelled.

He lifted his arm, and Selena moved into it, resting her head on his shoulder. She reached up to pull the pins out of her hair so that it could fall free. Then she lifted her mouth to his, and instead of kissing him, softly flicked the tip of her tongue across his lips. It was a gesture that usually aroused him, only this time he remained passive.

Selena realized that she would have to be careful. He was thinking of his wife, and if she were too aggressive, it might turn him off. She wasn't really worried, however, for if there was one thing she was good at, it was seduction. God knows, she'd had enough practice.

Moving gently and lightly, she touched his eyelids with the tip of her tongue, his nose, his cheeks, his lips again, his ears, and as she caressed his face with her mouth, her hand moved slowly to his groin. Deftly she unbuckled his belt, slowly unzipped his trousers, and sensuously, moved her hands around his penis.

He let out a deep sigh of desire, but he did not move. After a lifetime of his being the aggressor, he had learned the joys of being passive from Selena, and it was exciting. He felt his penis growing stiff with impatience, but he had learned from her that delayed satisfaction was far more intense and fulfilling. Slowly Selena stroked and fondled him with her fingers, and after a while she moved her head down and took him into her mouth. The ecstasy of her tongue moving up and down and around him was almost unbearable, and when she sensed that he was about to climax, she stopped and moved her mouth back to his, whispering, "Not yet, not yet."

Driven by desire, he pulled her closer to him, but she backed away. "No, relax, let me do it," she whispered. Gently she forced him to lie down, and she pulled his clothes from the lower part of his body. Then she stepped out of her full, heavy wool skirt and stood before him clad only in her silk blouse and black boots. She knelt down beside the couch and took him in her mouth again, but this time only briefly. Moments later, she mounted him and slid her moist and velvet vagina down over his hardness. Automatically he began to move to seek his relief from desire, but she cautioned him, "Lie still." And as he relaxed, she began to move slowly and rhythmically up and down, the friction of their bodies against each other creating that special electricity that brought them at last to a trembling and explosive peak.

After Dan emitted a last shudder of desire fulfilled, Selena relaxed and let her body go limp on top of him. As she always did, she kept him inside her until his hardness was completely gone.

"You're wonderful," he whispered, stroking her hair.

"You were fantastic," she replied. "You have so much control. It wouldn't work so beautifully if you didn't."

"I just can't believe how perfect your timing is. Every single time we've done it like that, we've come at the exact same moment. It's almost a miracle."

"I know. Nothing like that ever happened to me before you," she replied, hugging him and pressing her face into his neck and thinking about the lessons she had learned from her mother. "If you want to really please a man," Ginny had said, "always have an orgasm for him. Men are prouder of the orgasms they give than the ones they have themselves. If you can't manage to have a real one, then fake it. They'll never know. That's what God gave us instead of letting us pee standing up."

15

It's a Big City

Richard Terhune stood at the window in Milton Wise's office and looked down onto the street below. The huddled masses were streaming back and forth along Broadway below him. He refocused his eyes onto the dirty window-pane with its tacky wire mesh running through the filthy glass.

"Milt, you need a new office," Richard remarked, trying to avoid the real subject of their meeting.

The man sitting across from him leaned back into his ancient cracked red leather chair and lifted his cigar to his mouth with a smile. "Not much like the old place, is it, Rich?"

"No, it sure isn't. What are you doing here?"

"I've only got a few clients now, my friend, and they don't come to me. I go to them. I don't need a fancy office anymore, or a big staff. But I'm makin' money. Lots of it. Besides, I like to keep a low profile."

"Who're you working for, Milt?"

The heavyset man with gray hair just smiled and shook his head. "Not a proper question. You want me to go on with what we were talkin' about?"

Richard nodded. Listening had always been more important to him than talking.

"Look, you've gotta understand that I've got absolutely

no interest in this thing. None whatsoever. I'm just doing a favor passing this on to you, and I don't have any idea why my client is willing to pay so much, but he is. And I can't think of anybody I'd trust more than you to keep things quiet."

"This sounds like a job for the police, not an old lawyer like me," Richard protested.

"Don't try to pull that *old* stuff on me. You're the slickest shyster in the United States. You know, I've been told that you can be in a room where four separate conversations are going on at once and you can follow all of them. Is that true?"

"Flattering, but it's just not so. I can only follow two at the same time. Now level with me, Milt. Why do they want me specifically?"

"It's very important to my client to keep this all very quiet. Mike Fallon's daughter is missing. They want her back as fast as possible."

"You obviously know your way around the seedier parts of this town better than I do. Why the hell do they want me?"

Wise looked through heavy eyelids at Richard and replied, "I don't know for sure, but I can guess."

"By all means, make a guess."

"You're well-connected. You know a lot of people, both in politics and the not-so-savory circles, if that isn't redundant. I suspect this chick's got something she's not supposed to have. Information, maybe . . . and they want her back . . . fast. Before anybody even knows she's gone."

"Milt, who the hell is 'they'?"

"I can't tell you that. You know I would if I could . . . but client privilege and all that stuff. I'm still ethical, Rich."

"I don't believe we're having this conversation. Look, the answer is no. I'm too old and too rich to go around chasing runaway women. Besides, I'm up to my ears in this tax-evasion thing I'm handling for Billy Thomas. The

IRS has nailed him good this time. I don't know what the devil is wrong with him. I kept warning that asshole to play it straight, but he just has to cheat. It's in his blood, I think. The dough is rolling in from that television program of his, but it's never enough for him.''

"That's another thing." Wise cleared his throat. "You won't have to worry about Billy anymore. He's hired another firm to deal with the government. He's giving up the fight. Harvey Dalton is going to negotiate a settlement for him."

Terhune was angry and shocked at the pronouncement, but experience had taught him never to let anyone see his true emotional reactions. "Who told you that?" he asked.

"My clients asked me to have a little talk with Billy. I just warned him that the government might decide it wasn't an honest mistake and go after him for fraud. Billy didn't like the prospect of going to jail, because the fucker knows he's guilty."

"What business do you have talking to my client? I could take you before the bar for that."

"Look, Rich, take the case, will you, and save us both a lot of grief. I'm your friend. The price on this little lady's head today is two million buckeroos . . . but it goes down fifty grand a day. They're in a hurry. The sky's the limit on expenses. I know you need the money."

"What do you mean by that?" Terhune showed his anger finally.

"Look, you may be one of the country's best lawyers, but you've let yourself get in a bind. You bought too much real estate at the top of the market, and you're having a tough time making all the payments. You need cash, and you need it right now. You wouldn't be messing with the likes of Billy Thomas if you didn't. He doesn't represent any of those prestigious causes you've been playing around with lately. He's a sleazeball. It doesn't take a private detective to figure that out."

Terhune felt exposed and humiliated. Wise was right.

He did need the money, or he was going to lose some of the property he owned. He had to buy some time.

"Okay. Give it to me again."

"Mike Fallon's daughter left her home sometime in the last three days. Nobody knows exactly when, because she gave the servants a two-day holiday. Here's a picture of her. It's not very good, but it's all we have. Apparently she destroyed every photograph of herself as an adult before she left. She wore a hat with a heavy veil to her dad's funeral, so even the press doesn't have anything recent."

"As I recall, she used to be a drunk and a hellcat, right?" Richard asked.

"You got it. I could never understand why Mike Fallon was so damn protective of her. If she'd been mine, I'd have kicked her out on her ass the second time she went on one of those binges of hers. But old Mike made excuses for her at every turn. Some people said he was a saint underneath that steely facade. You believe it?"

"People are always talking about saints, but damned if I ever met one. And it certainly wasn't in character for Fallon to be so understanding and fatherly. He was a real firebrand from the time he inherited all that land out there in California. He sank oil wells everywhere and told anybody who complained to go straight to hell, including the government."

"You ever meet him, Rich?" Milt asked.

"Yeah, sure, but always in court. I lost every damned time, too. Once I even managed to have the judge step down because I was sure he'd been paid off, but I lost anyway. You'd probably think I was paranoid if I said I was sure he'd gotten to that one too, wouldn't you?"

Wise shook his head. "No, I wouldn't think you were paranoid at all. Remember the time he put the oil well right in the front yard of a house he owned in Beverly Hills?"

"I remember, because it was one of the few times he

didn't win. I don't think he cared much. The damn thing wasn't pumping enough stuff to make it worth the fight. Anyway, what's the big rush to find his daughter? It's fairly obvious that she left of her own accord, since she took care to cover her tracks.''

"Well, there's always the chance that somebody planned a very thorough kidnapping.''

"You think so?''

"Not for a minute. I think she took off,'' Wise replied.

"What did she take with her?''

"What do you mean?''

"C'mon, Milt, let's quit playing games, okay? Some woman inherits a bundle of money and then drops out of sight, leaving not a trace behind her. Kidnapped? No, or they wouldn't be offering *me* all the money in the world to get her back. Instead, they have you—and face it, you're not exactly the most powerful lawyer in the world anymore—offer me two million to find her fast and quiet. That's pretty big bucks for a broad everybody knows isn't the nicest or the smartest or the prettiest woman in the world. By the way, how old is she?''

"Forty, more or less. Here's the file on her. There's not much to go on. She's got a husband someplace, but I don't know where. Mike really kept her out of the public's eye. He was very protective.''

"Got any ideas where I should start? This file is more of a financial statement than a dossier. Didn't she have friends? Boyfriends? Girlfriends? What the hell did she do with her time?''

"She ran her daddy's house. She traveled with him, but in the last couple of years he stayed close to home. He entertained friends, and she was always there, I'm told. They were very close.'' There was a brief hesitation before he continued. "My client suspects she might be in New York. He wouldn't say why he thinks that, but I'd guess it's a good lead.''

"Jesus, she could be anyplace. It's a big city.''

"Nobody's gonna pay two million for something easy."

"Spare me your little homilies, Milt. I'll think it over."

"Costs fifty grand a day to wait, Rich."

"Yeah, well, that's the way it is. I'll call you tomorrow."

Richard got up and walked out of the office. He was disgusted with himself and the world around him. He'd never thought he'd spend the last years of his life grubbing for money. He didn't want the job. It was tainted. Why should he persecute some woman who wanted to disappear? Who was he to say she didn't have a right to go somewhere and start all over again? Maybe she had been waiting for her father to die so she could get away. It was pretty obvious that she never had a real life of her own.

Climbing into his limousine, Richard directed the driver to take him back to the Plaza. As he drove, he looked over the incomplete and sketchy personal file on Vanessa Fallon that Wise had given him. It seemed strange. She was the daughter of a very powerful and wealthy man, and yet she had apparently not received much media attention. She had inherited almost as much wealth as the Onassis daughter, but nobody knew her. Someone was interested in her, however, to the tune of two million dollars. Was it possible that whoever it was wanted her dead, not alive? Perhaps she had some very valuable information . . . on somebody important.

As Richard left the car at the hotel and hurried to the elevator that would take him to his suite, there was purpose in his step and commitment in his soul. Of course, he had to take the job. Not for the money, but for the challenge. He would find Vanessa Fallon and save her life.

16

First Love

Trish picked at her *truite fraîche à l'oseille*. It was the firmest, sweetest trout she had ever tasted, but she couldn't really savor it. She was too involved in trying to keep up with the conversation between Joe and Red to appreciate fully the excellent dinner being served by the Lutèce staff. What a waste to spend all that money and not pay any attention to the food or the wine. They might as well be eating hamburgers, she thought as she listened to Red and Joe discuss a campaign contributor who was pressuring them to support something that Red evidently opposed. Joe was not about to give up trying to convince him, however.

"You know, Red, if you go out on a limb, they'll saw it right off, and you'll be out of the campaign before you even get started," he warned forcefully.

"I know that, but I have to take the chance. I can't look like I'm waffling on an issue that's as important as this is. I wish I wasn't being pressed so damn hard, but I am. It's a little early to take sides, but I'm going to do it. What do you think, Delaney?"

Caught off-guard, Trish looked startled. It was the first time either had directed the conversation to her since the first glass of wine. "Why . . . I don't know . . . what kind of a stand do they want you to take?"

"Import quotas . . . attempts to keep foreign goods

from flooding the marketplace and taking jobs away from the people in the United States. Do you think they're a good idea?"

Trish took a sip of her wine before she answered. She knew the old saying that it's better to be silent and have people consider you a fool than to speak and remove all doubt. But what the hell. She had spent her whole life listening to others express their opinions. Maybe it was time for her to talk. "I think they're un-American."

Both men looked at her in surprise.

With his eyebrows raised, Joe asked testily, "Just how are they un-American?"

Trish was afraid to get in over her head, but she couldn't back down now. "Well, our system is based on the concept of competition, isn't it? We're always teaching our children that it's important to compete. It seems pretty uncompetitive to me if you ban some things from the marketplace. And besides, all it does is encourage higher prices and poorer quality. I feel that the goal of industry should be to compete on an even footing with the imports. Of course, I see it from the consumer's viewpoint, and we're the ones who have to pay."

Red picked up his glass and smiled wickedly at the irritation on Joe's face. Joe, however, was not to be bested in the discussion. "Any politician who'd espouse that kind of thinking would have labor on his neck. It would be suicide," he said emphatically, turning to the senator.

"I can't quarrel with that, but Trish also happens to be right, and you know it. The only thing the restrictions on the Japanese auto industry did was to make cars more expensive for everybody. Hell, the unions probably aren't going to back me anyway. They always go for the Democrat, so we might as well stop kidding ourselves. I'd like to think that everybody's going to vote for me, but I'll just have to settle for a simple majority. Now, enough of that. Let's find out what our smart lady friend here thinks of the abortion question, or do you not consider that fit conversation for the dinner table?" Red asked.

"Are you asking if I believe in abortion? No, certainly not. And I don't think that most women who have them do either. It's an extreme solution to a problem that they can't see any other way out of."

Trish paused and waited for a reaction. Seeing that she held their undivided attention, she was encouraged to continue. "I am terribly concerned, however, about the government being granted jurisdiction over a woman's body. Today it might be for the purpose of denying an abortion, but sometime in the future that same power could be used to force her to have one . . . right? As a matter of fact, I think that very thing is happening in China right now to control the population."

"Hear, hear." Red was obviously pleased with her response. "Have you ever thought about running for office yourself, Trish? You apparently have some pretty strong opinions about things."

"Me?" Trish laughed with pleasure and amazement. "Never. I even refused to run for president of the PTA. I'm really very unpolitical."

"I think you're going to be a great addition to my team. Now, would you like some dessert . . . or should we be on our way?" Red's eyes connected with hers, and she felt a tingling of anticipation.

Joe signaled for the check, and Red stood up. "Joe, have you got your car here?"

Joe answered that he did, and they all began to move toward the door. "Good. Then you go on home and I'll drop Delaney off at her hotel. I've got a lot of paperwork to do tomorrow, so don't call me unless something important comes up."

Once they were seated inside the limousine that was waiting for them at the curb, Red whispered into Trish's ear, "Okay, I'll ask you one more time . . ."

She looked up into his teasing smile and replied, "Not

everybody gets a second chance in life. I'm not missing this one.''

Red put his arm around her and pressed the intercom button to tell the driver, ''My wife and I are ready to go home now.''

As the car pulled away from the curb, Trish looked at Red quizzically. ''Your wife?''

Red shushed her and whispered, ''He's new on the job. He's never met Gloria. Besides, she's blond and just about your height. You know, I've married facsimiles twice. Tonight I'm going to have the real thing.''

A thrill of delight shivered through her body. Could this be happening, or was she just dreaming . . . again?

The car deposited them at the side entrance of a maisonette on Sutton Place just by the river. Red unlocked the door to the house, and without turning on any lights, guided Trish inside. He called to the driver to pick him up at eight on Monday morning and closed the door behind them.

They walked down a corridor lined with bookshelves that reached to the high ceiling and then entered a lovely large sitting room. Indirect lighting washed the creamy beige walls and gave the room a warm glow. The hardwood floors were partially covered by a large Oriental rug, and the overstuffed couches were upholstered in rich white on beige wool fabric. The other pieces were antiques, and Trish thought the paintings on the walls were Flemish. She vowed to spend time later—much later—going over them in detail. The room had a warmth and solidity that made it both beautiful and comfortable. Trish was impressed.

''What a wonderful room . . . did your wife decorate it?''

''Gloria? No. She's never even been here, although she did prevail on John Saladino to do it for me. It was expensive, but she said I should have the very best. She's always been one to judge something by its price.''

''Well, it's certainly beautiful. Why hasn't she ever been here?''

"I moved in about two months ago, and I haven't had a chance to invite her. She likes her big house on the Hudson River. It's been in her family for two generations. She has her horses there, and her tennis courts. She also has a pied-à-terre in Trump Tower for her visits to town."

"How do you keep your arrangement out of the press?" Trish asked, settling into one of the wing chairs in front of the fireplace.

Red turned on the gas logs in the fireplace, poured two glasses of brandy, and handed one to Trish. Slipping off his jacket and easing himself down onto the rug, he rested his back against her chair.

"I really didn't intend to talk about Gloria," he began, leaning against her legs. "I didn't want her to have any part of this night, but I suppose it can't be helped. She's there. Even if I could press a button and make her go away, I wouldn't. She's been very fair and good to me. We just couldn't make a go of it together. When she married me, she thought she was getting a good deal. She'd have a national hero as a father for her daughter. A man with a future with a capital F. She thought it was fun when I first ran for Congress ten years ago. Cute. Something to talk about at the Hunt Club over breakfast. But if you don't love politics, it's grubby business, and it gets tiresome pretty fast. By the time I was running for my second term, she'd had it. She went back to her home and told me she'd be *there* when I got finished with my little adventure."

"But didn't you say she'd agreed to help you if you ran for the presidency . . . and that you thought she'd like to be first lady?"

"Well, yes, that's what she says, but her attention span is very short. The only thing I can count on is that she won't cause me any trouble. I have a very close and loving relationship with Tessa, and she's the only thing in Gloria's life that has ever been really important to her."

"Tessa is her daughter by her first marriage, right?"

"Not exactly. Gloria never married Tessa's father. She had the baby in a convent in France, and she left her there until she was five years old. When Gloria's father finally died, she was able to bring her child home. She had been afraid that if he ever found out, he'd leave all those millions to his pet charities instead of his daughter. He died believing daddy's girl was a virgin."

"Oh my God, what a charade."

"People have done much worse for money. Gloria spent a lot of time in France. She never neglected Tessa. I came along at just the right time to help give Tessa a family. She's a beautiful and intelligent young woman . . . she's sixteen now, and I love her as if she were my own child. She's very excited about my plans. She's threatened to leave school to work on my campaign if I get the nomination."

"Red, I would have written to you when I read about your first wife's death, but you were still in the Army, and I had no way of knowing where you were."

"She was a terrific lady, Delaney. You would have liked her a lot. She was pregnant with our child when the accident happened. I was on temporary duty in Georgia, and she was in D.C. all alone. That was my first taste of disenchantment with the Army . . . before Vietnam."

"Vietnam? But you were a hero! You got the Congressional Medal of Honor over there," Trish protested.

"Right, but when I came home and was asked to speak before Congress, I felt frustrated by the situation over there and the response of the politicians. I realized where the real power in this country of ours is vested, and that's when I decided to resign from the Army and run for Congress."

"I'll bet the Republicans were happy to get you, weren't they?"

"Hell, yes. The Democrats made me a better offer, but my old daddy would have turned in his grave if I'd become a Democrat."

"I remember reading all about your first campaign . . . West Point graduate, football hero, Heisman Trophy, First Captain, Congressional Medal . . . and all this at a time when the military was very unfashionable," Trish commented.

"And I thought you'd forgotten all about me, Delaney. Why didn't you ever answer my letters?"

"I did. I answered all of them."

"That's funny. I never received a single one."

"I didn't mail them."

"Why?"

"I really don't know. I guess I just felt that you'd come back home someday, and we'd talk things out . . . the way we used to. It never occurred to me that your parents might move to Florida and you'd never return."

"As my mother would say, the Lord moves in strange ways. Here we are together again . . . . Tell me about you," Red said.

"Not tonight. We have better things to do than talk, don't we?" Trish put her hand on his face and turned it to hers. Leaning down, she kissed his lips softly. With one swift movement he pulled her down beside him on the floor, and as he held her in his arms, the years melted away, and she was sixteen again and in the embrace of her first love.

For a long time Red did nothing more than kiss and caress Trish. His lovemaking was tender and leisurely, unlike the eager young man she had once known, and she responded to him with passion. They undressed each other slowly and took time to admire each other's bodies. Red was still lean and sinewy with a light sprinkle of freckles almost everywhere, and she was surprised to see that his pubic hair was dark and not the same bright red as the hair on his head. When he began to stroke every part of her body, she was glad that she'd stayed slim.

"Hmmm, I always wondered how you'd look with your

clothes off. I used to daydream about you on my bed at the Point," he whispered.

"You've been part of my erotic fantasies all my life," Trish confessed.

"I'm not sure I can live up to all that," he answered, and he continued to touch her gently in all her secret places until she could no longer control herself and reached her climax. When she was finished, he continued to kiss her softly as he moved over her and slowly glided his body into hers. Sensuously, with a hypnotic and rhythmic movement, he moved inside her until she felt herself again begin to ascend. As he felt her spasm begin, he joined her in an orgasmic crescendo that left them both gasping.

Rolling over on his back on the Oriental rug, he pulled her on top of him. "Don't leave me," he whispered as he held her tightly, and she said, "I'll always be here when you want me." And the promise surprised her.

As they lay together in silent contemplation of the joy they had just shared, Trish thought back over the misery of the last few months. Just a short time ago she had felt that all the joy and trust had gone from her life. If she had learned one thing from her recent agonizing experience, it was that she must never despair. No matter how awful life could seem, it was always possible that something wonderful might be just around the corner.

17

A Maestro

Selena lay very quietly in the bed beside Dan. She wanted to be absolutely sure that he was sound asleep before she moved. It had taken a long time to inveigle him into bringing her to his home to spend the night, and she knew him well enough to understand that he would regret it when the booze wore off. She'd be lucky to get here again anytime in the near future, so she was determined to make the best possible use of this visit.

Dan was one of those men who got hornier as they got drunker, and he'd been all over her for what seemed hours. She thought he'd never wear out. But he was asleep at last.

Cautiously she moved her arm down the side of the bed and groped around on the floor for her purse. She was sure she had dropped it somewhere close by. Damn, she couldn't find it. With her luck, it probably got kicked under the bed when she was on her knees giving him that last blow-job. Shit!

Dan moved and groaned slightly, and she held her breath. God, she hoped he wasn't going to wake up and start mauling her again. But he turned over on his side and began to breathe heavily again, and she relaxed. Finally.

The lighted clock radio on the bedside table indicated three A.M. She felt as if she'd been there for two days.

Very slowly she inched her body off the bed and dropped quietly to the floor. On her hands and knees she began searching for the purse. Stretching out on her stomach, she waved her hand under the bed and found it. Thank God. The whole night would have been for nothing if she'd lost the damn purse.

Staying on her hands and knees until she was several feet from the bed, she inched her way toward the bathroom, which was twenty feet or more down a narrow hallway. Then, moving quickly, she stepped inside the lighted room and closed the door behind her. So far, so good.

She looked around the beautiful room with its marble tub and mirrored closets, contrasting it with the tiny cubicle that passed for a bathroom in her own apartment. Yes, indeed, this would do very nicely. It was just a matter of time before this would be all hers. She just had to be sure she didn't make any mistakes.

Cautiously she turned on the faucet to see how much noise it would make. Not too much. Did she dare take a bath in that glorious tub? She looked at her images in the mirrors and studied her naked body from all angles. As she turned her head to inspect herself, her long dark hair swished across her shoulders. God, she had a great body, she thought. Stepping closer to the mirror and putting her hands under her full, rounded breasts, she lifted them so that the dark red pigment of her nipples pointed up and then she ran her fingertips down her rib cage, along her tiny waistline, and over the roundness of her hips.

She smiled. Hers was not one of those nasty long-waisted anorexic bodies of the models who made so much money. No, photographers had never wanted to pay her for wearing clothes. They had only paid her for taking them off. She hated them for telling her the truth. They said she had a body that was meant to be seen naked . . . a body made for sex. There was no money to be made in posing nude, and she didn't like the way the fuckers expected her to put out just because she took off her clothes.

Her mother had told her never to give it away. Never. Maybe sex was the only real commodity a woman had, but Selena had learned that it wasn't enough. There was a glut on the market. Besides, she was going for bigger stakes. She was going to get Dan and his money and his house. Marriage was the only thing women could really count on to equalize their lot in a man's world. And Cake Halliday was a damn fool to walk away from it.

Selena turned on the warm water. While she was waiting for the tub to fill, she took a cosmetic bag from her purse and creamed her face, and then she brushed her long hair and braided it into a thick coil. When the tub was filled, she slipped her body into the warm water and luxuriated in it. There was nothing, absolutely nothing as sensuous and fulfilling as a warm bath. If men only knew how much more pleasing warm water was than their sweaty and brutal pounding, she thought as she lazily stroked herself until she came to a long and satisfying climax. Her first that evening.

Later, bathed and refreshed, she got ready to get back into bed, but first she opened the top drawer of the vanity table and pushed Cake's cosmetics to the rear. In their place, she put her own—several lipsticks, a mascara wand, a half-full jar of face cream, a rouge pot, and two tubes of makeup. She added a hairbrush with some black hair in it, and a comb, and in the medicine cabinet she placed her toothbrush and two prescriptions with her name on the labels. Just a little surprise package for Cake, if she was imprudent enough to return home. Then she crawled in bed and fell asleep immediately.

When Dan awakened Selena at seven the next morning, she felt rested. "Good God, Selena, wake up. We've got to get out of here," he said, leaning over her.

She opened her eyes slowly and smiled at him. "Dan, my goodness, I slept so well." She reached over to touch him, but he moved away from her and sat up on the edge of the bed.

"Come back to bed, Dan," she pleaded gently. "It's so nice and warm here, and I want to feel your body against mine. We don't often have a chance to make love in the morning." She lifted the blanket, offering her nude and inviting body to him, spreading her legs just slightly. A smile that promised forbidden delights lingered on her face, and she could tell that it was an enormous effort of will for Dan not to succumb.

"Selena, sometimes you make me feel like Ulysses. I need to lash myself to the mast to keep from falling under your spell. Come on, now, get up. I want to get us out of here before my wife's nosy friend sees us leave."

She knew better than to have a direct confrontation with him. No one ever won one of those. He was a tough and unbending bastard when he wanted to be.

"All right, if you insist. But just one hug and a kiss instead of breakfast," she pleaded sweetly, and she got out of the bed and moved toward him.

Afraid he would lose the battle with a touch, Dan turned his back on her and strode toward the bathroom. "Cut it out, Selena. Didn't you have enough last night? We've got to get to the office."

Selena smiled at the rebuff. She could see that he had started to have an erection as he walked away.

Dan was grim and silent on the drive to the office, and Selena could tell he was having some serious regrets over letting his mistress invade the sanctity of his marriage bed. She needed to say something to make him feel better about it.

Wisely not touching him or moving closer, she said softly, "You're the best, Dan . . . the absolute best."

He smiled and turned toward her. "You're pretty good yourself, Selena."

"True, but you're the one that counts. After all, even a Stradivarius doesn't give off sweet music unless it's played by a maestro."

18

Family Stability

Trish did not sleep well. The excitement of a dream ful-filled had stimulated her too much. After all those years of fantasizing about Red, he was now sleeping beside her, and she was having trouble touching reality. Was she still in love with him? Had she always been in love with him, or was she trying to make her fantasies real? Had all those years in between been unhappy? No, she could never believe that . . . never. What had happened had been won-derful. She'd had a good, fulfilling, useful life. Just be-cause it had all gone wrong didn't mean it wasn't right in the first place. She would never look upon her life as having been wasted, even though it had recently produced misery and disillusionment.

Light began to filter into the room around the edges of the heavy curtains. Cautiously she raised her head from the pillow to look at Red's face. As she leaned over him to try to make out his features in the semidarkness, she could feel his breath on her skin.

Suddenly his arms whipped out from the covers and he grabbed her, startling her so thoroughly that she yelped, "What are you doing?"

Holding her tightly, he pulled her over on top of him. "Lesson number one: never, never creep up on a combat soldier while he's sleeping. If he has a weapon at hand, he's likely to use it."

"I wasn't creeping up on you. I just wanted to look at you . . . to be sure you were really there."

"I'm here, all right . . . can't you feel me?" he whispered, and their second round of lovemaking began. It lasted most of the morning. They finally got out of bed at noon. Trish scrambled some eggs and made coffee while Red scanned the newspaper. By two in the afternoon they were in bed again, and they were still there at four when the telephone rang for the first time. It was Joe.

"Everything going okay, boss? You want me to take her home or anything?"

"Look, Joe, forget that stuff, will you? Let me find out if she needs anything. Trish, do you need anything from your hotel? Joe's on the phone, and he can pick up whatever you want."

Trish was uncertain what to say. "I . . . I don't know. How long do you want me to stay?"

Red smiled at her thoughtfully, then spoke into the telephone again. "Joe, are you at home? . . . Good, stay there for a while. I'll call you back."

Cuddling her close in his arms, he spoke softly. "Honey, let's talk about this. How much a part of my life do you want to be?"

"I don't know what you want me to say. You have to give me some idea of how you feel."

"Fair enough. You know I'm going to try for the presidency. Maybe I'm only kidding myself that the country needs me, but I really think it does. Perhaps all men who aspire to such a high position want to believe that it's not just lust for power, but a desire to do something good and lasting. Anyway, it's important to me to give it a try. So, unfortunately, I can't change my life right now, if I'm going to succeed. I have to maintain a semblance of family stability."

"Red . . . I would never want you to divorce your wife

for me. Can you understand that? The very last thing in the world I'm looking for is a marriage license. As you and I both know, they don't come with warranties."

"Trish, I love you now, but only time will tell if it's the real thing. Are you willing to hang in there with me to find out if we really love each other?"

"It's too much of a risk for you, Red. Suppose someone finds out about me? That would be the end of your quest."

"That's probably true, but it's a risk I want to take. I'm hoping it will show you just how important you are to me."

"I don't see how we'll manage."

"I've got it all figured out. You're going to be a very visible part of my campaign. The best way to hide is in plain sight. Besides, I think you'll be a great asset. You're attractive, intelligent, and unblemished by previous political activity. I want a woman nearby who will keep me attuned to her point of view. Most male politicians surround themselves with men advisers who tell them what women want, and then they wonder why they get into trouble."

"Red, I'm married."

"I sort of assumed that. What happened?"

"I can't talk about it. I'm pretty sure it's all over, but I just don't know. I have to let the wound heal first."

"I'll keep you busy. You won't have much time to think."

"What about sleeping arrangements?"

"I thought about that a lot during the night while you were asleep," he answered.

"I was awake and thinking too."

"You've got to move into a place in town that's more permanent. You can't stay in that fleabag of a hotel. It's not particularly safe, and I'll bet it's not comfortable. Joe tells me that Millie Burton has offered to let you share her apartment. That would be a good arrangement for you."

Trish suddenly felt a cold chill of exposure. "How does Joe know so much about me?"

"Hey, now . . . don't react like that. I'm in politics, remember? I don't like surprises of any kind. That's what Joe does for me: he keeps me informed of everything. It's one part of his job."

"Well, it gives me a very strange feeling to know that somebody's been spying on me," she retorted, and pulled away slightly.

"Come on, now, it's all part of the game. It's okay once you get used to it. Now, what about Millie?"

"How much does she know?"

"Millie and Joe will be the only people who know about our real relationship. We can't keep it just between us, even though I'd like it if we could."

"But Millie doesn't like Joe—she told me so."

"Makes no difference. They're both loyal to me. I really believe that. Besides, when you're in politics, you occasionally have to associate with people you don't like. And often it's good strategy to be surrounded by people who have different points of view and who aren't good buddies."

"Well, it all sounds very clandestine and manipulative, but I do want to be near you . . . for now. There's one thing I can't deal with, though."

"Tell me, Trish."

"Are you still sleeping with Gloria?"

Red released his hold on her and lay on his back staring up at the ceiling. "Only when she wants me . . . which isn't very often. A couple times a year maybe. That's one of the reasons Joe is so adept at . . . making arrangements. I like sex, Trish—I need it to keep me going. Life would be a hell of a lot simpler if I didn't."

"I see. . . . Well, I can't be part of a harem, Red. I'm sorry." Her voice broke, and she was angry with herself. Why, why was she setting herself up to be hurt again?

"Hey, wait a minute. I didn't ask you to be my whore,

goddammit. I want to love you, Trish, do you understand? If you're there for me, there won't be anyone else. I promise you that." He put his arms around her and held her tightly against him.

For the first time since that terrible day two months ago, she cried. Sobbing, she clung to him, and he kissed her tears and soothed her. He hoped that someday soon she would be able to tell him about the man who had hurt her so badly.

Later, Joe came by in his car to take Trish to the hotel to pack her things. That night, with more than a few misgivings, Trish moved into Millie's apartment.

19

The Sexy Rich Bitch

Vanessa's dinner consisted of a club sandwich on soggy white toast and a salad made with day-old lettuce and pickled beets. Everything tasted as bad as it looked, except for the wine, which she had chilled slightly in a bucket of ice the waiter had brought up with her meal. As she sipped desultorily on the wine, she switched on the television set and watched it without much interest. The alcohol began to affect her, and she became increasingly morose. What was she doing in this crummy hotel, eating this crap? She could be at home in her mansion with her cook and her servants. What was this obsession she had to sacrifice herself? Who cared anyway?

She was all alone in the world, and now that Mike was gone, she was useless. No, worse than useless, worthless. Damn, she shouldn't have started drinking. It was so hard to quit once she'd started. She remembered the time that she had wound up in the hospital after one of her severe drinking bouts, and the doctor had recommended strongly that she go to Palm Springs to an alcohol-abuse center, but Mike refused to let her go. He insisted that all she needed was a little self-control. God, he should have known how little of that she had.

She poured herself another glass of wine, and as she walked past the dresser mirror, she stopped to look at herself. Who was this ugly blond matron in the cheap robe? Where was the sexy rich bitch with the designer clothes? Angrily she stripped off her robe and stood looking at her nude figure. Her body was still good. A little thin, maybe, but the full breasts hadn't started to sag yet, and the waist was still narrow, the stomach flat.

As she stood looking at herself, the old urge for sex that booze usually brought on began to assert itself. She laughed. A little liquor was an aphrodisiac for her, but just a little too much worked to depress her sexual appetite. She'd had just enough, and now she felt very horny, dammit. She began to caress herself. First she touched her breasts until the nipples stood at attention. Then her fingers moved lower and lower until she could feel her clitoris stretching out with erection. It felt so good. She kept stroking, enjoying the feel of it and the view of herself. She tried to stop, to prolong the experience, but the desire for relief became too intense, and she watched and felt her body go taut in its orgasm . . . too quickly, much too quickly.

She drank some more wine and paced the room, still naked, still unsatisfied. Masturbation had never been fulfilling for her. It only served to make her want more. She needed to feel the thickness of a man's penis inside her.

Going to the closet, she took her money belt from a hanger and extracted a hundred-dollar bill, which she slipped under her pillow. Then she called room service again, and ordered their best bottle of champagne—to be delivered immediately, with two glasses.

Ten minutes later, there was a knock at the door, and a short, dark young man brought in the tray with the wine and the glasses.

As he walked to the table and set it down, he asked, "Would you like for me to open it for you?"

"Yes, if you don't mind. Would you like to join me in a

glass of champagne?'' Vanessa asked. ''I hate to . . . drink . . . all by myself.''

''Yes, ma'am.'' He looked up at her and saw that she had allowed her robe to fall open, exposing her breasts and pubic hair. He smiled. Tonight he'd get a big tip, for sure. There were some things he did better than serve food.

20

An Aging Flower Child

Joe dropped Trish's bags in the entry hall of Millie's apartment and left without even greeting Millie. The two women just looked at each other for a moment. Trish was embarrassed at the somewhat puzzled look on her hostess's face. It was an awkward but brief moment, until Millie abruptly ended it with a smile.

"Come on in and sit down. I think that before we do anything we should have a talk, okay? I know you're a little uncomfortable about all this, and you deserve an explanation. I've got a pot of herb tea all ready for us."

Taking Trish's arm, Millie led her down a hallway of highly polished and bleached hardwood floors into a small but well-appointed and cheerful kitchen done in white and gleaming chrome. She motioned for Trish to sit down at a table in the corner that was surrounded by windows overlooking the city. Everybody in New York seemed to have spectacular views, Trish noted as she eased herself into the chair farthest from the window. "Mind if I sit here?" she asked. "I'm still a little uneasy in these tall buildings."

"You know, I felt the same way when I came here— after living in California's earthquake country for ten years. Don't worry, you'll get used to it. Remember, Manhattan is built on rock. It's not like that nervous ground in California."

"I'll keep that in mind."

Millie poured two big mugs of dark hot tea and set one and a plate of granola cookies in front of Trish. "Here, this will make you feel better. You look exhausted."

Trish thought about the strenuous twenty-four hours she'd spent in bed with Red, and her cheeks flushed. How much did Millie know?

Millie caught the embarrassment on Trish's face and decided to be forthright. "Look, my friend, stop acting like the virgin who just lost her maidenhead. Remember, I lived through Berkeley in the sixties. We're the generation who started the sexual revolution, or whatever the hell that was. For God's sake, don't start acting like Hester Prynne. Scarlet letters are in short supply in this town. If you've got a good thing going with the senator, terrific. He's a lovely guy . . . . I just hope he doesn't hurt you too much. You know, politics is his real passion."

Trish looked into the kind face of the aging flower child and smiled. "Millie, you have a great capacity for friendship, don't you?"

"Remember the song . . ." And she began to sing, " 'What the world needs now is love, sweet love'—well, that's how I still feel. All those things we said and believed then, I still believe. And I try to live it. Not many of us do. Everybody's into greed nowadays."

"You're a good person, Millie. I feel awful about imposing on you like this."

"You're not imposing on me. This whole thing was my idea in the first place. Joe told me that Red was hiring a 'bird,' as he called you, and he was furious about the whole thing. When I met you, *I* was delighted . . . I had a feeling that you weren't just one of those one-night stands . . . so I told Joe that it would be safer to have you live with me than be alone. That way I could always cover for you. I let him go to the Senator and take credit for the idea, so he'd feel a lot more comfortable with the whole situation.

"God, do you have any idea how embarrassing all this is for me?" Trish wailed, and put her head in her hands.

"Come on, now. Take a taste of that tea and try one of my cookies. The tea will relax you—it has no caffeine—and the cookies are full of good things."

Trish did as she was told. The tea was dark and sweet and spicy. The cookies were heavy but rich and delicious. She ate one and reached for another. "Good grief, my appetite hasn't been impaired."

"You're going to be fine . . . and we're going to have fun together. I really don't like living alone. I lived in a commune once, and I just loved it. Day or night there was always somebody to talk to. I can't even have a cat in this apartment."

Suddenly Trish became more aware of her surroundings. The apartment was obviously an expensive place to live, for it was spacious and well-located. "God, Millie, I don't know if I can afford half the rent on this place."

"Sure you can. Half of nothing is nothing, right?"

"What? What are you talking about?"

"I don't pay any rent here. It's a co-op. I own it. All you have to pay is half the maintenance charge, which isn't all that much."

"But what about the mortgage payment?"

"Don't have one. When I sold this land to the developer, part of the deal was that I got my choice of an apartment—it was part of the sale."

"You owned this land? My God!"

"Now *I'm* embarrassed. It's always been tough to admit that I have a lot of money. The scarlet letter I wear is a dollar sign. I inherited the land from my folks. Dad tried to cut me out of his will, but he died before Mom did, and she was always sympathetic and loving. Even when I was part of the Haight-Ashbury scene, she never let me go. She just kept telling me she understood. She'd send me money so I wouldn't have to beg or fuck for bread. She was an angel, and I came home because of her."

Tears had formed in Millie's eyes, and Trish could see that Millie still grieved for her mother. "How long ago did she die?"

"Two years. . . . Come on, I'll show you around," Millie said, getting to her feet. She led Trish out of the kitchen into the dining area, which was large for a New York apartment but looked smaller because of the huge table and chairs and breakfront that were squeezed into it. Millie continued to talk. "You see, Dad died of cancer a year before my mother did, and Mother just couldn't adjust to life without him. He was a royal pain in the ass, but they were devoted to each other. Although most of the money came from her family, Dad was a brilliant surgeon, and he didn't need it. They lived well, but not outrageously, and the money just kept accumulating. I got it all."

"You were an only child?"

Millie shook her head. "My older brother died in Vietnam . . . that's when I got radicalized . . . and my father couldn't accept it. He said I was desecrating my brother's memory by protesting the war."

"Oh, Millie, how terrible for you."

"Yeah, well, I'm okay now. I made peace with myself, and my mother understood. See all this furniture?"

Trish smiled. "It would be hard not to notice it, Millie. Did it belong to your parents?"

"Good guess. Yeah. It was my mom's. All of it."

Millie took Trish on a tour of the apartment's three bedrooms and three baths. The large rooms were dwarfed by the heavy antique furniture everywhere. Millie explained. "One of these days I'll have the courage to donate all this stuff to a good cause, but it's been in my mother's family for ages. It's worth a bloody fortune, I suppose, but I just couldn't bring myself to get rid of all the things she loved when I sold the old homestead."

Trish looked at the rich and thick Oriental rugs on the floor and noticed that most of them were too big for the rooms and were rolled at one end against the walls. She wondered why Millie hadn't gotten a decorator to help her integrate the magnificent pieces of heavy walnut and mahogany furniture in the sleek modern apartment with its white walls and large windows. Everything was just shoved against the walls, making the place look more like an overstocked antique store than a home.

"Here's your room. If you don't like it, you can have the other bedroom, but that one's got even more furniture in it," Millie said apologetically. A beautiful four-poster bed, a massive carved walnut armoire, a dresser, and a rocking chair left little space to move around in, but the room was cheerful with its peach-and-green chintz coverlet on the bed and matching draperies.

As Trish unpacked, Millie commented on Trish's wardrobe in her usual honest way. "These clothes won't make it here in the winter. You'll freeze your ass. First of all, you've got to get a heavy coat, preferably a waterproof one, and some boots. Any day, the sky will open up and dump tons of snow or rain on us, and we'll probably have to walk in it because all the cabs disappear when the weather gets bad."

"That's a happy thought."

"Believe me. Now, are you all set here? There's lots of towels in the bathroom cabinet, soap, and stuff. Throw your dirty clothes in the wicker hamper. A woman comes in at ten every morning to clean. She'll also do any laundry you leave, but be careful about giving her delicate things. She throws everything into the same tub and uses hot water and bleach. I think it's part of her religion, because I can't get her to do it differently."

"Well, the least I can do is share her salary."

Millie emitted a deep sigh of despair. "Can't you get it through your head that I've got so much dough that I can't spend it in ten lifetimes? You know, I'm giving it away like crazy, but the damn interest rates are so high that I'm making it faster than I can get rid of it."

"Tsk, tsk, poor baby," Trish teased. "But I'm not a

charity, understand . . . and what you do for me isn't deductible.''

"Too bad. By the way, I'd appreciate it if you wouldn't mention the money to Joe. I'd hate it if he started kissing my boots. It would ruin our relationship, and I'd miss his hostility. Sleep well. I'll get you up at seven, okay?''

Trish took a long hot shower and then climbed into the huge bed. The sheets were cool and white and looked as if they'd been ironed. She turned out the lights and snuggled under a beautiful old puffy down quilt. How interesting life was when one had the courage to be adventurous.

21

The New Volunteer

Vanessa was the first to arrive at the campaign office in the morning. She found it still unopened but she didn't have to wait alone long, for Millie soon arrived in the company of another woman whom she introduced. "I want you to meet my new roommate, Trish Delaney. Trish, this is the new volunteer I told you about."

Trish smiled warmly. "Hi, it's nice to meet someone who's newer to this whole business than I am. If you have any questions, ask Millie. I don't have any answers yet."

"How do you do? I'm Mrs. John Fitzgerald, but please call me . . . Ann," Vanessa replied.

As they waited for someone to let them into the headquarters, the women sized each other up briefly. Trish thought that Ann seemed stiff and shy, and she determined to be extra friendly and try to put her at ease. Vanessa immediately noted that Trish's clothes were expensive, and she wondered who she was and why she had joined O'Shea's staff.

"Are you a native New Yorker?" Vanessa asked.

Trish laughed warmly. "Heavens, no! I just arrived in town last week. I'm from Los Angeles."

Vanessa tried to conceal her concern at the news that they both came from Los Angeles. "Really? What brought you all the way here?"

"I'm an old friend of Red's—the senator, that is. We went to high school together. I found myself at loose ends and decided to come to New York and do what I could to help him become president."

Trish's manner was not totally casual as she explained, and Vanessa felt at once that there was more to the story than the woman was telling. She didn't want to be paranoid, but she decided she would have to be very careful of Trish until she knew exactly what her situation was.

"Well, well, here comes our beloved leader to brighten our day and bring sunshine to our smiles," Millie said as Joe approached them.

"Good morning, ladies. Why are you standing out here in the cold? Don't you have a key, Millie?"

"Sure don't, Joe. That wimp Carl won't give me one, and he's always late getting here in the morning," Millie complained.

"I'll see that you get one. You too, Trish." He looked at Vanessa. "Hi, now don't tell me you're another old friend of the senator's?" Joe asked somewhat sarcastically, deliberately refusing to meet Trish's eyes.

Aware that Trish looked embarrassed and Vanessa confused, Millie stepped in quickly. "Joe, I'd like you to meet Mrs. Fitzgerald. She's going to do volunteer work for us, and she's planning to work the same hours as staff does . . . on the telephone. That is, unless you start flashing around the office again."

"Wash your mouth out, Millie. You're a long way from Berkeley. Welcome, Mrs. Fitzgerald. I hope you enjoy working here. If you have any questions, don't hesitate to ask me." Joe seemed preoccupied and uninterested in further chitchat as he unlocked the door and let them into the offices.

Millie went off to make coffee while Trish set to work scanning all the morning papers for any stories about Red to clip and reproduce for the files.

Vanessa started her fund-raising calls right away and the

morning passed rapidly. She found that she could be extremely persuasive. She'd had a lot of practice trying to please and persuade her father.

When they broke for lunch, everyone was extremely impressed with the responses Vanessa had gotten from voters—and the number of them who had promised to send money. She enjoyed their praise. It was a commodity that had been scarce in her life. However, when Trish and Millie invited her to join them for lunch, she declined. She didn't want to risk making a slip in casual conversation. For some reason, she was especially wary of Trish. She had a vague feeling that the woman was not whom she claimed to be.

Vanessa took a long walk during the lunch hour instead. She was beginning to feel that accomplishing her goal was not going to be as easy as she had hoped. She would have to wait for the right opportunity. It might take time, however, and she wasn't sure she had much of that left.

22

Down Memory Lane

Trish wandered around Red's house for half an hour waiting for him. He had called her at the office and told her that he was coming in to New York later that afternoon and would be free so that they could have dinner alone. She had stopped in at DDL's food show in Trump Tower and bought cannelloni, *insalata di funghi crudi*, and *crostata di ricotta*, the Italian version of cheesecake, for dessert. She resisted her first impulse, which was to go to a grocery store and get things to cook. But she was determined her relationship with Red was never going to be a domestic one. She'd already had one of those, and she was not eager for a reprise, especially since she'd been told so often that she had no talent for it.

She felt strangely comfortable in the town house. Perhaps because she knew that Red's wife had never set foot inside the place. Trish hoped she never would.

The sound of keys in the door interrupted her musing, and she hurried to see who it was. She checked the peephole first, and then with delight pulled open the door.

"You're here!" Red said, and the smile on his face showed his pleasure at seeing her.

God, he had the most marvelous face, she thought as he stepped inside the door and closed it behind him. Without giving her a chance to say a word, he took her in his arms and hugged her tightly.

"My God, Trish, I'm so glad to see you. Every minute we've been apart, I've thought about little except getting back here to be with you." Trish sighed and wished she could set the words to music—they sounded so beautiful to her ears.

"Red, I love to hear you say that, but it frightens me," she mumbled into the scratchy tweed of his sports jacket.

He pulled away and looked at her questioningly. "And why would you be frightened of my wanting to see you?"

"Because I'm afraid that it's all too temporary. I don't want to start needing to be a permanent fixture in your life. I want for us to enjoy each other, but not need each other. Is that okay?"

She looked down as she spoke, and he lifted her chin with his hand so that she was looking into his eyes. "Trish, life is temporary. Everything is temporary. Keep that in mind, always. Whatever is, won't be for long. People get into trouble when they begin thinking something will last forever, even though they themselves won't last very long."

"When did you start thinking like that, Red?" she asked curiously.

"A long time ago. It was the only way I could psych myself up to go into battle. It's easier to face death when you accept the fact that it's coming sooner or later." Then he laughed and put his arm around her. "Let's sit down there on the couch and neck."

As they walked toward the sofa, Red shed his jacket, tossing it on a chair. They settled down on the couch, and he put his arms around her while he continued to talk. "The realization that nothing lasts forever helped me through some pretty bad times. The worst, of course, was when my wife and child were killed in the automobile crash. I really thought my life was over . . . I wanted it to be over,

Trish. But it wasn't, and now I'm glad." He smiled at her as he reached down and touched her mouth with his lips. It was a warm, soft, and gentle kiss.

"Red, it's so amazing to me to find out that you're even more wonderful than I remembered you as being. I was afraid I'd discover that I had glorified you in my mind, but if anything, I did just the opposite. You're such a warm, caring, intelligent man, and I'm so happy to be here with you."

"I feel the same way, Trish. When you called me, I was almost afraid to see you. I thought you might be different from the terrific girl I once knew, and all my illusions would be shattered."

He kissed her again, but this time it was not as gentle or as sweet. This time it was more forceful, more passionate. For a long time they stayed together on the couch just kissing, until at last they were both at a fever pitch of passion, and he said, "Remember . . . this is the way it used to be."

Trish giggled. "I know. But take me to bed, will you? I feel like I'm going to burn up with desire."

"Good. Now you know how I felt when we used to sit in the back seat of the car and neck."

"You wretch. I used to feel that way too," she protested.

"You know what would be fun?"

"What?" she asked.

"Let's do it in the car . . . for old times' sake."

"Do you think we could?"

"Come on." He stood up and pulled her to her feet, and they went out a side door into the garage. He turned on the lights, and Trish looked at the car. "Thank God, it's a sedan," she observed. "I was so afraid there might only be a Porsche parked out here."

"I may be romantic, but I'm not crazy. Shall we take off our clothes before we get in?"

"No way. We'll do it the way we would have. Let's

go,'' she said, and laughed. Hand in hand, they got into the back seat of the Cadillac.

Red took her in his arms again and kissed her. It was a kiss of youth and passion and memory. His hand traveled up her skirt and tugged at her panties until he pulled them off. Then, slowly, he began to touch her, examining her body with his hand, exploring inside and outside. She had unzipped his pants and moved her head down until she could take him into her mouth. After a few minutes she raised her lips to his mouth again and said, ''I didn't even know about that then, did you?''

''Yes, but it seemed too exotic to even talk about, especially with a nice girl like you,'' he replied huskily.

Kissing her deeply again, he pressed her down onto the seat, and with some difficulty managed to arrange his long legs in such a way that he could slip himself inside her. As they moved together, Trish remembered the longing she had felt as a young virgin all those years ago, and she was lost in a trance of passion. She gave in to it completely, and soon found herself in the throes of a climax that seemed to go on for a long time. When it was finally over, she opened her eyes and saw that Red was watching her closely.

''Was it a good one?'' he asked with a smile.

''The best I've ever had, my love,'' she replied, and in moments she felt his body tense as he too reached the pinnacle.

When it was over, they looked at each other and laughed. ''You know, it's kind of cold out here,'' Red commented.

''I didn't notice. I had my love to keep me warm,'' she replied.

''Let's go get under the electric blanket and cuddle for a while, okay?''

''Do you think we'll ever get ourselves untangled?'' Trish giggled.

Laughing, they struggled to sit upright and get out of the car. As they went back into the warmth of the house, Red said, "It was a great trip down memory lane, but once is enough, don't you think?"

"Yes, for that car, but I thought we might have a go in the limo sometime," Trish teased.

"You're on. I'll bet the driver would enjoy the show."

23

Little Wisdoms

Dan set the telephone down, and a feeling of elation spread through him. He had just learned from his son, Rob, that Rob had received his usual letters from his mother and was unaware that anything was wrong. Dan decided Cake must intend to return home soon, or surely she would not keep up the appearance of normalcy for the children. That bitch Joyce was probably mailing the letters for her . . . or else Cake was somewhere nearby, watching him, waiting for him to make a mistake. Well, it wasn't going to happen. He had let Selena come to the house once, but he wasn't going to do it again.

He went upstairs to the bedroom and looked around to see if there were any signs that Cake had returned without his knowing it. It was possible that she was just next door. He supposed that was where he wanted her to be. Reluctantly he had to admit to himself that life hadn't been much fun since she left.

Opening her dresser drawer, he poked through it aimlessly. The delicate scent of sachet touched the air, and he closed his eyes, imagining her there. He picked up one of her satin slips, and rubbing it against his cheek, remembered the closeness of their early years together.

As he folded the slip to put it away, he noticed the edge of a spiral-bound notebook tucked under the lingerie. He pulled it out, taking care not to muss the neat folds of nylon and silk. On the cover, in Cake's handwriting, was "My Words . . . Little Wisdoms." She had never mentioned that she was interested in writing. He carried the notebook downstairs, fixed himself a Scotch on the rocks, and settled down in the study to read it, feeling curious as well as slightly apprehensive. Were there things there that he would prefer not to read?

The first page did not unsettle him much. It was titled "Truth" and was very short. "There is his truth, and her truth, and your truth, and theirs. But there is only one true truth, and that is mine." Nice little irony, he observed and turned the page. The writing on the next page was longer and less amusing.

> Accuse me, my love. Cry out the vilest lies.
> Call me any name you choose,
> So long as you speak not the truth.
> The cruel falsehood hangs only briefly in the air
> Quivering with indignation,
> But the sharp spear dipped in the poison of fact
> Cuts deep wounds which do not heal.
> So say what you like in the heat of battle.
> Accuse, belittle, revile, condemn,
> So long as you speak not the truth.

Dan wondered just when Cake had written that. He was a little uncomfortable and not sure he wanted to go on. He had the feeling that perhaps she had suffered more than he thought when he harped at her about her lack of organization. On the next page he read:

"As the winds and rain erode the mountain, the thoughtless, unkind words of one's beloved erode the spirit. And so, where once stood the majestic peaks of pride and self-respect, now lies only the humble dust."

"Jesus!" he exclaimed softly. He put the book down and sipped his drink, trying to remember some of the

disputes they'd had. Her writing made her sound so meek
and down-trodden, and she hadn't been that way at all.
More often than not, she'd fought back defensively. He
began to read again.

"You broke my arm," I cried in pain and anger,
"Sorry," you said, but the cast was stiff and white.
"You broke my heart," I cried, hurt and bewildered,
"Sorry," you said, but the wound did not heal.
An arm in time will mend; the bone will knit as new,
But where is the cast to hold the pieces of my heart
together?

Good grief, he'd never laid a finger on her. Was she
trying to say that she'd rather he'd beaten her? What the
devil was wrong with her?

"Don't be down and weep and cry," they tried to
comfort me.
"The world goes on, it will not end, though you're
betrayed by your best friend."
But I know best why I am sad.
I lost the friend I never had.

Dan was now completely hooked on his wife's words.
He could tell by the difference in pens and writing that she
had composed the poems over a long period of time. Most
of them had a sad or slightly wry tone. There were many
pages, and impatiently he turned to the end of the book.
He needed some clue as to her recent state of mind, and he
found what he was looking for on the last page.

A river of sorrow flows through me.
It once was a river of life,
Carrying the air to me,
A humiliated, despairing wife.
A river of sorrow flows from me

I've opened the gates to the sea
And when it turns red,
He'll know I am dead,
And never again will I be.

There was one more couplet at the bottom of the page,
and it was entitled "Last Line."

The fear that I felt of leaving,
Has gone with him.

Dan put the book down and went back to the bar for
another drink. He was upset and angry. Cake had obviously been so miserable that she had actually thought
about killing herself. Was he to blame for all the unhappi-
ness she had written in that damn little book? Why did he
have to carry the burden of responsibility for her state of
mind anyway? Marriage was a damn one-way street. The
husband was expected to provide for all the physical needs
of a family. Was it also his job to keep everybody happy
and content?

Looking for relief and justification, he walked out to the
room in the garage to look at the paintings Cake had been
messing around with for years. He had never let her hang
any of them in the house because he didn't like them. He
pulled one out of the bin to look at it again, to try to see
some of the joy that painting them seemed to bring her.
One by one, he studied them, but he saw nothing to
change his original impressions. The colors were nice,
bright and bold, but in his eyes the paintings looked like
child's work. The paint was streaked across the canvas in
bold strokes, making rainbows that stretched across the
sky in some; in others, geometric forms were piled one on
another. Why didn't she ever try to paint a picture that
looked like something?

He walked back into the house, feeling a little less
morose. If nothing else, those damn canvases had cheered

him up a bit. When she came back, maybe he would encourage her to continue painting. Take some classes. He would much rather have her in the garage painting than writing that damn morbid poetry. God, he missed her.

24

Old School Chum

Richard Terhune was disgusted with the entire operation. He had people strung out all over the city looking for Vanessa Fallon, but he hadn't had a lead that was worth a nickel. He was getting too old and tired to do this kind of shit. All he really wanted was to go to a nice restaurant for a good meal and a glass of wine. Perhaps Trish would be free. She was a pleasant woman, very uncomplicated and good-natured. He called her and learned that she had checked out of the hotel. Fortunately, she had left a number where she could be reached. At the new number, a woman answered and called Trish to the phone.

"Richard, how nice to hear from you. I thought you'd be back in California by now," she greeted him.

"I wish I were, but since I'm still here, I wonder if you could have dinner with me tonight."

"Oh, I'm sorry, but Millie and I just started to fix ourselves something."

"Millie is the one who answered the phone? Please bring her along. I'd love to meet her."

Trish turned to Millie. "Millie, would you like to go to dinner with a friend this evening?"

Millie shook her head. "No, you go on by yourself. I'll be fine."

Trish was insistent. "But I'd like for you to go. Richard

is such a terrific person. We'll have a lovely time together." She then spoke into the phone. "We'd love to, Richard, but nothing fancy. We don't really feel like dressing up. We had a big day at the office."

"You've started work already?"

"Yes, and it's really exciting. We'll tell you all about it at dinner." Trish gave him the address, and Richard said he'd be there in less than an hour.

He started into the bathroom to shave, when the telephone rang. It was one of the men he had put on the street to find Vanessa Fallon. "Hi, it's Bob Reed. I think I got a lead on this Fallon chick for you."

"Terrific. Where is she?"

"Well, you told me you'd heard she was a real live one, so we started talking to the bellboys in some of the smaller hotels. We heard about one who got laid by a dame who paid him a lot of dough. I showed him the picture, and he said maybe, but she had short blond hair."

"Women change their hair every day. Find out as much as you can about her. What name is she registered under?"

"Mrs. John Fitzgerald, that's all I know."

"Where is she now?"

"In her room. I haven't made any attempt to talk to the desk clerk yet. I'll take a picture of her when she leaves in the morning and put a tail on her, then I'll try to get into her room to search it."

"Be sure to put somebody there to see that she doesn't leave the place tonight."

"From what I've seen, she never goes out in the evening."

"Good work. Keep me posted."

Richard put down the telephone, feeling elated. It might be a false lead, but he couldn't keep his hopes in check. He had come to the conclusion that he ought to take the money and run, although his curiosity wouldn't let him leave it at that. This was the strangest deal he'd ever been involved in, which was saying a lot. Perhaps he ought to call his office in the morning and have them research Mike Fallon's will. It was surely in the probate mill by now, and it might shed some light on the situation.

After a quick shave and a change of shirts, Richard called for his car. It was a night to celebrate, and he was looking forward to seeing the delightful Trish Delaney again.

When Millie and Trish came down into the lobby to meet him, Richard tried to conceal his surprise at Millie's costume. She was wearing boots that had seen better years, a voluminous denim skirt that reached almost to her ankles, and a thick knitted poncho draped over her shoulders. Her long lank hair was pulled into a ponytail, and her face was bare of makeup. She looked like a ragbag beside the trimly neat and fashionable Trish. He wondered how the two ever got together, and as soon as they were seated at Il Menestrello waiting for the wine to be poured, he broached the subject.

"Well, Trish, the last time we dined together you were staying at a rather modest hotel, and now you're situated in a very fashionable apartment. It looks as if New York is agreeing with you. Have you and Millie known each other very long?"

Trish shook her head. "No, but I feel as if I've known her all my life. We've become very good friends, and we see a lot of each other, since we work together."

"Ah, yes, tell me about your new job," he responded.

Millie spoke up. "Trish is the women's coordinator for Senator O'Shea's presidential campaign."

Richard's eyebrows shot up in surprise. "Really? I'm very impressed. If nothing outrageous happens during the primaries, I think he's a shoo-in for the nomination."

Trish's eyes sparkled with pleasure at her friend's assessment. "I hope you're right. He'd be such a good president. I can't imagine anybody who could be better. But I'm afraid Millie is making my job sound much more important than it is.''

The brightness of her eyes and the wonder in her voice did not escape the courtroom veteran. Trish Delaney was especially enthusiastic about her candidate. ''Tell me how you got involved in his campaign,'' he asked.

''Well, I knew Red in high school,'' she began, and Richard noted the slight flush that appeared on her cheeks, ''and I asked him for a job and got it,'' she finished somewhat lamely.

Millie broke in to cover for her. ''Trish came along at just the right time. Joe Franklin, Red's campaign manager, was looking for someone to work with me and coordinate the staff workers with the volunteers. As soon as I met her, I knew Trish would be perfect, so I recommended that she be hired. It was a good move. The place has really been humming since she came with us.''

''Well, O'Shea's a good man, and if he gets the nomination, I'll probably sign on too, although it will be quite a departure for me. I'm usually a Democrat, though I have bolted on a few occasions. Never in the presidential bid, however. Red O'Shea might be just the one to convince me. Ah, here's the wine. I hope you like it.''

Trish and Millie allowed Richard to suggest dishes for them, and he had ordered a bottle of Brunello, which was dark red and mellow. By the time they were on the second bottle, they were all good and close friends and laughing and talking easily together. Millie invited Richard to have dinner at their apartment one night soon, and he said he would count the hours until he heard from her.

As the limousine took him back to the Plaza, Richard filed an important little bit of information in his head. If his instincts hadn't deceived him, he would bet that the Mr. Clean of politics, Red O'Shea, had a serious girlfriend. Trish Delaney was not the kind of woman a man as ambitious as O'Shea would play around with unless there was something important between them. And he was pretty sure by her manner that something was going on. Old school chum. A likely story. One could never tell when information like that could be useful.

25

Mystery Woman

Vanessa stopped at Trish's desk and watched as she sketched a layout for a poster. She stood there for several minutes before Trish, who was totally absorbed in her effort, noticed her and looked up.

"Oh, I'm sorry. I didn't see you," Trish apologized. "When I get involved in something, I really lose myself in it."

Vanessa smiled. "Every real artist I've ever met has had that kind of concentration. You know, that's an awfully good layout for a campaign poster. Why don't you show it to Joe?"

Trish sighed. "I've tried several times to show him some of my ideas, but he just tells me to get busy on the telephone and try to shake loose some more campaign contributions. He says they're paying a high-priced group of professionals for artwork and don't need amateurs to waste their time."

Vanessa shook her head. "He's a jackass. I know a talented artist when I see one, and you're good, really you are."

"Thanks, anyway. But Joe's a lost cause. Maybe I'll show them to . . ." she started to say "Red," and suddenly realized she would be making a serious gaffe and finished, " . . . Millie." Then she quickly changed the subject. "Ann, how are you doing on the women's clubs?"

"Pretty well. I've scheduled luncheon speakers for several organizations. I talked to Joe about training some women to go out on the stump, and he promised me a list of some of the bigger contributors. We're going to form a special committee of women who will meet with the candidate personally. We'll give them speeches to read and coach them on where he stands on the issues."

Trish was impressed. "My God, that's great. You've only been here a couple of weeks, and already you've managed to get so much done. I think you should be in charge of women's issues. I haven't accomplished anything."

"Well, I would be a lot more effective if I could talk to the senator myself."

"Why don't you ask Joe to set it up for you?" Trish asked.

"I have, but he says the senator's too busy."

"He is, but I know he'd find time to talk to you. Let me see what I can do."

"Can you manage it?" Vanessa asked skeptically.

"I don't know . . . maybe. You see, I went to high school with Red. I know him pretty well. The next time I talk to him, I'll mention it and see what he says."

"When will that be?" Vanessa suddenly saw Trish in a new light. Perhaps she'd been wrong to concentrate her efforts on impressing Joe. How dumb not to guess about Trish. Her father had told her that most politicians were womanizers, because the drive to get elected often translated itself into a strong sexual drive.

Trish began to feel a little discomfited. "I have no idea. I only talk to him occasionally."

Millie arrived and the conversation ended. "Oh, hi, Millie. Where've you been all morning?" Trish asked in relief.

"I went to the county registrar of voters to pick up the latest listings, and I had to wait. Is Joe in yet?" Millie responded.

"Not yet, and it's almost lunchtime," Vanessa responded. "If he doesn't get on the ball and get those names to me, I'm going to be angry. The first women's-club luncheon I've scheduled is only a week away, and we haven't got our speakers' group organized yet."

"Let's go have lunch," Millie suggested.

Trish stood up. "Great idea. Ann, would you like to join us for a change?"

Vanessa shook her head. "No thanks. I'm on a diet. I'm skipping lunch today and having my hair done instead."

Millie and Trish put their coats on and left the office. As they walked toward the coffee shop where they usually ate, they discussed Ann. "There's something about Ann Fitzgerald that's very strange," Millie said.

Trish laughed. "You've been saying that every day since she started working there. You've got to admit she's a great worker."

"Yeah, yeah, I know, but she's skitzy. One minute she'll be super nice and sweet and playing that 'little-me' role of hers, and the next, she puts on her organization hat and starts taking charge of everything and telling everybody what to do."

"Yeah, maybe, but you have to admit that place needs somebody besides Joe to run it. He tries to be everywhere at the same time, and he just can't function as office manager and serve as Red's right-hand man as well."

"You're right. You know, Ann could really whip that place into shape if Joe would let her. She's a born leader. I bet in one of her early lives she was the coxswain on a slave ship."

"Very funny. But say what you will, I like her. In fact, I'm going to ask Red to meet with her."

"What the hell for?" Millie asked indignantly.

"Because she's asked Joe to set up a meeting, and he won't. She needs to get that women's committee organized, and she can do it faster with Red's help."

"My little chickadee, I hope you haven't let your secret out to her, have you?"

"Don't be silly, of course not. I just told her he was an old friend from high school."

Millie shook her head. "That was a serious mistake. A very serious mistake."

Trish was unnerved by Millie's gloomy assertion. "Aren't you being a little paranoid, Millie? What could she possibly deduce from that innocent piece of information?"

Millie walked for at least twenty steps before replying. "The exact same thing that I did when Joe told me you were an old friend of the senator's—that you were sleeping with him."

Trish's heartbeat accelerated. "But how could you possibly come to such a conclusion on so little information?"

"That's the way the world is, Trish. That's what everybody thinks about men and women who are friends. We haven't reached the stage yet where friends can be just friends. In fact, we're regressing. Two women used to be able to be close friends without any kind of sexual shadows on their relationship. Now they're suspected of being lesbians if they live together."

"You're depressing me, Millie. I think your blood sugar is low. Let's have something fattening for lunch."

"I can relate to that."

When they returned to the office, Joe was waiting for them. "Where the hell have you two been?"

Millie raised an eyebrow as she replied, "Eating, Joe. It might be breakfasttime for you slugabeds, but it's lunchtime for us drones."

"Cut the sarcasm and come into my office, both of you. And Ann," he called, "will you please join us?"

Millie made a face as she remarked to Trish, "The mystery woman gets a 'please.' "

When they walked into his office, Joe indicated they should be seated in chairs he had pulled up close to his desk.

"Listen, I have a very interesting proposal for you. Red and I talked it over this morning, and we made a decision. How would you like to come out of the closet?"

Millie, who was ever suspicious of any of Joe's ideas, was quick to retort, "Who the hell ever said we were in the closet? We're not gay, you know."

Joe smirked. "Don't be crude, Millie."

Trish spoke up. "Just what do you mean?"

"Well, as you know, the female vote has become very important in this campaign. We think we ought to introduce you three to the media. We're going to think up some important-sounding titles for you and present you as the women who are running that aspect of Red's campaign. So, what do you think?"

"Fine with me," Millie responded, a tad sarcastically. "I always wanted to be a star."

"I'm not interested," Trish said. "I think the focus should be on Red. Besides, we're all amateurs, and we might come off looking just that way—amateurish."

Vanessa looked decidedly unenthusiastic. "What happened to our idea of having women who are big donors or wives of important supporters form a committee to act as window dressing?"

"That's still on the fire and will take a little longer to get going. This is something we can go forward with immediately and get some good press coverage out of," Joe answered.

A cold fury suffused Vanessa's voice as she responded before either Trish or Millie could speak. "There's absolutely no way that I would participate in that kind of circus. I came here to work behind the scenes, and that's where I intend to stay. My . . . husband would be very upset if I made a spectacle of myself. Besides, I'm very shy and would probably make an idiot of myself. It makes me nervous to talk in front of people."

All eyes turned to her in surprise. Nothing she had done had indicated that Ann Fitzgerald was shy or retiring. On many occasions she had made it quite clear that she felt she was the most articulate and well-educated person in the office.

"Come on, Ann. It was your idea to have a women's committee, and I think you have an obligation to see it through. And let's cut out this shy crap. Visibility is part of the political process," Joe persisted.

"Well, it isn't for me," she snapped. "I'm not the candidate. Red O'Shea is."

"Yes, but if you want to be on his team, you have to go along with what he wants, or you'd better find somebody else to work for," Joe replied.

"Joe!" Millie cried out. "Don't talk to her like that."

Vanessa's air of authority seemed to crumble before their eyes, and to the surprise of everyone in the room, she was suddenly at a loss for words. She started to say something, then cleared her throat and tried again. "I'm sorry. I must have misled you. I'm afraid I have to refuse." She stood up, looked around at Trish and Millie, and said, "I must go." Without another word, she hurried from the room.

"Nice work, Joe. We've probably lost one of the most effective and creative people we've ever had in here," Millie snapped as she followed Vanessa out of the room.

"What did I do?" Joe asked Trish in amazement.

"Joe, sometimes I think you're a little thick in the head. You know damn well why I don't want to do it. I'm sure Ann has her reasons too, and they may have nothing to do with what she said. Are you sure Red knew about this proposal?"

"Well, I mentioned it to him. He said to talk it over with you first."

Trish got up to leave. "Tell him you talked it over, and it just won't work. Unless you can use Millie alone. I'm sure Ann and I would be very happy to back her up . . . but no media appearances for us, understand?"

"Millie's the wrong image alone. I need all three of you, because you're different types, and I want to hit everybody with someone they can identify with."

"You're crazy, Joe. Suppose word gets out that I'm

having an affair with Red?'' Her cheeks burned as she said the words.

Joe looked at her defiantly. ''That's the reason, my dear lady, that's the reason. If I can get you identified as one of a group of workers, there'll be less chance that you'll get singled out.''

Trish laughed. ''Forget it, Joe. No matter what you say, I know the only thing you're thinking about is a cute little press conference with these attractive little housewives doing their darling little thing to attract attention. *People* magazine would eat it up. So would the *National Enquirer*. Red O'Shea is a serious candidate dealing with serious issues. Let's keep him that way.''

As Trish walked out of his office, she bumped into Millie, who announced, ''Ann's gone.''

''Did she say anything before she left?'' Trish asked in astonishment.

''She just said, 'Good-bye. It's been nice knowing you.' But she looked upset and pale.''

''Come on, get your coat. Maybe we can catch her.''

They hurried out onto the sidewalk, but Vanessa had disappeared into the midday crowd. Trish walked for two blocks in one direction, Millie in the other, but the woman was nowhere to be seen.

Later, on their way home after work, they discussed the matter dolefully.

''I was right, Trish. Ann really is a mystery woman.''

''Maybe she just doesn't want anybody to know what she's doing or where she is. I can certainly understand that, can't you?''

''Not really. Why would someone who's trying to hide go to work in a highly visible place like the campaign office of the media star of the political world? Come on, there has to be more to it than that.''

''I guess there is, but unless she comes back, we'll never know.''

"Don't say that. You know what a terrible curiosity I have. Do you know where she lives?"

Trish laughed. "No, I don't, and if I did, I wouldn't tell you. Leave the poor woman alone."

That night, just as they were about to turn off the late news and go to bed, the telephone rang. Millie answered. It was Vanessa.

"Hi, Millie. It's me . . . Ann. I need a big favor."

"Sure. What can I do?"

"I need your help. I can't stay in this hotel any longer. Is there any chance that I could sleep on your couch for a few days?"

"Hey, I've got an extra bedroom. You won't have to sleep on the couch. And you can stay as long as you want. Okay?"

Her voice sounded relieved. "Okay. Can I come right away?"

"Sure. Are you all right?"

"I will be, once I get there. I'm on my way."

Millie put down the telephone. "That was Ann. I think she's in trouble. She's coming over here . . . to stay. She sounded frightened."

"You know, I thought she looked more afraid than angry this morning," Trish said.

"So did I. I wonder what's going on. Do you suppose she's got a jealous husband looking for her or something?"

"Maybe," Trish answered quietly.

Millie's eyes lighted up. "Hot damn. Now I won't have to die not knowing."

"Not knowing what, Millie?" Trish asked.

"Why she's a mystery woman . . . what else?"

26

Out of Time

Earlier, when Vanessa had put on her coat and hurried out of the campaign office, she hailed a taxi and told the driver, "Take me for a drive around Central Park."

"Sure, lady. For how long?"

"Till I tell you to stop," she snapped.

"It's your dough," he replied peevishly.

She was extremely agitated and needed some time to calm down. She was furious at herself for having lost control and revealed too much. Now all three of them knew that she had something to hide, and that was the last thing she wanted anyone to suspect. She was sure that there had been a concerted effort mounted by now to locate her, though there had been not one word in the media about the disappearance of Mike Fallon's daughter. Which had not been very cagey of them. They were often quite good at outsmarting themselves, as her father had frequently observed. If they had been open and honest about her disappearance, she might have thought that there was honest concern for her welfare. But by keeping it quiet, they had revealed to her that they were threatened by her disappearance, and she was certain her life was in danger.

Over the past few days she had begun to wonder if she had made a serious error. Instead of disappearing, perhaps she should have announced that she was taking a vacation. It was possible that she would have been believed and no one would have been at all suspicious. On the other hand, the people she was dealing with were a trifle paranoid anyway, and they might have had her followed wherever she went. No, she had taken the safest course. Surveillance would have been too tight, and she'd never have been able to give them the slip.

She was running out of time. She'd been playing around too much, trying to be too clever. If she was going to go through with it, she would have to work more quickly and more directly. She shouldn't have walked away from the campaign office. She had to use Trish Delaney, one way or another.

Why was she suddenly feeling so frightened for her own safety, when for most of her adult life she hadn't cared whether she lived or died? She put her face in her hands. She had to pull herself together. She had allowed that stupid Joe Franklin to frighten her and make her lose her composure. God, she needed a drink, but she had to put that out of her mind. She couldn't start on the booze again, or she'd be dead for sure.

The cabbie was watching her in his rearview mirror. "You okay, lady?"

She lifted her head. "I'm fine, thank you. You can take me to the Maybelle Hotel now."

"But we ain't gone through the park yet," he protested.

She smiled ruefully. "Well, why not? Go on, one turn around the park and then to the hotel. It's a lovely day."

The cabbie looked at her in his rearview mirror but said nothing. It was a lousy day. It was cold and cloudy, and the wind was blowing, sending the wind-chill factor below zero. This was one loony dame. He hoped she wouldn't stiff him for the fare.

Later, as she walked through the lobby toward the elevator, the room clerk called to her. "Oh, Mrs. Fitzgerald. I have some wonderful news for you."

"For me?" she asked curiously.

"Yes, I'm not supposed to tell you this . . . I promised I wouldn't, but my wife insisted. I didn't want to spoil the surprise, but she said it wasn't right for a husband to walk in on a wife without letting her know he was coming."

"What are you talking about?"

"Your husband. He's back in town. He was here not more than an hour ago."

"What do you mean . . . my husband?" she asked, her knees weak with shock.

"He wasn't even going to tell me who he was, but I got it out of him."

"Uh . . . what did he say?" Vanessa asked, smiling, but her heart was pounding and her hands began to shake.

"He wanted to be in your room to surprise you when you came in this evening. Of course, I couldn't let him do that. I told him you never came back to the hotel until six in the evening, and he said he'd be here then. I had no idea you'd be here early today."

Vanessa tried to hide her agitation. "Oh, thank you, for telling me. John is always playing these little jokes on me, but this time I'll be one up on him. I'm going right to the beauty shop and get myself fixed up." She smiled sweetly. "You tell your wife thank you . . . she understands how women feel about things like this." She reached into her purse and took out a twenty-dollar bill.

"Here, take her a little gift tonight . . . and, please, if my husband shows up early, don't let on that I know. He'd be so disappointed if he thought his surprise had been spoiled."

Vanessa hurried to the elevator and went to her room. Quickly she jammed everything she could into her handbag. The large amount of cash she carried was always in the money belt around her waist. She pulled a sweater on over her blouse, put on her coat and gloves, and took one look around the room, realizing she would never see it or anything else there again. She was sorry that she would have to walk out on the bill, but she didn't dare pay it. The clerk must not suspect that she would never return.

As she passed through the lobby, she waved coyly and called, "I'll be back in a couple of hours, in case he gets here early."

Not daring to look around, she ducked into another cab. Even if someone were watching her, she wouldn't recognize him. They would never send anyone she knew.

"Where to, ma'am?" the cabdriver asked. He was young and courteous.

"Let's drive around the park a few times while I decide," she answered. She had to figure out someplace she could go to hide.

27

Golden Headaches

Selena was not happy with the way things were going. Try as she would, she could not get Dan to take her to his house again. It had been three weeks since Cake had left him, and in that time they had been in bed together only twice, which was unusual. The damn idiot was brooding over his wife's absence and had lost his libido. Selena had tried everything she could, every trick her mother had ever taught her and some she had invented herself, but Dan was simply not interested.

For a while she suspected that he might have another woman on the string, but she dismissed the notion. All the telltale evidence was missing. She knew the signs well and often wondered how wives could be so stupid as to miss them. A sharp eye, a sensitive nose, and a little intelligent watching were all it took to ferret out a cheating husband or lover. Once she was safely ensconced as his wife, she would make sure that he never had a chance to stray.

Damn Cake. She had messed up all of Selena's cleverly calculated plans. It had never occurred to Selena that the stupid bitch would walk out and leave things hanging. Now Selena had to battle the memory of a good wife instead of the reality of a dull woman. After the little talk Selena had had with her, Cake was supposed to have wept and confronted her husband with the evidence of his cheating and demanded a divorce. Still, since that had not happened, Selena was not one to waste her time brooding. She must work out a new plan. She just wished she could talk to her mother. Ginny would know what to do. Why not? After all, she wasn't that far away.

That afternoon, after she had made her plane reservation, Selena asked Dan if she could talk to him privately. With a wary look in his eye that warned her not to get too close, he consented. She sat down primly across from his desk and said nothing. When he looked up from the plans he was studying, he saw that she was sitting quietly with her hands folded, and there were tears in her eyes.

"What's wrong?" he asked apprehensively.

"I need a favor, Dan," she replied meekly.

"Oh? What?"

"I talked to my mother in Tucson last night, and she's very ill. I'd like to spend some time with her, if it's all right. I know there's a lot going on in the office right now, but I'm sure Delia would be able to fill in for me."

Dan was immediately relieved. He was getting tired of Selena's watchful eyes and her demands for attention. A few days of separation would be refreshing. "Of course. I hope it's not serious. Is there anything I can do?"

"I don't know if it's serious or not. She would certainly never tell me if it is. I'll just have to go there and see for myself."

"Okay, what day would you want to go?"

"Well . . . I was hoping it would be all right if I left this afternoon."

The imminence of her leaving distracted him. For three years she had been there to handle all the miserable details for him, and the prospect of a disruption in his routine was worrisome. "Well, uh, sure. Have you spoken to Delia yet?"

Selena realized that Dan was worried, and she decided to feed his apprehension a little more. "Yes. Of course, she's pretty busy with the Tahiti project, but she said she'd be happy to do whatever she could. I'll try not to stay away too long, unless . . .'' She let her voice drift off and lowered her gaze, ostensibly to prevent her tears from showing. It was a delicately tuned performance. When she left Dan's office, Selena was certain that for the first time in two weeks, she truly had had his attention. Maybe that wife of his wasn't so dumb after all. Selena had never believed that absence made the heart grow fonder, but perhaps she had been wrong. It had been her experience, up until now, that men were susceptible to whatever was available.

Selena left the office almost immediately and hurried back to her apartment to pack a small suitcase. She had arranged for the airport limousine to pick her up, and by five o'clock she was on her way to the plane. The flight was a short one and at seven-thirty they landed in Las Vegas.

''The Savannah,'' she told the cabdriver as she settled back in the seat to enjoy the drive down the famous strip. God, it seemed like a long time since she'd made the big move out of here to Los Angeles. It had been only four years, but it seemed a lifetime. When she left Vegas, she had left a lot of baggage behind, and she had never regretted the decision, although life hadn't been easy in L.A. She'd had to force herself to study typing and short-hand. Although she had detested it, she'd become the most skilled student in the secretarial class and had landed the job with Dan's firm right after graduation. The combination of all her skills had brought her from his office to his bed, but it would be a longer jump to marriage, and she had to be sure she didn't make any fatal errors.

The cab stopped before the big old casino hotel she knew so well. She paid the driver and carried her bags through the crowd of people playing the slots to the cashier's cage, where she inquired, ''Is Ginny around?''

The woman looked at her sharply and asked, ''Are you a new girl?''

In spite of herself, Selena laughed. "I wouldn't exactly say new."

The woman in the cage pressed a buzzer, and within seconds a security guard was at Selena's side asking, "Got a problem, Liz?"

"Says she's one of Ginny's girls. I never saw her before."

God, Selena thought, nothing ever changes in this place. Everybody who walks in is just a piece of meat to be screwed or fleeced. "Look, just tell Ginny Selena's here, okay?"

The guard took her elbow as he said, "Come on over to the office. I'll check it out."

Within a few minutes Selena was cleared and in the elevator on her way to the fourth floor. When the elevator doors parted, a bosomy redhead was standing in the hall waiting for her. "Baby," Ginny said, gathering Selena into her outstretched arms.

"Ginny, you look just the same. I don't think you've aged a minute since I left." They hugged each other and walked toward a suite a few doors down the hallway. As the door was closed behind them, Selena looked around at the familiar yellow-and-chartreuse interior, heavy with satin brocades, gold leaf, and crystal chandeliers and sconces. Las Vegas Baroque, she thought to herself.

"Have a chair, honey. What'll you have to drink? My God, that smog in L.A. must be agreeing with you, you look gorgeous," the older woman declared. Selena laughed and stepped back to study her mother.

Ginny Shaw did not look anywhere near her fifty-four years, though she was a voluptuous woman of grand proportions. Her hair was rich and dark red with the help of henna, her face was unlined and heavy with makeup, and her waistline was still there. She was dressed in a flowing caftan of chiffon in a bright red and blue floral print, and her hands were decorated with long red acrylic fingernails and rings with stones too big to be real diamonds.

"What have you got?" Selena asked. "I could use something."

"Something, honey? You still prefer a joint to a high-ball, or have you graduated to coke yet?"

Selena shook her head and sank onto the down-upholstered sofa. "None of that stuff anymore, Ginny. I'm straight. You still keep Dom Perignon in your refrigerator for special clients?"

"You bet your life I do. Let's have some to celebrate your homecoming." She looked directly at her visitor. "Are you here to stay?"

"No, I'm not, but don't you think I'm worth a bottle of champagne anyway?"

Ginny smiled as she replied airily, "Yes, indeed you are, honey. I've missed you." She sailed toward a small refrigerator hidden behind cabinet doors near the window and pulled out a bottle of champagne. With a quick twist of her powerful hands, she popped the cork and filled two of the wineglasses sitting on a silver tray on top of the television set. Handing a glass to Selena and lifting hers in a toast, Ginny said, "To your homecoming." She took a sip and then sat down in a chair. The smile was gone as she asked, "Now, why have you come back?"

Selena took several long swallows of her wine before she answered. Ginny was nothing if not direct. "I just wanted to see you, that's all."

"Cut the bullshit, Selena. In your entire life, I never knew you to do anything that wasn't calculated to get you something. Is it money?"

"Not at all. Money is the least of my worries. I have a good-paying job as a secretary."

Ginny snorted and got out of the chair to refill their glasses. "You can't make good money with your hand wrapped around a pencil, baby. What else have you got going for you?"

"I'm not turning tricks anymore. I told you when I left that I'd never do it again, and I haven't."

"Are you sleeping with your boss?"

"Yes, but he's in love with me, and he's going to divorce his wife—"

Ginny looked up at the ceiling. "Lordy, lordy, didn't I ever manage to teach this girl anything?" Then she looked at the daughter she had raised and loved, and her voice hardened. "How many times have I told you that a smart woman never gives it away—never, ever. That's how you wind up alone and poor and in the gutter. You make 'em pay—either with cash on the line or a marriage certificate, but you make 'em pay, or you'll get nothing, nothing at all."

"Times have changed," Selena protested. "No woman saves it for her wedding night anymore. Men expect—"

"Expect, hell. They've always expected it, and if they can't get it for free, they have to pay. Huh, don't tell me that times have changed. For a while there, I was worried that all those liberated women would put me out of business, but it didn't work that way, and my girls are busier than ever."

"You still take customers yourself?" Selena asked.

"Occasionally, when I want to, but I don't even have to screw old Jimbo upstairs anymore. He sold the place to a group of businessmen, and they're really happy with the money I'm producing. You know, it's not gambling that the men come here for, it's the thrill of doing something bad—away from their wives. Why don't you come back, baby? You were the best. I'd always planned for you to take over for me when I'm ready to chuck it all and retire. You'd have money . . . lots of it. Of course, I still plan to leave you what I have if I don't spend it all before I go. I'm plannin' to live at least another fifty years, however, so don't hold your breath."

"Ginny, no matter what happens, I'm never coming back. I love you because you're my mother, but I intend to get married. I just need some advice so that I don't make any mistakes."

Ginny shook her head, and the big sausage curls piled on top quivered. "It's a waste, baby, a fuckin' waste. You have everything it takes, just like I did. It was just a job to you, and that's the only way to make this kind of life work for you. Who's the john you're after?"

As Selena talked about her relationship with Dan and about Cake's leaving, Ginny listened without comment.

"Now he's avoiding me. I think he's forgotten how much she annoyed him and remembers only the good things. What should I do?"

"You really want this guy, honey? Do you think you could be happy with somebody who sounds as dull as he is?"

"He's handsome and he's successful. He works all the time, and I've enjoyed working with him ever since I realized the money coming in from the business could be mine too someday."

"You could have your own business here too, honey. You wouldn't have to answer to anybody."

"Ginny, I was good only because you taught me so well, but I hated it. I hated every goddamn trick I ever turned. Sure, I understand that every woman is a whore in one way or another, but wives can have headaches, and hookers can't."

"God, I hate those terms. I told you never to call yourself a hooker."

"Sorry, it just slipped out, but the point I'm trying to make is that I don't want to do it ten times a night. A married woman only has to fuck a couple of times a week."

Ginny howled with laughter. "Sweetie pie, that's the kind of thinking that's made me rich. Where oh where would we be if wives didn't get those golden headaches? Tell you what. Let's go downstairs to the lounge. I've got a special table there, and we'll have dinner and talk. How long are you going to stay?"

"I don't know. A day or two, I suppose."

"Good. Want to make a few bucks while you're here?" Ginny asked with a wink. "I'll let you keep it all."

"I don't think so, Ginny. I'm out of practice."

"It's just like riding a bicycle. Once you learn how, you never forget."

28

Damn Fools

Vanessa's mind was like a jungle filled with animals scurrying about looking for sanctuary in the face of an oncoming hurricane. She had been discovered, and she was more frightened than she had expected to be. She had set out on her quest without fear because she accepted the fact that she was doomed whether she failed or succeeded, and living wasn't all that precious anyway. But working and living with a new identity had made life desirable again, and she had even postponed doing what had to be done in order to prolong the pleasure.

Now her hours were numbered. She would have to make contact with Red O'Shea personally—and soon—and tell him everything. Although she had not intended to, she would have to involve Trish and Millie, too. They were nice people, and it seemed unfair to drag them into a mess of such ominous proportions, but if her father had taught her anything, it was that the end justified the means. How ironic to be invoking her father's principles. He had none.

She remembered the hatred that had existed between her father and her husband. Cliff did not measure up to Mike Fallon's standards, if indeed anyone ever could. Cliff was gentle, intellectual, and satisfied with his job teaching history to high-school students in a slum neighborhood. A real man of principle.

Mike Fallon, on the other hand, had made his fortune pumping oil from the ground wherever he could find it. He used the wealth he amassed to acquire more. He bought property, politicians, and people, and he believed with all his absent heart that profit made any deed proper. He gloried in his wealth, because it gave him power over others. He was aggressive and instinctive and delighted in forcing people to do as he wished. He wanted control of everything and everyone around him, and he would tolerate no view of life that was different from his. He considered those who did not agree with him to be damn fools. Not once in his life had he entertained the thought that he could be wrong about anything.

Looking back, Vanessa knew that she should never have married Cliff, but she was young and ignorant and foolishly believed that marriage would put her out of her father's reach. It hadn't, of course, and she managed only to hurt innocent people. Recalling the day he caught up with her—the worst day in her life—was still painful after almost fifteen years.

The telephone call from her father had brought her hope and happiness. For the first time since the birth of her baby daughter, Claudia, her father called and asked to come for a visit. Vanessa rushed around the small apartment, trying to make it look tidy and attractive, but there was so much clutter with the baby's things and Cliff's books that she wasn't very successful. She knew how disgusted Mike would be. And she was sure he was still angry with her for defying him. Mike had a powerful ability to carry grudges.

The baby started to cry, and Vanessa sat down to nurse her, hoping she would be finished by the time he got there. But Claudia continued to be fussy, and when the doorbell rang, Vanessa was still in her housecoat.

When she opened the door to let her father in, the sight of the tall, handsome, powerful man that she had worshiped all of her life brought tears to Vanessa's eyes.

"Mike," she said softly, "you look wonderful."

He smiled and replied, "And you look like shit. What the hell are you doing in this dump?"

"Please, don't start our visit like that. I'm so happy to see you. Come on in."

He strode past her into the room without touching or kissing her or even glancing at the baby. He looked around at the room briefly and with contempt and then sat importantly on a chair in the middle of the room.

"Mike, this is Claudia, your first grandchild. Wouldn't you like to hold her?"

He shook his head. "No. Kids never interested me much."

"I know. I never got any attention from you until I was thirteen." Her voice was heavy with rancor, and she was angered at his rebuff of her beautiful baby.

"I want you to come home where you belong. That's why I came." He looked directly into her eyes, and his voice had the ring of a god's.

She was surprised and deeply affected by the possibility that he missed her. She knew that it was not easy for him to admit. "Mike, I'd love to come home, you know that, but Cliff wouldn't . . . I know he wouldn't."

"The hell with that wimp. Leave him and come back to me." He looked into her eyes, and Vanessa realized with horror exactly what he meant.

"I can't. Don't you understand that I'm a wife . . . a mother . . . I have a child now. Even if I wanted to come back to you, I couldn't." She held the child more closely to her, suddenly feeling threatened by the power he had always held over her.

"Put the baby down, Vanessa," Mike ordered in the low commanding tone that warned her to obey him.

Silently she went to the bassinet in the dining room, where, gently, she put Claudia down on her stomach and rubbed her back until she fell asleep.

Mike watched Vanessa in silence. When she straightened up, he moved to the couch and beckoned her to sit beside him. As she sat down, she knew what would happen, just as she had known all those other times when she and her father lived in the big mansion alone except for the servants. And as always, she knew she would not have the will or the strength to stop him from doing what he wanted to do.

He put his arm across her shoulders and pulled her close to him. The smell of his after-shave evoked a mixture of memories. Vanessa tried to will herself to resist, but she couldn't. She had been under his spell all her life, and she still was.

Gently but hungrily he kissed her as he stroked her breasts. She closed her eyes, knowing she should try to resist, but knowing she was too afraid of him. She surrendered herself to him because as violent and erotic as his using her would be, it would soon be over, and he would go away and leave her in peace for a while. She felt the housecoat being pulled from her body as he lifted her in his strong arms and carried her to the bedroom.

Without bothering to remove his clothes, her father opened his pants and with a quick thrust entered her body and reclaimed it as his. Pressing himself deeply, he moved back and forth inside her, and she tried to ascend to an orgasm. She knew that he would not finish until he had proved he could still control and satisfy her. The baby began to cry, and Vanessa was distracted and unable to concentrate, but Mike did not stop his demanding movements inside her. She tried to focus, to ignore her child's cries, but she couldn't. She just wanted the ordeal to come to an end.

Suddenly another voice burst into her consciousness. She opened her eyes and saw her husband standing at the foot of the bed holding their baby.

"What the hell is going on in here?" Cliff demanded in a voice that was hushed with anger and betrayal. "Get out of my wife and get out of my bed!"

Ignoring the intrusion, Mike proceeded to have his orgasm, and when he was finished, he pulled away, got to his feet, and defiantly zipped his pants. Looking squarely into the eyes of his furious and shaking son-in-law, he sneered. "You little twerp. You can never be man enough for her."

Looking out at the beauty of Central Park with unseeing eyes, Vanessa felt again the anguish and the humility of that awful moment. Filled with self-hatred and guilt, she had had no choice but to submit to the will of the two men in her life. She gave up her child to her husband, who demanded she do so, claiming she was sick and unfit to be a mother. In his humiliation, it never occurred to Cliff that Vanessa might be a victim who needed his support to escape. Meekly she went back to her father's house in exchange for his promise to let Cliff take the child peacefully. Mike, of course, had been eager to fight her husband for custody of Claudia, but Vanessa would have no part of it. The last thing she wanted was for Claudia to come to puberty in her father's house. His desire for domination would surely destroy her too.

There were times, such as now, when Vanessa ached to see her daughter, but she did not know where Cliff had taken her. She suspected that her father knew their whereabouts, but she was afraid to discuss it with him. She never wanted him to know how much she loved her child. He was already aware of most of her weaknesses, and he never failed to use them when it suited him.

During the last long years of servitude, she had tried to convince her father and herself that she was happy to be with him. It had been the only way to survive, but the denial of her resentment caused an ugly sore to fester in her soul, try as she would to ignore it. Sometimes, however, her demons would take over and force her to rebel in a self-destructive way. She would sneak out into the night and use alcohol and men in a vain attempt to punish her father. Instead, she only succeeded in punishing herself.

She always returned home, fearful that if she didn't, Mike would reach out and seek vengeance against Claudia or Cliff. Alive, her father was much too powerful for her to defy. But he was dead now, and he could not stop her. All by herself she was going to destroy his evil dream. It was the least she could do.

Later that evening, from the telephone booth in a small restaurant near Times Square she called Millie and asked for asylum.

29

Dirty Little Drama

When Vanessa arrived at Millie's apartment, the two women greeted her warmly and didn't press her for an immediate explanation.

"Where's your luggage?" Trish asked.

"I won't need anything. If it's all right with you, I'll just borrow a robe and a nightgown. I won't be able to leave the apartment until I accomplish what I came here to do."

"Oh?" Trish responded, but Vanessa offered no further information. Millie showed Vanessa to a bedroom, leaving her to take off her coat and settle in. After a few minutes Vanessa joined them in the living room, where they were talking about the campaign over a glass of burgundy. Vanessa accepted a glass of wine and sipped it quietly. They waited for her to begin.

"I wish I didn't have to bring either one of you into this mess, but what I'm doing is very important, and I need your help," she said at last.

Trish was the first to respond. "We'll do whatever we can."

Millie was a little less enthusiastic. "You sound a bit cloak-and-daggerish, don't you think?"

"That's not too far from the truth. But I can't tell you

exactly what's going on. The only person I can tell is Senator O'Shea.''

Millie and Trish were surprised by her announcement. ''What does it have to do with him?''

''Please, Trish, don't ask, okay? What we need to figure out is some way that I can meet with him in private. It has to be done in such a way that nobody will ever know that he's talked to me personally. I think he had better come here, because I don't dare set foot outside this apartment until I've talked to him, or I might not . . .''—she hesitated and then finished—''live to meet him at all.''

''Who's out to get you, Ann?'' Millie demanded to know.

''There are . . . men who want to stop me from seeing the senator. If they're successful, I'm afraid your lives will be in as much danger as mine is.''

''Jesus Christ, how dare you drag us into your dirty little drama!'' Millie exclaimed.

''I'm sorry. I only came to you now because you're probably already in danger by the mere fact that I've been seen working with you, and I don't want to drag anybody else into this,'' Vanessa explained.

''That's not exactly true,'' Trish countered. ''You seem intent on involving the senator too.''

''Believe me, if he weren't already involved in this up to his neck, I wouldn't go near him.''

The two women looked at each other in silence. Millie and Trish were beginning to wish that they had never seen Ann Fitzgerald. There was a ring of ominous truth in her words.

Millie expressed their thoughts. ''Look, Ann, I don't know what's going on with you, but I personally want to stay out of it.''

''I'll try my best to keep you out, but I can't guarantee anything. You'll just have to go along with me and believe that it's important to all of us to keep me safe for a while.

Now, when can we get Senator O'Shea over here to talk to me?"

Trish's defenses were up now too. "He never comes here. Why should he?"

Vanessa looked at her solemnly, and although she was tempted to reveal what she suspected, she refrained. "I'm sure you can think of some reason to get him here."

Millie understood the meaning in her tone, and she bristled. "Just what the hell do you mean by that?"

Vanessa backed off quickly. "Nothing, absolutely nothing." She would have to try another approach. "I know for a fact that he has a . . . shall we say, weakness for women, and I thought perhaps . . ." She paused and then continued, "You may not believe me, but I know a good deal more about him than either of you do, and I've never met the man."

Trish's face flushed with embarrassment, but she said, "What do you want us to do? Red is on a swing through the Midwest and won't be back for a week."

"I know, but if you'll just let me stay without anyone knowing I'm here, we can work it out. Then, when he gets back to New York, you can bring him over here for our meeting."

"How do we know that you're not one of those crazy terrorists trying to set Red up?" Millie asked.

Vanessa just smiled. "I don't think you really believe that, do you, Millie? But if it will make you feel any better, please feel free to search me and my handbag. I promise you I have no weapons . . . nor do I have any accomplices. What I am doing I am doing alone. Honestly, it's in your interest as well as the senator's to help me."

"All we have is your word," Millie observed.

Vanessa nodded, and Trish said with a sigh, "I guess we'll just have to go on that."

That night, none of the three women slept easily in her bed, and the next morning, as Trish and Millie waited for the bus to take them to the office, Millie expressed her misgivings.

"Boy, I hope we're doing the right thing."

"So do I, but I'm not going on faith alone. I fully intend to tell Red the whole story before I lead him into some kind of trap."

"Smart lady."

"I must admit it's pretty exciting, though." Trish laughed.

"That's true. Do you think I was too tough on her last night?"

"Well, you were a lot less friendly than you usually are. You don't like her, do you, Millie?"

"She didn't know who Joanie Caucus was, and that makes her automatically suspect."

"What do you think this big secret of hers is?"

Millie smiled wickedly. "I think she's just got the hots for the next president of the U.S. of A. You heard her say she knew he had a weakness for women. She's a political groupie."

"Really? Well, then, I guess that makes her one of us."

"Speak for yourself, John," Millie teased. "I have no designs on the senator's bod . . . I just want to fuck his brain."

30

A Sentimental Journey

Dan was relieved when Selena left town to visit her mother. He was beginning to regret that he had ever gotten involved with her. Still, he hated going home to an empty house. Even more he hated dealing with the cleaning woman, the gardener, the monthly bills, and the damn laundry. He was also tired of eating in restaurants. But above all else, he was beginning to feel lonely. He called his son, Rob, almost every evening to find out if he'd had a letter from his mother, and was pleased when Rob said yes.

The police, of course, would have nothing to do with the case once Dan admitted that Rob was receiving letters from Cake. They informed Dan that it was not a crime to leave one's home. Finally he decided he had to know where she was, and went to the office of a private detective agency that his attorney recommended.

Dan was slightly disappointed that the office of Ralph Spiegel, private eye, was nothing like Sam Spade's. Located on the tenth floor of a new building in downtown Los Angeles, it was neat and modern and uncluttered. Spiegel didn't look the part either. He had a shining bald head, bright blue eyes that peered myopically through his rimless glasses, and hands with short stubby fingers.

He asked all the usual questions about Dan and Cake's

relationship, and for the first time, Dan expressed aloud his concern that Cake might have found out that he was having an affair with his secretary.

Spiegel listened and made no comment. He asked Dan to supply him with pictures, a list of all her friends and acquaintances, and her vital statistics. He assured Dan that with the help of computers, he would be able to check out the possibility of her having met with foul play.

"Mr. Halliday, from what you've told me, I think it's likely that she left you for the reason stated. I feel sure that you will hear from her eventually. I don't want to take your money unless you're really anxious to get this situation straightened out quickly. Don't you think you should give her a little more time?"

Dan shook his head. "No, I need to find her and talk to her. I can't live in limbo."

The detective nodded. "Very well. If you want me to begin right away, you can make out a check for five hundred dollars. Hourly rates and expenses will be charged against that until it is used up; then I will ask for another five hundred, and so on, until we find her or you decide not to continue. If you want to go ahead, fill out this form, and we'll get started. The sooner you can supply me with the pictures of her and other information I requested, the faster I can get back to you."

Dan gave him the check, filled out the form, and went home immediately. For the rest of the day he rummaged through the boxes of pictures of his life with Cake, searching for good photographs of her. It was a sentimental journey.

As he poked through the shoeboxes stuffed with pictures Cake had never managed to organize into albums, he remembered with nostalgia and pleasure the occasions the photos depicted.

There was Cake coming out of the hospital carrying Rob. What courage she'd shown during her pregnancies.

She'd felt nauseous most of the time, but she'd never complained.

He picked up the snapshot of Cake and Trina just after their daughter had won the third-grade kite contest. Cake had worked for two evenings helping Trina make a pink kite with glitter and ruffles. It hadn't flown very high, but it won the "most-beautiful" prize. Cake was always ready to help the children with artwork and crafts. She got as much enjoyment out of it as they did, and Trina, of course, had turned out to be an extremely talented artist.

A picture of the four of them on a boat on Yellowstone Lake made Dan recall how he'd chartered the launch to take them fishing, and that the children had caught their limit in the first half-hour. Before that time, Trina would never eat fish, but she enjoyed every mouthful of the ones she had caught herself. The cook at the lodge had prepared their trout for them, and it had been a memorable dinner.

Each picture he picked up was a reminder of the happiness they had shared as a family. Why had he let it all slip through his fingers?

That night before he went to sleep, he vowed to get rid of Selena. When he found Cake, he would convince her that their marriage was too good to discard. They had shared too much not to be able to put the pieces of their lives back together again.

Three days later, Selena flew back to Los Angeles refreshed and with renewed determination not to be cast aside. Ginny had, as usual, made her feel better about herself. Too bad her mother would never get to meet Dan.

The moment she got off the plane, Selena headed for the telephone and made an appointment to have her hair and her nails done. Ginny had reminded her how important it was to take care of the tools of her trade. When she returned to the office the next day, Selena wanted to look refreshed and beautiful.

She arrived at the office early, carrying a bunch of

peach gladioli for Dan's room. She arranged them in the black ginger jar on the credenza by the window. Then she polished his desk, sharpened the pencils, and put everything in perfect order, giving the room a pleasing harmony and serenity.

Dan arrived earlier than the rest of the staff, and he was startled to see Selena gazing out of his window at the view of the city.

"Selena! When did you come back?" he asked abruptly and without welcome.

She sensed immediately that he was not happy to have her return, but she refused to let it bother her. She smiled serenely, walked to him with arms open, and when he did not respond, she gently kissed him on the cheek and brushed past him.

"Last night. I have a lot of things to take care of here, and they were worrying me," she replied as she headed toward the door to her office.

"Like what?" he asked suspiciously.

"Nothing that would really interest you. I can handle them on my lunch hour. You won't mind if we don't lunch together today, will you?"

Dan shook his head. "No, no . . . of course not. I have things to take care of myself."

Just before she closed the door behind her, she turned and smiled sweetly and coolly at him. "It's good to be back, Dan. I really missed . . . being here."

When she had gone, Dan slumped into his chair and tried to analyze his feelings. Last night he had been so sure of his course of action, but this morning things looked different. He hated the thought of having to train another secretary. Selena was both efficient and unflappable, and she never made mistakes or let him make them. The hell with it. He'd just explain to her that he wanted to keep her in her job, but they'd have to stop sleeping together. Eventually he would have to find the courage to fire her, but not right now. Someday.

Selena sat down at her desk and punched on the computer. She needed to find out in detail what had happened with all their contracts the last few weeks. She knew her allure for Dan Halliday was not all in the bed. He needed her smarts and her efficiency to keep him on top of things. She had to reassure him that he was getting more than he was giving to their relationship. He didn't want a lovesick drone draped around his neck.

For the rest of the day she was cool, businesslike, and quiet. When it was time for the office to close and she left him with only a friendly good night, he seemed puzzled. She smiled secretly all the way home.

"Always do the unexpected, honey. Don't ever let a man think he can predict what you're gonna do. Keep 'em guessin' all the time. They'll appreciate you more," her mother had told her. Old Dan was probably really surprised that she hadn't pressed him for sex. Maybe he would even suspect that she'd picked up another lover. Of course, she'd never do anything dumb like that. It would queer the whole scheme if she did. A man like Dan could never stand sharing his woman. She couldn't take any chances. She wondered if dull little Cake had found herself another cock. Not bloody likely.

31

Chicken Little

Trish and Millie had made jokes about Ann Fitzgerald being a mystery woman, but Trish no longer felt there was anything funny about it. That night, when Trish went to bed, sleep eluded her completely. She tossed and turned and conjectured until she was too agitated to sleep. She tried to convince herself that none of it was her responsibility. Why did she always feel that whenever she found herself in some curious or untenable situation, somehow it was up to her to find a solution? Too many years of being a housewife and mother, she supposed.

The hell with it, she finally concluded. It was up to Red, after all. She would tell him the whole story and let him decide for himself whether to meet with Ann.

On the way to the office the next morning, Trish learned that Millie was just as concerned as she was.

"I don't like it at all. What's this big mystery that she can't even give us a clue to? The whole thing smells funny. I thought it over and decided we ought to talk to Joe about it first."

Trish reacted in a way that surprised Millie. "No, absolutely not! I think I ought to talk to Red first."

"But why? Joe's job is to act as a screen for Red to keep the crazies from getting too close. Suppose she's some kind of a nut?"

"Look, last night we made the decision to tell Red first. Let's go with it." The tone of Trish's voice signaled to Millie that the discussion was over.

Later that morning in the office, Trish went into Joe's office to talk to him. "Joe, when Red calls in from Chicago this morning, will you let me talk to him for a few minutes? It's important."

"He'll be pretty busy, and he probably won't be anywhere he can talk privately," Joe replied curtly.

Trish was exasperated, but she was learning to live with Joe's disapproval. "This is business, Joe, and it's important," she replied.

"Well, then, if it's business, you can tell me what it's all about, and I'll decide if it's important."

"I think I'd prefer to let Red decide. After all, he's the candidate, I believe."

Without waiting for a reply, she wheeled around and stalked out of the office. She was getting fed up always having a go-between insinuating himself between her and Red.

Was it that way for the president and his wife too? Was the intimacy in their relationship confined to their moments alone in the bedroom? She wasn't sure she could tolerate living like that.

Trish didn't go to lunch with Millie in case she might miss Red's call. But it was almost four o'clock before Joe called her into his office to say the senator was on the phone. Joe hesitated as if he were hoping she would let him stay, but she waved him out before she spoke.

"Red, it's so good to hear your voice. How's the windy city?"

"Windy . . . and cold outside, but inside, it's been warm and inviting. I've been getting extremely good response from the politicos here. How are things back there?"

"Fine, but something's happened here that I need to talk to you about in private. When will you be in New York again?"

"You sound pretty serious. What's up? Joe's not giving you a hard time, is he?"

"This has nothing to do with us. There's somebody who needs to talk to you. She says it's vital."

"Who?"

"I really don't think we should be talking about this on the telephone. It's too public."

"Tell Joe to send you to Pittsburgh day after tomorrow. We can talk privately over lunch. He can send some campaign stuff for me to read and sign. I'm sure there's a lot I need to be briefed on anyway. Tell him to arrange flights for both of us out that night, as close together as possible. I'll go on to Washington, and you can go back to New York. D'you mind doing that?"

"Not at all. I'll see you then." Trish was elated.

"It's been a long week away from New York."

"Yes, it has." Their words were formal, but both of them understood what the other was trying to convey.

"Put Joe back on the line. I'll see you in two days. 'Bye, Delaney."

Trish called Joe back to his office and hurried to Millie's desk to tell her the news.

Millie was impressed with Red's response. "Whee-ooo, he's some terrific guy. He didn't ask questions, just took you at your word, huh? He must have a lot of trust in you."

Trish smiled. "It amazes me. He actually treats me like an equal."

"What the hell's so strange about that? You are one, you know. An attractive and intelligent lady. By the way, who's going to make the calls to these women's groups now that our friend's not here? I've tried and bombed out. I just don't have much rapport with the ladies who lunch."

"Okay, okay. I'll get back to work. It's just so much fun being an executive."

That night over dinner Trish told Vanessa about her

plans to fly to Pittsburgh to make arrangements for the meeting with Red.

"I wish you could meet with him sooner than that," Vanessa said moodily. "I may not have too much time. I need to talk to him as soon as possible."

"Look, Ann, you've put us on the spot, particularly since we don't know what the hell we're getting into in the first place. You don't tell us anything. You won't leave the apartment. Jesus. What do you expect?" Millie protested.

"I'm doing the best I can, but if you're in such a hurry, perhaps you should talk to Joe—" Trish began, but Vanessa cut her off in mid-sentence.

"No! Absolutely not! And please do not tell Joe Franklin anything about it. You haven't said anything to him, have you?" There was a look of agitation on her face.

"No . . . no . . . we've told no one. Honestly," Trish reassured her, and was glad that she had followed her instincts about Joe.

"Please, I hope to God you didn't tell Joe I was staying here. Did you?" Vanessa asked again, and both Millie and Trish were startled by the look of naked fear in her eyes.

"No, we didn't, but that was because of Trish. Look, Ann, why don't you let us in on this little secret of yours. I think I'm entitled to know what the shit we're getting into. This is, after all, my apartment, and I want to know what the hell is going on," Millie demanded.

"I need a drink," Vanessa said, and got up from the couch and went to the cabinet where the liquor was kept. She pulled out a bottle of Rémy Martin.

"Help yourself," Millie murmured sarcastically.

"Anybody want to join me?" Vanessa looked very distressed, and they noticed that her hands were shaking.

Neither woman answered. She poured herself a generous portion of brandy and sat down with the glass. After taking a sip, she looked at them with a direct and defiant gaze.

"All right, if you insist, I'll tell you this much, but only to keep Millie from running around like Chicken Little, although I have to admit I also feel like the sky is falling. You see, I have certain vital information that I must give only to Senator O'Shea. It's a matter of life and death, and I'd like to tell you what it is, but it would be dangerous for you to know right now. I'm sure when everything is straightened out, the senator will be grateful to me for informing him and to you for making it possible.''

She paused to take another drink, and there was silence in the room as Trish and Millie digested the fact that they were now deeply involved in something dangerous. There was no doubt in either of their minds that she was telling them the truth.

"You see, if I'm successful in passing on the information I have, then everything will be okay. There'll be no need to eliminate me . . . or you . . . because their rotten secret will be out, and there'll be nothing to protect. Understand? And every day that I waste brings them closer and closer to us.''

"Who the hell is 'them'?'' Millie asked.

"That's part of the secret, Millie. And believe me, if I told you, you wouldn't be able to sleep either.''

"But what about Red? Aren't you endangering his life too?'' Trish asked.

Vanessa laughed. "His life was put on the line the minute he decided to run for president. It goes with the territory.''

32

In Full Measure

In Pittsburgh Trish was met by a limousine driver who took her to Red's campaign headquarters. She was greeted by a woman named Marcia Hunter, who showed her around and told her about the operation. Playing her part, Trish explained how they were organizing the women's speakers' bureau, but her heart wasn't in the conversation. All she could think of was: when was she going to see Red?

At one o'clock, the senator finally called on the telephone. "Hi, how was the trip?"

"Fine. What happened to our lunch date?" Trish asked.

"Got some problems. Can you stay over for dinner? I'm sure I can get away by five."

"That should be all right. My plane doesn't leave until midnight anyway. Where will I meet you?"

"There's a terrific restaurant called Tambellini's. Tell the driver to get you there by six. See you."

He ended the conversation abruptly, and Trish was forced to spend the rest of the day discussing women's issues with the volunteers in the office. Her enthusiasm for campaign strategy was difficult to maintain, but she hoped her anxiety was not too obvious.

When she arrived at the restaurant at last, Trish was taken to a private table away from the others. She ordered a glass of wine, but it was gone and she was halfway through her second one before Red finally arrived.

"Sorry to keep you waiting all day, Delaney, but this is a tough town to crack. How's the wine?""

"It's fine, but I'm on my second glass and beginning to feel a little light-headed."

"Then let's order dinner right away. The fish here is great."

She let him order for her. Food seemed so inconsequential when she was with him. His presence electrified the air and imbued everything with a feeling of excitement. Was this what the word "charisma" meant? Did everyone share her feelings about him? It was a disturbing thought, which she did not want to explore.

Red was full of campaign talk, and she listened distractedly. Finally, as the salad was served, there was a lull and she broke in.

"Please, Red, let me tell you why I'm here."

Looking at her with eyes that seemed more gold than brown, he nodded slightly. "You're so serious. What's wrong? I hope you're not going to tell me you're tired of me already." His voice reflected his concern, although he was trying to keep it light.

"No, Red . . . never that. I wish we were somewhere more private so that you could take me in your arms. I miss you when we're apart." She paused. "Something very strange has happened."

Forgetting that they were in a public place, Red took her hand in his. "What's wrong?" he asked.

She told him about Ann Fitzgerald's ominous insistence that she needed to see him. When she was finished, Trish asked, "Do you think this is some kind of a plot against you?"

He smiled, but he did not treat her concern lightly. "It might be; it might very well be, but we have to find out, don't we?"

"What should we do?"

"Tell her I'll be back in New York tomorrow night, very late. I'll call you when I get in, and we'll arrange to meet somewhere."

"But she says she can't leave the apartment."

"She'll have to. I can't walk into any kind of a setup all by myself. If what she has to tell me is that important, she'll go where I tell her to."

"You're absolutely right. I'll tell her that. I just hope I'm not putting you into some kind of danger."

He gave her hand a small squeeze, and then he dropped it as the waiter returned to the table. "Don't give it another thought, Miss Delaney. I can handle it."

Once the waiter retreated, Red continued, "I just don't like the idea of your being involved in something that might be messy. Delaney, am I asking too much of you to be with me in this quest?"

She smiled at him. "Like the song says, it's a glorious quest, Red, and I'm honored to be part of it. I believe in you. I always have, and I always will."

Very softly he replied, "I love you, Delaney. I always have, and I always will."

When she got on the plane to New York alone that evening, her courage and her joy had been restored in full measure. Life was not meant to be lived in fear and reluctance. She had chosen her course, and she was not going to back away now. Red loved her and needed her, and that was more than she could say about some of the people who had occupied her life. Life with him certainly wasn't going to be dull.

33

The White Knight

The day after Richard Terhune had dined with Trish and Millie, he received a call from the man who thought he had spotted Vanessa Fallon.

"What have you found out, Bob?"

"Not much, except the maid caught me trying to enter her room," Bob Reed explained. "I told the desk clerk I was her husband, and he told me she always got back by six and stayed in her room till morning. I'm going to get a bite to eat and return in an hour or so just in case she's early today. I've got a camera ready to snap some pictures."

"Good work. But don't let her see you. If she's anything like her father, she'll outsmart you and get away if she suspects anything. Did you pay the clerk to keep his mouth shut about your inquiries?"

"No problem. I'll put the fifty on my expense account."

Terhune set the telephone down and decided to call Milton Wise. Before he turned over any information, he had to try once more to find out why it was so important to find Vanessa Fallon.

"Milt, how're things going?" Terhune asked when the telephone was answered.

"You tell me, Rich. You're the one on the trail. The amount of your fee is dwindling fast. It's nearer one than two now."

"I can subtract, Milt. I called to tell you I might have some news by tonight, but there's one question that I want you to answer before I turn this lady over."

"Go ahead. I'll answer it if I can, but you know I'm not really part of any of this. I'm just doing a job like anybody else," Milt replied.

"Hm, of course, the 'Good German' response. Why the big price on Fallon's head? And is it just a sham or will they really pay off? And with that kind of dough, why me? There's a slew of extremely good private investigators who could have done the job for a lot less. All I've done is hire some of them myself."

"You want me to guess? There's no way I can give you a real answer, because I just don't know."

"Give me your guess."

"Well, I personally think they don't want the right hand to know what the left hand is doing."

"Terrific. I love platitudes. What exactly does that mean?" Richard asked.

"Only one person knows that she's split, and he wants her back before somebody in his own little circle finds out about it. Will he pay off? Yeah, I'm sure he will."

"By circle, I take it that you mean Mike Fallon's group of wealthy cronies," Richard speculated.

"No comment. Call me when you've got something."

"Wait, Milt. What are they going to do with her when they find her?"

"Not part of the deal, Richard. I assume they plan to take her home."

"Do you think somebody means to harm her?"

"The broad's a little nuts, I hear. Maybe they don't want her runnin' around and sullying the family name. I've been assured that it's all for her own good, or I wouldn't touch it with a ten-foot pole," Wise assured him.

"I always worry when people assure me that they're doing something for someone else's own good. But thanks anyway, Milt. I guess I'll just have to take your word for it."

Richard put down the telephone and went to the window to look out over Central Park. Winter had settled in on the city, and he could see that the lake was beginning to ice up at the edges. He shivered. Cold weather was so damn bleak and hostile. Some people were energized by it, but he was not one of them. He had always been thin, with not enough fat to keep his bones warm. He needed to go back to California, where he could loll in the sauna or soak up the sun's rays.

In the meantime, he'd take a long hot shower and try to wash away some of the bad karma that had surrounded him from the moment he had taken on this assignment to find the lost heiress. Although he wanted to believe that it was a clean job, years of experience with people would not let him. He had seen too much sin in the hearts of men. Perhaps when he found Vanessa Fallon, he would talk to her before turning her over to her father's friends. He needed to know why there was such an exorbitant price on her head. He had gotten through almost sixty years of life without getting any blood on his hands. He was too close to the pearly gates to let it happen now.

He stripped off his robe and got into the shower. Bullshit, it was all bullshit. He couldn't afford to play the white knight anymore. He needed that money or he was going to lose everything.

He waited all day for the call that would tell him if the search had ended. At eleven that evening, it finally came.

"Bad news," Bob Reed informed him. "She never came back to her room."

"The room clerk told her, right?"

"He swore he hadn't seen her until I waved a hundred-dollar bill under his nose. Then he admitted he told her I'd been there. Trouble is, he suspects I'm not her husband now, and he clammed up. He threatened to call the police if I didn't let him alone."

Terhune sighed. "Well, you know what to do. Keep me posted."

What a wasted day this had been, he fumed, sitting around in his hotel suite all day like a buzzard circling a carcass that got up and walked away.

Maybe he had spent too much of his life with the slime of the world, and it was now rubbing off on him. Nonsense. He had been a force for good too. He had believed in and supported worthwhile causes, with both money and professional effort. Not all of his life had been devoted to defending hoods and creeps, but there was no escaping the fact that was where he had earned the money. What was so different about the job he was now doing?

As he got into bed, he decided he would call Trish Delaney and invite her to dinner again. He'd get two good theater tickets too. That way, he could avoid having to invite her strange friend along. He much preferred to dine with Trish alone, but if that couldn't be arranged, then he'd just have to put up with Millie. He tried not to admit to himself that he was infatuated with Trish. She was the only bright light on the horizon. He chuckled. What would she think if she suspected that he might have more than a friendly interest in her? She might be scared off. He'd always been successful with women because his timing was right, so he had to be careful not to rush things. Right now, she was probably involved with the senator, but that, of course, could not last long. Once Trish realized that there was no future there, she'd back away. She wasn't the type to be a camp follower. Yes indeed, timing was very important . . . in everything.

34

Her Highness

As Trish walked through the apartment door, Millie greeted her in a fury. Her anger spilled out in a torrent of words: "When the maid arrived this morning, Ann tried to keep me from letting her in. When I insisted, she locked herself up in her room and refused to come out."

Trish tried to smooth over the situation. "Now, don't be so upset. I'm sure it's just that she's afraid of being seen. Perhaps you ought to give Maria a vacation till she's gone."

"Fine with me, but I don't intend to clean up after her highness. You should see the mess she made in the bathroom. She dropped a glass and broke it and didn't even bother to pick up the pieces. I almost cut my damn foot off."

"Come on, now, it's not like you to let little things bother you. She's on edge, and we just have to be patient with her. It won't be for much longer. I'll get her, and we'll all sit down in the living room and talk . . . like friends. Okay?"

Wrapped in an old robe of Millie's, Vanessa emerged from her room looking haggard and messy. There were dark circles under her eyes. She was smoking a cigarette and carrying a glass of brandy, and it was obvious it wasn't her first glass of the day.

"So . . . what happened? Where's the senator?" Vanessa asked, and her words were slurred.

"Well, I told him how urgent you felt it was that you meet him, and he agreed."

"So when's he coming?"

"He won't come here. It's too much to ask of him, Ann, can't you see that? He doesn't know who you are or what you want with him, but he's offered to meet you alone in a place that he chooses. It's only fair."

"Then piss on him. I'm not doing this for me, goddammit, I'm doing it for him, the asshole. In fact, I'm risking my fucking life to talk to him anyway," she snapped, and lifted the brandy snifter and drained it in one swallow. She slammed the empty glass on the table so hard that the delicate stem split, and Millie jumped out of her chair.

"That's it! I've had it with you, you bitch. That glass belonged to my mother. How dare you come in here and treat us like your servants? We've been trying to help you and all you've done for the past three days is drink my brandy and complain."

Trish had had enough of both of them. "Calm down, Millie. I'm sorry about the glass, but she's obviously not herelf. Can't you see she's had too much to drink?"

"That's pretty damn obvious. God, I can't stand drunks," Millie protested, but her fury was ebbing.

Trish turned her attention to the culprit. "Look, Ann, why don't you go to bed and try to get some sleep. When that liquor wears off, we'll be able to discuss the situation like civilized people. I've had a long day, and I'm exhausted. This trip was for your benefit, and I did the best I could. We all have to make some accommodations. Nothing in life is exactly as we choose it to be."

"No, I can't sleep. I want to talk." Vanessa tried to pull herself together, not too successfully.

"I'm not sure you'll remember what I tell you. Maybe some black coffee would help," Trish said, but Vanessa shook her head vehemently.

"No coffee. I need another glass of brandy."

"Ann, please. You came to us for help, and we're trying to give it to you, but you've got to stop drinking so heavily. Now, here's the plan. Senator O'Shea will call me tomorrow night and tell me where we are to meet him. You and I will take a cab. I gave it a lot of thought while I was on the plane. No one will see you leave the house. Tomorrow I'll buy you a brown wig the color of Millie's hair. You can wear her boots and her clothes. Wrapped up in that huge poncho of hers, no one will suspect it's anyone but her. I'll take you to talk to Red, and you can do whatever you want after that."

Vanessa said nothing. Even though she'd had a lot to drink, she understood what was being said.

After a short silence Millie asked, "So, what do you think?"

Vanessa got to her feet, looked at both women with contempt, and turned to go back to her room. "I'll think it over," she declared.

When she had closed the door behind her and they were alone, Millie let out more of her anger, but Trish tried to appease her. "Look, Millie, it's the booze that's turned her into such a royal bitch. Alcohol does that to some people. We mustn't lose sight of the fact that she's a very frightened woman."

"Has it occurred to you that if you walk out of this building with her, whatever's laying for her out there might go for you too?"

"Good grief, Millie, you talk as if there's a werewolf or something just waiting to pounce on her. You know, I've looked around a lot, and I haven't seen anybody or anything that looks suspicious, have you?"

Millie shook her head. "No, and I've been pretty paranoid about looking, too. Sometimes I think maybe she's just loony and we've been sucked into her fantasies."

"Wouldn't it be terrific if that were the case? I think the worst thing that could happen would be to find out that she's on the level and that she really does have some terrifying secret to tell the senator."

"Yep. That's a thought not to sleep on. Cross your fingers that it will all be over in a day or two and we'll still be alive," Millie replied, but the smile on her face indicated that she was not really worried.

"You know, Millie, in spite of your anger with Ann, I think you're enjoying all this intrigue and excitement as much as I am," Trish said accusingly as the two set to work to clean up the broken glass.

"Yeah, you're probably right. Life can get pretty boring."

"Speaking of boring, have you ever thought about getting married?" It was the first time that Trish had asked about Millie's personal life.

"I used to think about it all the time, but not anymore. There's too much competition out there for the good guys, and I don't want one of the bad ones. I've had a lot of men in my time, and there are very few that I'd want to share a meal with, much less a life."

"Millie, that's a cynical and defeatist attitude. It's not like you at all," Trish protested.

"Trish, you're the closest thing to a virgin I ever met. C'mon, now, tell me, how many men have you slept with?"

Trish smiled with a trace of embarrassment. "Only two," she answered.

Millie laughed. "See, I was right. Have you got any idea how many I've screwed?"

Trish shook her head no.

"Neither do I. I'd need a computer to figure it out."

They laughed and said good night.

35

Sexual Excitement

With a minor amount of encouragement, Dan agreed to meet Selena at the apartment for what he assumed would be their usual sex break. When he arrived, however, she was still dressed.

Selena had decided that the time had come to confront Dan as Ginny had encouraged her to do. She was sure he needed her now more than ever, and she had to make the most of his wife's absence. Any day, Cake might return and make life difficult. Selena wanted not only to re-awaken Dan's lust but also to bind him to her more closely.

As he walked in, loosening his tie, his first words were, "Let's get going. I have to get back for that call from Stevenson."

Selena looked directly at him without moving from the couch where she was sipping a glass of wine and paging through the latest issue of *Fortune*. "Sit down, Dan. I want to talk first." She'd learned long ago that men were far more prone to make promises before sex than after.

Dan was annoyed. "We can talk in the office. In the apartment, we fuck. Let's go."

Damn him, she was tired of being ordered around. "Sit down, Dan. There's more to making love than sticking your cock into somebody. I need to talk to you."

The low, husky tone of her voice sheltered the nastiness of her words, and he was more intrigued than offended. Selena always managed to be interesting. He poured himself a glass of wine and sat down.

After a brief pause she looked up at him with her incredibly huge dark eyes and said, "I know that life hasn't been easy for you lately, and I don't want to add to your problems, but there's something we have to discuss . . . right now."

Good God, now what? he wondered.

"While I was visiting my mother," she continued, "I had time to think about us and our relationship, and I've come to a decision. As she so often does, my mother helped me get things into perspective. I'm sure you can appreciate that, because you've always been very close to your mother too." Her manner was sincere and earnest, but in truth, she was quite aware that it had been Cake who had attended to Dan's family obligations.

"I made a promise to my mother, and I know you'll understand how important it is to keep it," she added, and his head nodded almost imperceptibly in agreement with her. "My mother insisted that I ask you this question. Dan, did you mean it when you said you loved me and wanted to marry me, or was it just bedroom talk?" Her words were direct but her voice was tremulous, and she even managed to squeeze a small tear into the corner of her eye.

Dan was uncomfortable. He didn't know what to say, because in truth he didn't know the answer. He had been sincere at the time; he was pretty sure of that.

Selena watched him closely, looking for signs of wavering as Ginny had instructed her. "Pin him to the wall, sweetie, because it's now or never. If he doesn't care if you walk, you've lost the ballgame, and you better quit wastin' your time with him. Trust me, I know what I'm talkin' about." Selena had believed her and decided to take the risk.

"Selena, what do you want from me?" Dan finally asked.

She reached over and took his hand and forced him to look into her eyes. "Dan, I want somebody to love and to take care of, but I must have an emotional commitment from you. If you're not willing to give me some assurance, then perhaps I should go back to the office and clean out my desk and leave. I can't keep my life on hold any longer."

There, she had said it. She hoped she hadn't played her hand too strongly.

Dan looked at her and knew she wasn't bluffing. She had never been one to make idle threats. If he said the wrong words now, she'd go, and he'd be alone, both at home and at the office. Suddenly Cake seemed very far away. It was funny, but for the last few days he'd been having trouble remembering her face, and whenever he tried to recall details of their sex life, his intense encounters with Selena closed in and blotted them out almost entirely. Cake had been warm and willing, but Selena was exciting and a little dangerous. She was perfect in all the ways that appealed to him. She was, perhaps, a bit calculating, but then, admittedly, so was he. Dammit, he didn't want to lose Selena, not now anyway. Suppose his wife had left him for good? As independent and arrogant as he appeared, Dan Halliday did not like being alone.

"I don't want you to leave me, Selena." The words came out of his mouth almost as if they had a will of their own, and he wondered just how much of a commitment he had offered.

Selena smiled her secret, knowing smile. He'd said enough, for now. "That's all I wanted, Dan. That's all."

She stood up and began to unfasten the tiny buttons on her silk blouse. "Let's make love," she said softly. "It's been a long time since we've touched each other, and I need to feel your body inside mine."

Later, in bed, after she had aroused him with her tongue,

she pressed him to lie on his back. Moving her lips up his torso until she reached his mouth, she whispered softly, "Now I'm going to take you inside of me, and I'm never going to let you go." Lifting her body on top of his, she settled herself slowly until her moist warmth encircled and held him tightly. He tried to move, to satisfy himself, but she would not let him. She pressed her body down tightly on his, letting all her weight fall on him. "No," she commanded, "I'll do it." And then, moving slowly and sinuously, she arched her body in a climax just as he began to have his.

When it was over, she held her position. "You were wonderful. You have the most beautiful cock in the world, and now it's all mine. I'll never understand how your wife could have abandoned it, if it treated her as well as it does me. Tell me, my love," she whispered, "was sex with her ever as good as it always is with us?"

He could not bring himself to discuss the intimacies he had shared with Cake. They'd had many special moments together, and he wanted to keep them private. "It was different, Selena, very different," was all he would say.

The answer did not bother her. Gently she rolled away from him and stretched her body alongside his, touching him from shoulder to toes. "Dan, I think it's time we started sleeping together . . . every night."

"Where?" he asked suspiciously.

"Why not here?" She wanted to suggest his home but decided it was premature to do so. "I'm the only person who knows your schedule . . . and I promise not to tell," she said impishly. "I'll even cook dinner for us this evening. Okay?"

"Okay," he answered, suddenly ready to surrender himself to the ministrations of someone who would take care of things for him. He was getting tired of dealing with the everyday details of meals and laundry. He needed to be free of all the mundane problems of living so that he could concentrate on his work, as a man should. He got out of bed and went into the bathroom to shower.

Selena arose feeling secure and triumphant. "Men are nothin' but little boys with bigger cocks and whiskers," Ginny had said with a smirk. Selena decided she was right as usual. As she got dressed to follow him back to the office, she vowed to take care of Dan better than his wife or his mother ever had. At least for now.

36

Joe's Apartment

Trish and Millie went to the office the next morning, but neither of them could concentrate on anything. When a call came in for Trish, she was disappointed to hear Richard Terhune's voice. Not that she didn't enjoy hearing from him, but she was anxious to hear from Red and resolve the situation with Ann.

"A friend just gave me two wonderful seats to *Glitz*—it's the hottest new musical on Broadway—and I was hoping you'd join me. We'll have dinner first, of course. How about it? Are you free?" he asked.

"Tonight?"

"Right, can you make it?"

Disappointment, not real but feigned, colored her answer. "Richard, how sweet of you, but no, I'm afraid tonight is impossible. I would love to see that show, but I just can't," she replied. The last thing she wanted to do was to go out and try to be charming when her head was filled with the drama of Ann and Red's meeting. She liked Richard, and so she chatted with him amiably for several minutes to keep him from feeling rejected. When she hung up, it occurred to her that she was acting like a young girl keeping two guys on the string, and she laughed at herself. She wasn't playing the mating game anymore. Richard was just a friend. Certainly it was possible to have male friends, especially at her age—and at his—wasn't it? The thought that Richard might be courting her did not please her. How awful if he ever made a pass and she had to reject him. Good grief, life was never simple.

Millie interrupted her reverie. "Was that Red?"

Trish shook her head. "No, it was Richard Terhune. He wanted me to go see *Glitz* with him tonight. I told him I couldn't."

"I'd call him a dirty old man, but I know you'd yell at me. Can't you see he's got the hots for you?"

"Cut it out, Millie. He's just lonely."

"Yeah, lonely for a little nooky. You know, some of those old geezers get pretty horny. Even when they can't get it up."

"Well, you'd know more about that than I would, given your vast experience," Trish retorted, but her tone was teasing.

"Hoo, hoo . . . my God, you're getting a mean mouth. I think you've been hanging out with a bad element."

Trish nodded her head in mock agreement. "Between you and Ann, I've been corrupted, I suppose."

"Not me, I was talking about him." Millie jerked her finger over her shoulder, indicating Joe, who had come up behind them and was listening to their conversation.

"What's going on here? You two haven't done a damn bit of work for two days."

"Joe!" Trish protested. "I was in Pittsburgh yesterday."

"Exactly. I've got Red on the line. He wants to talk to you. Take it in my office, and close the door."

As Trish hurried away, Millie remarked, "I didn't hear the phone ring," and Joe replied sarcastically, "You should try keeping your mouth shut and your ears open for a change."

Millie was not offended. "Look, Joe, let's not forget that I'm worth every cent you're paying me."

"I know, I know. And sometimes I've even considered

putting you on the payroll just so I could have the pleasure of firing you."

"You're such a doll, Joe. I'd like to stick some pins in you."

Trish closed the door and picked up the telephone. "Red, where are you?"

"I'm in Washington, but as soon as they take this roll-call vote, I'll be on my way back to New York. How about bringing your friend to Joe's apartment at nine tonight?"

"Oh no, Red, I know she would be terribly upset if she knew that you'd brought someone else into this. She's already unhappy that you won't come to our place."

Red sounded a bit impatient. "Look, explain to her that I've already arranged for Joe to be somewhere else. He thinks that it will be just you and me there. Tell her I've told him nothing about her."

Trish was apprehensive. "Is it really okay, Red? I wouldn't want to be responsible for misleading her."

"It's okay. Take my word for it."

Trish wanted to say she trusted him above anyone else, but the words wouldn't quite come out. A small voice reminded her that she had been wrong before.

"I'll see you at nine, then. I just hope everything works out all right," Trish said, feeling very unsure.

She went out and found Millie waiting to find out what had been arranged. "Millie, I need a break. Let's get out of here for a little while."

"Good idea. I'll tell Joe we're going to lunch. Besides, we have some shopping to do, don't we?"

"Yes, we do. Maybe we better check the Yellow Pages before we leave. We need to find a wig."

As soon as they were out on the street and away from the eyes and ears in the office, Trish told Millie of the conversation and the plans for the evening. Millie was not pleased with the arrangements. "Jesus, there'll be hell to pay. Ann won't go there. I know she won't. She doesn't trust Joe Franklin any more than we do. She made a number of nasty remarks about him when she was working here, and it was his talk about putting the three of us in the limelight that precipitated her walking out.''

''I tried to tell Red that but he wouldn't listen. I guess I can't really blame him. After all, the only thing we know about her is that she's difficult . . . and secretive,'' Trish said.

''True . . . and she drinks too much, and she's a pain in the ass.''

''Well, we'll just do the best we can to convince her. You know, there are a lot of crazies who go after people in public life.''

''Yeah, you're right. Come on, let's go find a wig that matches my gorgeous tresses. That bitch is so unpredictable that she just might fool us and decide to be cooperative.''

37

I've Never Been Without Her

When Dan got back to the office, he received a call from the detective, Ralph Spiegel. It was a short but unsettling report.

"Mr. Halliday, I've got the information here that you wanted. Do you want me to come in to see you or would you like to have it on the telephone? It's pretty cut-and-dried."

"What does that mean?" Dan asked.

"Well, it's just this. Your wife made no attempt to cover her tracks at all. What I did, you could have easily done yourself. I feel a little guilty taking your money."

"Well, what did you find out?"

"Your wife bought a ticket to New York on Pan Am and boarded the economy flight the night she left your house. She checked into the Talbot Hotel the next morning. She used, and continues to use, her maiden name. She got a job in the campaign office of Senator Jonathan O'Shea, and she now lives with a woman named Millie Burton, who is a volunteer in that office. Millie Burton is apparently a well-heeled woman, because she was the owner of record of the land on which the apartment house was built. She sold it to the developer for a pretty handsome sum, I imagine. Do you want me to go any further? I've got the addresses and the telephone numbers in the report."

Dan's words were clipped as he replied, "No, that will be quite enough. I'd appreciate it if you'd send the report to me by messenger. Tell him it's to be delivered only into my hands. When I receive the final bill for your services and expenses, I'll send a check. I appreciate your efficiency and promptness."

"No problem, Mr. Halliday. It was a pleasure doing business with you."

Dan sat back in his chair to think. He signaled Selena and told her to hold his calls for a while. He had to decide what he was going to do with the information he had just received.

The facts were not easy to digest. Cake had obviously left in a fit of temper. It was a dramatic ploy to get him to come after her and bring her back, but through either stupidity or lack of interest, he had not understood the game and his part in it. Well, if it was an eyeball-to-eyeball stand, he would not be the first one to blink. She could wait until hell froze over, for that matter. She was bound to come to her senses one of these days, wasn't she? Certainly, by Christmas, when Rob came home from school . . . or at least in May, when Trina would return from her year abroad.

Dan became more uncertain. Was it possible that Cake had made a new life for herself and was enjoying it? Would she want to come back to be just his wife again? Dammit. He needed someone to talk to . . . but who? Certainly not Selena. He was not stupid enough to think she would give him any advice that would not be self-serving. Perhaps he should go see his mother and talk to her. She was growing extremely feeble, but her mind was still alert. At least it had been the last time he had gone for a visit.

He rang for Selena, and when she appeared, he announced, "I'm going to be out of the office for the rest of the day. I think I'll go visit my mother."

"I'd be happy to go with you, but I think I should stay

here to deal with the Stevenson people, don't you?'' Selena wondered just how much the news about his wife had bothered him. She had held the key open on the phone so that she could hear everything. It was one of her methods of staying informed on every aspect of his life.

Dan's mother was asleep when he arrived. He took a chair beside her bed and held her tiny, fragile hand in his. It saddened him to remember how strong and capable she had once been. She had been a clever and dexterous woman. She could fix almost anything, unlike most of his friends' mothers, who waited until their husbands came home and asked them to make repairs. She had been a special and admirable mother. She always said she liked Cake so much because she reminded her of herself, but it was only kindness that made the comparison. Cake had never been as capable or organized as his mother had been.

"Mother . . . are you awake?" he asked softly, and her eyelids fluttered briefly.

He repeated the question, louder this time to force her to attention. She opened her eyes slowly, and although a smile briefly touched her lips, she said nothing.

"Mother, I've found out where Cake went. She's in New York," he began, and without waiting for her to comment, he told her everything that he had learned from the private investigator. As he spoke, he saw that her eyes stayed fixed on his intently, and when he concluded, he asked, "Do you think I should find Cake and talk to her and get this thing settled once and for all?"

Her eyes did not blink, nor did she make any sign that she had heard or understood. He tried again and again, but he could get no response other than the intent stare. At last he moved away from the bed and sought out the head nurse, who was not very comforting.

"I know, Mr. Halliday. She has not spoken for several days. It's possible she's had another small stroke."

"Can't she hear and understand me at all?" Dan asked in horror.

"I really don't think so, but I believe it's important to keep talking to her as if she can."

"Good God."

The nurse recognized his agitation and pain. It was a look she saw frequently on the faces of children, husbands, and wives when they realized that the person they knew and loved had gone without quite dying. Her voice was gentle. "I'm so sorry, Mr. Halliday. She was a charming lady. We miss her too."

"You're talking as if she's already dead," he said bitterly. He wasn't ready to let her go.

"In a way, she is. Her body is still here. By law we must keep it alive as long as we can, even though we know that her spirit is gone."

"Is that why you have a tube down her nose?"

"When she stopped eating, we had no choice but to insert an NG tube. We couldn't let her starve to death."

"Is she in pain or uncomfortable?" He needed some kind of reassurance.

"I don't think so."

"But you're not sure?"

She did not answer his question, and he turned to go back to his mother. Her eyes were closed, and when he kissed her good-bye, she did not open them. For the first time since he was a young man, a prayer formed on his lips.

"Dear God . . . take care of her . . . and help me. I've never been without her."

38

Mission Incredible

When Trish and Millie arrived home after work, Vanessa was waiting for them. Although she looked tired and drawn, she was dressed and her hair was combed, and she did not seem to have been drinking. She was smoking a cigarette, and her hands were shaking.

"Anything new?" she asked in greeting.

"Well, for one thing, we found this terrific wig. How about trying it on to see if we can make you look as dumpy as me?" Millie said.

Vanessa ignored the wig in Millie's hand and stared at Trish. "Well, did you hear from the senator or not?"

"Yes, I did. Just let us get our coats off and sit down, okay?" Trish sounded a little testy. She was on edge too. After all, she was going to be the escort on this mission incredible.

"Okay, okay. Be coy. I'll see you in the living room." Vanessa whirled around and stomped away. Millie and Trish looked at each other with raised brows, but they hurried to follow her.

Trish sat down on the couch. Vanessa was standing by the window, nervously taking deep drags from the cigarette in her hand. Until she had moved in with them, they had never seen her smoke, but now she was never without a cigarette.

"Senator O'Shea wants me to bring you to Joe Franklin's apartment at nine tonight. He'll be there alone." Trish's announcement was made as matter-of-factly as possible.

Although they expected a burst of anger, none was forthcoming. Vanessa was silent for a long moment, and then, without turning from her gaze out the window, she asked, "He won't come here, then. Is that it?"

Trish started to explain, but she knew it was futile. Either the woman would go or she wouldn't. It was up to her to decide. "No, he won't. It doesn't make sense for him to risk it."

"Does Joe Franklin know anything about my staying here with you or this meeting?" Vanessa turned to Trish and looked at her with a steady and piercing gaze.

Trish shook her head, and then in a somewhat embarrassed voice replied, "No, he thinks that Red is meeting me for some kind of an . . . assignation."

For the first time, Vanessa's stern look broke, and a sardonic smile spread across her lips. "Well, well . . . I was right after all. Little Miss Priss and the pompous Dudley Do-right. A match made in heaven. I wonder what the honorable Mrs. O'Shea would say about that."

It was all Millie could do to keep her mouth shut, but she did, for the look on Trish's face had changed from embarrassment to mirth, and she laughed out loud. "See, you fell for it just as I said you would. I figured if you bought it, then Joe would be no problem. You know what a jerk he is, and it's just the kind of thing he'd understand. That's all he thinks women are good for—a quick roll in the hay. It would never occur to him that we might have something else to offer."

To Trish's delight, the comic aspect of it all convinced Vanessa everything was all right. She stubbed out her cigarette and said, "Okay, let's get on with it, then. Where's the wig?"

Laughing and joking like three sorority girls, the women spent the next hour dressing Vanessa in Millie's clothes.

Millie assumed responsibility for the transformation, even to coaching Vanessa on how to walk. Their difference in height caused the only significant problem. Vanessa was four inches shorter than the tall, lanky Millie.

Vanessa suggested that they hem the skirt so it wouldn't sweep around her ankles, and Trish put some cotton in the heels of the boots to lift her up a little. Millie decided that Trish should wear flat shoes and hunch down a little to make Vanessa look taller.

By eight-thirty Vanessa was as ready as it was possible to make her, and suddenly, as Millie called down to have the doorman summon a cab, the lark was over. It was serious business again.

As they were about to go down to the lobby, Millie asked Vanessa, "Are you planning to come back here when you're finished?"

"Probably not. I think I'll go right to the airport and get on the first plane home."

As they hurried out the lobby and into a waiting cab, Trish looked around to see if anyone was watching them. The street was dark and deserted. Trish gave the driver Joe's address, and they were on their way. As they rode through the night, Trish wondered how far this drive was going to take her away from the world she knew. A year ago, if anyone had told her she would be living in Manhattan, indulging in high-level political intrigue, she would have laughed. Well, life was pretty funny.

39

The Need for Money

Richard Terhune picked up the telephone to call Milton Wise. It had been two weeks now since he had agreed to look for Vanessa Fallon, and the trail had suddenly gone completely cold. She had dropped out of sight, since Reed had been stupid enough to reveal to the room clerk at the Maybelle that she was being sought. If it weren't for the fact that the hotel employees had all identified Mrs. John Fitzgerald as the missing Vanessa Fallon from a picture that had been doctored to give her short blond hair, Richard would have kissed the whole deal good-bye. The reward was dropping fast, and soon it wouldn't be worth his while to continue.

"Milt, it's Terhune. I need to talk to you about this Fallon situation," he began.

"I thought you had her nailed. What happened?"

"The investigator who found her made the mistake of thinking that fifty bucks would keep the room clerk's mouth shut. She took off and left everything in her room. What the devil is she running from?"

"Beats the hell out of me. She's got a lot of dough in her own name. Her father left her everything he owned, including stewardship of a massive trust. You've heard of it, the Heartland Trust," Wise replied.

"Yeah, but what does it do?"

"I'm not sure. Scholarships, grants, I think. Fallon kept a lot of his dough in it."

"Milt, tell me, how did you get involved with this thing anyway?"

"Look, I'm really only on the periphery. One of my clients, who must remain nameless, as the old saying goes, asked me to contact you. All I can tell you is that he's very legitimate."

"Is he a relative or something? What's his connection?"

"He's a friend of the family."

"How did you get involved?"

"I owed somebody a favor, and he knew that you and I used to be pals."

"Have you talked to him lately?"

"He calls me every day. I wish you'd hurry up and find that chick and get me off the hook."

"Well, tell him that I've got to have some money for expenses. I've got a lot of people working on this, and they don't work on speculation. You also tell him that either the clock stops on that reward, or I'm out," Terhune declared.

"Don't do that yet, Rich. There's still a lot of dough on the line, but the time element is important to him. My client wants her found as quickly as possible. You'll really be putting me in a bind if you quit now." Richard detected a note of anxiety in Wise's voice.

"Then tell your client that I need my expenses covered now. And also, I need something more to go on. Ask your client if he knows why she's in New York."

"I'll see what I can do."

Richard put the telephone down and poured himself a glass of tomato juice from the bar in his suite. He looked around. He was sick of the Plaza Hotel, New York City, and Milton Wise. The telephone rang, and he picked it up, hoping that Wise had good news for him. It was not Wise but one of the investigators working the city for him.

"Brad, got some news for me?" Terhune asked.

"Sure do. I took that doctored picture of Vanessa Fallon and started showin' it around, and I got lucky. A woman who works at a small restaurant on Third Avenue said she'd seen the woman in the picture working in Senator O'Shea's campaign headquarters. The waitress has delivered sandwiches there a coupla times and talked to her. I checked the place, and Joe Franklin, he's the chief honcho there, identified her as Ann Fitzgerald, a volunteer worker. He wanted to know who was lookin' for her, and I said her husband. He bought it and said she'd walked out a few days ago when he asked her to do some p.r., and she hasn't been back since."

Richard could not believe what he was hearing. O'Shea! That's where Trish and Millie were working. He asked, "Did you talk to anybody else there?"

"Not yet. The two women that Franklin said knew her the best had left the office early. But I'll check them out first thing in the morning."

"Good work. Did you get any reaction when you told the guy her real name?"

"I never give out any information that I don't absolutely have to. People get funny ideas, especially if they find out you're looking for somebody who has a lot of dough. They start trying to figure out how they can get a little of the action and fuzz things up."

"You're a smart man, Brad, and worth every cent you're planning to bill me for. I'll take it from here."

Richard was excited as he dialed Milton Wise's number. He didn't want to call the deal off right now, when he was so close.

"Milt, have you talked to your client yet?" he asked.

"I'm waiting for his call."

"Then, I've got some interesting news you might pass on to him. I've found out that Fallon's daughter has been working in Senator Red O'Shea's campaign office as a volunteer. I just happen to know two of the women who work there. With any kind of luck at all, I should have her located by tomorrow.''

"Terrific. Still want me to try for the expense money?''

"Of course. Call me as soon as you hear.''

Richard put down the telephone and decided to wait for Wise's information before he called Trish. He considered her a friend and an honest woman and was sure he could talk her into helping him.

Milton Wise's call came about half an hour later. He sounded strangely upset and angry.

"What happened, Milt?'' Richard asked.

"Deal's off, Rich.''

"What do you mean, the deal's off?''

"That's what I said. Don't ask me any questions, because I haven't got any answers. I gave him the information, and he said to tell you there wasn't a deal anymore.''

"What about my expenses and my time?'' Richard asked furiously.

"No dice. He said he was out of it, that's all. I'm sorry, Rich . . . I feel responsible.''

"You are responsible. Either tell me who the fuck this mystery client of yours is, so I can go after him myself, or by God, I'll take it out of your hide . . . in court! As an attorney, you should know that a verbal contract is just as binding as a written one. Who does that bastard think he is? He can't call the deal off now that I've found her!''

"Send me the bill, Rich . . . for everything. I'm sorry, what else can I say?''

Richard slammed down the telephone. What the fuck good was it to get his expense money back when he really needed the big money? All these days wasted, and he'd lost the fee on the Billy Thomas IRS case too. What a mess! Despite his fury, his curiosity was aroused. What was the reason for the sudden pullback when he was almost there? Was the whole deal a sham, or was there more to it? Maybe it would be worth his while to find out more on his own. Especially since he couldn't afford to keep paying the private investigators. He was going to get to the bottom of things and find out who the bastard was who had reneged, and if nothing else, threaten to expose him.

In the morning, he would call Trish and tell her it was important to meet with her. He would tell her what he knew, since there was no longer a privileged client-attorney relationship—if in fact there had ever been one. His instincts had told him to stay away from this deal, but he had ignored them, and it served him right to get stiffed, he decided. Even now, however, the thought of all that money intrigued him. It would have been so nice to make enough on one fast deal to put him back where he started, before he decided to become a real-estate tycoon. Shit, why wasn't he satisfied with what he had? Why did he always want more? The lure of easy money makes villains of us all, he reflected.

He picked up the telephone to call in all his sources and tell them the deal was off. There were a lot of calls to make. If Richard Terhune was to continue being one of the best-connected men in the country, he'd have to pay everybody off handsomely. What the hell, Milt was going to foot the bill. It would be good for him. Next time, Milt would think twice before sucking him into something shady.

Milt must be losing his touch. Richard had never known him to be so far out in left field.

40

Crazy Lady

Trish and Vanessa rode to Joe's apartment in silence. When they arrived, Trish paid the cabbie, and Vanessa hurried into the building, keeping her face down in the poncho as if she were shielding herself from the cold wind. They rode the elevator to the eleventh floor in silence and knocked at the door. Red opened it immediately.

"Come in." He closed and locked the door behind them, then asked Trish, "Did you help her dress? She's not likely to have a gun, is she?"

Vanessa laughed without humor. "Don't worry, Senator O'Shea. I'm not going to try to assassinate you. That would be the last thing on my mind. You can *frisk* me, if you'd like to—that might be fun, as a matter of fact."

"I'll take your word for it. Okay, now, what do you want to tell me that's such a big mystery?"

"Got something to drink?"

"This isn't my apartment." His voice was cold and impersonal.

"Okay, then, do you mind if I smoke?"

"Look, what kind of a game are you playing? And what do you want to talk to me about?" Trish was surprised to hear him sound so cold.

"I want to talk to you alone. There's no reason for Trish to hear what I have to say. As a matter of fact, there's every reason for her not to hear it."

"Do you want to stay or wait in the bedroom, Delaney?" Red asked impersonally.

"What do you want me to do?"

"You'll be sorry if you stay, Trish. Your life won't be worth any more than mine is . . . although I've got to admit that if anybody—anybody at all—knows you've been here, you're sunk anyway," Vanessa stated flatly.

Trish looked at Vanessa and was torn by indecision. There was something terribly frightening about her words and the deadly tone of her voice, which indicated to Trish with unbearable certainty that they were true. Should she put herself and perhaps her loved ones in jeopardy because her curiosity demanded satisfaction? She decided against it. "I'll wait in the bedroom."

Trish walked away, feeling cowardly and contemptuous of herself. Where had all her courage gone?

For half an hour she sat on the bed in the tiny, drab room, trying to keep herself from pressing her ear to the door to make out the words in the steady hum of the conversation going on in the living room. Occasionally the resonant timbre of Red's voice would send a phrase or a word through to her, but she could make no sense of it. The one thing she could tell was that whatever was being said, Red was taking it very seriously.

At the end of half an hour, Red opened the door. His face betrayed his shock and concern, and when he swept her into his arms and held her tightly in front of the startled Vanessa, she knew that he had heard something terrible.

"Delaney, I'm sorry, so sorry. If I'd had any idea what this all was about, I would never, ever have allowed you to be involved in it," he exclaimed.

Vanessa was sitting on the couch smoking a cigarette and drinking a brandy. "Well, well, so I was right the first time." Her manner was mocking and not kind. Trish wondered why Red had revealed their relationship in front of someone whose behavior was so strange and mysterious. What could she have possibly told him?

"Was I right in bringing her here, Red?" Trish asked.

"Yes . . . I don't know. I wish to hell I had never heard a word she said, but yes. You'll never know how important it was. You're a real heroine."

"What about me . . . Red? Don't you think I did good too?" Vanessa asked mockingly.

"Yes, you certainly did. Now, what are we going to do to protect you?"

"Just get me out of here and onto the first plane to Los Angeles. Once I'm safely back in my home in Hancock Park, nobody will know for certain where I've been. They'll think I've just been on another one of my sex-and-booze binges. I just wish I'd brought that documentation with me. I feel sure it's still there, but I was in such a rush to get out of L.A. . . ."

"Without it, there's nothing I can do. Everything you've told me is just a very grim fairytale without it," Red warned.

"You believe me, don't you?" Vanessa asked.

"I wish to hell I could say no. But, yes, I can't think of any reason for you to say what you did if you didn't believe it to be true."

"Good. Because I can't go to anybody else, and it would be a shame if I'd risked my neck in vain. What happens if I can't get the papers?"

"Try. I'd like nothing more than to blow this whole thing out of the water. But I can't do it without proof."

"It's going to be tough. I hope that people will believe that I've just been gone on one of my legendary binges, distraught over the death of my beloved father. I know for certain that I'm the only one who knew that he kept records, and I think I can locate them. For reasons I won't go into, they'll be very hard to get at."

"I don't have to tell you how valuable those records are, not only to me but also to the people who were involved with your father. Did anybody know just how much you knew about this?" Red asked.

Vanessa shook her head. "I didn't know anything at all until just a couple of weeks before he died. When he finally admitted that he wasn't going to live much longer, he told me everything and ordered me to carry on for him. He said he'd come back from the grave to haunt me if I didn't."

"My God," Red exclaimed.

"He didn't believe in Him either, Senator. But you know what, I'm not at all sure that he won't find some way to get me . . . either in this life or the next. I just want to be sure that if there's a heaven or a hell, we're not in the same place." She got to her feet. "Well, I'll do my best to figure out a way to get what you need, but it won't be easy. I'm sure the goons will be watching every move I make, if I even make it back to Los Angeles alive. By the way, I'd better call the airlines and see what time I can get on a plane out of here, much as I hate to leave such charming company."

"Is there anything I can do to help you, Ann?" Trish asked.

"It's not 'Ann,' my dear. You might as well know now that I'm the notorious Vanessa Fallon, daughter of the late Mike Fallon. Nobody can help me do what I have to do, but thanks anyway."

Half an hour later, Vanessa left the apartment and hurried downstairs to a waiting taxi. She had a reservation on a flight to Los Angeles, and she had to rush to make the plane.

Trish was curious and asked Red, "What is it that she's going to try to get for you?"

"Names, lots of names. Dates. Locations. Contacts. I need more than just the word of a bitter and vengeful daughter. You know, my dream of being president isn't so wonderful anymore, now that I've talked to Vanessa Fallon." His voice was wistful and sad.

"But why . . . why should it affect your run for the presidency?" she asked.

"Because I believe what she had to say. She told me a lot of things about herself, her relationship with her father, her reasons for doing what she did. There was no reason for her to lie. Of course, it's always possible that she's just a crazy lady, but I don't believe that, do you?"

Trish shook her head. "Not for a minute. She's a little strange and sometimes not very nice, but there was an urgency about her that I found very affecting."

"So did I . . . goddammit." He paused then and a guilty expression crossed his face. "Trish, I'm sorry, but I lied to you. I wanted to know what she had to say, and I couldn't take a chance on meeting her alone. Joe was listening. I was afraid that if she learned he was in on it, she might be scared off."

"Joe! Where is he?" Trish was furious with Red for having lied to her.

"He was in the kitchen with the tape recorder going. He's probably gone downstairs to make sure that she got into a cab safely."

"I see," she replied coldly, feeling used. "You could have told me. I can be trusted, you know, and I would have understood your need for safety. But you made me a party to your betrayal of Vanessa's confidence, and I don't like it one bit." She looked away from him to hide her angry tears. "Well, it's been a long day, and I want to go home. I'm sure Millie's worried half to death."

"I'm really sorry, Trish. I wish I could have done things differently, but I had to protect myself. You understand that, don't you?"

"Not really. I'm pretty new to all this intrigue. People seem to make life so much more complicated than it really is. Just tell me one thing, Red. Why were you the only one Vanessa could go to?"

"Someday, when it's all straightened out, I'll tell you why she couldn't trust anybody else."

As they got to their feet, Red took Trish in his arms for a reassuring hug. "Are you going to hang in there with me for a while?" he asked.

"For a while," Trish replied, but there was little enthusiasm in her voice.

Red opened the door, and she started out of the apartment, when she suddenly remembered, "My purse. I left it in the bedroom." She brushed past him hurriedly. "I'll be right back."

"I'll go ring for the elevator," Red said, and stepped out the door. Suddenly there was a sharp thudding sound. Trish whirled around to see Red looking at her with a surprised and horrified expression on his face. He clutched his neck and blood spurted from between his fingers. He was still on his feet, but his knees were beginning to buckle.

Trish raced to him and grabbed him around the waist. With all of her strength she pulled him back into the room and heaved the weight of both of their bodies against the door, slamming it shut. Letting him fall to the floor, she scrambled to turn the key and thrust the dead-bolt lock shut. Thank God for the paranoia of New Yorkers who only felt safe behind multiple locks. Another whooshing sound raced past her shoulder, and she realized that someone had just sent a bullet through the door. Instinctively she dropped to the floor beside Red, where she lay in panic. He was unconscious and it took a moment before the sight of his life's blood seeping from him shocked her into action and out of her numbing state of fear. She tried to remember her Red Cross training, and words like "stanch the flow" and "shock" came back to her.

She needed something to apply pressure. She looked around the room and saw nothing, but she was afraid to get to her feet for fear another shot might blast through the door and hit her. Wriggling on her stomach, she made her way across the room to the bathroom, where she grabbed all the towels in sight. Then, feeling secure, since nothing more had happened, she got to her feet and raced back across the room. Pressing the towels against the wound in Red's neck, she tried to stop the flow. God, she needed help immediately! She left him again and went to the telephone and dialed 911.

"Hurry, please. Senator O'Shea has been shot, and I think he might be dying!" She heard herself repeat Joe's address and wondered from what little segment in her mind she had managed to remember it. As soon as she was assured that they were already on their way, she returned to the man whose life she wanted so desperately to save.

Crooning a litany of soothing words to try to comfort him and herself, she held him in her arms and pressed the towels against the wound. Oh God, would they ever get here?

A long six minutes later, there was a knock at the door. She leapt to her feet to open it, although she called out first, "Who is it?"

"Paramedics. Open up."

As she slid the bolt back, she hoped they were who they said they were. The door opened, and two men in uniform rushed past her toward Red. Joe came in right behind them.

"Thank God you're here, Joe. Somebody shot Red just as he was going out the door!"

"Jesus Christ, is he dead?" Joe asked trying to see over the backs of the men swarming around the senator's body.

"I don't know."

"Did you see who did it?" His voice was tense, and he had taken her arm in a grip that threatened to cut off all circulation.

"No! I pulled him inside and slammed the door shut. They shot right through it." Her voice seemed distant. Who was that talking for her? she wondered.

"Think, Trish, think . . . how did it happen? Did Red say anything to you at all?" Joe demanded.

"No! I just saw the blood. I went back to get my purse, and Red opened the door . . . and it happened. I grabbed him and pulled him inside and locked the door. They shot right through it." She felt as if she was babbling hysterically.

She looked up to see a policeman standing behind Joe, listening. Joe turned and reacted quickly. "Quick, officer, get some help here. Somebody tried to assassinate Senator O'Shea. The assassin might still be here in the building!" The officer turned and shouted to another policeman at the door, "Radio for some help here, right now!"

Trish was relieved when Joe's attention was turned away from her. She moved closer to see what was being done to save Red. The paramedics moved quickly. One of them had started an intravenous, and the other was tying a compress to the wound. When the medic finished, he contacted the hospital on his mobile radio and told them to have a surgeon ready.

"Is he going to be all right?" Trish asked.

"I think so, ma'am. He's losing blood, but his vital signs are okay. We've got to get him to the hospital fast. Are you his wife?"

Joe intervened. "No, she's a campaign worker, and I'm his manager. I'll call his wife immediately. Take good care of him. That's Senator Red O'Shea."

"Yeah, I recognized him. Well, we're on our way."

When they were alone, Joe put his arm around Trish's shoulder and said, "Nice going. You saved his life, you know."

"Joe, I think you ought to call Gloria and tell her to meet you at the hospital. Do you think it'll be all right if I go over there too?"

"I think it might look a little strange if you didn't." He went to the telephone and called Gloria. She took the news well and said she would drive into the city immediately.

As they drove to the hospital, Trish began to feel numb and remote from the horror she had just witnessed.

"Joe, why would anybody want to kill Red? Do you think it had anything to do with Ann . . . Vanessa's visit?"

Joe shook his head. "Naw, I don't think so. In my opinion, she's a crackpot trying to make herself look important."

"Really? I think Red believed her story."

"No he didn't. He's just a pushover for women. I think that whoever shot him will turn out to be a Hinckley-type character. Those are the only kind who are ever successful assassins, because they work entirely alone, and they don't have any apparent reason except what goes on in their heads. You know, there's no way you can stop a guy who's willing to die himself."

"But this person got away," Trish protested, and she felt anger bringing her back to life.

"They'll get him, don't worry." He reached over and covered her hand with his. "You should be proud of yourself, my friend. You saved Red's life. If he pulls through this, you'll be a real hero."

"Oh my God, Joe! Will anyone start wondering what I was doing there alone with him?"

"No way. I already thought about it, and here's the story. You were with me, but I was downstairs getting the car when it happened. Just stick to that story. Gloria will be at the hospital, and we'll try to focus media attention on her. Now, trust me. I'll take care of everything."

Trish smiled shakily at him and said, "Thanks, Joe. God, I hope he doesn't die!"

"So do I! But just think, if he pulls through this all right, he'll be more popular than ever. Look what happened to Reagan after he was shot. He rocketed up in the polls."

Trish looked at Joe's face and wondered if he had any concern for the human being or if all he cared about was the candidate. God, she detested Joe Franklin.

41

You Shouldn't Be Alone

Dan did not return to the apartment after his visit to his mother. Selena had cooked a special dinner for him, and she waited for two hours before calling his home. She managed to keep the anger out of her voice when he answered.

"Dan, honey, did you forget that I was cooking dinner for you tonight?" she asked sweetly.

"No, but I've been pretty upset. I visited my mother, and she's . . . gone.

"She died?"

There was a long pause, and Selena could tell that he was trying to regain his composure. Men like Dan would never let anyone hear them cry.

"Not really, but she doesn't know me anymore, and she isn't speaking."

"How awful for you. You shouldn't be alone. I'll be right over."

Without waiting for his protest, Selena put down the telephone, grabbed her purse and coat, and dashed out of the apartment. As she closed the door behind her, she could hear the telephone ringing. "No way I'm going to answer you, Dan. I'm coming whether you want me or not."

She got into her car and sped to the freeway. She had to

get to Dan before he had a chance to do something rash,
like leaving the house. Not heeding the speed limits, she
maneuvered her car skillfully across the Ventura freeway
to Woodland Hills, where Dan lived. Traffic was light,
and twenty minutes after her last words to him, she was
ringing his doorbell. Dan opened the door immediately,
and she could see that he was agitated.

"Selena, I don't think this is the time or the place . . ."
Dan began, but she ignored him and backed him into the
house by opening her arms to embrace him. Mindful that
his neighbors might be watching, he stepped into the house
and closed the door.

"Dan, I'll just bet you haven't had a bite to eat, have you?"

He shook his head and started to protest, but she ignored
him and sailed toward the kitchen. "Well, I'll take care of
that right now. I'll get you fed and settled before I leave."
By announcing that she did not intend to stay, she quieted
his fears and his protests. One thing at a time, she calculated.

There wasn't much to work with in the kitchen, but she
scrambled some eggs and threw together some biscuits
from a box of mix she found in the pantry. There was a
bottle of Chardonnay in the refrigerator, and she opened it
and poured a glass for them both. Handing Dan his wine,
she led him into the study, where he settled down in an
easy chair in front of the television.

"Now, you just sit there and relax. I'll bring you something on a tray. We'll talk later."

She brought his dinner to him, and while he ate it, she
built a fire in the fireplace, refilled his glass with the cool
white wine, and then settled down on the floor at the
hearth, facing him. The firelight provided a halo around
her dark hair, which she had let fall loose from its knot,
and she posed herself so that the shadows and flickering
light would make her look more beautiful and alluring.

When Dan had finished the eggs and the hot biscuits,
Selena refilled his glass and said, "Now, tell me what
happened at the hospital this afternoon."

Without intending to, Dan found himself not only telling her all his anxieties and fears about his mother's living death but also revealing everything he had found out about his wife's whereabouts. It was almost as if another person, not he, were speaking. Surprisingly, he was relieved when he had finished. It had been a long time since he had felt free to confess anything personal to another human being. In the last few years he had even refused to share his innermost feelings with Cake, although when they had been lovers and newlyweds, he told her everything. He couldn't remember exactly when or why he'd stopped.

Selena listened without speaking, afraid the sound of her voice would break the spell. The Dan she was hearing was a different man than the one she had pursued. He sounded weak and humble and confused, and she realized that he was far more vulnerable than she had suspected. But wasn't that just what her dear mother had always told her? The bigger they acted, the smaller they felt. She must not, however, let herself feel too sorry for him, or, God forbid, fall in love. Once you loved somebody, you could never control him properly.

When Dan finished, Selena touched his hand lightly with hers. "I know how you must feel. Mothers are very special people. I just hope for your sake, and hers, that she isn't suffering."

He put his head in his hands. "God help me, what should I do?"

"There's nothing you can do, except be patient. And that goes for the situation with Cake too. I don't think she's coming back. At least, not for a long time."

"But suppose her leaving was just a gambit to get me to follow her and bring her back?"

"If that's what it was, would you want her back on her terms? She didn't just leave, she humiliated you, walking out and leaving you with guests on your hands. She's a selfish woman. You've worked hard all your life for her. You built her this beautiful home . . . bought her expensive clothes . . . and look how she repaid you. The first time she had some cash of her own, she took off. She took your own mother's money and used it to spite you.''

"But I cheated on her, Selena. Day after day, I chose your body over hers. Do you realize that I almost stopped having sex with her altogether? Maybe once or twice a month, just to keep her from suspecting anything.'' Selena's heart skipped at the news. Good grief, if she'd only known how much power she'd had then. Had she overplayed her hand now?

"You're not the first man that's happened to, you know, Dan. It happens all the time. You're not the same man you were when you got married. You've grown, and Cake didn't . . . or couldn't . . . or wouldn't. It's not your fault that you fell in love with somebody else.'' He didn't look at her.

"Come, Dan,'' she continued, "I think it's time we got you to bed. You've had an exhausting day, and tomorrow is coming too soon. You know the Stevenson contingent will have their knives out to slash your plans to pieces, and you'll have to be in good shape to fight them off. There's a lot of money riding on them, and you can't afford to let them cut too close to the bone.''

She got to her feet and took his hands to pull him out of the chair. As he stood up, he wrapped his arms around her and held her closely. She let her body fall sensuously against his, and she could feel that he was becoming aroused by her touch. She stood very still. What happened next would be crucial. Finally he pulled away and looked at her.

"Come to bed with me. I need someone to hold me tonight.''

She said nothing as they walked toward the stairs with their arms around each other, but in her mind echoed one word: *"Bingo.''*

Long after Dan had fallen into a deep sleep, Selena lay on her back looking into the darkness. The future seemed much brighter than it had just a few days ago when she had detected signs that Dan was beginning to miss his wife. Men. They thought they were such pillars of strength. Hmpf. Pillows of gelatin was more like it. How funny that women had become known as the weaker sex. Women, who had to be everything. Strong, enduring, pliant. She thought back to her pregnancy and shuddered. Thank God she'd been able to have an abortion. Jesus! Just once a man should have to know what it was like to have to worry about that.

Although she dreaded the prospect, Selena knew it was essential that she get pregnant with Dan's child as soon as it was feasible. With her help, Dan was going to be even more rich and successful than he now was, and there was no way that she would allow his other children to have exclusive claims on what would rightfully be hers.

Not that she cared about children particularly, but they were a good way to anchor one's position in a household. God knows she'd have gotten Dan away from Cake a long time ago if he hadn't been so damn worried about what his brats would think.

She rolled over on her side and faced away from the man sleeping beside her. Dan Halliday was a lot better than most of the men she'd known in her life. He was good-looking, clean, extremely bright, and he enjoyed the good things in life . . . as she did. A man with a lot of money and no yen to enjoy it might as well be poor. She had long ago decided that she would only choose a man with whom she could live in a style that would bring some joy to her life. She had no intention of marrying an old fart and being miserable while she waited for him to die.

Dan was important to her because he was a rare commodity. It would have been nice if he hadn't been married, but that was Cake's tough luck. Successful, intelligent men who were single were almost nonexistent. Marriage was too good a deal for a smart man to pass up.

Now, if Cake would just stay out of the way for a few

weeks longer, Selena could carve out her own little niche in this household. She wondered how long she should wait before suggesting that they pack Cake's things away. Too bad all those nice clothes were about three sizes too big. Cake was tall and wore a ten . . . or maybe even a twelve.

Selena ran her fingertips along her body, lightly touching her hip bones, her flat pelvis, and her slim thighs. Good things come in small packages, she exulted, and wondered why any man would be interested in a woman who was as big as he was. Selena was a petite size four, and the only ample parts of her body were her breasts. She cupped them in her hands and then ran the palms over the nipples, which came obediently to attention. She loved her round, full breasts. They had cost her plenty. Because she'd been so flat, she'd had to have three operations to get implants big enough. But it had been worth it, not only because they made her physically desirable to men but also because her figure pleased her now too.

She pressed her fingers around the breasts, feeling and testing. She often wondered if Dan had ever suspected that the globes he was so fond of kissing and caressing were really just bags of chemicals surrounded by skin. She chuckled silently at the thought. She never intended to tell him.

It was getting late, and she needed to go to sleep. She couldn't afford to be tired and cranky. Not for a while anyway. She'd have to be sympathetic and caring and sweet and positively darling. She would wear her mantle of womanhood with grace and dignity and devotion. She would kiss his feet if necessary. Why not? She'd already kissed everything else. But he would feel cared for and loved and nurtured. And if he was good to her, she would continue to make him feel that way even after she had that golden band on her finger.

42

One-Night Stand

Gloria O'Shea swept into the waiting room of the hospital forty-five minutes after Joe and Trish had arrived. As soon as she walked into the room that Joe had commandeered to keep them away from the press, Trish felt herself shrinking. Gloria was beautiful, far more beautiful than her pictures had shown her to be. She was tall and slim and golden-haired, and carried herself with grace and hauteur. She gave Trish a glance that withered her, not that it was cold or filled with hatred, it was just that in one chilling look she let Trish know that they were not equals.

"Joe, what the hell happened to Red? He's not dead, is he?" Gloria demanded, and Trish was fascinated by the servile and meek tone of Joe's response. She had never seen him cower before.

"No, he's not, Gloria. Somebody shot him in the neck as he was about to leave the apartment—" he began, but Gloria interrupted smoothly, "Not somebody's jealous husband, I hope." There was a brief flutter of humor in her voice.

"Uh, oh, no, no, nothing like that," Joe responded. "He was talking to somebody about a . . . well, you don't want to know about that. I'm pretty sure it was an assassination attempt by some crazy, but we're not giving out anything because we don't know."

Without looking at Trish, Gloria asked coldly, "Was *she* the woman he was talking to?"

Joe had regained his composure now and was operating at optimum level. "Oh, no, I'm sorry. This is Trish Delaney. She works in the office. She's in charge of helping to get women interested in Red's campaign. Trish Delaney, this is the senator's wife, Gloria O'Shea."

"How do you do?" Trish responded softly.

Gloria acknowledged the introduction, glanced at her briefly, and then turned her attention back to Joe. "Where is he?"

"He's in surgery. We don't know yet how bad he is. It was a neck wound, but the gunman only got one shot at him because of Trish's quick action."

"I see. Give me the details," Gloria told Joe as her eyes appraised Trish again.

"Our strategy meeting was over and I had gone downstairs to get the car out of the garage to run Trish home. She and the senator were on their way out the door when he was shot. Trish managed to pull him back inside and shut and lock the door, or I'm afraid they might have both been killed. Whoever fired the shot sent another one through the door before he took off."

"Go on."

"Trish administered first aid and called the paramedics. I didn't know what had happened upstairs until I saw the ambulance. I called you right away."

Gloria's expression softened and became more thoughtful as she surveyed the woman who had saved her husband's life. After a moment she commented, "Well, thank you . . . Miss Delaney, is it? Whatever can I do to repay you for saving Red's life?"

"Nothing. Anybody would have done as I did," Trish replied, and her face grew hot with embarrassment.

"Uh, Gloria, I think it might be a good idea if you sort of let on that you know Trish. That might divert the press from wondering why she was alone in my apartment with us. It was all perfectly innocent, but you know how they are," Joe said, and smiled.

Trish wanted to stuff her fist down Joe's throat. Gloria listened to him coolly and then turned her gaze back on Trish thoughtfully. "And just why should I do that, Miss Delaney? Especially if there's nothing to cover up."

"I really don't know, Mrs. O'Shea. Ask Joe. It was his idea, not mine."

"Well, I'll give it some thought. How long have you been working on his campaign?"

"Not long. A few weeks. I think he would be a great president, don't you?"

Gloria sat down on the couch and crossed her legs. "Not really. I would much prefer that he give up the whole thing, but then he doesn't much care what I think."

Gloria continued to stare at Trish, who tried not to wither under her gaze. Even Joe seemed uncomfortable with the air of tension in the room.

Suddenly Gloria noticed the large brown stain on Trish's light blue jacket. "Good God, is that blood all over your sleeve?"

Trish looked down at it, and the memory of Red's blood spurting from his neck returned in all its horror, and she grasped the stain tightly, just as she had grasped him to stop his bleeding. Her heart pounded, and a cold perspiration broke out on her forehead. She looked up at Gloria in terror. "Yes . . . that's his blood!"

Without warning the impact of the terror she'd denied because she had to save his life hit her with the force of a tornado. She got to her feet, but her legs would not support her. She looked at Gloria, and all she could see was Red's face the moment after he'd been shot, and then there was nothing but merciful darkness as she sank to the floor unconscious.

Gloria sprang to her feet and went to help her. "Call the nurse!" she snapped to Joe, who rushed out of the room to find someone. He was back in moments with several hospital attendants. Gloria was kneeling beside Trish, holding her hand, when they arrived.

Quickly they checked her out. "I think she's just fainted," a nurse commented. "Get a gurney in here immediately." As Trish was being lifted onto the gurney, she regained consciousness. "Red!" she called out hysterically, and began to cry, saying his name over and over as they wheeled her away sobbing.

The expression on Gloria's face was a mask of ice. When she was alone with Joe, she turned to him, and her voice was steely. "You were lying, weren't you, Joe?"

"What do you mean?" he asked.

"She isn't just a campaign worker, is she? Tell me the truth, you son of a bitch."

"Look, it's nothing, understand? She's nobody for you to worry about."

"Don't take me for a fool. That woman is no one-night stand," she snapped as she strode toward the door. "Come on, Joe. I think it's time we met with the press, don't you?" She looked directly at him, and her smile had the glitter of shiny new razor blades.

Joe was completely disconcerted. "What are you going to say, Gloria?"

"I'll think of something."

43

The Evil Influence

When the plane to Los Angeles was finally airborne, Vanessa relaxed, lighted a cigarette, and ordered a double brandy. The excitement of the day had put her nerves on alert, and she needed to calm down. She hoped that she'd gotten away clean, but she was afraid she hadn't managed to fool anybody, nor had she accomplished anything by engaging in what now seemed a perfectly ridiculous charade. She should have known that Red O'Shea would demand proof of some kind to support her wild claims.

She didn't intend to give up yet, however. She was Mike Fallon's daughter, and she had more than a streak of his stubborn determination. She was a descendant of a long line of men who were strong and tenacious, and the daughter of a man who had become almost a legend because of his ability to build fortunes. Her father had made millions in oil before he turned to real estate. He seemed to have an almost uncanny knack for investing at the right time, and better yet, he always knew when to sell. It was often said that Mike Fallon had sold his soul to the devil in exchange for inside information. She was probably the only person who really believed that story to be true.

She wondered if she should call Jim Danton when she got home or if she should wait for him to call her. The old curmudgeon had been Mike's most enthusiastic cohort during the years when their nasty plot was being hatched, and now that Mike was gone, she was fairly sure that Danton had taken over command of the operation.

Danton had embraced Mike's nefarious scheme with a religious fervor that almost matched his devotion to his church. Mike had told her that much of the violence in their plan had been Danton's inspiration, which hadn't surprised her. Vanessa had always detested Danton and tried to avoid him because of his obvious relish in lecturing her about the sins of fornication and liquor.

One time when she and Mike were having an unusually acrimonious fight, she had threatened to reveal their incestuous relationship to the pious Danton, but Mike had merely laughed and told her to go ahead. "He won't blame me, you little asshole," Mike had declared. "It will only confirm his suspicions that you're the evil influence in this house. Don't you know the old fart still believes we'd all be in the Garden of Eden if that nasty temptress hadn't waved her sexy apple in front of poor Adam?"

What a thing to think about now. Time was supposed to make the bad memories fade, but since her father had died, she found it harder and harder to remember any of the good things he had said and done. All she could remember was the tyranny.

Lighting another cigarette, Vanessa wondered if it was a death wish that had her hooked on the miserable habit again. She had stopped smoking a year ago when she was told that the emphysema that made an invalid of her mother at an early age was manifesting itself in her lungs too. At the moment it seemed silly to worry about her long-term health when she might not make it beyond the next couple of hours.

She finished her brandy and was tempted to have another one but didn't. She had to keep her mind clear in order to plan her moves. She would have to find someone who could extract the information she needed from her father's computer. She regretted that she had failed to learn anything about computers when he was alive. Mike had tried to tell her that they were fun to play with as well as being the wave of the future, but as with so many things that he had espoused, she rejected the idea and swore that she would have nothing to do with a ram that didn't produce wool or a byte without teeth. Pity. Now she had the chance to do something significant and worthwhile in her wretched life, and she didn't have the skills or knowledge to do it. And she was running out of time. If they didn't already know what she was up to, they probably would very soon.

One thing she had going for her was the fact that nobody else knew that her father had put everything in his computer. Night after night, when the house was dark and the servants had retired, he would sit in front of his terminal for hours, logging in data and planning his strategy. He became obsessed with the machine to the point that he preferred its company to his daughter's. But then, she had ceased to be of value to him after surgery had left him impotent. He never admitted it, of course, nor did she ever try to make him feel diminished, but the doctor had given her all the details when he told her that Mike would probably not live more than six months.

Vanessa closed her eyes and remembered his last weeks of excruciating pain. She had tried so hard to be a dutiful and loving daughter, even though she knew he hated her for feeling well when he felt so miserable. He was determined to live long enough to see his plans come to fruition, but the disease proved stronger than his will. When he died, Vanessa had come close to believing in a just God. It was almost as if there had been divine intervention to prevent his evil scheme.

She dozed for a while in the darkened plane as her thoughts roamed through the past. If she survived this quest of hers, she would call Cliff and beg him to let her see Claudia once more, if only from a distance. The passing years had done nothing to ease the grief of losing her only child. Were there words that she could say to Cliff that would soften his resolve and his hatred? Was there any way that she could convey to him the depths of her loss and her loneliness? Probably not.

The plane landed in Los Angeles, and she decided against taking a limousine home. It would be better to take a taxi to the big house in Hancock Park. If someone was still there watching, it might be assumed that she was returning from one of her binges. She looked at herself in her purse mirror. God, would Stevens let her in? She certainly looked nothing like the woman who had walked out of the house two and a half weeks ago. She'd have to go to the hairdresser's first thing in the morning and have her hair tinted back to its natural dark shade. She had to remove all traces of Ann Fitzgerald.

As the taxi pulled up into the circular drive of the massive stone house, Vanessa stared at the turrets stretching dark against the starless sky and felt suddenly depressed. The mansion was big and ominous, and there were no lights bidding her welcome from the leaded-glass windows. Stevens took a full five minutes to answer the bell.

"Stevens, it's me . . . Vanessa. Open the door!" she called to the eye in the peephole.

The elderly butler recognized her voice and responded with alacrity. It was not the first time that she had disappeared and returned unexpectedly. "Miss Vanessa? Is that really you?" he asked, squinting at the bizarre appearance of the woman who walked through the door.

"It's me, all right, Stevens. A little worse for the wear, but that's not unusual, is it? Go on back to bed. I'll talk to you in the morning. Anything happen while I was gone?"

"No, ma'am. It's been very quiet around here. Just a few telephone calls for you."

"Did you leave the messages on my father's desk for me?"

"No messages, ma'am. The gentleman who called didn't leave his name."

"Just one person called me?" she asked incredulously.

"I believe so. But he called twice every day. Once in the morning and again in the evening."

"I see. Well, when you hear from him again, be sure that I get the call. Good night, Stevens."

"Can I fix something for you, ma'am? You look a bit . . . tired."

"Nothing, thanks."

Vanessa stood for a moment in the middle of the huge entry hall, staring at the floor, an antique mosaic that her father had smuggled out of Italy to adorn his own private palace. Sighing, she pulled her body up the wide circular staircase that had once graced a manor house in England; its banister of polished ebony wood seemed to grow richer with the years of waxing and wear. As her feet touched the magnificent deep blue Persian rug that covered the steps and she passed the Aubusson tapestries, the paintings of Renoir, Matisse, and Seurat that lined the wall along the stairway and in the gallery above, her depression deepened. She did not even glance at the opulence around her.

The treasures were not confined to the entry; every room was an exquisite setting for the work of countless artists and artisans. The bedrooms were filled with rich walnuts and mahoganies, furniture created by skilled craftsmen of the past. The curtains were all genuine lace imported from Europe, and the brocades were of finest silk. Mike Fallon's enormous wealth had allowed him to indulge in a lifelong orgy of acquisition, and he had filled his house with priceless art, paintings, sculpture, and antiques, both bought and purloined. He had paid the best decorators to organize and display his treasures, and he had succeeded in surrounding himself with a glorious past, a heritage bought and paid for with lots of new money.

Now that she was back in this mansion, Mike's control of her seemed to manifest itself again, and Vanessa realized that she was still his prisoner. Suddenly a dazzling thought blazed across her horizon, and she paused at the top of the stairs and turned to look at the bright lights that twinkled and shimmered from the heavy crystals of the gigantic Baccarat chandelier dominating the entryway.

Damn! She didn't have to live here anymore! She didn't have to be Mike Fallon's dutiful daughter, his unwilling concubine, the object of his contempt, his slave anymore. She could sell the house, the sculpture, the paintings, every damned thing. It was all hers now. With one beautifully bold gesture she would call in the auctioneers and wipe Mike Fallon's monument to himself off the face of the earth. What an exhilarating idea. Why hadn't she thought of it before? Why had she felt that she must continue to be her father's captive? He could never hurt her again . . . never. She had finally come into her own by simply surviving.

Later, as she settled herself into the warm scented water of her huge pink marble tub, Vanessa studied the surrounding onyx walls of her huge bathroom with its gold fittings and beveled mirrors. She was consumed with the hope she felt rising and rustling the tattered leaves of her emotions. She would rid herself of all this! Perhaps she should let the intrigue go, too. It was really none of her concern anyway. She was free now, free to make friends and lead a normal life without the shadow of her father and her past servitude haunting her. It was time to find out if there was any joy in the world. She was anxious to get started. After she'd sold the house, she'd move to New York for good and begin her new life.

44

The Crush of Bodies

Joe and Gloria walked out of the hospital through the front doors, past a contingent of policemen keeping the photographers and the reporters at bay. Gloria's lips were set in a thin line as the lights of the television crews blinded her and a dozen microphones were pushed toward her face.

She said nothing, waiting for Joe to handle the situation, which he did almost immediately.

"Please, please, don't crowd Mrs. O'Shea. She's been through a difficult time, and I'd like for you to treat her with some respect. As you know, the senator was shot and wounded by an unknown assailant. He's in surgery now. He lost a lot of blood, but the doctors are hopeful that he'll be all right. It happened just as he was leaving my apartment after a campaign meeting. There were no other witnesses. Ms. Trish Delaney, who is on our staff, was in another room when it happened. She returned to see the senator just as he was falling, clutching his throat where the bullet lodged. Her quick thinking saved his life. She pulled him into the apartment and slammed the door shut. The assailant sent another bullet through the door but failed to hit anyone. Ms. Delaney dialed 911 and within minutes the paramedics and police arrived. We have no idea who the assailant was. Now, we'll answer a few questions, and as soon as the senator's surgery is finished, a member of the hospital staff will talk to you. Okay?''

"Where's Ms. Delaney?'' a reporter with a microphone asked.

"She's under sedation. She acted brilliantly and bravely, but now she's having some kind of delayed shock. She won't be available to speak to you until she is feeling better.''

"Mrs. O'Shea, where were you when you heard the news?''

Without smiling, Gloria responded tersely, "I was at our home. Joe telephoned me immediately after the paramedics put my husband into an ambulance, and I got here as fast as I could.''

"Did you see your husband?''

"No, he was already in surgery when I arrived.''

The questions were hurled at them for ten minutes, and finally Joe called a halt. Gloria was getting testy, and it had become obvious that she was ready to tell them all where to go. With the help of the police, they managed to escape the crush of bodies and microphones and retreat into the hospital again.

When they were away from the cameras, Gloria said to Joe, "That's it, do you understand? I will not submit to anything like that again . . . ever.''

"I know, and I'm really sorry, but we just had to do it.''

"I don't have to do anything of the sort. Now, find out where that woman is.''

"Why?''

"Because I want to know if she's all right.''

Gloria marched back to the room where they'd been talking and sat down to wait. Joe spoke to the nursing staff and came in a few minutes later.

"She's been admitted to the hospital. They've got her under sedation. The nurse said Trish was sleeping and they'd probably send her home in the morning.''

"Good. Now, as soon as Red's out of surgery, I am going home, and you'd better make damn sure that none of that horde follows me."

Joe nodded, but wondered how he could control the press if they decided to pursue her.

Trish lay on the cool hospital bed, drifting in a daze. Her body felt heavy and relaxed, and the memories of the past hours seemed to be fading away. Funny, her face felt wet but she couldn't understand why. She was too drugged to realize that her eyes were still producing a flood of tears, although the hysterical sobbing had finally ceased.

At last she drifted off into a dream-filled and troubled sleep that lasted for about three hours. Awaking suddenly, she was confused for a moment until she remembered where she was and what had happened. She rang for the nurse, who responded immediately.

"Please turn on the lights," Trish asked.

"Of course, but you ought to try to get some rest," the nurse cautioned.

"No, I've got to get up. Please, is Senator O'Shea out of surgery yet?"

"I really don't know, but I can find out."

"Is Joe Franklin still here in the hospital?"

"Who's Joe Franklin, honey?"

"Just find out about the senator, please. Hurry."

When the nurse had gone, Trish picked up the telephone and dialed Millie. She was probably worried to death about her.

The telephone rang only once before she heard her friend's voice. "Hello."

"Millie, it's me," Trish began, but her voice broke with a sob.

"Are you okay? I heard on the news that you were in shock. Want me to come over to the hospital?"

"No, I'll be all right. Oh, Millie, it was just awful."

"Look, don't talk about it now. Try to get some rest,

and I'll be over there first thing in the morning . . . that's just a few hours away. Then I'll bring you home."

As they were talking, the nurse came into the room, followed by Joe and Gloria, who approached the bed.

Trish told Millie to come early and put down the telephone.

"Are you feeling better now?" Gloria asked, and her voice was kinder than Trish remembered.

Trish nodded, and then Joe said, "Trish, the FBI and the police want to talk to you. Are you up to it yet?"

"My God, Joe, can't you let her alone for a while?" Gloria asked.

Joe ignored her protests. "They need to know if you saw the gunman, because if you did, they want a description as soon as possible."

Trish shook her head. "I didn't see anybody. I don't even think Red saw anybody. It happened so fast. It was like a shot out of nowhere. How is he?"

"He's in the recovery room, but he hasn't returned to consciousness. The doctor said he'd make it. He's a very strong man. They said I could see him as soon as he was awake," Gloria said, and then hesitated before continuing, "Thank you . . . for being there." Quickly she turned and walked out of the room.

Gloria's words stung Trish more than they would have if she'd been nasty and unkind, and she felt miserable. There was no way, absolutely no way that she could continue to see Red now, and her involvement with him seemed shameful.

"Don't take it so hard, Trish. She's usually not that nice," Joe remarked, seeing the look on her face.

"Joe, I want out of here . . . as soon as possible."

"Take my advice, and stay put. You're in no shape to meet the press. One look at you and they'd know the whole story. I'll get you out of here in the morning. Then, when you've got your act together, you can make a statement."

"What about the police?"

"Don't worry about it. I'll tell them that you didn't see anybody and can't give them any information that will help. They will want to talk to you, but maybe they'll wait until tomorrow."

"Thanks, Joe. I wish I could help them find that bastard who shot Red."

"Yeah, well, they'll find him sooner or later. Thanks for saving my candidate. I'd be out of a job, you know, if you hadn't thought fast."

"Joe, you don't think . . . it couldn't have been Ann . . . Vanessa, could it . . . who tried to kill him?"

"No, it couldn't. She was in a cab on the way to the airport when it happened. Besides, I told you I think she's nothing more than a loony dame."

When she was alone again, Trish picked up the telephone once more. It was about midnight in California, and she wanted to make the call that would take her back to sanity and morality. Dan answered the phone on the second ring.

"Hello, Dan? This is Cake. I'm coming home."

45

Sorry

Selena took a long, leisurely bath. The water was warm and relaxing, and she was in no hurry. Dan had already fallen asleep, and she had sneaked out of bed as soon as she heard his breathing become heavy and regular. Selena had a passion for cleanliness, and she never slept well after having sex if she didn't bathe herself. Ginny had drilled into her the need for cleanliness, and Selena tried not to remember how many times a night she'd had to wash away the traces of one man's passion in order to be ready for the next encounter. She shuddered. Never again.

The events of the evening had worked out even better than she'd hoped they would. Instead of sleeping in the apartment with Dan, she was ensconced in his house, at last. Of course, it would have happened sooner or later anyway. She'd never intended that they would stay in the apartment indefinitely.

Suddenly she heard the telephone ring. Damn. Standing up, she reached for a towel, as she heard Dan's voice answer. She dried herself as quickly as she could, but by the time she reached the bedroom, the conversation was over. Dan had turned on the light and was sitting on the edge of the bed.

"Who was that?" she asked, but the answer was in the

expression on his face, which was a lot happier than she would have liked.

"Cake. She's coming home."

Years of masking her true feelings helped Selena through the next difficult moments. "Oh? When?"

Dan shook his head. "She didn't say exactly. She just said soon."

"Well, where was she calling from?" She had trouble keeping the irritation out of her voice.

"I didn't ask her. New York, I guess."

Selena wanted to shake him, but she had better sense. "How distressing for you," she murmured as she sat down on the bed beside him. She could not force herself to make the next step easy for him. If he wanted her to go, he'd have to tell her.

"I know it's a pretty rotten thing to ask, but I think maybe you ought to go back to your apartment," he said at last.

"Right now?" she asked, trying to keep any trace of bitterness out of her voice and her manner.

"I wouldn't ask if I didn't think you'd understand. I'm in a really tough spot."

"I know you are, and I won't make it any worse. I'll get my stuff together." She went back into the bathroom and cursed silently. God damn Cake Halliday, she swore softly. Couldn't she do anything right? If she had to come back, the least she could have done was to walk in unannounced and find out that she'd been replaced. But no, the miserable bitch had been thoughtful enough to call first and give her husband warning to clear the decks.

At two o'clock in the morning Dan walked Selena out to her car and stood there as she climbed into it. Not once did she let down her guard and reveal her true feelings at being so handily kicked out, though she seethed with anger. She would remember this night, and she'd make him pay, one way or another.

"Good night, Dan. I'll see you in the morning at the

office. Don't forget, you have an early appointment with the Michaelides Foundation.''

"Right." He turned to look at her, but didn't lean down to kiss her. "Sorry about this, Selena."

She smiled and said nothing, but as she drove away, she declared out loud, *"Sorry* doesn't help, you son of a bitch.''

46

The Connection

It was seven o'clock in the morning when Richard awakened stiff and cold. Jesus, why hadn't he undressed and gone to bed like any sensible person his age would have? Well, at least he'd had some rest, and his mind would be sharp. He called room service and ordered breakfast along with the morning papers. As he stripped off his clothes and shaved and showered, thoughts of the frustration of the evening before returned to irritate him. Damn that squirrelly woman Millie. He had tried all evening to reach Trish, but every time he called, her roommate answered the telephone and refused to give him any information about Trish or where she was. He had cajoled, threatened, and wheedled, but Millie stonewalled him until about midnight, when he finally gave up and dozed off.

As Richard emerged from the bathroom, the waiter arrived and wheeled in the table with his usual juice, coffee, scrambled eggs, and morning newspaper. He started to eat, but stopped when his eye caught the headline in the *Times:* "SENATOR O'SHEA SHOT BY UNKNOWN ASSAILANT." He read on, his breakfast forgotten. Sure enough, there was Trish's name. She had been present and had called the paramedics and was credited with saving the senator's life.

Shit! That was it. That was the connection. O'Shea wanted to be president. Whoever was looking for Vanessa

Fallon didn't want her to get too close to O'Shea. And Trish was getting caught in the middle of something she had no business being near. He picked up the telephone and dialed her number. Millie answered again.

"Millie, is Trish back yet?" he demanded.

"No . . . have you seen the papers?" she asked.

"Yes, I certainly have. I told you last night that you might be involved in something risky, didn't I?"

"So you were right, but Trish won't be home until later today. She went into shock when it was all over, and they kept her in the hospital. I'm getting ready to go pick her up now."

"Wait ten minutes. I'll come by for you in my car, and we'll both get her. You hear me, Millie? You wait for me."

"Okay, Okay, I'll be here."

They had to wait two hours at the hospital while Trish was interrogated by the police and the FBI. When she was released, Richard spirited her out through the emergency entrance to avoid the press. As the limousine carried them away, Trish thanked him for saving her from the television cameras.

"You know, you're going to have to face them eventually, or they'll begin to make up stories that have nothing to do with the truth," he warned her.

"I know, but I'm just not prepared for that yet. They frighten me."

"Don't let them. The press will love you if you'll just be your own charming self. You're a heroine, you know," he assured her.

"I feel as if I've been through the wringer. I was so afraid he would die before I got help. It's a memory that's going to haunt me forever."

Richard's voice showed his genuine concern for her welfare. "That's only natural. You've had a harrowing experience. It'll take some time."

"I know, and I'm sure I'll be fine. While Millie was

helping me get dressed, she said you wanted to talk to us about Vanessa Fallon. Why? Are you one of the people who's trying to find her?''

"It's a long story. Why don't we have dinner this evening, and we'll talk about it. There's something I want to look into this afternoon. Maybe I can get some information that will clear things up.''

"Honestly, Richard, I don't think I'll feel like going out. Once I get back to Millie's apartment, I'm going to stay there until my knees stop shaking, and then, as soon as I know that the senator is out of danger, I'm going home.''

"Giving up the big city, are you?''

She smiled. "Not really. I live in Los Angeles.''

"I'll be going back there too in a couple of days. Now, what do you know about Vanessa Fallon?''

Millie spoke up. "She's a bitch when she drinks, and I don't like her, if you're talking about a woman I know as Ann Fitzgerald.''

"Richard, we just can't tell you anything much more than that. I'm sorry.''

"Where is she?''

"As far as I know, she left New York last night and went home.''

"After she saw the senator?''

Millie spoke up. "No comment.''

"Well, I think it would be a good idea if you had me around when you meet with the press. Okay?''

"Joe Franklin said he'd handle it, Richard. I think I should let him. I don't want to do anything that might interfere with the senator's campaign. But thank you for everything.''

As soon as the women left the limousine, Richard picked up the telephone and dialed Milton Wise's office and spoke to his secretary. "This is Richard Terhune. Will Milt be in his office this morning? I have something very important to discuss with him.''

"I'm sorry, Mr. Terhune, but he hasn't come in. I've been trying to reach him at home, but there's no answer. I don't know what to do. The bailiff just called from Judge Wilson's court. Mr. Wise had an important court date this morning, and he hasn't been there either."

"Give me his home address. I'll go over and check on him."

"I'm sorry, sir, but I can't give out that information."

"Never mind, I know about where it is anyway. I've been there many times for dinner. It's on East Sixty-fifth, right?"

"Yes . . . it is."

Richard directed the driver to the area and sat back to think. He was worried. It was not like Milt to miss a court appointment, but then, he seemed to be doing a lot of things lately that were out of character.

Even though the traffic was bad, the limousine pulled up at the apartment building within ten minutes. It was a private building with a security guard in the lobby.

Richard walked up to his desk and asked, "Has Mr. Wise left for the office yet?"

"I don't think so. Do you want me to ring him and see if he's there?"

"Please."

The guard picked up the telephone and dialed the number. There was no answer. "I'm sorry, sir. He doesn't seem to be in."

"How long have you been on duty?" Richard asked.

"I came on at seven."

"You're sure you didn't see him leave the building this morning?"

"No, he didn't leave after I came on, but he could have gone out earlier . . . or maybe he never came home last night."

"Then I think that if you have a key to his apartment, we should go upstairs and have a look. He might be ill and need assistance."

The guard demurred, but Richard was forceful and insistent, and eventually he got his way. Together he and the guard investigated, but the apartment was empty, and there was no indication that anyone had slept there the night before. The place was clean and tidy.

The guard scratched his head. "You know, it doesn't look as if anybody's been here since the maids left yesterday afternoon."

"Does Mr. Wise often stay out overnight?"

"Not unless he tells us he's going out of town. He's very security-conscious."

As Richard got back into his limousine, a feeling of anxiety swept over him. He tried to shake it off, but it would not go away. Milton was his one link to the identity of the man who had hired him. He needed to find out who that was.

He went back to his hotel room and called his office on the coast to get the names and telephone numbers of some of Milt's friends in New York. While he waited for his secretary to call him back with the information, he scanned the *Times* and the *Wall Street Journal* and then turned on the television set to the news station. After headlines about international and national events, including the senator's condition—which was improving—the newscaster intoned, "The driver of the sports car pulled from the East River late last night has been identified as prominent attorney Milton Wise. Wise, who was apparently driving alone, is suspected of having fallen asleep at the wheel while driving on FDR Drive. An autopsy will be done to determine the cause of death."

47

Wanting Somebody Else

The evening after Trish returned from the hospital, she was called by reporters and representatives of several talk shows, who asked if she would be willing to be a guest the next day. Millie took the calls and declined for her, saying she was not up to it at that time and to call Joe Franklin at the campaign office.

The next morning, Trish read in the newspapers that Senator O'Shea was doing so well that he had been moved out of intensive care and was being allowed a few visitors. Joe Franklin, who was interviewed on the morning news, assured everyone that the senator was doing fine but that he would not be available to the press while he was in the hospital. Trish's name was not mentioned.

Trish wanted to know more, so she tried to reach Joe, but was told he was too busy to talk to her. Suddenly she realized that perhaps she had become a liability to the campaign. Though she made several more calls to Joe, none of them were returned.

Richard telephoned to say that he wanted to come over and talk to them. He also advised Trish to let no strangers into the apartment. When Trish told Millie that they had to stay in, Millie asked, "Trish, what the hell did Ann . . . Vanessa tell Red?"

"I don't know. I chickened out and went in the other

room while they were talking. Something told me I didn't want to know what was going on. Are you disappointed in me for being such a coward?''

"Not at all. I think it was smart. But I am a little surprised that Red didn't tell you before the meeting that Joe was listening in the other room. You might have goofed and said something nasty about Joe."

"Red was just protecting himself, and I was really glad that Joe was around after the shooting. He did a good job of keeping things under control. Although it would be nice if Joe had found the time to call us and tell us exactly how Red is doing."

"What do you think Richard's found out?"

Trish shrugged. "I don't much care anymore. I just want out of this. I'm feeling a lot of guilt right now. I have two children, you know. My daughter, Trina, is studying art at the Sorbonne in Paris and my son, Rob, is at the University of Oregon. I have no right to get myself involved in something that might affect their lives. Millie, I'm going home."

"Isn't that a pretty sudden decision? What's the big hurry?" Millie asked.

Trish got up and walked over to the window. After a few minutes of thought she replied, "Guilt, pure and simple."

"What the hell for?" Millie demanded.

"I'm ashamed of myself. I acted like a selfish, self-centered baby. And I just hope my children never find out—"

Millie interrupted indignantly, "What's wrong with them finding out that their mother is a human being?"

"But not a very moral one. When things got tough, I ran away. In one dramatic move, I was going to punish my husband for cheating on me and find my lost love, and instead, look what happened."

Millie spoke soothingly. "You've got nothing to be ashamed of, believe me."

Trish wiped her eyes and took a swallow of coffee. "Maybe. Maybe not. Anyway, there's no future here for me . . . with Red. He has his own rainbow to follow. I realized when I met Gloria last night that I was no better than Selena."

"Who's Selena?"

"My husband Dan's secretary. Selena came to me and told me that Dan had bought and furnished an apartment so they could be together and that he intended to divorce me but was only holding off until the kids were on their own. She said she was telling me out of kindness so that I could make another life for myself before I got too old."

"Jesus . . . and you believed her?"

"Not at first. I couldn't believe Dan would do that. He's always been so prim and proper. But I followed them after work . . . and she was right. She'd go there first . . . fifteen minutes later, he'd arrive. It was sickening."

"You poor thing."

"Please don't pity me. I never wanted to be a pitiful woman."

"You're not. You're a terrific lady, don't you know that?"

"You're too kind. But anyway, I cried a lot. It was the deceit . . . the lying that upset me the most. I couldn't bear the thought that for months we had been in the same bed together, night after night. He had touched me . . . kissed me . . . and all the time, he was wanting somebody else. Finally I decided to play my little scene. I made everything in the house neat and tidy, just the way he liked it. I arranged a lovely dinner party, and ten minutes before he came home, I left."

"Really? Why'd you do it that way?"

"I guess I wanted to punish him in some way for being so deceitful, or maybe I didn't want him to think there'd been foul play. I couldn't bring myself to write a note, but I left all sorts of clues. I got on a plane and came to New York. I also made it easy for him to find me and come after me . . . but he didn't. So I know where I stand with him.''

"Then why are you going back?"

"To get everything settled, one way or the other.''

"Why did you latch on to Red? Surely you must have known there was no future with him.''

"I wasn't looking for a future. I was trying to find the past.''

Millie was confused. "I don't understand.''

"Red and I were high-school sweethearts. We were very much in love. We wanted each other so badly, but I was . . . afraid. I never forgot him. He was an unresolved element in my life.''

"But things worked out with him okay, didn't they?''

"I'd like to say yes, because I really love Red. I always have, and I probably always will. I guess that's why I could never forget him, and when my marriage started collapsing, he was the one I ran to. He's kind and generous and . . . well, elegant in such a natural and spontaneous way. He's so different from Dan. My husband is humorless, ambitious, and a perfectionist. I used to think I complemented him because I was none of those things. How stupid. Anyway, I'm too old to believe that love conquers all. Sometimes it gets in the way of the things you need to do.''

"When are you leaving?''

"Tomorrow. I called Dan last night and told him I was coming.''

"What did he say?''

"He said all right.''

"Are we still going to be friends?''

"Of course, and as soon as the campaign is over, I want you to come out for a visit.''

"Great. I'll meet you in San Francisco and show you where I used to hang out in the sixties.''

Early the next morning when Richard called, Trish told him that she was leaving, and he insisted on coming to drive her to the airport. Once more she tried to contact Joe, but again without success. She called the hospital and was told that the senator was doing fine but that he was taking calls only from his family. When she put down the telephone, she shivered. She had apparently been left out in the cold. Hero today, gone tomorrow, she reflected.

Trish was glad that Richard would be taking her to the airport. He was the first friend she'd made here in the big town, and it was fitting that he would be the last to say good-bye.

48

Defuse the Situation

Richard Terhune was nattily dressed as always, but Trish thought he looked tired and concerned.

"Richard, come in. You're early. I'm all packed and ready, so why don't we sit down and have a cup of tea?" He followed her into the living room. "Is Millie around?" Richard asked.

"She's in the bedroom. Did you want to talk to her?"

"Not yet. Trish, I'm very concerned that you . . . we've . . . gotten involved in something that's not very nice. I don't want to frighten you, but you need to be aware, and you need to give me some information so that I can take steps to defuse the situation or extricate us from it," he began.

"Please, Richard, don't frighten me anymore. I just want to go home and try to forget the last few days," Trish protested.

"Several weeks ago, Milton Wise, an old friend of mine, an attorney I've known for years, offered me two million dollars to locate Mike Fallon's missing daughter. You know who Mike Fallon was, don't you?" Richard persisted.

"Sure. He was a multimillionaire oilman, among other things, wasn't he?"

"Right. Well, the offer was made on behalf of someone who insisted on remaining anonymous."

"Two million dollars? Good heavens, but why you? You're not a detective, are you?"

"No, but over the years I've made some extraordinarily good contacts. Anyway, whoever it was wanted to find her in a very big hurry. The fee shrank by fifty thou each day that passed without her being found. One of the men working for me located her at the Maybelle Hotel, but he was careless, and she slipped out without him seeing her. The next tip was that she was working for Senator O'Shea. I told Wise that I had friends working there, you and Millie, of course, and that I would probably contact Vanessa in less than a day."

Trish said nothing. She was apprehensive and afraid that somehow she might give away something that she shouldn't. "Then what happened?" she asked.

"When my friend Wise called his client and mentioned that Vanessa was working for the senator, the whole deal was called off . . . finished. I was left holding the bag for a lot of money I'd spent."

"Why would they do that? You hadn't really located her yet."

"Right. I complained, of course, and Wise offered to pick up the bill for all my expenses. I felt sure that I ought to warn you and Millie to stay away from Vanessa Fallon if her path crossed yours again. I think she's big trouble."

"Why do you say that?"

"Yesterday morning I went to see Wise after I brought you home from the hospital, but I couldn't find him. Then I learned that they'd fished his car out of the East River. They said he probably fell asleep at the wheel. I know better. I spent most of yesterday with the police and the coroner. When the autopsy is completed, I'm sure they'll find that he was attacked. Or maybe his car had been tampered with."

Richard's voice was tense and his words were clipped.

Trish felt that she was back in the twilight zone again. Was this all really happening?

"You think he was murdered?"

"Milton Wise was the only one who knew the identity of the man who was looking for Vanessa Fallon. When I found out about the attempt on O'Shea's life, I was determined to make Wise tell me the name of the man who had hired me to find the Fallon woman."

"And you think he was killed to silence him?" Trish asked.

"Yes, I do."

"What does this all have to do with me?"

"I don't know how much contact you've had with Vanessa Fallon. I hope that it wasn't much. There's something going on here that's very sinister. If you know anything . . . anything at all, please tell me."

Trish was torn with indecision. Her first reaction was to tell him everything, but she was afraid. "Richard, would you mind repeating all this to Millie? I really think she should know."

"Whatever you say."

Trish brought Millie into the room, and Richard repeated his suspicions. When he finished, the two women looked at each other, and Trish asked, "What do you think?"

Without hesitating, Millie answered, "Go for it."

Trish told Richard everything that she knew about Vanessa Fallon, including the fact that she had met with Red O'Shea shortly before someone tried to kill him and that Vanessa had returned to Los Angeles to get further information for Red.

"Good God," he exclaimed, and his face was ashen.

"It's pretty scary, isn't it?" Millie asked.

"Scary? Scary? You bet your sweet ass it's scary. All of you women are in serious danger. Do you realize that? Vanessa Fallon was obviously trying to impart some very sensitive information to Red O'Shea. And somebody powerful was determined to stop her. I suspect that anyone who's been near her is tainted.''

"God, what are we going to do?" Trish asked.

"Does anybody know your married name or where you live?" he asked.

"Only Red."

"What name did you use to make your plane reservation home?"

"Halliday. I, uh, decided to go back to being who I really am."

"Good girl. I'll take you to the airport and see that you get on that plane safely. Now, what about you, Millie?"

"I'm not afraid. I think it'll look even more suspicious if I suddenly drop out of sight. I'll just go to the office in the morning and act as if nothing unusual has happened. I'll tell everybody that Trish and her husband have reconciled, and she's gone home. What d'ya think?"

"I think you ought to have some protection."

"Like what—carry a gun? No, I hate them."

"No, I'll arrange to have somebody watch you, okay?" Richard asked.

"I think you should let him, Millie. I really do," Trish urged.

"All right, but what about you? You're going back to Los Angeles, and that's where Vanessa is, isn't it?" Millie reminded her.

"She's right. Maybe you better stay here, and I can have you both watched."

"Look, don't get the idea that I'm brave or daring or anything like that, but I just don't think anyone will be interested in me once I'm no longer involved with Red O'Shea. I'll just be an obscure little Woodland Hills housewife shopping for groceries. Besides, I don't know anything that could harm anyone."

"It's not what you know that's important. It's what people think you might know that's dangerous," Richard insisted.

"I'm going home. I've already called my husband and told him. Please, just leave it at that. We've got to get started, or I'll miss my plane."

Millie said, "I hate to see you go. Promise me you'll call me often."

"Thank you for everything, Millie. You've been a wonderful friend. I'll miss you too. And be careful."

Richard carried Trish's suitcase down to the limousine, and when they were on their way to the airport, he cautioned her again, advising her not to tell anyone where she had been. She promised to be careful and thanked him for his concern and for his friendship.

He put his arms around her and hugged her. "Trish, my dear, you are a very special woman. Promise me that our dinners together will continue in Los Angeles."

"Of course they will. I'll call your office and leave my address and telephone number. And thank you for everything."

He kissed her on the cheek. "Take care, now."

An hour later, she was settled in her seat on the plane as the crew prepared for takeoff. She looked around at the passengers seated near her. Funny, she wasn't afraid at all. Whatever horror and intrigue had happened had touched only Trish Delaney, not Cake Halliday. She felt sure that nothing that had happened to her on her adventure in New York would follow her home . . . except her memories. The good ones—the ones of her times with Red—she would pack away with the memories of her high-school days an take them out only when she needed them.

49

With My Memories

The day after Vanessa returned home, the call came in from the man Stevens had mentioned. When she answered the phone, Vanessa heard the booming voice of the man she most feared now that her father was gone.

"Well, Vanessa. Where you been keepin' yourself? I haven't heard a word from you since your daddy's funeral. How you been, girl?" Jim Danton's voice indicated nothing.

"Not too well, Jim. You know, life hasn't been the same for me. I suppose I'm having a little trouble adjusting to being alone," she answered. She would try the pitiful approach and see what his reaction would be.

"What's wrong? Anything I can do to help?"

"Well, maybe. I've been thinking of putting the house on the market. You know, it's hard living here all alone . . . with my memories."

"Whew . . . selling that house will be a big step. Where you plannin' to go?" A slight measure of suspicion put an edge on his question.

"I don't know. I thought maybe I'd do some traveling. Go to Paris, London, I don't know. I was even thinking of getting a job. I feel so useless."

"Well, hard work never hurt anybody. I always felt that Mike was wrong to keep on supporting you like he did. He should have made you get out and learn what it took to earn a livin'. Parents don't do kids any favors by coddlin' them too much."

"Mike didn't coddle me, Jim. He wanted me to stay home and take care of the house and keep him company, you know that. It was especially important after he found out he had . . . cancer." She let her voice drop so that she would sound as sorrowful as possible.

"Old Mike sure did suffer there at the end. He deserved better'n to die like that. He was a good man, and the best friend I ever had."

"I guess the only comfort we can get is that there's some higher reasoning that we just don't understand." That answer should appeal to the sanctimonious old buzzard, Vanessa thought.

"Yep, the Lord moves in mysterious ways. But your daddy was a fine man. 'Course toward the end, he did sorta have a few wild ideas, but we just played along to keep him happy. No sense tellin' a dyin' man that he's a little tetched, is there? Now, what can I do to help you, girl?"

"I don't know, Jim. For the past few weeks I've been trying to figure out what I wanted. I tried going back to some of my . . . old ways, but it just isn't any good anymore." She tried to sound contrite.

"You broke your daddy's heart tearin' around like that . . . drinkin' and whorin'. Mike told me all about pickin' you up in dives and bringin' you home to dry out. You were mighty lucky he didn't just let you kill yourself." His voice was scornful.

"He told me that you advised him to do just that," she accused him.

"That I did, little girl . . . that I did. I never thought you were worth a bucket of piss."

"Well, my father did, Jim. You know he left me everything, including control of all the trusts and all of his money. I've decided I'm going to step into his shoes and start managing things myself. I appreciate the kind offer you made after Mike's death to take over for me, but I don't want to impose on you. Besides, as you know, Mike always hired good men to advise him. Anyway, it's time I started learning a little about finances myself. I might even hire a tutor from the university to help me learn more about finance and balance sheets.'' She deliberately chose to ignore Danton's insults. She needed to convince him that her primary interest in life now was her inheritance. Money was the only thing that the old coot really understood.

''Well, that's sure a switch for you. All you were ever interested in was spending your dad's money. You never seemed to care much where it came from.''

''Now that it's mine, I may feel differently. I need a little advice. Would it be better taxwise to donate my father's collection of art to a museum, or should I try to sell it?''

''What d'ya want to do that for?''

''Because there'll be no place to keep it if I sell the house. And I can't stay all alone in this big mausoleum, Jim. I just can't.''

''Your daddy loved that place.''

''Yes, but he's dead, Jim.''

''Well, if you insist on gettin' rid of it, then I think you ought to lend the stuff to a museum for a while. Then you can donate it piece by piece so that you spread the deductions out over the years. Those paintings are mighty valuable.''

''That's an excellent idea. Now, could you recommend a good real-estate agent?''

When the conversation finally ended, Vanessa poured herself a stiff glass of brandy to try to wash away the vile taste in her mouth. She hated Jim Danton, but she was afraid of him too. She just hoped she had managed to convince him that she was no threat to him or his evil project. The son of a bitch was dangerous.

She sat down on the couch and picked up the morning *Times*. The headline that leapt out at her almost stopped the beating of her heart. "SENATOR O'SHEA SHOT: UNKNOWN

ASSAILANT ATTACKS PRESIDENTIAL HOPEFUL.'' Good God! She read on and found out that the attack had taken place immediately after she left him and Trish. Fortunately he had survived and was in serious but stable condition. Her hands shook as she poured herself another drink.

She was certain that she had spent the last half-hour talking to the reptile who had arranged the whole thing. He knew she had gone to New York to spill the beans, but why had he let her go? Why try to kill O'Shea and not her?

Jesus, she had no time to waste. Had Danton believed anything she'd said? Probably not. But why had he tried to insinuate that the whole scheme had never been a serious one anyway? Was he really uncertain about her trying to stop him? She had no answers. She had to continue on the assumption that he still didn't know.

She looked at her watch. Damn, it was past three. She could not let a whole day go to waste. She started to call the university but changed her mind. No, she'd go to one of those computer stores and find some child genius who would be interested in a lot of money very quickly.

At the first computer store Vanessa tried, there was only the proprietor and his wife. They were friendly, but from Korea or Vietnam, and neither was fluent in colloquial English. The next stop was better. It was a large store with a lot of young people buzzing around. She asked for the manager. A tall, dark young man with a trim mustache came out of the office.

"May I help you?" he asked.

"Yes, I need someone who is familiar with the IBM computer. It belonged to my father, and he is now dead. There's some vital information that I need that's stored there . . . it's very confidential, you understand, and very important. I would pay very well."

"Well, I think anybody here could help you. It might take some time, however."

"I want the most experienced and resourceful person you have. Time is something I don't have a lot of . . . but as I said, I'll make it very worthwhile." She emphasized the last two words and smiled prettily.

"There's a young man who works in the back on repairs. He really needs the money. He's always asking to work extra shifts. Where is the computer located?"

"In my home."

"Do you know the model?"

"I have no idea, but he's had it for several years, and I guess things have changed a lot."

"I should say so! Let me bring Chuck out, and you can talk to him yourself. If it doesn't work out, let me know. I can always find someone else. We have a lot of young kids who hang around here all the time, and they're really sharp."

The man disappeared into the back room and two minutes later emerged with an incredibly handsome young man with sandy hair and bright blue eyes. She had expected to see a Woody Allen clone, but this young man looked as if he would be more comfortable on the football field than sitting at a computer terminal.

"I'd like you to meet Chuck Ferris. Chuck, this is the lady I told you about. If you'd like, you can use the demo room over there to talk." He indicated the room behind a large window, and then he left them.

"How do you do, Chuck. My name is Vanessa, and I hope you can help me." She explained what she wanted, and he was interested.

"I'd love to give it a try, but I can't guarantee I can do it. I could really use the money. How much will you pay?"

"How much do you need?"

He smiled and shook his head. "How high's the moon?"

"Okay, here's the deal. If you're successful in getting the information that I need out of the computer, I'll pay you five thousand dollars. If you can't do it, I'll pay you five hundred to let me know as soon as possible. Time is very important. What do you think?''

''I think I just died and went to heaven. Sure, I'll take it on. When do you want me to start?''

''Now . . . tonight . . . as soon as possible.''

''I've got to finish a job in the back. I get off work at five, and tomorrow's my day off. You want me to start this evening?''

''That would be terrific. Don't bother eating. I'll see that you're well fed while you're working. Here's my address. It's extremely important that you tell no one what you're doing. I'll explain it all when I see you this evening.''

The young man's extreme good looks had given Vanessa the excuse she needed. She would let the servants and everyone else think she was having an affair with him. It might even be necessary to seduce him—just for the sake of appearances, of course.

As she maneuvered the car through late-afternoon traffic, her spirits rose. Her life had taken on a decidedly interesting edge, and she was enjoying the risks she was taking. Not that she hadn't taken risks before, but they had never been like this. Just drinking and doping and screwing around in the ghettos of Los Angeles never produced the kind of high she was getting from trying to foil her father's cronies.

She used to think it would serve her father right if she were found dead in the slums, but now that he was gone, the need to punish him by abusing herself seemed foolish. She would outsmart him . . . she alone would outsmart all those men with all their millions. And in the process, she suspected that she might also save her immortal soul. If she still had one.

50

Other Plans

Selena tried to keep her emotions under control, but it was difficult. The old nagging doubts about her place in the scheme of things were back in full force and throbbingly painful. It was as if the gods had decreed that life wouldn't ever work for her. Had she been born under some evil curse?

Dan's wife's imminent return had not really taken her by surprise. That's the way it had always been for her. Whenever she thought she finally had the situation in control, it blew up in her face. Her mother had always laughed it off. "Life's what happens to you while you're busy making other plans," Ginny always said, but Selena refused to believe it.

Even when she was a little girl, she had believed that if she just tried hard enough and was smart enough, she could shape the world and the people in it to be as she wanted them to be. She had been successful manipulating people and events, but never in anything that seriously mattered to her. Dan was just the latest in a series of disappointments in her schemes. Unfortunately, he was the most important.

Selena decided not to panic. If Cake returned and told Dan that she planned to stay—that would be the time to start worrying. She'd save her tears for that. Now she had to be cool.

She arrived at the office early the next morning to find Dan already there, intently leaning over a drawing board examining a blueprint. She walked over to him and touched him on the shoulder.

Smiling sweetly, she said, "Good morning. I see you couldn't sleep either."

Dan shook his head, and she was relieved to see that he felt a bit shameful. "No, and I'm sorry about last night. It wasn't a very nice thing to do, was it?"

Of course it wasn't, you son of a bitch, she thought, but said, "It was the best thing to do, really. You needed to be alone to get accustomed to the change of situation. I understand completely. I just hope that everything works out for you the way you want it to."

"Thanks, Selena, I don't know what I'd do without you. I sent a note to the payroll clerk to increase your salary."

"Really, that's not necessary, Dan. I'm extremely well paid now. Besides, I've never placed a dollar value on our relationship." It was difficult to keep the bitterness out of her voice.

"The raise has nothing to do with us personally. It's entirely for your work here in the office. I want you to understand that."

"Well, then, all right. But you know how much I enjoy working here. It's difficult to think about leaving and starting all over again somewhere new," Selena sighed.

"It's premature to be thinking about that now. No matter what happens, you'll always have a good job here in this firm. I hope you won't let any personal feelings interfere with our business relationship."

You bastard. You want to have your cake and eat it too, she fumed, and was not amused by her inadvertent pun. "Dan, I think you ought to know that if everything is over for us, I may have to leave." Her voice softened, and she looked directly into his eyes. "I don't think I could handle seeing you every day . . . working with you . . . talking to you . . . if I could never touch you . . . or kiss you . . . or make love to you." Her tone was sensual, her lips moist and quivering, and her eyes glistened with emotion. "I'm sorry."

She turned and hurried into her own office and closed the door. That should give the bastard something else to think about today besides his wife's return. If he had trouble with the house and the garden, just let him contemplate steering the course in the bedlam of this office. Little by little he had abandoned all the details to her, and if she had to leave, he'd have one hell of a time keeping things going. She'd make sure of that.

51

Lost Loves

As the plane glided onto the runway and touched down, Trish tried to focus on the coming meeting with Dan, but her mind kept slipping back to New York and Red. The long-term effects of his injury had probably not been determined yet, and she hated it that she could not be with him now when he needed all the love and encouragement he could get. She wasn't sure that Gloria would give him enough, but one thing he did not need right now was the complication of the other woman. And that's all she was or ever would be. The lure of power and the presidency were more competition than she could handle. God knows she hadn't even been able to compete with a bitchy little secretary.

Well, now she had been both wife and other woman. She hadn't been too successful in either role, but did that make her a failure as a woman? Dammit, no. If she had learned one thing in this strange and exciting experience, it was that she had some value in and of herself and was not to be measured only in terms of her relationship to some man. She was a woman who had left her husband and had done something worthwhile. Now she was coming home, but not on her knees.

Since it was early in the afternoon, Trish decided to talk to her friend Joyce before she called Dan. Strange that she would be more eager to see a friend than to see the man who had fathered her children. On the other hand, Joyce had never betrayed her.

The house was cool and still as she walked through the familiar rooms. Everything looked just as she had left it, and yet she had the feeling that she was walking through the rooms of another woman's life. How long had she been gone? . . . Only a few weeks, but it seemed to have been a whole other lifetime.

She walked into the kitchen and found it clean and tidy. Either Dan had brought his sense of order into the house or Selena had.

Trish carried her suitcase up the stairs and into her bedroom. The bed was made, and everything looked exactly as it had the night she left. Sniffing the air, she smelled perfume. Selena had been here. Maybe not as recently as last night, but surely not long ago.

Going into the bathroom, Trish picked up the towel that hung at her side of the dressing table and held it to her nose. No perfume there. Only the fresh smell of clean laundry. Casually she pulled open the top drawer of her dressing table and saw an array of unfamiliar cosmetics. She laughed, and whispered, "You bitch." Selena was so damned obvious. Why did she find Selena amusing now, when just a short time ago she considered her to be threatening and invincible? Because I'm not Cake anymore, and I don't want to be, she concluded.

Trish left the house and went across the street to ring Joyce's doorbell. She needed to talk to someone she could trust. She hoped Joyce would be home.

Suddenly the door was thrown open, and a delighted and astonished Joyce yelled, "Cake, for God's sake, did you just drop out of the damned sky?"

Hugging each other, the two women made no attempt to keep their tears of joy hidden.

"Sort of. I just flew in from New York."

"God, let me look at you. Wheee . . . that's some expensive suit you've got on. I just bet you didn't get it at Macy's."

"Saks, actually."

"Come on in. I just now fixed myself a fresh pot of tea. Have you eaten?"

"Yes, on the plane."

They sat and talked for several hours. Trish told Joyce all about her Manhattan adventures, discreetly omitting the part about Vanessa Fallon.

Joyce was suitably impressed. "Was Red O'Shea what you expected? I mean . . . was it like old times?"

"Much better than I dreamed. You know, Joyce, I really went back there hoping to have an affair with him just to punish Dan for cheating on me with Selena. Red was also an old longing that had never been fulfilled. I almost wish I'd been disappointed. I loved every minute I was with him, but I have sense enough to know when to get out. I fell in love with him all over again, but there's no future in that. He wants to be the president of the United States, and he should be."

"I heard on the news that he's doing fine. One of his representatives said that he was doing so well that he had decided to hold a small press conference in his room day after tomorrow."

Trish smiled. "See what I mean? He's a political animal with all the right instincts."

"He looks pretty sexy to me."

"He is, Joyce. He is."

"How come they let you leave town. Won't the press be on your tail, since you were with him at the time it happened?"

"Joe—he's Red's aide-de-camp, sort of—told me he'd take care of it. I was in the other room getting my purse when Red was shot and saw nothing at all. I gave my statement to the police, and Joe told them I was his friend, not Red's. There's always the chance they'll call me, but I don't think so. Red's wife was there almost immediately. You know, the press is not the watchdog you imagine it is. They can be diverted and manipulated easier than you might think.''

"Cake, I can't believe this is you talking. You sound so damn worldly and sophisticated. I think this trip was good for you.''

"Was it ever. I don't feel like a victim anymore. And by the way, everybody in New York called me Trish. You know, I never really liked 'Cake.' My parents called me Patty, but the nasty little boy next door started calling me Patty Cake . . . it got shortened to Cake . . . and it stuck. It sounds so sweet and gooey. When I started high school, my friends called me Trish, but my family used Cake, and so did Dan. Anyway, I'm not coming home as Cake. She disappeared one dark and dreary night, never to be seen again. Call me Trish. Please.''

"I'll try, but don't get mad at me if I slip occasionally. Have you talked to Dan yet?''

"Not since I called to tell him I was coming home.'' Her voice was quiet, and she stared intently into her teacup.

"It won't be as bad as you think. He missed you, Cake . . . Trish. He was really desperate, and I must confess I treated him like shit,'' Joyce gloated, "and loved every glorious minute of his misery.''

"I'm not going to call him, I'll just be there when he walks into the house.'' Trish stood up. "Well, I'd better be on my way. If my car still runs, I want to go out to the hospital and see Dan's mother. She's been on my mind and my conscience since I left. I'll talk to you tomorrow, okay?''

"I'm glad you're back . . . Trish,'' Joyce said.

'I'm not sure I am . . . but it's awfully good to see you,'' Trish replied.

"Are you going to stay?"

Trish smiled. "I really don't know. It all depends."

At home, Trish went to the garage, where her beloved old station wagon sat waiting for her. Dan had tried to get her to trade it in on a new car, but she had insisted it would be like trading in an old friend for a new one. It had taken her and her children and their friends many places. It had transported Rob's sabot to the bay, Trina's Girl Scout troop on camp-outs, and thousands and thousands of bags of groceries. No, it would be her car until it was too old and infirm to be driven, and then she would send it to the graveyard for a proper interment.

She was pleasantly surprised when the car started immediately. Dan must have driven it occasionally to keep the battery charged.

The sun had broken through the clouds, and the temperature was climbing into the seventies as she drove onto the freeway. It felt good to be behind the wheel of a car again. In New York, people rarely had an opportunity to drive peacefully down the highway. She enjoyed driving and had missed it.

Trish's second surprise was not a pleasant one. The sight of Dan's mother, the woman she had grown to love almost as much as she had loved her own mother, upset her. For a long time Trish sat by her mother-in-law's bed, holding her frail wisp of a hand. As she listened to her labored breathing, Trish tried to will her mother-in-law back to life and consciousness. She wanted so much to speak with her one last time. It was painful to accept the fact that although her heart was beating, Elizabeth's spirit was gone.

As she left, Trish stopped at the nurse's desk to inquire about her mother-in-law's condition, and the nurse told her, "She's been like that for over a week now. Her heart is failing too. I'm surprised she's hung on this long. She must have a very strong will."

Trish managed to hold back her sobs until she reached the car, and then her tears came in a rush of pent-up emotion. Resting her head on the steering wheel, she wept . . . for Dan's mother, who was her friend . . . for her illusions, which were gone . . . and for lost loves.

52

It's Your Funeral

Richard Terhune decided that it was time to confront the issue head-on and made his way to Columbia Presbyterian Hospital. The newspapers and television stations were reporting Senator O'Shea out of danger, and Richard wanted to talk to him. He figured there was an outside chance that he could talk his way past a few nurses.

Security was tight. Even though there were few policemen around, Richard could tell by all the men floating around the place in three-piece suits that both the Secret Service and the local constabulary were on the alert. He suspected that some of them were from the FBI too. It wasn't going to be easy.

He stopped at a front desk manned by volunteers who received and delivered flowers.

"How do you do? I had some flowers sent to Senator O'Shea this morning. Do you know if they've been received?" he asked.

The woman answered with a smile, but her tone was a trifle exasperated. "I really couldn't tell you, sir. We've had so many deliveries of flowers to him that he just can't accept any more. He's asked us to send them to the children's ward."

"What a nice gesture." As Richard spoke, he glanced down at the list in front of her and saw that O'Shea was in room 430. Years ago he had learned that reading upside down was a very handy skill to acquire.

As soon as the elevator door opened onto the fourth floor, Richard knew he was in the right place. The corridor was swarming with security personnel. He went directly to the desk to announce himself. He had learned never to act suspicious when he was near men wearing shoulder holsters.

"How do you do? I'm Richard Terhune, and I would like to speak with Senator O'Shea's assistant, Joe Franklin. I was told by his office that he was here with the senator."

"There's no one with him right now, although he had several visitors earlier today."

"Well, then, would it be possible for you to take the senator a note for me?"

"I suppose that would be all right."

Quickly Richard took his business card from his pocket and wrote on the back, "Representing Vanessa Fallon . . . can we talk?"

He handed it to the nurse, and she walked to a room halfway down the corridor where a policeman in uniform was posted outside the door. She was inside only about thirty seconds and then returned to say, "Senator O'Shea wants you to come right in . . . but please, we're limiting his visitors to ten minutes."

Richard smiled at her as he hurried away. "Thank you, nurse. I'll remember your kindness."

Before he entered the room, a policeman did a thorough check for weapons. O'Shea was propped up in bed reading. He looked pale, and his shoulder was in a cast.

"Come in, Terhune, you old bastard. The last time we saw each other you were advising Armand Harrison to take the Fifth before my committee on organized crime. Don't you ever get tired of keeping crooks out of the reach of justice?" He spoke in a hoarse stage whisper.

"Well, Senator, it's nice to see that sniper didn't damage your spirit. Mind if I sit down?"

"Be my guest. You'll have to do the talking. It hurts when I do. What do you want?"

"Has the room been swept?"

"It's clean. The FBI took care of that."

"And you trust them? Pretty naive, Senator. Remember J. Edgar? He was the biggest bugger of them all. Anyway, I thought you should know that I put your friend Trish on the plane for Los Angeles yesterday. I also think you should know that Milton Wise is dead." Richard proceeded to tell the senator everything that he knew.

Red listened silently, making no comments. When Richard was finished, there was a long pause before Red responded. "I appreciate your concern, but there's nothing you can do. The only thing I'm at liberty to tell you is that if I can't get this thing solved soon, I intend to withdraw from the presidential race."

Richard was astounded. "You can't be serious. You're practically a shoo-in for the nomination and probably the election. People everywhere have crossed party lines to support you."

"I know that, but I may have no choice. Believe me, this is not anything that I want to have happen. My options are limited . . . but I appreciate your concern. When you go back to Los Angeles, check on Trish, if you can. None of this has anything to do with her, but I'd hate to see her get caught in the cross fire."

"So would I, and I'm a little worried about those thugs who forced Milt's car into the river. I hope you can convince them she's not involved. By the way, did you get a look at the gunman who shot you?"

"I didn't see anybody." The senator's manner was flat and calm, but not totally convincing. "Besides, whoever did it wasn't important. I want the man who hired the gun."

"Look, Senator, don't underestimate your enemy. It might be fatal. Is there any chance that Trish might be used as a pawn to force you to do something?"

"No. She wouldn't be involved. This has nothing to do with her. I'm an old soldier, you know. So don't worry. I was trained never to underestimate my enemy."

"Then it's your belief that Trish is safe? Are you sure I shouldn't put someone on her to watch her?"

"Take my word, she'll be fine as long as she stays in Los Angeles . . . and away from me." Richard sensed the regret in the senator's words. "And I'd advise you to do the same."

"Thanks for the advice, but it's a little late for me to start playing it safe. Someone killed a good friend of mine, not to mention cheating me out of my time and a lot of my money. I intend to see that they don't get away with it."

"It's your funeral, but good luck. By the way, do you still own all the judges in California?"

Terhune shook his head and smiled. "You know, Senator, everybody accuses me of buying judges. People just don't want to accept the fact that I'm the best damn lawyer in the country."

"You're good, I'll admit, but you have rotten taste in clients."

"Innocent people don't want to pay my price. The guilty ones have to. Nice to see you're okay." Terhune turned to leave the room but stopped at the door for one last remark. "By the way, I hope you don't drop out of the race. I intend to support you."

"In that case, be extra careful. I'd like to have you on my team."

Richard walked out of the room and down the corridor to the elevator. He was perplexed. How could O'Shea be so sure that Trish was safe? Suddenly he had the answer. Of course. She had not heard the information that Vanessa had imparted to O'Shea, and in some way the senator had managed to convey that knowledge to . . . whom?

It was time to go back to Los Angeles. Richard wanted to talk to Vanessa Fallon.

53

Time-Honored Ritual

In her own house again, Trish walked upstairs to the bedroom. Why did she feel like a stranger here? She looked at the bed and wondered how many times Selena had lain between her sheets. Morbidly she pulled back the spread and the blanket. It had been made perfectly; the sheets were pristine and unwrinkled.

She started to unpack her bag, but premonition stopped her. Was she really coming home to stay, or was this just a brief stop on a journey somewhere else? How had it happened that prim, proper little Cake Halliday had become a restless wanderer?

She walked downstairs to the kitchen to fix herself a cup of tea. It was almost eight o'clock. Dan had probably stopped for a quick dinner at Devin's, and would be home soon.

Taking her cup of tea into the family room, Trish settled on the couch in front of the television set. She turned the set on, but she barely watched the colored picture flicker and move. She wasn't really paying attention to anything that happened on the screen. Her thoughts were thousands of miles away in a hospital room. She was sorry she had not been given the chance to have one last talk with Red. She would miss him terribly. He was like a bright fire in the winter, warming and comforting, and a little dangerous. He was so easy to love.

Finally she heard the door to the garage open, and her heart began to beat furiously. Dan was home, and the encounter that she dreaded was about to take place.

"Dan," she called. "Is that you?"

"Cake? Where are you?"

"In here . . . the family room." She walked toward the sound of his voice. The moment they saw each other, a dramatic tension filled the air. They both stopped in their tracks and stared. A smile crossed Trish's lips, unexpectedly, gratefully. God, Dan looked wonderful. He was even more handsome than she had remembered. The familiarity they had once shared warmed her, and she felt an impulse to take him in her arms and hold him. But then she decided that she wanted *him* to welcome *her* home.

His response was less than she hoped it would be. There was no smile on his lips, nor were his arms open to embrace her.

"Well, this is a surprise. You didn't tell me that you were coming home right away."

Her eyes dropped from his in disappointment. "Yes, I know. Sorry about that late call. I hope I didn't interrupt . . . anything," she said, the old bitterness creeping back into her tone.

Now it was Dan's turn to look away. "Not at all." There was a long pause, and when they looked at each other again he asked, "Why did you do it, Cake? Why did you leave me like that in the middle of a dinner party? Do you really hate me so much?" His voice was sad and his eyes pleaded for an answer.

"I couldn't hate you, Dan . . . ever. No matter what happens to us, you will always be an important part of my life. You're the father of my children." Her voice broke, and she was in tears. Without further talk, Dan strode toward her and took her in his arms. Quietly he led her back toward the couch, where they sat down and clung to each other until her sobs had subsided. Then, gently, he turned her face up to his and kissed her eyes, her nose, her cheeks, and her mouth. The last was a long, lingering kiss filled with memories of youth and passions past and almost forgotten. For a long time they held each other, kissing and caressing, and Trish thought to herself that kissing her husband was much like wrapping herself in her favorite old robe and putting her feet into a pair of well-worn but comfortable slippers. It was warm and familiar and comfortable.

After a while they got up from the couch and went to their bedroom, where they undressed and got into bed together. Then they made love.

Every action was performed the way it had been for the last twenty years. Dan kissed her and stroked her. She held him in her hand until he was engorged and ready, and then she guided him gently inside her. If there was anything different, it was that perhaps their kisses were longer and more engulfing than usual, which was a relief to them both. Neither had any words for the occasion.

Ordinarily Dan waited for Cake to have her orgasm before allowing himself to release, but as the minutes passed and nothing happened, he let himself go.

When it was all over and they were lying beside one another with his arm under her head, Dan said, "I'm glad you're home. I missed you."

Trish wanted to tell him that she was glad to be home and that she'd missed him too, but she couldn't bring herself to say the words. She had never been very good at lying. She realized one thing about herself. She had gone to New York to have an affair and punish her husband, but she had returned still carrying a heavy load of hostility. Even now she couldn't find it in her heart to forgive him for betraying her.

54

Ripe Mangoes

Vanessa had her cook prepare a hearty dinner of roast beef, browned potatoes, and apple pie with ice cream. That sturdy young man would enjoy a filling meal, she decided. What a handsome specimen he was, and what a nice household pet he would make, she thought, but then scolded herself for being diverted. She needed his brains, not his cock. Still, time and opportunity permitting, she wouldn't pass up the chance to check him out at both ends.

Chuck Ferris arrived on schedule, but he was not as tempted by the meal as she'd expected. "I'm a vegetarian," he responded when the juicy piece of meat was presented to him. A quick response by Stevens, however, saved the day. A huge salad with avocado, half a loaf of French bread, and a quart of ice cream were produced. Chuck declined any of the rare Bordeaux too. "I think alcohol's poisonous to your body. I used to drink beer when I was a kid in high school, but I never touch any of the stuff now."

"My, my . . . what a good little boy you are," Vanessa said mockingly. "Tell me . . . do you abstain from sex too?"

He answered her without any embarrassment, "No, I don't. That's one thing I don't think should be done in moderation.'' Vanessa raised her eyebrows. The lad was full of surprises.

''I'm sure glad my girlfriend feels the same way, because I also believe in monogamy. One man, one woman, you know,'' he proclaimed earnestly.

''To be sure. Now, if you've had enough to eat, let's get started. The computer is housed in a room just off my father's study.''

As he walked down the long corridor toward the study, Chuck was suitably impressed with the paintings on the walls. ''I guess that's a real Van Gogh there, isn't it?'' he asked.

Vanessa laughed. ''Yes, it is . . . and that's a real Seurat . . . a Renoir . . . a Matisse, and when you get into my father's study, you'll see a genuine Rembrandt behind his desk.''

Chuck was openmouthed. ''Are you kidding?''

''No shit, honey, no shit.''

The study was large and dark and lined with bookshelves to the ceiling. At the far end of the room a hand-carved mahogany spiral stairway led to a catwalk that wound around the room and gave access to the upper shelves.

''Jesus, what a collection of books. It looks like the library at the university.''

''Good choice of words, because that's where I plan to send them all. When the house is sold, of course.'' Vanessa went to a small door set into the shelves. It too was heavily carved of dark wood, and was unobtrusive. Inserting a key into the lock, she opened the door and peered into the dark room beyond. As she hit the switch, bright fluorescent light flooded the room.

''Good God,'' Chuck exclaimed when he saw the computer. ''A Fifty-one Hundred! An antique!''

''My father always wanted to be the first to have everything,'' she said, ''and it's been here for several years. As I remember, he spent a lot of money to have someone teach him how to use it. He was a brilliant man, and he couldn't stand the thought that technology might pass him by. Do you think you can use it?''

"I don't know . . . I think so. I took a class on the history of computers, and we spent some time at IBM. Besides, it will be fun to try. After all, it was made by a man, certainly it can be used by one. Give me a few hours to play around. This thing uses tapes, as I recall, to store data. Where are they kept?''

"They're in that file over there. Fortunately, I found the key to it. It's already unlocked.''

"Okay. If I have any trouble, I'll call you. What kind of information are you looking for?''

"I'm looking for a list of names, dates, agendas, meetings, et cetera.''

"What was the subject of the meeting?''

"I really would rather not say.''

"Look Mrs. Fallon, I can't operate in the dark. If you want me to talk to your computer, I need to know the language.''

Vanessa grew nervous. She took a package of cigarettes from the pocket of her satin jacket and started to put one in her mouth.

"Please don't smoke in here, Mrs. Fallon. It's a small room with no windows, and—''

"I know, I know, smoking gives you cancer,'' she interrupted him, but she replaced the cigarette in its pack.

He smiled. "Right. I need code words, subjects, key phrases . . . things like that. Do you want to think it over while I play around in here?''

"Yes . . . let me go through my father's desk and see what I can find. I'll be right out here if you want me for anything. Should I leave the door open?''

"If you don't mind. I get kind of claustrophobic in rooms without any windows.''

Vanessa sat down at her father's desk, and for the first time since he had died, she opened the drawers. She had never been allowed to touch anything on his desk when he was alive, and she felt intrusive. The ghost of Mike Fallon had not been exorcised yet. He was still haunting her, and she became the five-year-old who had been spanked for spilling ink all over the blotter on her father's desk once again.

Closing her eyes, she heard his roar of anger and the pain of her mother's pitiful pleas for mercy for her errant child. "Mike, please, please don't hit her. She's just a child. She didn't mean to do it. I promise I'll never let her near your desk again. Just don't hurt her. She's a good girl." And the supplicant's words faded, as she felt those huge hands push her mother away and grab her. He lifted her high in the air and shook her until she felt her teeth quivering. Then, there was the terror and the humiliation as he ripped her panties from her bottom and stretched her across his knees. Even now she could feel the slap of his large hand as it came crashing down on her buttocks again and again.

Vanessa closed her eyes and rested her head in her hands. Pressing her fingers against her temples, she tried to strangle the memory of that hideous day. Why did she allow him to torment her still? He was dead. God had punished him with suffering and pain, but it hadn't helped her. Wherever she went, he pursued her. Time after time he'd told her that she belonged to him. She was his chattel, his property, his slave . . . his child. His.

Vanessa picked up the antique glass inkwell and held it in her hand. Slowly she turned it upside down so that the dark fluid would pour out and stain the leather of the desktop, but nothing came out. The ink had dried long ago. "You win, Daddy . . . again," she whispered.

Inserting the key on her chain into each of the drawers, she unlocked them and began searching for something that would help Chuck. As she skimmed through her father's papers, she tried to recall any dropped clue, unusual expression, some half-remembered word. But nothing came to mind. The alcoholic daze in which she'd lived for so

many years severely restricted her memory. Maybe she
would have to undergo hypnosis to dig out the words she
needed.

At midnight she roused herself from a drowsy stupor
and went into the room where Chuck was still working.

"How're you doing?" she asked.

"Having fun. God, this thing is really primitive. Say,
does the word 'mango' mean anything?" he asked. "It
keeps coming up, but when I try to use it to enter a file, it
aborts. Got any ideas?"

Vanessa shook her head. "No, not really. My father had
them in the house all the time. He loved them, he said it
was like eating sweet perfume."

"Hmmm, let me try 'perfume' . . . 'sweet' . . . no, that
isn't it. Can you remember anything else about them?"

"Let's see . . . well, he liked them to be very ripe, and
he usually ate them in the morning for breakfast, but I
can't . . ."

As she spoke, Chuck entered the words "ripe mangoes"
into the computer, and suddenly the document appeared on
the small screen.

"Here, take a look and tell me if this is what we're
looking for."

Vanessa peered at the screen as Chuck let the document
scroll up so she could read it. "That's it, I'm sure that's
it," she exclaimed.

"Terrific. Now, do you want everything out of the files
with that code name?"

"Everything, everything. Young man, if you can print
out all the information I need, you won't have to worry
about money for a while. As a matter of fact, for being
able to do it in one night, I'm going to give you a bonus.
Now, get going on it."

"Gee, thanks, but five is plenty, really."

"Don't be a fool, Chuck—take the money and run.
How soon can you have the information printed out?"

"It all depends on how much there is . . . and cross your

fingers that the machine doesn't break down before we get finished. It's old and not as sophisticated or reliable as the current versions."

"Get to work. I'm going upstairs to get dressed. Just come out into the entry hall and call me when you're finished."

Vanessa hurried out of the room and raced up the stairs. She wanted to get the papers out of the house as soon as possible. She decided not to try for the airport. If someone were watching, it would be too clear a signal that something was going on. She would have to make contact with Trish or Millie. And she didn't dare call them from her house for fear her telephones were bugged.

Two hours later, Vanessa heard her name being called, and she hurried downstairs. Chuck handed her a sheaf of papers. "Here you go. All done. I hope it's what you were looking for."

Vanessa scanned the pages quickly, and as familiar names and places leapt out at her, she knew she had what Red O'Shea and the United States of America needed. It had been almost too easy.

"Come on back into the study, Chuck. Would you mind shutting down the computer and locking the room up for me? If it's all right, I'm going to go in to the safe and get the cash for you. I'd prefer not to write a check because I don't want anyone to know that I've given you that much money, okay? You won't have to tell the IRS about it then either."

"But that would be against the law."

"Have it your way. I need something else from you, however. I want you to drive me to a pay telephone so that I can make a call.

"You don't want to make the call from here?" His voice sounded wary and somewhat suspicious.

Vanessa realized that he was getting a little nervous about her, but years of practice and deceit had made lying as natural to her as breathing, and she was very inventive.

"Don't worry, Chuck. It's just my ex-husband causing me trouble. I'm trying to get custody of my daughter and he's trying to prove that I'm not a fit mother. Understand? I have to be very careful about what I say and do. I'm pretty sure my telephone is bugged. He'll go to any lengths to keep us separated."

"He must be a real jerk."

"He really is, Chuck. He's made my life a living hell. All he ever wanted was my money. And now he's using my child against me." The story was getting better and better. Time to quit while she was still ahead.

"That's really tough. Sure, I'll take you wherever you want to go. You can come over to my place to make your calls if you want to. My roommate works late at the bowling alley, and you'll be all alone."

"Thanks, but I'd better not. You've been a real godsend, you know that, young man?"

"I'm just glad I can be of help."

Vanessa went in to the safe where her father had stashed thousands of dollars in cash for emergencies. She counted out six one-thousand-dollar bills, put them into an envelope, and took another ten for herself.

Dashing upstairs to her bedroom, she changed into a pair of jeans and a cotton shirt, stuffed the sheaf of computer printouts inside her shirt against her back, and put on a windbreaker. The printout felt sticky and bulky, but it was not noticeable. Then she hurried back downstairs to the study, where Chuck was waiting for her.

"Okay, let's go. I think all the servants have turned in for the night, so let's be very quiet. I don't want anyone to know I've left the house. I closed my bedroom door and turned off my telephone. What time is it, anyway?"

"It's two in the morning."

"Let's go. Don't open the door until I shut off the security system. You go out first and get in the car. I'll turn off all the lights and then I'll join you. Get in on the passenger side and leave it open for me. If anybody's watching or listening, they'll hear and see only one car door close. Okay?"

"Sounds pretty sneaky."

"Yes, well, I'm pretty sure my husband is having me watched closely, and I don't want to be seen in the middle of the night with a handsome young man. Now, get going."

Everything went smoothly. When she got into the car, Vanessa slid down in the seat so that it looked as if Chuck were alone when he drove through the massive iron gates. A few minutes later she asked him to check to see if any cars had followed.

"I'm not sure. There's a car back there. Want me to find out?"

"Please." Damn. She was being watched.

Chuck slammed his foot down on the accelerator, and the car began to speed down the quiet thoroughfare. He turned several corners rapidly. "He's staying with us. Want me to try to lose him?"

"No, that's a professional back there. Find a bar that's open."

"A bar?"

"Yes, and don't ask questions."

Chuck drove toward downtown Los Angeles, and when they passed a seedy bar on Third Street called Hinkey's, Vanessa snapped, "That's it. Now, floor it around that corner. As soon as we're out of his vision, slow down so I can jump out."

"But you might get hurt!" he protested.

"Just do as I say, goddammit!" she ordered furiously.

With his lips set grimly, Chuck did as he was told. He wheeled around the corner at top speed and circled the block. When he was sure she would have enough time to get out before the pursuing car had them in view again, he jammed on the brakes. Vanessa threw open the door and jumped out, barely managing to stay on her feet. Running into the darkened alley, she pressed herself against the wall. Chuck accelerated the car again and raced away. Within seconds the other car wheeled into view and passed in hot pursuit. Vanessa smiled.

She waited a few minutes until she was certain she was in the clear and then she began to walk rapidly toward the bar. The street was deserted, but she kept looking over her shoulder to make sure she was alone.

When she arrived at the entrance, she hesitated. She'd spent a lot of time in dives like this, but tonight was the first time she'd ever been in one stone-cold sober. It was frightening.

55

The Only One Who Knows

Richard Terhune had left New York the morning after his visit with O'Shea. He had made some inquiries and learned that Vanessa Fallon was back home in her father's house in Hancock Park. It was time to confront her with what he knew and try to get her confidence.

When the plane landed in Los Angeles, he went directly to his office. A mound of letters and calls covered his desk, and although he wanted to ignore them, there were several that demanded immediate attention. He returned his accountant's call and listened patiently to his complaints, and then he returned a call from Trevor Houseman, who had been Milton Wise's partner until they'd had a falling-out several years ago. Trevor had left New York and established a firm in San Francisco.

"Trevor . . . Richard Terhune. How've you been?"

"Thanks for returning my call. Tough about Milt, wasn't it?"

Terhune sensed that Houseman had something to tell him. "Yeah, do you know anything about what might have happened to him?"

"That's what I called about. Coupla weeks ago Milt called me. He said he was working on some kind of a deal with you and if it worked out he'd have the money to buy out my share of an office building we bought in Manhattan a few years back.''

"Did he tell you anything else?" Richard asked.

"Yeah, but I don't want to be quoted on this, understand? It's strictly off the record. I'm not accusing anybody or implying anything.''

Richard sensed that Houseman's information was important. "Of course. Go ahead.''

"Well, when he told me about getting the money, I got sort of sarcastic. That building's been appreciating in value pretty rapidly, and it would take a lot of dough to buy me out.''

"And?" Richard asked, beginning to be interested in the story.

"I didn't believe Milt had enough money until he told me that Jim Danton was also involved. You know who he is, don't you?" Houseman asked.

"Of course. Did he say anything else?" Richard's mind was clicking off facts, and everything was dropping neatly into place.

"No, in fact, he got pretty upset after he told me about it. He said that Danton would be furious if word got out that he was involved. He made me promise to keep my mouth shut.''

"Why are you telling me this?"

"I don't know what kind of deal you're in with that old buzzard Danton, but his politics just don't seem to jibe with yours. And I don't believe for one minute that Milt ran his car off a bridge. He was a maddeningly cautious driver.''

"I agree. And thank you for calling me, Trevor. All I can tell you is that the information you just gave me is very important. Danton's name is the missing piece in the puzzle. As soon as I get it all put together, I'll call you, okay? And don't tell anybody else.''

"Hell, you don't have to worry about that. I intend to stay as far away from this as I can. You know, Milt and I had our problems, but he was a good guy, and I'm sorry things worked out between us the way they did.''

"I'll be in touch." Richard put down the telephone, anxious to end the conversation so he would have time to think. The circle was growing smaller. Vanessa, her father, now her father's closest friend—but what the hell was the connection with the senator? If there ever was a politician who would not appeal to the extreme right wing of the Republican party, it was Red O'Shea. And Fallon and Danton had never been anywhere near the center.

Next, Richard buzzed his secretary and asked her to telephone Vanessa Fallon. As he waited, he tried to fit the pieces of the puzzle together.

A few minutes later, his secretary called on the intercom and said, "I'm sorry, but Miss Fallon is not at home. The butler said he didn't know when to expect her back. I left your name and number."

"Try again in a couple of hours . . . and keep on trying until you get her."

Terhune looked at the stack of work on his desk and decided to tackle it. There was nothing more he could do until he talked to Vanessa Fallon. Tomorrow morning he would call his good friend Ted McCormack, who was a superior-court judge in Manhattan. He would tell him that he'd heard Danton might be involved in Wise's murder and let him take it from there. After all, if anyone had two million bucks to spend looking for somebody, it was Danton. It was rumored that the old boy had socked away billions he'd made from government contracts with his armament factories and from the building companies that were so successful in getting military installation contracts. He was a wily old bastard who professed to have high moral and religious values, as long as they didn't interfere with business.

The two-million-dollar price on Vanessa's head still bothered Richard, however. In spite of his enormous personal wealth, Danton was notorious for being a penurious son of a bitch. If Danton had put up the money, whatever information Vanessa had was worth at least twice that amount.

Terhune sent his secretary home at six and continued to try to reach Vanessa Fallon until about ten that evening, but there was no response.

Finally he gave up and went home. His body was still on New York time, and he was exhausted. Passing up dinner, he undressed and fell into bed. The sound of a telephone ringing awoke him from a deep sleep. It was three in the morning, but the voice on the other end brought him to attention.

"Richard, it's Trish. Thank heaven you're back in L.A.! I'm sorry to awaken you, but I need your advice."

"Trish, are you all right? Where are you?"

"I'm at home, here in Woodland Hills. Vanessa just called me. She's in some bar in downtown Los Angeles and wants me to meet her there as soon as possible."

"Is she drunk?"

"I don't think so. She told me she had something very important for Red, and she won't give it to anybody but me."

Terhune was alarmed. "How did she know where to find you?"

"She called Millie and got my telephone number. She says it's urgent."

"Trish, let me go with you."

"Dan's offered to go, but somehow I don't think it's fair to get him involved in this . . . and since you already are involved, I thought—"

"I'll come pick you up."

"No, that will take too long. I'll have Dan bring me to the Century Plaza Hotel. You can pick me up there at the car entrance."

"How long will it take you to get there?"

"Half an hour. The freeway's clear now, and Dan is a fast driver."

"I'll be there."

Richard put the telephone down and hurried into the bathroom. Since the Century Plaza Hotel was just five minutes away, there was time to shower and shave. What an interesting turn of events, he mused as he turned on the water.

56

No Place for a Lady

With some reluctance, Vanessa put her hand on the door and pushed. God knows what was waiting for her inside the bar, but she had to get off the street as quickly as possible, and she needed to use a telephone. She hoped there was a public one in the bar in working order.

The place was not crowded. In the dingy room lighted by only a few neon signs advertising various beers, three old men sat lounging at the bar. No trouble there. At the end of the room sitting at a table were two men that might be a problem. One was young and black and slightly built. The other was a white man, but he was huge. He had muscles that had gone to fat, he was dirty, and he looked at her through eyes that seemed to be sizing her up like a lean piece of meat.

Vanessa walked straight over to the bartender. "I need change for the telephone. Where is it?" she asked briskly. Mike had taught her the importance of erecting a facade of self-confidence and control whenever she felt the least bit threatened or afraid. This was quite obviously no time to be timid.

She handed the bartender a five-dollar bill, but he shook his head. "Don't have much change, lady."

"Then pour me a whiskey . . . double, straight."

Slamming a glass on the bar, he poured the whiskey,

and took her five-dollar bill. He gave her two quarters in change and a look that defied her to complain.

She picked up the glass, took a small sip, and almost gagged. The whiskey was pure rotgut. She wanted to throw it in his face, but instead she merely asked where the telephone was. He nodded toward the back of the room, and she turned and strode purposefully toward it, looking neither right nor left. She was grateful that the wall phone was not in the rest room where someone could easily follow her, although it wasn't bloody likely that any of the seedy bar patrons would move off their filthy asses to help her in any case, she thought sourly.

She dialed the long-distance operator and called Millie collect in New York. She spoke softly, but Millie sensed the urgency in her voice and gave her Trish's Los Angeles number right away.

As soon as she had it, Vanessa called Trish.

"Sorry to get you out of bed, but I've got to see you right away. I've got those papers for your friend, but there's no way I can deliver them to him because I'm being followed. You're going to have to do it for me. Can you meet me tonight? I'm in Hinkey's Bar on Third near Vermont."

"It'll take me a while to get there."

"For God's sake, hurry, Trish. This is no place for a lady." Her voice was low so that no one could hear her, and she cupped her hand around the mouthpiece as she spoke.

"I'll do my best," Trish responded. When the conversation ended, Vanessa looked around to see if anyone was listening to her before she replaced the receiver. To her chagrin, the two men who worried her were watching intently. Pretending that there was still someone on the other end of the line, Vanessa raised her voice just enough so that it could be heard and said, "Thank you so much for calling the police. How soon will they be here to pick me up?" She waited a moment as if listening for a reply, and then said, "Good. I'll tell them everything." As she walked back to the bar to get her drink, she did not avoid looking directly into the eyes of the men staring at her. As Mike always said, if you look straight at people, they'll assume you've got balls, even if you haven't. She wondered how long she would have to keep up the charade.

The bartender was drying glasses on a filthy towel, and her stomach churned at the thought that she'd have to put one of the glasses to her mouth. It was a miracle that she'd survived all those terrible binges she'd gone on. The good Lord protects drunks, she decided, when He should really be watching the children.

The bartender spoke. "I never seen you around here before."

She smiled enigmatically and said nothing. She tasted the liquor in the glass again, but it was too disgusting to drink. It would be a long wait. Leaning toward the bartender, she asked softly, "Have you got any coffee? I better not be drinking when the police arrive."

He poured her a cup of burned black coffee and pushed it toward her. "That'll be a buck more," he said through yellow, decayed teeth. She put another five-dollar bill on the bar, and he gave her four ones in change, which she didn't pick up. Let him think she was going to order more, she decided.

Out of the corner of her eye Vanessa saw the two men get out of their chairs and move toward her. Her muscles tensed to defend herself, and as they approached, she remained rigidly seated on the barstool, exerting a great effort of will not to look around as they passed behind her. When they were gone, she breathed a deep sigh of relief mixed with a measure of triumph that her inspired remark about the police had sent them scurrying. Bitterly she reflected that it wasn't the first time she'd played a little game of make-believe to protect herself. In her father's house, it had been her only salvation.

57

Fast Company

"I'm sorry I can't tell you more, Dan, but I have to hurry," Trish said as she headed toward the bathroom to dress.

"I'll be ready in five minutes," he informed her, and there was no more conversation. Trish's mind was filled with the news that Vanessa needed her to transport information secretly to Red. She was excited and eager to go back to the life she had enjoyed, and she experienced a wonderful feeling of importance.

Dressed in a pair of good wool slacks, boots, a silk blouse, and a warm sweater, Trish stood at a mirror running a comb through her hair. She put her cosmetics into a small bag and jammed it into her large shoulder bag. She avoided making any kind of contact with Selena's cosmetics. Somehow, they seemed to belong in that drawer now more than hers did.

On her way out the door, Trish grabbed a raincoat. If she had to go directly to the airport, she'd be ready.

Dan was waiting in the car when she scurried out of the house, and they sped off immediately.

Dan was the first to speak. "I wish you'd tell me what the hell is going on.

"This has nothing to do with us. It's political, I suppose. I really don't know what it's all about, except that it has something to do with information Vanessa Fallon gave O'Shea. Now she's got the documentation, and she can't risk taking it to him herself.''

''Aren't you sticking your neck out? Whoever took a shot at a senator of the United States wouldn't be above doing the same to a housewife from Woodland Hills.''

''You're right, and I'm scared. That's why I called Richard Terhune. He'll know what to do, and I trust him.''

''You're traveling in pretty damn fast company. I hope you know what you're doing.''

''So do I. Dan, I might not be back home for a while.''

''What do you mean by a while?''

Trish did not want to make a commitment that she might regret. ''I don't know, Dan. I wish everything could be just the way it was, but I don't think I'm the same person I used to be.''

''What about the children? They have a stake in what happens to our marriage, don't they?''

''Of course they do, but I don't feel like going into it tonight, okay? There'll be plenty of time when I get back.''

''Will you answer one question for me?''

''If I can.''

''Did you leave because of my . . . relationship with Selena?''

''Of course I did, Dan. Why else would I have walked out of my home . . . away from my family and everything I loved?''

''How did you find out?''

Trish was exasperated. Why did he persist in this discussion right now when she was preoccupied with the job she had to do? ''Selena told me. She had to outline it for me because I was too stupid to see things for myself. And that told me a lot about my relationship with you . . . and my view of myself . . . a lot of things I didn't want to know.''

"How long did you know before . . . you left?"

"I don't want to tell you, it's too awful."

"I need to know."

"I lived with it for six miserable, humiliating weeks."
Just talking about it made her cringe with embarrassment.
"I didn't have the courage to let you know. In my anger
and humiliation, I tried to pretend that everything would
work out all right if I just ignored it until it went away.
Every day I prayed that you would get tired of her and
come home to me, your true love." Tears were falling
from her eyes as she spoke, but her voice had a bitter
edge.

"I didn't want to hurt you."

"What do you mean, you didn't want to hurt me? How
noble of you. All along, you just had my best interests at
heart. How stupid of me not to see it."

"You're still furious with me, aren't you?" Dan said.

She tried to calm herself, but the anger bubbled up and
spilled over. "Yes, yes I am. There were times I wanted
to kill you, but what was worse, sometimes I wanted to
kill myself. I thought it was all my fault. Somewhere, I
kept telling myself, I had failed. I hadn't kept the house
clean enough, I hadn't been a good enough cook . . . I
was getting old and ugly. It took me a long time to realize
it was you who were to blame. You were self-centered and
selfish and self-indulgent. But you've always been that
way. When you added deceit to your list of shortcomings,
it became unbearable to live under the same roof with
you."

"Did you have an affair with O'Shea while you were in
New York?"

"Do you really want me to tell you?"

"Yes."

"Good God, is that all that's important to you? Aren't
you interested in the fact that I became close and good
friends with the man who is going to be the president of
the United States? That he found me intelligent enough

and interesting enough to confide in me and let me run part of his campaign? Don't you want to know that I think he's the most brilliant, most charismatic, warmest, most human man I've ever met? Is it still important to know whether he possessed my body when you know that he still possesses my mind and my spirit?''

"You did have an affair with him, then?"

"It's none of your business, Dan. The day you put that cock of yours inside your secretary was the day you relinquished all rights to know what goes on in my life. God knows, I'm no prude, and I believe that everybody's entitled to live his own life in his own way, but if fucking Selena was so goddamned important that you were willing to risk our marriage for it, then our marriage wasn't very important to you, was it?''

"I never heard you use that kind of language before, Cake. You're like a different person.

"Just once in our lives, let's argue without focusing the attention on my failings. In fact, this discussion is at an end. There's the hotel, and I've got important things to do.''

"Our marriage isn't important?"

"It used to be. I'm just not sure that I can live with a man who brings out such anger in me. Marriage wasn't meant to be an adversarial relationship. Thanks for the ride, Dan. Don't worry if you don't hear from me for a few days.''

As Trish opened the door and got out of Dan's car, a dark blue Plymouth sedan pulled up behind them, and she recognized Richard behind the wheel. Without looking back at her husband, she walked over and got into Richard's car.

"Goodness, I expected a limousine," she laughed. "You look like one of us common folk in this car.''

"That's exactly why I own it. Sometimes I need to go to parts of the city where I don't want to stand out like a sore thumb. Neither my Mercedes, nor my Rolls, nor my limousine is very good for that."

"Here's the address of the bar."

"That's not a good part of town. What the hell is she doing there?"

"I got the feeling that she was trying to get away from someone."

"I hope nothing happens to her before we get there."

"I hope nothing happens to any of us," Trish remarked.

"Don't worry. I came prepared." Richard opened his jacket to show her that he wore a shoulder holster with a handgun. "I learned to carry one of these years ago. I've dealt with some pretty gruesome characters."

"Why did you get involved in criminal law?"

"Money, my dear young lady, money. I love money, and I love to spend it. Men facing life in prison or worse pay their attorneys vast sums of money, and they rarely haggle about the price.

"You try to picture yourself as a very cynical, materialistic person, but you're not. You spend a lot of time on causes that don't pay you a thing. I know. I found out all about you."

"Just hedging my bets, my dear. If there's a heaven, I don't want to pave my way too efficiently to hell. Now, tell me exactly what Vanessa said."

58

A Very Hot Potato

Richard pulled up in front of the bar, and as they got out of the car, he took a quick look around to make sure they were alone. The street was deserted. Taking Trish's arm, he hurried her inside. Vanessa was seated on a barstool smoking a cigarette and holding a cup of coffee. She said nothing to them until they were close to her.

"Who the hell is this?" Vanessa asked, her eyes narrowing with suspicion as she looked at Richard.

"Vanessa, this is Richard Terhune. I brought him along because he knows everything that I know about your situation, and I trust him," Trish explained.

"I hope to God you're right, my friend, or we're both in big trouble," Vanessa replied.

"Come on, we can talk in the car," Richard suggested, but Vanessa did not move.

"No, I don't want all of us to leave here together. If I've slipped up and we're being observed, it would be better if we left separately. I've already called for a cab," Vanessa replied. "It should be here any minute. Trish, have you made a reservation on a plane to New York yet?"

Trish shook her head. "No, I left the house as soon as you called."

"Then let's find out when the next flight leaves," Vanessa

said, getting off the stool and walking back to the telephone. Trish and Richard followed her.

"Why don't I call someone and charter a private plane, then we won't have to wait for a scheduled flight. I'm pretty sure nothing leaves until at least seven or eight in the morning," Richard suggested.

Vanessa was adamant. "No! Absolutely not. I don't want a big deal made of this. Trish can just slip quietly into New York, and nobody will know about it, we hope. A private jet would be too damn conspicuous."

"Well, I don't like the idea of Trish wandering around an airport all night by herself carrying something that is obviously a very hot potato. Just what, by the way, is this thing she's supposed to take to the senator?"

"You mean you really don't know what it is? You're not just playing dumb? Did you know my father at all?"

"Everybody knew your father, but I was never one of his friends or admirers. I didn't like his politics," Richard said somewhat impatiently.

"Well, I have a list of names, places, and agendas that I promised I'd get for Senator O'Shea." As Vanessa spoke, she looked around the room to make sure once more that no one else was listening. "O'Shea didn't think my story was totally credible, at first. He thought I was some paranoid crackpot, but I guess that bullet he took in the neck made a believer of him."

Richard looked at her skeptically. "Okay, try me. Maybe I'll be a little easier to convince."

"Not now. There's the cab," Vanessa said, and nodded toward the door, where a driver was just coming in.

"Anybody here call a cab?" the man asked.

Richard walked toward him. "Yes, we did, but we're not quite ready yet. Why don't you go outside and wait for us, okay?"

The man smiled. "Whatever you say, mister."

Meanwhile, Trish, who had reached American Airlines

on the phone, made a reservation for Margaret Evans on the first morning flight to New York.

She was a little nervous. "The first flight doesn't leave until eight-thirty. It's after three now. By the time I get to the airport, I'll still have four hours to wait."

"I don't like this at all," Richard complained. "I think it would be better if Trish went home and I took these papers to O'Shea."

"But I want to do it, Richard, really I do."

"She has to," Vanessa agreed. "I'm not sure O'Shea would believe they were genuine if somebody else brought them to him, and if anything is going to be done, he has to believe that what I told him is true."

"And what was that?" Richard asked.

"It's a little complicated. Tell you what, take me home with you, and I'll tell you all about it. I was followed from my house tonight, and I managed to give them the slip, but I'd rather not go home until after Trish has delivered the papers. Then it won't matter, because the shit will have hit the fan, but good."

"Vanessa, are you aware that I was offered two million dollars to find you in New York?" Richard asked.

She smiled, but one corner of her mouth turned down in a slight grimace. "I'll just bet you were. How come you didn't take it?"

Richard laughed shortly. "God knows I tried, but I was fired, and then the man who hired me was pulled out of the river. Ever hear of Milton Wise?"

Vanessa shook her head. "No. Is that why you're involved in all this now?"

"No, I called him," Trish interjected. "I'd already told him everything I knew."

"I'm interested in getting to the bottom of this whole affair," Richard explained. "A good man was killed—probably to keep his mouth shut. The only people I want to see get away with murder are my clients. Besides, I have a fierce curiosity."

"The cab's waiting," Trish announced. "If I'm going to take it, hadn't you better give me the papers and let me leave?"

"Come in the rest room with me," Vanessa said, and Trish followed her into the dark, foul-smelling toilet area.

Vanessa pulled the papers out of her shirt and handed them to Trish. "Here, stash them somewhere," she said.

"Help me. I'll put them in the same place. Tuck them under my bra in the back to hold them in position."

When they were finished, the two women emerged to find Richard talking to the bartender.

"What was that all about?" Vanessa asked suspiciously.

"He just asked me if I had a sandwich job going with you two. He said he'd never seen either of you around before."

Trish looked bewildered, but Vanessa enlightened her. "He thinks we're hookers, Trish. Tsk, tsk, and I thought I had him convinced I was calling the police."

Richard interrupted, "Trish, you'd better get in that cab and put some distance between you and Vanessa. I'll watch when you pull away to make sure you're not followed. If you are, I'll follow you to the airport, so don't worry. If you're clear, I'll meet you in New York at the Plaza Hotel in the Oak Bar for cocktails Tuesday night at eight, okay?"

Trish nodded and hurried out the door.

As her cab pulled away, Richard watched for signs of another car following her, but he saw nothing.

"I think she's clear. Let's get out of here, Vanessa."

"Good idea. The guy who was following my car might get smart and come back to this neighborhood to look around."

They drove to Richard's in silence, both occupied with their own thoughts. Richard hoped he had done the right thing letting Trish go on her own, and he wondered about the strange quirk of fate that had gotten him involved in something that was absolutely none of his business, especially when he already had so many problems of his own. But his old friend Milt was dead, and that proved to some extent that this wasn't all just a fairytale hatched by some crazy, overindulged daughter of a rich son of a bitch.

Richard glanced at Vanessa, and although it was too dark to see, he was sure that the haunted look was still in her eyes. He had a hunch that her story was going to be a doozy, and he was looking forward to it. You're a nosy bastard, Terhune, he said to himself.

Checking his rearview mirror, he noticed that there was a car following him. When he accelerated to see if it would keep pace, and it did, he turned a corner rapidly. The car stayed with him. Well, well, so someone was watching after all, he said to himself. There was no point in alarming Vanessa unnecessarily. He was almost pleased with this new development because it lent credence to Vanessa's fears and at the same time indicated that Trish had gotten away safely. Whoever was following them thought that Vanessa still had the papers. Richard chuckled. Good. Now just let that creep try to follow him through the tall iron gates at Century Woods. Richard knew all he had to do was stay ahead of the fucker until they got there. He stepped on the accelerator and headed onto the Santa Monica Freeway. In less than fifteen minutes they would be home free.

59

Arrangements

Selena put down the telephone and leaned back in her chair. Now, how should she use the important piece of information she had just received? She looked up at the clock. It was after nine and Dan hadn't arrived at the office, nor had he called to tell her why. Unusual behavior for him, but then, he was not acting himself at all nowadays. She picked up the telephone to call him at home, but there was no answer there either.

As she was mulling over her next move, Dan suddenly opened the door and walked in. She got to her feet and smiled warmly. "Good morning, Dan. I was getting a little worried about you . . . are you all right?" she asked. He looked terrible. His eyes were puffy and his face was the color of ash.

"I'm fine. Get me some coffee, please."

He strode into his office and closed the door before she had a chance to tell him about the phone call.

She hurried back to the coffeepot and filled his mug with the hot black liquid, splashed a small amount of milk in it, and walking carefully so as not to spill any, went back to his office. He sat slumped in his chair, looking morose and depressed. He was obviously not ready for any kind of a business meeting.

She set the coffee down on his desk. "Dan, would you like for me to call Blair Foster and postpone your meeting?"

He seemed not to have heard her. "Cake's gone again, Selena. This time for good." Dan said.

Selena did her best not to demonstrate her real feelings at the news. "Oh . . . are you terribly upset, Dan?"

So wrapped up was he in his own self-pity that he was barely aware of her presence or her voice. "Twenty years, two kids . . . and she walked away from it all . . . just like that. I'm small-time stuff now that she's been moving with the high and the mighty."

Selena stood quietly listening to every word and filing it away in her memory. Amazing, Cake had actually done exactly what Selena had hoped she would do. Finally. When a long moment had passed and it looked as if Dan weren't going to say anything more, she moved closer to the desk and said in a hushed voice, "Dan, I have something more important to talk about than Cake's leaving."

After a moment he looked up at her, and their eyes met. She finally had his attention, although she could tell that he could not believe there was anything more important than his wife's desertion.

"Dan, the convalescent hospital called a little while ago. It's about your mother."

"What . . . about my mother? Is she all right?"

"I'm so sorry I have to be the one to tell you, Dan . . . she died early this morning."

"Oh God, no," he said softly, and buried his face in his hands.

Selena moved across the room and around Dan's desk. First she put her hand on his shoulder, and then when he did not resist, she leaned down and put her arms around him.

Sorrow filled her voice as she spoke words that would comfort and reassure him. "I'm so sorry, truly I am. I know how much you loved her, and what a terrible loss you're feeling. She was a wonderful mother, and she was very proud of you and your success. She used to tell me on the telephone how happy you had made her over the years. Now, I don't want you to worry about the details. I'll take care of making all the funeral arrangements. Everything will be done beautifully, just as she would have wanted it.''

With soothing motions she ran her fingertips over the back of his neck as she crooned the words of solace. "I'll always be here for you, no matter what happens. I'll never leave you.''

60

One's Adversaries

"We're landing at Kennedy, Ms. Evans. Would you like a hot towel to freshen up?" The stewardess touched Trish's arm.

Trish took the towel and pressed it to her face. Her hands were shaking slightly from the sudden awakening. Nervously she thought about the delivery she still had to make, and about seeing Red again. It would be her first meeting with him since the paramedics had taken him away.

When the plane landed, she was the first out the door, and she strode through the terminal quickly. She was anxious to get the papers into Red's hands. Since she did not have to wait for luggage, she hopped into a taxi, gave the driver the name of the hospital, and sat back to look at the lights coming on in the city. It was almost five in the evening. Taking a mirror out of her purse, she checked her appearance. Would Red be as glad to see her as she was to see him?

At Columbia Presbyterian Hospital Trish stopped at the desk to make sure she would be admitted to the senator's room. Security was probably very tight.

"I'm sorry, ma'am. Senator O'Shea was released this morning."

Trish's heart sank. Now what would she do? She'd have to wait until the next morning to track him down.

"Perhaps you could tell me where he went. I've just brought some papers for him from . . . Washington. Is he at his home here in Manhattan?"

"I'm sorry, I really can't say."

Trish went back outside and waited for a taxi. The night was cold and damp, and she was shaking with nerves. She felt utterly alone. Finally a cab arrived, discharged its passengers, and she got in. She gave the driver Red's address on Sutton Place with only a dim hope that he would be there. As she had feared, the house was dark.

She got back into the cab. It was time to take another person into her confidence. She hoped Millie would be home.

"Trish! For God's sake, what're you doing back in New York so soon?" Millie yelped. There was no question about the delight in her voice as she hugged her friend.

"I just couldn't stand all that warm weather in California. I missed the suffering," Trish replied, and there was joy and relief in her voice.

"Come on inside. You're staying with me, aren't you?" Millie asked.

"If it's okay. You haven't got a live-in boyfriend or anything, have you?"

Millie closed the door behind them before she answered, and a wide smile lighted her face. "Well . . . not exactly . . . not yet, anyway," she whispered.

Trish was surprised that her little joke had hit so close to home. "No kidding . . . already? I just left. What happened?"

"Come on in and take off your coat. I just opened a bottle of burgundy."

"That sounds wonderful. I slept all the way from California, and I'm wide-awake now," Trish said, and was startled to hear another voice say, "Well, well, look who's here. I didn't expect to see you again so soon."

Trish whirled around and saw Joe Franklin standing at the entrance to the living room with a glass of red wine in his hand.

"This *is* a surprise, I must say," Trish gasped. "I never expected you two—

"Shut your mouth or you'll catch flies, my grandmother used to say. Come on in and sit down." Millie took her by the arm and propelled her to the couch.

"What are you doing here in New York?" Joe asked with only casual interest.

"I . . . uh . . . couldn't work things out with my husband, I'm afraid," Trish answered somewhat lamely. Something told her to tread cautiously.

"That was pretty fast, wasn't it?" Millie asked, and Joe added, "You didn't give it much of a try."

Trish accepted a glass of wine and sipped it gratefully. She needed time to gather her wits. "Mmmm, that tastes wonderful. Well, no. I suppose I didn't. I just realized immediately that it had been a terrible mistake to go back. We got into a bitter fight, and I walked out in a huff."

As she talked, Trish decided to tell her story and divert them. "You see, I left my husband originally because I found out he was having an affair with his secretary. At first I was afraid to let him know that I knew . . . I was so terribly insecure. But as time passed, I began to realize how foolish I was being. I really had nothing to fear. I had already lost the husband I loved." She stopped to take a sip of the wine and think about what else she would tell them. Strangely, it didn't hurt to talk about it anymore.

"Anyway, after Red was shot and I met his wife, I decided that I didn't want to be the other woman in his life . . . in anybody's life. I planned to go back to Dan and give it another try."

"Then why did you leave him so quickly?" Joe asked.

Millie shot him a withering look and interjected, "I think that's her business, Joe."

"It's okay, Millie. Well, for one thing, I found the other woman's cosmetics in my dressing table, but that wasn't what was important. I realized that I could never trust him again. My basic response to his overtures of love and kindness were hostile and cutting. I don't want to live with someone who makes me behave like a shrew."

"Are you coming back to work on the campaign?" Joe asked.

Trish shook her head. "I don't think so. As much as I loved the job and believe in the cause, I think it would be too uncomfortable. By the way, is Red recovering as well as the newspapers say he is?"

"He's doing fine. He was moved out of the hospital this morning."

"Really, so soon?"

"There's a big problem, Trish," Millie said softly. "He's lost his voice."

"Oh no . . . what will that mean to his candidacy?" Trish asked.

Joe shook his head. "We don't know. He was recovering just fine, when suddenly he couldn't make any sounds. The doctors said that there wasn't any specific reason . . . but the bullet had come close to the voice box and the vocal cords. It's possible there was some delayed swelling of the tissue which in time will correct itself. We'll just have to wait and see."

"Poor Red . . . what a rotten break. Are you going to be able to keep this out of the newspapers?"

"That's why he was moved. We didn't want anybody sneaking into his room at the hospital and finding out. The vultures would have swooped in and counted him out before he had a chance to find out what shape he's really in," Millie added.

"Where did you take him?" Trish asked.

"He's at Gloria's . . . her big house on the river. The

place is crawling with security men, and she's about to have a fit. She's been trying to get him to withdraw from the race, but he won't do it. She has no understanding of his desire to become president and, as she describes it, 'a sitting duck for every loony with a pistol.' " Joe's words indicated his amusement at Gloria's fears.

"Do you think that what Vanessa told Red had anything to do with the shooting?" Trish asked.

"Not at all. Red and I are both convinced that it was some crackpot. Anybody running for president attracts that kind of stuff . . . it can't be helped, especially when someone close to him sets him up." Trish chose to ignore the accusatory tone of Joe's remark.

"But somebody took a shot at him . . . and even tried to shoot through the door to finish him off. And that happened right after Vanessa left. Don't you think that's a little strange?" Trish persisted.

"Coincidence, pure and simple. Remember, Vanessa walked down that hall, probably right past the gunman, without anything happening. Whoever it was had probably followed Red to my apartment and just got a lucky shot, like Lee Harvey Oswald did," Joe replied matter-of-factly.

"Has Red said anything more about who the gunman might have been?"

"He doesn't know. No one has come up with an answer to that," Joe replied.

"Are you going to go see him, Trish?" Millie asked.

Trish paused before replying. "Well, I'd like to see him and get matters straightened out between us. I'd hate for him to believe that I ran out on him when things went bad . . . but no, I suppose not. It would be too awkward for me to go to Gloria's house."

"You want me to take him a note?" Joe asked.

"No, thanks. He doesn't need me to complicate his life any further." Trish yawned. "Would you two mind awfully if I went to bed? I feel emotionally drained and totally exhausted. Is my room still the same one?"

"You bet it is. I'll have your name carved on the door. Where's your luggage?"

"It'll be here in the morning. Apparently the skycap didn't get it on the plane." There was no need to tell them that her visit had been intended to be a short one. "I have my cosmetics and toothbrush, and I can sleep in my slip."

"I'll get you a nightgown and robe."

Joe got up. "Well, I know you two want to talk, so I'll be on my way. Let me know if there's anything I can do. I might phone a few people and help you get a job."

"That's very kind of you, but I'm not ready to deal with any big decisions yet, and please don't rush away on my account. It's still early," Trish protested.

"It's time for him to go. G'night, Joe. I'll see you in the morning," Millie airily dismissed him as she led him to the door. Trish walked to her room and tried not to look at them, but out of the corner of her eye she saw them kiss. What had changed Millie's mind about Joe so suddenly?

Trish was brushing her teeth when Millie came in, carrying a gown and robe. "Here, these should do you till tomorrow."

Spitting the toothpaste out of her mouth, Trish asked, "When did you two start being so cozy?" Her manner was frostier than she had intended it to be. After all, it was really none of her business, but Millie did not take offense. "Weird, isn't it? Right after you left, Joe called. He seemed all broken up about the shooting. He asked me to go to dinner with him . . . said he was lonely. I went . . . and before you knew it, we were here in the sack. God, it felt good. Do you have any idea how long I've been celibate?"

Trish could not hide her disapproval. "I thought you didn't like him."

"So, maybe I was wrong. He's really a nice guy."

"He's married, Millie . . . he's got two kids."

Millie smiled. "I know, but then, so is Red, and you

hopped in the sack with him. Sorry, I didn't mean that the way it sounded. I'm not looking for a big romance like you were. I just want a little hanky-panky. Sleep in, if you want to. I'm going in to the office early. We've been deluged with calls and mail since the shooting."

"Be careful, Millie. I never intended to fall in love either."

"It was inevitable, Trish. You're one of those innocent broads who can't sleep with a guy unless she's in love. And falling in love is what gets women in trouble."

Trish laughed. "You're right up there with Plato and Aristotle, Millie. A real philosopher. A bit skewed, maybe, but deep. I'm glad to be back. I missed you."

When her hostess left the room, Trish returned to her nightly ablutions and her plans. She had hoped to enlist Millie's help, but something warned her to be wary. She would have to find a way to get to Red without help from anybody. There was absolutely nobody she could trust absolutely. No, that wasn't quite true. There was one person she could go to without fear, and that was Gloria. Strange. In some situations, one's adversaries were more reliable than one's friends.

61

Easy Answers

When Richard and Vanessa arrived at the entrance of his condominium, he waved to the guard, who opened the heavy iron gates for them to drive through. He checked his rearview mirror and saw the car that had been following him had continued on Century Park West. Good. Living in a gate-guarded community had more advantages than just making it impossible to be served with a subpoena without warning. He drove along the short winding street lined with large early-California-style buildings only three stories high and tall trees and shrubbery. As he approached the building where he lived, he touched a transmitter to open the gate into his garage and drove inside. He got out of his car in a lighted area, keeping his hand on the pistol under his jacket. If anyone was waiting to jump him, he had a surprise of his own.

He led Vanessa to the elevator, which carried them to his penthouse.

Anyone less accustomed to enormous wealth and magnificent surroundings than Vanessa would have been awed by the size and grandeur of Richard's home. The ceiling soared to twenty-five feet in the living room, and a wall of windows looked out over the lights of the city. The room was richly decorated with marble and exquisite furnishings, all of which looked as if they had been custom-made.

The penthouse reeked of money lavishly and well-spent Richard had never wanted to live in an old man's house cluttered with memorabilia, so when his wife died, he had sold the big house in Beverly Hills and put almost everything on the auction block. If one wanted to stay young, he believed, one had to think young . . . to do as young men did. And so he lived in this beautiful and stylish aerie. And it suited him.

Ignoring her surroundings, Vanessa plopped herself on the nearest couch and took off her shoes. "I could use a brandy," she announced.

Richard poured a hefty measure of cognac into a large Baccarat snifter and handed it to her silently. He poured himself a glass of chilled San Pellegrino water and watched as his guest curled her legs up under her and took a long and grateful swallow of his best Paradis cognac. She set the glass down and took a cigarette out of her purse and lit it. After a deep drag she asked, "We were followed, weren't we?"

"I'm not really sure. There was a car tailing us for a while, but I lost him a couple of blocks before we got here. It could have been a cop car out looking for drunk drivers at this hour," he lied, hoping to get her to relax and talk.

"I hope you're right."

"Would you like to wash up or take a nap or something? I have a lovely guest room where you'd be very comfortable."

Vanessa shook her head. "Thanks, but the brandy is enough for now. It's very good, by the way."

"The cognac in that glass is more than a hundred years old."

"Imagine, a dumb bottle of booze will last longer than we will." She swirled the bronze liquid in the glass and continued. "I don't feel like resting. I need to talk to someone. I need to tell my story to someone who might take me seriously."

Richard sat down on the couch across from her and said, "I must warn you, I'm a very cynical person, but I'd certainly like to hear what you have to say."

"You know what, the whole fucking world is cynical. For most of my adult life, I haven't been on speaking terms with the truth, and yet hardly anyone except my dear old dad ever disputed me. But now, when I need to tell the truth, nobody wants to believe me." Her words were not spoken in anger or frustration but in wry irony.

"Vanessa, if I were to write a novel about some of the true situations that I've witnessed, nobody would believe it, because real life is so damned incredible."

Vanessa listened appreciatively and then remarked, "You're an attractive man, Mr. Terhune. Wanta fuck?"

Richard laughed out loud at the unexpected and flattering proposal. "My God, you really are a hellion. I'm glad you're not my daughter. No, thank you, but I appreciate the offer. Now, tell me the story that nobody else will believe. Maybe you'll get lucky."

"What do you think of Red O'Shea?"

"I like him. I think he's a bright, honest politician, and I also think he'll be a great president . . . if he recovers and gets elected."

"Exactly. That was the plan. It was so perfect. So reasonable."

"Whose plan?"

"My father's. Red was the candidate he'd been waiting for for the last twenty years. Ever since John Kennedy was assassinated."

Richard was incredulous. "My dear woman, your father was somewhere to the right of Attila the Hun. O'Shea's far too moderate and reasonable a man to appeal to the doctrinaire politics of Mike Fallon."

Vanessa smiled knowingly. "True, but he was my father's candidate anyway. You see, Dad felt that the world was going to hell. Little by little he saw his country being eaten away by turmoil, and he hated it. Crime on the streets, races mingling, homosexuality being flaunted. He tried influencing politicians. He donated heavy sums of money to them, but it didn't do any good. Life, especially in the cities, just kept getting worse. Nobody seemed to be able to straighten things out or to make life safe and comfortable the way he felt it used to be. He insisted that order had to be brought to the United States.''

"What's so awful about that? We're all trying in some way to make things better," Richard insisted.

"Not with the same goal that my father had. You see, he believed that money could buy anything, including law and order. He began to contact men who felt much the same way as he did. You know, there are a lot of people in this country who have a great deal of money, but no one before my father was able to weld them together as tightly as he did, with a common purpose, and a plan to accomplish something. Do you have any idea how much power money really has when there is enough of it?''

"Well, fortunately for the world, most of those people with money have only one goal, and that is to keep it and make more.''

Vanessa's eyes narrowed. "Too bad you didn't know my father intimately. He was a forceful, persuasive man.''

"What does this have to do with Kennedy's death?''

"Remember the paralysis that afflicted the nation when he was shot? For four long days everybody in the country sat in front of their television sets and mourned. I did. Didn't you?''

Richard nodded silently, and she continued, "Suppose during that time the vice-president had declared a state of emergency. Suppose that he announced he had information that the nation was about to be taken over by enemies within. And just suppose that the chief justice of the Supreme Court, the secretary of state, and ten governors had been assassinated within hours of Kennedy's death. How much power would Johnson have had?''

"My God, are you telling me that O'Shea was going to be set up?"

"You're a quick study, Terhune. No wonder you're the bane of prosecutors. Yes, exactly. Senator O'Shea has that same charisma . . . he's bright, he's witty, he's a national hero . . . my God, he was even a football star. He would be the first president to have a love affair with his constituency since JFK. My father and his friends were just waiting for the messiah. Nobody would have really cared if Nixon, Ford, or Carter had gotten it, and my father was sure that the people would never elect an actor to be president. He hated actors. But Reagan was elected, and do you remember the pandemonium when he was shot? For several hours everybody was in a panic, and even the secretary of defense thought he was in charge. So just imagine a situation that was deliberately designed for a takeover. Don't think it couldn't happen."

"What was the plan?" Richard's voice had become tense. This entire affair had seemed unreal to him until now, and he was hypnotized by the enormity of it.

"First of all, you must keep in mind that my father felt he was doing something that was good. He considered it to be his personal crusade to clean up the country. He felt that the criminals, the drug dealers, the murderers, the hookers, and the pimps should be eliminated. He hated attorneys like you who helped criminals to get back on the streets. He believed that the good hardworking citizens of this country would be a lot happier if their cities and their children were safe. And he didn't think that freedom was too high a price for them to pay."

"Sick, simplistic minds always find easy answers to everything," Richard snapped angrily.

"Add to that money, lots and lots of money, in a society that runs on dollars. Mike Fallon believed that everyone had a price, including Red O'Shea."

"What was his price to buy his own death?"

"Well, of course, he wasn't to know what was in store

for him in the long run. In the short run, all that would have been asked of him was that he accept Clarence Tuttle as his vice-presidential running mate. In exchange for that, he was to have received fifty million dollars in campaign funds. O'Shea could then have devoted all of his time and energy to the issues and not had to worry about raising money.''

''Jesus Christ . . . Clarence Tuttle! He's a joke. He's been running for the presidency for twenty years. No one takes him seriously anymore.''

''That's why he was perfect. All he ever wanted to was to be president—he would be willing to pay any price to succeed. And my father and his friends would be in charge.''

''Did you tell O'Shea all this?''

''I certainly did, but he insisted that he had to have a list of the names of the people involved. If the plan was as widespread within the government as it would have to be for this to succeed, he said it was imperative to know who could be trusted and who could not.''

''And that's the information we sent Trish to New York with? Good God, her life is in danger.'' Richard was on his feet and furious.

Vanessa spoke with deadly calm. ''Correction. All of our lives, my friend.''

Richard spoke with authority. ''Let's go. We're getting on the next flight to New York. Do you have an extra copy of those names?''

''No, but I'm sure we could get one out of the computer. I could call the young man who did it for me last night.'' Vanessa was infected by the urgency in Terhune's voice.

''Call him,'' he snapped, ''as fast as you can.''

''We'll have to wait until the computer shop opens. I don't have his home telephone number.'' She looked at her watch. ''It's almost six A.M. now. They should be open by nine or so.''

Richard didn't feel like waiting, but there was nothing

else he could do. "Do you want to try to get some sleep, or should I make some coffee and we can talk more?" he asked.

"Coffee, and would you mind turning up the heat? All of a sudden, I feel very cold." Somebody had finally understood, and for the first time, the reality of the situation descended on Vanessa with a crushing weight of responsibility.

The computer shop opened at ten o'clock, and Vanessa called to speak to Chuck, but she was told he wasn't scheduled to work that day. She got his home number and dialed it. A woman answered, and when Vanessa asked for Chuck, the woman broke down and began to cry.

"What's wrong?" Vanessa demanded.

"Chuck was killed last night. He lost control of his car, and it broke through the guardrail on the Santa Monica Freeway overpass."

Vanessa put down the telephone and looked at Richard. "God help me," she whispered, "I've killed him!"

62

Suburban Housewife

When she was certain that Millie had gone to bed, Trish turned on the light at her bedside table and took the sheaf of papers that Vanessa had given her from under the mattress where she had stashed it when she undressed. If she was going to pass them along, she might as well have a look and try to figure out what the big mystery was all about. More than once in the past few days she had regretted her decision not to sit in on Vanessa's conversation with Red. There was no question that she had gotten herself involved in something complicated and frightening. It was time to find out what it was.

The papers were printed in old-fashioned computer type, which was difficult to read, and the light was not bright. She put on her reading glasses and began to scan the pages.

The first set seemed to be minutes of meetings. The first date was January 11, 1972. There were only four people present: Jim Danton, Raymond Hawthorne, Bill Tracey, and Mike Fallon. The meeting took place at a home in Los Angeles, and the only business conducted was the agreement that each member would put up one million dollars immediately to begin the funding of the project, which was to be called "Matrix."

The next meeting did not take place until November

1976. There were twelve in attendance, and their names were listed, but none of them were familiar to Trish. The business that was conducted was the assessment of all members for another million dollars each. There was no dissent. Jim Danton was appointed to collect the money in cash. The only information that seemed irrelevant was the note that Jimmy Carter had just been elected to the presidency.

After that, the meetings began to be held more regularly. There were names of those in attendance, and the list grew longer with every meeting. As she perused the names, Trish occasionally would see one that seemed vaguely familiar. What the devil was Matrix, anyway?

Impatiently she skipped to the last page. The last meeting had taken place less than a year ago. Only twenty people had attended, but her heart stumbled and almost stopped when she recognized one of the names. "Joseph Franklin" leapt off the page at her. Good God . . . what did that mean?

Her hands shaking, Trish got out of bed and went to her purse. She took a small piece of paper out of her wallet. Early in their relationship, Red had given her a list of telephone numbers where he could be reached in an emergency. Perhaps one of them was Gloria's. She picked up the telephone and began to dial. When the first number did not answer, she remembered it was his office. The second one was the number of his house on Sutton Place, and she knew he wasn't there. The telephone rang several times at the third number before she heard a man's voice say, "Hello."

"Hello . . . this is an emergency. Please put Senator O'Shea on," she said softly.

"Please speak up. I'm afraid I can't understand what you're saying."

"Please tell Senator O'Shea that Trish is calling."

"One moment, please."

Trish said a little prayer that Red would get her message, but the voice that came on the line was certainly not his.

"This is Gloria O'Shea. What in the world do you want with Red at this time of night, Miss Delaney?"

"Gloria, thank God it's you. I must see Red as soon as possible. It's vital . . . please help me." The urgency and the desperation in her voice were effective, and Gloria responded.

"Where are you, Trish?" Gloria asked.

"I'm in Manhattan . . . at Millie's apartment. I'm in danger. I've got to get out of here as soon as possible."

"Give me your address. I'll send a car with a security agent to pick you up and bring you here. Do not leave the apartment alone, do you understand? The men will come to the door and get you." Her voice was stern and commanding. "It's almost eleven now. They should be there by midnight."

Trish gave Gloria the address and as soon as she hung up the telephone she began to put her clothes on. She returned the papers to the inside of her blouse, but they seemed to be burning a hole in her skin. She moved as quietly as possible. With a little luck, she could get out without Millie hearing her, she hoped, and then she realized she had a problem. She would have to go down to tell the doorman to let the agent in, so the intercom wouldn't wake Millie. She didn't want her to know she was leaving. Trish was certain Millie could be trusted, but her association with Joe was a definite problem.

When she was ready, Trish turned out the light and began to sneak down the hall toward the living room. As she passed the door to Millie's bedroom, she stopped to listen. Everything was quiet, and Trish felt a few pangs of guilt. Why was she suspicious of her friend just because she'd slept with Joe Franklin? Millie was surely only being used by Joe, who had heard everything that Vanessa had told Red, since he'd been taping the entire conversation.

Millie really knew nothing about it. The importance of her mission loomed large and heavy. God, she'd be so glad to get these papers into Red's hands. How the hell had Cake Halliday, suburban housewife and mother of two, ever gotten involved in political intrigue?

63

Alone in a Shark Tank

Terhune's nerves were rocketing messages so rapidly from his brain to his fingertips that he felt his hands begin to shake, and his knees were threatening to buckle under him. Vanessa, too, seemed to have gone into a state of shock.

"My God, that beautiful young man is dead, and it's all my fault. I should have known that I was being watched . . . I should have known . . ." she moaned.

Richard tried to calm her, although he knew she was right. "Come on, now, Vanessa, it's possible that the kid had too much to drink."

"He didn't drink . . . he didn't even eat meat." She had collapsed into the chair, and her face had acquired a blue-white tint. The circles under her eyes darkened. She looked as if she needed oxygen. Quickly he walked toward her, took her arm, and pulled her to her feet. "Get up, Vanessa," he commanded her. "Get out of that chair this minute! Pull yourself together. We've got to fly to New York as soon as we can, or you may have another person's death on your conscience. And in Trish's case you *will* be guilty!"

Under other circumstances he might have felt pity for Vanessa but not now. Trish was all alone in a shark tank, and she needed him to pull her out.

Richard picked up the telephone to find out when the next flight left but before he dialed, he slammed it down again. He turned to Vanessa and said, "My limousine and driver should be downstairs now waiting to take me to the office. Let's go."

"Where?" she asked.

"To New York, on the first flight that will get us there."

Vanessa got to her feet. "What are we waiting for?" she asked, but her voice was heavy with resignation and despair. She had done some mean and wretched things in her life, but she had never wished anyone real harm. Now she felt responsible for the death of a charming young man, as well as the fact that Red O'Shea had been set up and shot after she talked to him, and she wasn't sure she could handle that heavy a burden.

Richard took her arm and propelled her out of the room, down the hallway, and out the door without speaking another word. When they were in his car, he directed the driver to take them to the airport immediately.

"Did it ever occur to you that your house might have listening devices?" Richard asked.

She shook her head numbly. "Pretty stupid of me, wasn't it? That's probably how they knew that Chuck had gotten the information out of the computer . . . and that's why he died. Whoever was following us last night didn't see me jump out of the car. They were trying to kill me too, but why did they wait so long? I was allowed to pass safely through the hallway just minutes before Red was shot, and then they let me leave New York and come home. Why?"

"I can guess. They wanted you to find out where your father had stashed the information. Did anyone know about the computer?"

"No, absolutely not. He never told anybody about it. It was his toy, and he kept a log on the operation just for fun. . . . No, that's wrong. That's what he told me, but in truth, he loved having control over people. In spite of the fact that he was the chief architect of the conspiracy, I'll bet he wanted that information available either to keep everybody in line . . . or maybe even take credit for it if the whole preposterous thing worked.''

"The way Nixon kept the tapes, although they proved to be his undoing.''

"I suppose so. Have you got a bar in this limo?''

"Sure, what do you want?''

"Anything, and how about cigarettes? I smoked my last one in your apartment.''

Richard pulled open the small bar, took out a glass and a small decanter, and poured out a couple of ounces of Scotch. "Sorry, no ice . . . and definitely no cigarettes. Those things will kill you.'' He looked at her and smiled, and she smiled too. "That's right. We are trying to protect our health, aren't we?''

When they reached the airport, Richard went into the TWA terminal and arranged for two seats on the next flight to New York.

In the Ambassador's Lounge, where they went to wait, Vanessa had another drink, but when she asked for a third, Richard asked her to refrain.

"Look, my dear lady, if you get drunk, you'll damn well be on your own, understand? I have no intention of playing wet nurse to a souse. We've got a lot to do when we get there.''

When the jumbo jet finally lifted off the runway, Richard breathed a sigh of relief. They were on their way, and his nervousness had given way to excitement. He wanted to help Trish, but he had another, equally driving motive, and that was to see those papers. If Red O'Shea didn't have the guts to blow the whole thing open, then he intended to do it. He had finally found a crusade with a reachable goal. He was tired of the work he was doing and sick of defending so many sleazy people.

He took a cup of coffee from the hostess and leaned back in his seat, sipping the hot liquid. Would society have been any better if he had stayed in the district attorney's office and prosecuted criminals instead of going into private practice to defend them? Although he didn't want to admit it, he knew he could have had fame as a prosecutor, but he wanted fortune too. Hmph. Some fortune he'd amassed. At the moment, it could be counted only in terms of how much money he owed other people.

It was after nine P.M. when the plane landed at Kennedy. Richard immediately commandeered a taxi and directed the driver to go to Columbia Presbyterian. When they learned that the senator was no longer there, Richard guessed at Trish's path and gave the cabbie Millie's address.

"Do you think she went there?" Vanessa asked.

"It seems logical. Red was already gone by the time she got here. We've got to track her down."

"We're the only ones who know she has the papers. I'm sure they think I've still got them, since neither I nor the papers were in the car with Chuck when he crashed last night."

"Don't forget that a car followed us to my place," Richard added.

"I think we managed to confuse them."

"I wouldn't bet the farm on it."

They arrived at Millie's shortly before midnight and the doorman rang, awakening her from a sound sleep, although she was alert by the time they reached her apartment.

"Is this some kind of convention?" Millie asked.

"Millie, Trish is in jeopardy, and I've got to find her immediately," Richard announced without preamble.

She smiled. "No problem. She's in here asleep. She came in and practically went right to bed."

"Thank God," Vanessa murmured.

"Would you mind awakening her?" Richard asked, determined to make sure she was all right.

"Is it really urgent? She looked bushed when she came in," Millie said reluctantly.

"Yes, it is," both Richard and Vanessa said in unison.

"Okay . . . I'll knock on her door." Millie pulled her bathrobe tighter about her waist and walked toward Trish's door. She knocked softly . . . then louder. When she received no response, she called to Trish. Richard and Vanessa stood listening, and the room was charged with fear and apprehension. Finally Richard strode toward the bedroom door and pushed it open. Millie turned on the lights. Trish was gone.

64

The Fast Lane

On the way to Gloria O'Shea's estate, Trish sat in the back seat of a dark sedan between two neatly dressed broad-shouldered young men. She hoped they were the Secret Service agents they said they were. They certainly looked the part.

The car sped across the nearly deserted streets of the city. Trish tried to figure out what direction they were heading, but she had spent practically no time on the highways leading out of Manhattan, and she soon lost her bearings.

About forty minutes later, they turned into a long drive-way leading to a huge stone house. Floodlights shone on the long porch with its imposing Doric columns. As their car pulled up, they were greeted by another man dressed just as Trish's escorts were. He opened the door and helped her out.

"Miss Delaney, Mrs. O'Shea is waiting for you."

Relieved that everything was going as planned, Trish got out of the car and followed the Secret Service man through the massive oak doors into a marble hallway dominated by a grand staircase. The place looked like a castle. No wonder Gloria preferred living here. She must feel like a queen, Trish observed.

She was directed through a door to the right of the stairs. "Mrs. O'Shea is in the library." He opened the door, and she entered, but he did not follow. Gloria was sitting behind a huge desk. "Come in, please, and sit down," she said in greeting, and indicated a large leather armchair next to the desk.

Intimidated by the size and the richness of her surroundings, Trish quietly did as she was told. She looked around at the high ceilings and at the rows upon rows of books. Stained-glass windows, which were lighted from outside, cast a glow of warm colors into the room. Two long couches in front of the enormous stone fireplace were covered in a buttery soft suede in a warm rust color. Everything in the room reeked of power and money and tradition, and it made Trish feel like a humble peasant who had been summoned by the lady of the manor.

Gloria was dressed to fit the role in a rich dark purple dressing gown of velvet sashed with a gold rope. Her blond hair fell loosely about her shoulders, and she looked as if she had just put on fresh makeup. Roll the cameras, Trish observed silently, the drama is about to begin.

Gloria removed her small gold reading glasses, closed the book she had been reading, and turned to Trish. "Welcome to Xanadu . . . are you impressed?" she asked with a sly smile.

"That would be putting it mildly. I feel like Pussy Cat."

Gloria looked puzzled. "What?"

"Pussy Cat, you know, the one in the nursery rhyme—'Pussy cat, pussy cat, where have you been? I've been to London to visit the queen.' Do you have a mouse I can frighten under your chair?" Trish asked with a laugh.

Gloria was amused. "No mice, but a few hobgoblins, I suppose. Trish—may I call you Trish?—I'm glad you're here safely. I've had a room prepared for you in case you have to remain with us for a day or two. I really don't think that under the circumstances you should take a chance on being alone. There are a lot of dark forces abroad in the land.''

''Don't say that. I'm already frightened out of my wits. Does Red know yet that I called?''

Gloria shook her head. ''No, I didn't want to worry him. He's very upset, as you know. The doctors cannot guarantee that his voice will return, and if it doesn't . . .''

''He can't run for president,'' Trish finished.

''Exactly, but as you know, that doesn't make me unhappy. It's a terrible job, at best . . . but it's his life. Whatever happens, I think you should know that I will not stand in his way, but I want no part of it. If he persists on this dangerous course, I intend to remove myself and my daughter from it entirely. I will not have my daughter endangered, nor do I want her followed everywhere by agents. It is a perfectly miserable situation for young adults to have their lives and privacy violated by constant and unremitting surveillance. Any man who runs for the presidency puts those who love him in jeopardy. If Tessa were really his daughter, I would have to tolerate whatever happens, but she is not.''

''Why are you telling me this?''

''Because you're entitled to know what the true situation is between Red and me. I know you're in love with him.''

''And you're not?'' Trish asked.

''I thought I was at one time, but what I really wanted was to create a family. I married Red to complete my household, but he was the wrong choice. Of course, my daughter loves him, but he is too ambitious and independent. He doesn't fit in with the way I live, and I have no intention of changing that.''

''What will Tessa think?''

''Tessa's an adult now, and she understands that Red and I just don't fit together, although I will admit that I wish it were different. He's a charming, warm man, and as you know, an excellent lover.'' She looked directly at

Trish, who dropped her gaze in acute embarrassment and could say nothing.

"Anyway," Gloria continued, "this shooting incident stunned me into realizing that the pursuit of the presidency is an enterprise too perilous for me, or more specifically, for my daughter."

"If you divorce Red, it will hurt his candidacy," Trish protested feebly.

"That's his problem," Gloria stated flatly, and got to her feet. "Now, I'll take you to Red's room. He's still very weak. I have nurses around the clock for him."

"Why was he taken out of the hospital?"

"He's safer here, and he just needs time now to recover."

"But if you're worried about violence . . . why did you let him come here?"

"Because he needed my help. Besides, the Secret Service has moved in with full force, as has the FBI. We're quite safe."

Trish followed her out into the hallway and up the staircase. As they walked down a long gallery lined with portraits, some of which were very old and imposing, Gloria remarked, "Don't be too impressed. These aren't my ancestors. My grandfather was an artist, and he couldn't bear to part with any of his paintings."

They approached a man sitting outside one of the doors. Gloria spoke to him. "Jeffrey, this is Miss Delaney. Is the senator sleeping?"

"No, ma'am. The nurse just told me that he'd been awake for an hour or more." He looked apologetically at Trish. "I'm sorry, ma'am, but I'll have to check you out with this metal detector before you go in."

"Is that necessary?" Gloria asked. "This is a close personal friend of his."

"It's perfectly all right," Trish replied as he ran the small detector over her.

He nodded. "Fine. Go right in."

Gloria opened the door for her. "I'll be in my room if

you need anything," she said, and left. Trish went through the door into the huge bedroom.

There was only a small reading light on, illuminating the book Red was holding. He was propped up in a hospital bed, and he peered at her through the dim light.

His face was pale and drawn, but his eyes were bright with joy. "Trish," he whispered hoarsely when he recognized her, and beckoned her with the arm that was not bound up in a dressing. Because he had always been so strong and big, she was devastated by the way he looked. She put her arms around him, and they clung to each other without speaking. Out of the corner of her eye Trish saw the nurse approaching, and she pulled away slightly, embarrassed that their very private moment had been observed.

"Jean, leave us alone, please," Red said. The nurse nodded and quietly left the room, closing the door behind her.

When she was gone, Red took Trish's hand and pulled her to him. She sat down on the bed, and their lips touched each other's, tentatively at first and then with a deep, searching hunger. When at last he released her, she gasped, "You're in better shape than you look."

"I'll get better faster now that you're here."

"Red, I brought something for you . . . some papers from Vanessa.

He looked annoyed and rasped, "What are you doing with them? Why didn't she bring them herself?"

"Don't use your voice like that. It'll only make it worse. She couldn't come. She was being followed."

"What about you?"

"Apparently I wasn't, because I got here without any trouble."

"Let me have them," he demanded. He was business-like and cross. Where had the wonderful, warm moment of welcome gone?

Quickly she pulled the papers out of her blouse. They were warm and slightly damp. She had been more nervous than she realized. "Here they are." As she handed them to him, he asked, "Did you look at them?"

She nodded that she had.

"And?" he asked.

"I didn't undestand them, but there's a Joseph Franklin's name mentioned. What does that mean?"

Without answering her, he turned the light up brighter and began to read. She sat down in the chair by his bed and watched and waited. His eyes narrowed with interest and displeasure, and she tried to read his emotions as he studied the material. After about half an hour he looked up and stared at her thoughtfully for several seconds before speaking.

"You've done me and your country a great service, Trish," he whispered. "However, for your own safety, I think we should keep your part in this just between us."

"Well, that's fine with me, but I do think I'm entitled to know what it's all about, don't you?" she asked.

He pursed his lips in thought and then nodded. "Come sit by me so you can hear me easily, and I'll tell you everything."

He explained the plot just as Vanessa had told it to him, and when he was finished, Trish asked, "But who shot you and why?"

"Think about it. . . . One person knew what I knew about the plot. That same person knew that you didn't." He paused and waited for her to figure it out.

"Joe! Of course. Did you know?"

"No, but I suspected. He was the only one who knew what Vanessa had told me. He also knew that you didn't know anything and so, thank God, he did nothing to harm you. If you had sat in on that meeting, he would have been after you too."

"Why did he let Vanessa go? She walked out of that apartment building all alone and totally vulnerable, and she was the one who held the key to the whole thing."

"They needed her to uncover the documentation so that it could be destroyed. They didn't know that it even existed until Joe heard her tell me that it did, and I think he panicked when he took that shot at me. If he'd waited and talked it over with his friends, they'd have set me up a little more professionally—permanently.''

Red's whispery voice was showing signs of strain, but Trish had to know more. "What are you going to do now?"

"The longer this thing is kept quiet, the greater danger every one of us is in. I'll go public immediately, and then Vanessa will be out of danger, because she'll no longer be a threat to anybody.''

"What about Joe?"

"I hope they hang the son of a bitch!''

"Joe was at Millie's apartment when I arrived. They're sleeping together. Do you think she's involved in this?"

Red shook his head. "Knowing Joe, I'd guess he's just using her to try to find out about Vanessa.''

Trish breathed a sigh of relief. "I'm sure you're right. Now, what's the next step?"

"Tell the FBI, and they will inform the president. Now that I know exactly who is involved, I know whom to avoid. I feel sure the Department of Justice will handle it from here. Once the people planning this insidious scheme know that we have the documentation, the heat will be off us and on them. The last thing they'll want are dead bodies littering the landscape and making their conspiracy look very real.''

"What about Joe?"

"He's the first. I'm sure that they'll have no trouble pinning the assassination attempt on him once I tell my story. I'm going to see that he gets picked up right away. . . . And tell your friend the lawyer that this is one criminal I don't want him to defend. Now, give me a good-night kiss and go get some sleep. Ask the guard to come in, please.''

As Trish left his room, the nurse said to her, "Mrs. O'Shea asked me to show you to your room.'' Trish followed her down the hall to a luxurious large bedroom dominated by an antique four-poster. She closed the door and collapsed on the bed, tears of relief filling her eyes. She was sobbing and she didn't understand why. Life in the fast lane was a little too tough.

65

She Doesn't Trust Me

Richard, Vanessa, and Millie were all worried. Where the hell had Trish gone?

"Did you hear the telephone ring?" Richard asked Millie.

"No, I didn't, and I'm not a sound sleeper at all. The security system was still armed when I got out of bed, which means that she left of her own free will."

"Do you think she went to the hospital to see Red?" Vanessa asked.

"No, I'm certain that she tried there first, just as we did, and came here to Millie's when she found out that he had been checked out," Richard declared.

"Then where did she go this late in the evening?" Vanessa asked, and then turned to Millie. "Did Trish mention that she was on an errand for me?"

Millie shook her head. "No, and I'm really upset about that. Obviously, she doesn't trust me anymore."

"How come? I thought you were such buddies."

"I wish I knew."

"I think she knew where to find Red and went there," Richard suggested. "She doesn't strike me as reckless enough to take off without having a specific destination in mind."

"God, I hope so. Say, let me call the doorman and find out if she left here alone." Millie picked up the in-house telephone. The doorman said that, according to the log, Trish had left the building less than half an hour before Vanessa and Richard arrived.

"Was she by herself?" Millie asked.

"No, ma'am. Two men picked her up in a car. They identified themselves as Secret Service agents."

Millie thanked him and immediately repeated the message.

"You didn't hear the telephone ring at any time . . . you're sure about that?" Richard quizzed Millie.

"No, and it rings right at my bed."

"Then the men came in response to a call she placed, and I assume she called the senator. That's the best we can hope for," he conjectured.

"Now what'll we do?" Millie asked.

Richard answered, "Well, I don't know about you, but I'm going to the Oak Bar in the Plaza Hotel tomorrow evening. If Trish doesn't keep our eight-o'clock appointment, I'm going to the police."

66

More Important Things

Trish was awakened by someone shaking her arm slightly. "Ms. Delaney . . . Ms. Delaney . . . time to get up."

She opened her eyes and looked at her strange surroundings. A young woman in a maid's black uniform stood over her.

"I'm Cleora, Ms. Delaney. Mrs. O'Shea asked me to awaken you. She wants you to join her for lunch. Would you like me to draw a bath for you so you can freshen up a bit?" Her manner was friendly and courteous, and her accent British.

Trish shook her head to clear away the cobwebs of the sound sleep that had enveloped her. "No thanks. I think I need a nice brisk shower to help me wake up."

When Trish emerged from the mauve-tiled bathroom, Cleora handed her a beautiful gray silk kimono and a pair of silver slippers. "I've taken the liberty of having your underthings laundered. If you'd like to slip into this robe, I'll have them ready for you by the time lunch is over."

Trish wrapped the kimono around herself and sat down at the dressing table to brush her hair and put on a little makeup. She felt that she ought to try to live up to her part in the drama that was unfolding.

When she was ready, she followed Cleora down the stairs and into the morning room, which was surrounded by windows looking out over the river. The day was bright with afternoon sunshine.

"Please sit down here, Ms. Delaney. Mrs. O'Shea will join you shortly. May I bring you something to drink?"

"Coffee, please . . . black."

A cup of thick, dark coffee was poured immediately. Several newspapers were lying on the credenza, and Trish picked up the early-afternoon *Post*. As she sipped her coffee she glanced over the front page. Suddenly a headline brought her up sharply. It read: "SENATOR O'SHEA ACCUSES AIDE." The copy went on to say that Joe Franklin had been taken into custody and that Senator O'Shea had requested that the head of the FBI come to his mansion for a high-level meeting about an alleged conspiracy. After their meeting, they had promised to hold a joint press conference.

Shocked, Trish put down the paper. How could it all have happened so quickly? So absorbed was she in the revelation that she did not notice that Gloria had slipped into the room and sat down across from her to watch her reaction to the news.

"So, what do you think?" Gloria asked.

"I'm stunned. But why the publicity, so quickly?"

"For safety . . . no other reason. The sooner light is shed on this nefarious little scheme, the better off we'll all be. These nasty plots flourish only in the dark."

"I guess Red told you everything," Trish said.

"He felt I was entitled to the truth . . . and I must say that I admire your courage. I would never in the world have risked my life as you did."

"Don't praise me too much. I really didn't understand what it was all about until last night," Trish admitted.

"You're too modest. Now, shall we have breakfast or would you like to have lunch?" Gloria asked.

"I don't know whether I can eat or not," Trish said.

"Nonsense . . . you must eat. You're a heroine, my dear, and you've got to keep up your energy. Let's start with a glass of champagne. I want to propose a toast to a very courageous woman.'' She called the butler and asked him to bring them a bottle of Dom Perignon. The bottle was immediately produced, offered in a silver wine bucket. When it was served, Gloria raised her glass in a salute.

"To you, my dear woman. I only regret that circumstances make it impossible for us to be friends.''

Nodding her acknowledgment, Trish lifted her glass in a salute, and then sipped the bright liquid. "When my clothes are ready, I would like to leave, Gloria. Could you arrange to have me taken back to Manhattan?''

"Of course. Whenever you're ready. Would you like to see Red before you go?''

"I guess he has more important things to do now. Is he up to all this?''

"He's positively thriving on it, the damned fool.''

The two women's eyes met in understanding.

67

The Devil's Advocate

Millie and Richard arrived at the Oak Bar in the Plaza Hotel the next evening, hoping that Trish would remember the date Richard had made with her. They had read the newspapers and were elated that Trish had succeeded in delivering the documents.

They decided to order a bottle of wine to celebrate, once they were settled in a corner table away from the piano.

"I'm sorry we had to leave Vanessa locked up in the apartment. She really wanted to come with us," Millie said.

"I know, but she's a very valuable witness, and I think we ought to keep her hidden until the government gets its act together. She's going to have to be very careful for a while," Richard stated.

"Do you think she's safe there?"

"I think so. Her enemies are in total disarray right now. They're too busy trying to figure out how to put some distance between themselves and Mike Fallon to worry about her. She's really not much of a problem to them now. The smart thing for them to do would be to ride it out and insist that it was Mike Fallon's fantasy, and they had never considered him to be serious."

"You mean they might wriggle out of it?" Millie asked.

"If I were the attorney, I could damn well assure that they would."

"I don't know whether I like you or not, Richard Terhune."

"That makes two of us, Millie," he said sardonically.

"Well, I'm glad to see you didn't forget our date," Trish said. She had walked up behind them without their noticing.

Both Richard and Millie sprang to their feet with cries of delight and surprise. The three of them hugged and kissed each other.

"Trish, my God, I'm so glad to see you," Richard exclaimed. "If anything had happened to you, I would never have forgiven myself."

"Everything went off without a hitch, thanks to Gloria, Red's wife. Where's Vanessa?"

"We made her stay at my apartment. Richard thinks she still might not be safe," Millie explained.

"I'm so glad I'm finished with the whole rotten mess. I feel sorry for Vanessa," Trish commented.

"You know, in my long experience with people, I've learned that some of us have very strange auras. I sensed that about Vanessa right away. There's a feeling of pain and tragedy surrounding her. She's destined for turmoil," Richard observed.

Trish shivered. "How awful." She turned to Millie. "I hope you're not too upset about Joe."

"Fuck Joe," Millie snapped bitterly, and then she laughed. "But I already did that, didn't I? I should have followed my intuition. I never really liked the guy, so could somebody please explain to me why I went all gaga over him when he started making passes and treating me as if I were some hot, desirable chick?"

Trish put her hand on Millie's arm. "Hey, we all make mistakes. I made one that lasted twenty years."

"I'm sorry you couldn't work things out with your husband," Millie said.

"It was really all my own fault. I didn't even want to give it another try, I guess. I'm not sure I'll ever get over being angry with him."

"Have you made any decisions?" Richard asked.

"That's a good question. I think I ought to go back home to L.A. and get things settled one way or the other. The children know nothing about the trouble between us yet . . . so that's a bridge I still have to cross."

"What about Red?" Millie asked.

Trish looked somewhat guiltily at Richard before answering. "I'm afraid that's over. There's really no room in his life for me and I intend to be very adult about that. I'm not exactly a lovesick teenager anymore. You see, Richard, Red and I were childhood sweethearts. I came to New York to see him when I found out that my marriage was in trouble. We hit it off . . . rather well, I'm afraid, but I guess it was just never in the stars."

There was a long silence, which Richard finally broke. "Trish, did you look at the papers that you took to Red?"

"Yes, I must confess that I did. I didn't understand much, but I gather it had to do with a lot of meetings that took place over a period of years. The members of this little group invested enormous amounts of money in their scheme. I didn't recognize any of the names . . . except Joe's . . . and I still don't understand his part in the whole thing."

"That's easy to figure out, Trish. He was a plant. He was being paid to help the senator get elected, to get close to him and to be in the know on everything. I'm pretty sure that if they had been successful and Red had become president, Joe would have been his chief of staff in the White House . . . and in a perfect position to help run things after the assassination."

"He's a beast!" Millie snapped vehemently.

"Let's not malign the four-footed creatures who walk the earth. Men have done far worse things than beasts have. Joe had very grandiose and ambitious plans," Richard said.

"But why? What was the reason for any of it? I should think that men who had so much money would want to spend it helping people who are less fortunate," Millie said.

"Well, I've spent my life playing the devil's advocate, so maybe I can understand their motives a little better than you can. I think these men thought they were doing something good. They were trying to put the country into some kind of order. Because we are such imperfect creatures, a free society run by men is by its very nature a chaotic one. Successful leaders understand that, and they just try to muddle through and do the best they can. An orderly society is a totalitarian one," Richard explained.

Trish smiled. "Well, I can relate to that. I've never been much good at keeping things in perfect order."

"Well, say what you will, I still think they're monsters. They would have destroyed the country and made prisoners of us all."

"I agree with you, Millie," Richard said, "but you can't deny that a lot of your freedom has already been taken away by the hoodlums. Do you really feel safe riding the subways? How often do you venture out on the streets after dark alone?"

"Richard, what the hell do you know about it? I'll bet you've never even been on the subway. Life itself isn't safe. It never was and it never will be. Even the pilgrims had to watch out for the bear in the woods," Millie countered. "If I stay home, it's because I choose to, not because I'll be in violation of some damn curfew."

Trish felt she'd heard all the political discussion she wanted to for the moment. She finished her glass of wine and said, "Enough. Pretty soon one of you will begin pounding the table. Besides, I think we should go have dinner before I get tight. Richard, can we go into that lovely dining room where you took me the first night we met? You can take turns dancing with Millie and me.''

"It would be my pleasure. Let's go."

"I want to have fun tonight, because tomorrow I'd better go back home.'' Trish giggled. "Look at me, I'm getting to be a real jet-setter.''

"No, no, Trish. That term is out. Very out. You're bi-coastal,'' Millie announced.

68

Fame

At Trish and Millie's insistence, Vanessa called the Department of Justice and asked for protection. She offered to be a government witness and tell them everything she knew. Within an hour, she was picked up by two FBI agents and taken into protective custody.

The newspapers and the tabloids trumpeted her story, and she became the heroine of the hour. Her picture made the front page of most newspapers and the cover of *People* and the *National Enquirer*. She was interviewed on television by Barbara Walters, who asked, "Was there something in your relationship with your father that made you want to get revenge on him by revealing his part in the scheme?"

Vanessa, who had lived in the shadowy recesses of her father's life, suddenly found herself enjoying all of the fame and notoriety. She flashed an innocent smile. "Not at all. I loved my father very much. I could never have done anything to hurt him." A small tear escaped from her eye. Only she knew what a bravura performance she was giving. By the time she got to Phil Donahue, she had developed a character and a performance that enchanted everyone.

After a while, Vanessa began to believe what the media said about her, and she saw herself as a noble figure. It was time, she decided, to track down Cliff and find out if he would relent and let her see their daughter. First she tried Fairfield, Connecticut, where his parents had lived, but she had no luck. She engaged a private detective who found them in New Hampshire. The call was not easy for her to make, but she did it after several days of procrastination.

When she got Cliff on the telephone, he was cold and unforgiving. He was not impressed the slightest with her new role as heroine and savior.

"No, Vanessa. There's no place in Claudia's life for you now. She thinks you're dead. Resurrecting you would serve no purpose except to make me look like a liar. She's a very bright young woman, and I know she'd start to ask questions. Eventually we'd get caught in a bunch of lies, and the whole truth might come out. I'm sure you don't want that any more than I do."

"Please, just let me meet her . . . we could tell her that I was an old friend of her mother's," Vanessa said, and hated the begging tone in her voice.

"No, Vanessa. One lie just leads to another. Haven't you learned that by now?"

For the first time in fifteen years, some of the burden of guilt she'd carried was lifted. "Cliff, in all of these years, did it ever occur to you that I needed your help when you ran away from me? I was your wife. How could you leave me like that?"

"You were never my wife. You were your father's whore." The bitterness in his voice was as thick now as it had been then, but it didn't hurt her as much anymore.

"Yes, I was, and I stayed with him for all these years to protect you and my daughter from his wrath and his wickedness. In case you don't know it, he could have destroyed you and taken Claudia away from you if I'd let him. The least you could do is let me have one look at my child." Her voice was angry. She was tired of being a victim.

"No, Vanessa. The law would never have given her to a

man like him. You stayed with him because you wanted to, not because you had to. Don't try to impress me with your nobility. I'd appreciate it if you wouldn't call me anymore. If you really care about your daughter, leave her alone." He slammed down the telephone.

Vanessa fixed herself a gin and tonic and tried to forget her father's words that rang in her ears constantly: "You poor bitch . . . you're nothing without me."

She drained her glass and poured another. "Yes, I am something, you bastard. Just watch me!"

69

Wife and Mother

Trish arrived at her home unannounced just one week after she had left. She had stayed in New York for a quick briefing by authorities, but Red had managed to keep her in the background, for which she was extremely grateful. Vanessa was obviously glorying in the publicity, but Trish was happy to remain unknown. After all, her family still didn't know anything about her involvement.

She showered and put on a sweater and skirt. It was good to get back to a full wardrobe of clothes again. She sat down at the telephone to call her son. It took a while to reach him, but the tone of his voice startled her. "Mom, where the devil have you been?"

"What do you mean, Rob?" she asked.

"Why weren't you at Grandma's funeral?"

Trish's heart almost stopped in shock. "Oh, Rob, I didn't know she'd died. I . . . I've been out of town."

"I know. Dad told me, but he wouldn't explain anything. I flew in for the funeral, but I had to leave again the next morning so I wouldn't miss a test Friday. What's going on? Are you and Dad having trouble? He acted so weird the whole time I was there. He just said that when you got back home you'd explain everything."

Trish was caught completely off-guard and couldn't find

her way through the series of emotions that Rob's announcement had triggered.

"Rob, honey, I'll tell you everything . . . but not now. I'm still in shock over your grandmother's death. I loved her as much as I loved my own mother." She was trying to keep herself in control, and not succeeding very well.

"I'm really sorry to throw it at you like that, Mom. Want to call me back later?"

Sobbing, she said yes and put down the telephone. After all the wonderful years she'd enjoyed her mother-in-law's love and friendship, Trish felt incredibly sad not to have been there to say good-bye. She was also upset that her son and daughter knew she'd gone off, but didn't know her reasons. She lay down on the bed and wept until her eyes were swollen and her body was drained of the pent-up emotions of the past few months. What had happened to her life?

When she was certain that her emotions were in control again, Trish called Dan's office. Selena, of course, took the call.

"Selena, this is Mrs. Halliday. Please put my husband on the line."

"I'm sorry, Mrs. Halliday, but he's not here. Shall I have him call you when he calls in for his messages?"

"Please," Trish replied through clenched teeth.

"And where can he reach you?"

"At home," Trish snapped, and slammed down the telephone. She could not control the bitterness she felt toward Selena. It would serve Dan right if she left him to the clutches of that manipulative witch. Selena was just what he deserved.

Dan returned the call less than an hour later.

"Cake, when did you get home?"

"Early this afternoon. Dan, why didn't you try to reach me to tell me about your mother's funeral?"

"I'm sorry about that, Cake, but I was too broken up. I

let Selena make all the arrangements, and she didn't know where to find you. Rob came down.''

"I talked to him. Did you call Trina?''

"Rob called her. There wasn't time for her to get back. As you know, Mother wanted no fuss, and I had her cremated the next day, just as she'd planned. She was a great lady, Cake. We'll all miss her.''

His voice was soft and gentle, and the sorrow he felt touched Cake. "She loved you so much, Dan. You know that, don't you?''

"She loved you too, Cake.''

For the first time, the bonds of their life together and the love and the family they shared pulled Trish closer to her husband.

"Cake, why don't you meet me at La Scala? Let's talk things over while we have a nice dinner together. All right?''

"All right, Dan. It will take me a while to dress and get there. Seven-thirty?''

"I'll see you then.''

It was almost eight by the time Trish gave her car to the attendant at the Beverly Hills restaurant and went inside. Dan, waiting in one of the booths near the entrance, was deep in conversation with the sommelier about the wine selection. She tried not to let it annoy her, but he always made such a big deal of choosing the wine. Moving quickly, she seated herself before he could get to his feet.

"Sorry I'm late, but the traffic is terrible on the Ventura Freeway.'' It was a small lie. Actually, she had gone over to talk to Joyce, who had helped her put things into perspective.

Dan leaned over to kiss her, but Trish offered only her cheek. The moment of warmth she'd felt on the telephone seemed to have evaporated at seeing him again.

"It's good to have you back, Cake. Was the trip a success?''

"Haven't you read about it in the newspapers?''

He looked mystified. "The newspapers?"

"Yes, you know, the big scandal about the plot to take over the United States . . . you know, Senator O'Shea?"

"Sure, but what did that have to do with you?"

"I was the courier who carried the evidence across the country to him," she said quietly, with pride in her voice.

"Why would you do a dumb thing like that? You could have gotten yourself killed."

"That's probably true, and at the time, I must confess I didn't know exactly what I was doing. But I did it, and I'm glad. Matter of fact, I'm rather proud of myself."

"Really? I didn't see your name mentioned anywhere," he said, and she could tell from his manner that he didn't quite believe her.

"I know. Red wanted to keep me away from the publicity and the hassle."

"Thank God for that. It would look pretty strange, a wife and a mother dashing around the country doing cloak-and-dagger stuff."

When the wine arrived, Dan somberly swirled the liquid in the glass, sniffed it, tasted it, and then pronounced it fit for consumption. Cake decided to change the subject.

"Dan, you know how sorry I am that I wasn't here for the funeral. I hope you believe me. I loved your mother."

For a long moment Dan said nothing. He just kept staring into his wineglass as if it were a crystal ball that could give him answers. Finally he said, "Mother told me that she'd given you her savings."

"Yes, she did. She told me she wanted me to feel the same sense of security she had felt knowing that there was a little money that was hers alone."

"Don't you think it was callous to use my mother's money as you did?"

"How do you think I used it, Dan?"

"To walk out and leave me." He finally raised his eyes from the glass to look at her accusingly.

Trish looked away. "You're right, Dan. That's what I

spent it on. I still have a couple of thousand left. I'll give it to you tomorrow.''

"No! If she'd wanted me to have it, she would have given it to me herself. It's yours."

"Dan, why didn't you try to find me?" she asked, unable to conceal the hurt in her voice.

"I did. I hired a private detective, as a matter of fact. It cost me a lot of money."

"But you never came for me. Didn't you want me back?"

"I wasn't sure. Maybe I just wanted you to come home of your own accord."

"How do you feel now?" she asked.

"I've given it a lot of thought, and I think we ought to pick up where we were. I want to go back to life as it was."

"What about Selena? Where does she fit into things?"

"She's my secretary. That's all."

"You can't believe she'll agree to that. Dan, didn't you promise to marry her?"

"We all make mistakes, Cake. I'm sure she knows I never meant it seriously."

As Trish listened to him talk, visions of Dan and Selena making their plans together filled her mind. "Dan, do you really think we can ever go back?"

"I think we should try . . . for the children's sake."

"It's a little late to think about the children. Besides, I don't want them to live their lives just to please me, nor do I intend to live my life just for them anymore. They're adults. I'll be there if ever they need me. But as for us, it's over. I know that now."

"And you don't want to give it one more try?"

"No. Because I could never trust you again. It's that simple. As far as I'm concerned, our relationship can never be the same. Besides, I know now that you never really liked me. You tried too hard to make me over into your image, but you failed. It's true that I'm changed somewhat, but not enough to suit your image of what a wife should be. Marry Selena. You two are more alike than we ever were.''

"What are you going to tell Rob and Trina?'' Dan asked apprehensively.

"The truth. Are you afraid of that?''

"I just don't want all the blame, that's all.''

"Then let's tell them that we both fell in love with somebody else.''

"And is that true? Are you in love with somebody else?''

"If being in love means that I'd go almost anywhere he wanted me to go just to be near him, yes. Unfortunately, it's not that simple. There's no place in his life for me. God willing, he'll be the president one of these days.''

"Where do we go from here?''

"Well, let's begin by having dinner, and then we'll go home and start packing your things. I think you should move out as soon as possible. You still have that apartment near your office, haven't you?'' The sly smile on her face and the mocking tone in her voice let him know that she knew what had gone on there.

"I'll move out tonight.'' There was stolid acceptance in his voice.

"I'll put the house on the market soon. I want this to be an easy divorce for both of us.''

"You've already decided that divorce is the answer? Well, I certainly won't oppose you. As a matter of fact, we might as well let John Davenport represent both of us. It will cost a lot less money,'' Dan said.

"Not on your life. I'm not crazy, Dan. John is your buddy, not mine. When I said easy, I meant fair and equal. I'll get Richard Terhune to suggest someone to represent me.''

"How do you know Richard Terhune? His kind will charge you a fortune.''

"Richard's a close friend of mine, Dan. And I trust him.''

Later that night as she lay all alone in the big bed she had shared with her husband, Trish lost some of the self-confidence she had displayed earlier in the evening. Life was not going to be simple, and she wasn't at all sure she'd like being totally on her own.

70

Glory

As Trish looked out the window at the trees in her yard, at the magnolia in bloom, she felt a wrenching sense of loss. It was her last day in this house, and she would be leaving behind her garden and reminders of the most important years of her life.

She stopped packing the dishes and walked outside. The air was filled with the freshness of spring, and everything looked new and bright. It was appropriate that she would be setting out on her new life today. Standing on a garden chair, she pulled a magnolia blossom from the tree and held it to her face. The last time this tree had bloomed, she had been someone else. A happy housewife. Where had that woman gone?

Time to finish up. The van would be here soon to pick up her belongings and move them to a condo in Santa Monica. The apartment was much nearer to UCLA, where she was now a fulltime art student.

Shaking out a sheet of newspaper to wrap a glass, Trish saw Red's face smiling out at her. She had not spoken to him again since the night she had delivered the papers. She had wanted to call him when Millie had revealed that he was withdrawing from the race for the presidency because of his voice, but she had resisted the impulse. Damn Joe Franklin; he had not succeeded in killing the man, but he'd managed to assassinate the candidate. And then the bastard had made a deal for immunity by becoming a government witness. As Richard had suspected, Joe's shooting Red was a spontaneous move. Joe had known nothing about Vanessa Fallon's disappearance until he overheard her conversation with Red. Joe had been acting on his own when he shot the senator. Now he sought protection from the very government he had set out to destroy.

Millie also informed Trish that Red's voice was beginning to come back and that Gloria had filed for a divorce. Gloria released a statement saying that Red had been a faultless husband but that she did not like political life.

As soon as Dan moved into the apartment, Selena joined him. They planned to marry once Dan's divorce was final. Selena had gotten exactly what she wanted, but Trish was certain that they would make each other miserable.

The children had taken the news of the breakup amazingly well. Trish had hoped that Trina would come to live with her, but she had declined. Both Trina and Rob had insisted on places of their own, and she had no intention of opposing them.

Trish spoke to Millie at least once a week on the telephone, and she kept track of Vanessa through the gossip magazines that couldn't seem to get enough of her. Vanessa loved her newfound fame, and she was constantly doing things that would bring her publicity. The latest was a big romance with an androgynous young British rock star. In the latest issue of *Star* there was a picture of Vanessa in a leather dress and dyed green hair. Trish hoped she was enjoying herself.

Richard Terhune had been Trish's biggest disappointment. When it was announced that he had taken on the task of proving Jim Danton innocent of any conspiracy charges, she had been furious. She telephoned him to protest, but he contended that even rich men were entitled to be defended. She refused to accept the premise or to forgive him.

The doorbell rang and startled her. The movers weren't expected until ten, and it was only eight-thirty. Damn. She had wanted to get out of the dirty old housecoat she was wearing before they arrived. She hurried to the door and opened it. Instead of moving men, Red O'Shea stood there grinning at her.

"You don't look quite like I remember you," he said, and snickered nastily.

Suddenly realizing what a fright she looked, Trish covered her face with her hands, but they were black from the ink on the newspapers and she made herself look worse. "Oh no!" she moaned.

"Hey, that's not the welcome I expected," he complained.

"I don't want you to see me like this. Go away—come back in an hour," she wailed.

Red stepped into the house. "No way. I want to see you at your very worst." He pulled her hands away from her face, which was now covered with black smudges. He sighed. "Well, I guess this is it . . . and it's pretty bad, I must admit." Then he took her in his arms and kissed her lightly on the nose. She looked up at him defiantly.

"How come you never called me?" she demanded.

"I was busy. Why didn't you call me?" he retorted.

She grinned. "I was busy too."

"Are you divorced yet?" he asked.

"Almost. How about you?"

"Almost. Let's get married." The expression on his face had changed from amusement to tenderness.

"You haven't given up your plans to run for the presidency, have you?"

"No, but that's at least four years away . . . maybe even eight. I'll still be young enough. And when I go for it, I'll need you alongside me to keep me out of trouble."

"Will the divorce be a problem for you?"

"Times have changed. After all, Reagan was divorced. Besides, I believe the American people would prefer to elect a president who was honest in his personal life as well as his public one. As long as Gloria and I were hanging in there trying to keep up appearances, I wasn't being honest with anyone. When you came back into my life after all those years, it was even worse, because I love you . . . I always have and I always will.''

Trish was so overwhelmed by Red's words that she was speechless. He reached down and brushed her lips with his and said, ''Well, how about it? Are you going to marry me and have a go at the big race? Whether we win or not doesn't matter. Gandhi said that glory lies in the attempt to reach one's goal, not in reaching it. Will you buy that?''

''Red O'Shea, I'd buy anything from you. Even a used car.''

They both laughed as he held her close. ''Let's go upstairs,'' he said softly.

''But the moving men will be here for the furniture any minute,'' she protested weakly as they walked through the house with their arms around each other.

''They can take the bed last,'' he replied.

⊘ SIGNET

SIZZLING HOT . . .

☐ **ROSES ARE FOR THE RICH by Jonell Lawson.** Autumn McAvan wanted money, power—and vengeance on the ruthless Douglas Osborne who had killed the man she loved. On a quest that takes her to the heights of glamor and passion, she learns to use her beauty as a weapon to seduce and destroy both him and his handsome, dynamic son. The only thing she has to fear is love. . . .   (141091—$3.95)*

☐ **GOLDEN TRIPLE TIME by Zoe Garrison.** From starlet to studio boss, Kit Ransome had created scandals in bedrooms—and boardrooms—all the way to the top on the big-money side of the camera. But now someone has raised the stakes on the industry's favorite golden girl. In five days she must save the biggest picture of her career . . . and the love of the only man who ever made her really feel like a woman. (141504—$3.95)*

☐ **THE STUD by Jackie Collins.** Tony Blake was all things to all women . . . to the lithe model who balled him in an elevator and them made him *the* man to see in the world's wildest city . . . to the starlet who couldn't get enough of what he was overendowed with . . . and to the ultimate pussycat who gave him everything—except the one thing a stud can never get. . . .   (132351—$3.95)†

☐ **THE DIAMOND WATERFALL by Pamela Haines.** She had sold herself for their cold sparkle . . . It was their wedding night and Lily and Robert had a sumptuous suite in the finest hotel in Nice. She caught sight of herself in the glass, weighted down with diamonds, rubies, sapphires, emeralds, and it was then that he took her, and she felt only the pain of the stones pressed into her soft skin. . . .   (136489—$3.95)†

*Prices slightly higher in Canada
†Not available in Canada

Buy them at your local bookstore or use this convenient coupon for ordering.

NEW AMERICAN LIBRARY,
P.O. Box 999, Bergenfield, New Jersey 07621

Please send me the books I have checked above. I am enclosing $_____ (please add $1.00 to this order to cover postage and handling). Send check or money order—no cash or C.O.D.'s. Prices and numbers are subject to change without notice.

Name_____

Address_____

City_____State_____Zip Code_____

Allow 4-6 weeks for delivery.
This offer is subject to withdrawal without notice.